About the Authors

Clare Connelly was raised in small-town Australia among a family of avid readers. She spent much of her childhood up a tree, Mills & Boon book in hand. She is married to her own real-life hero in a bungalow near the sea with their two children. She is frequently found staring into space – a surefire sign she is in the world of her characters. Writing for Mills & Boon is a long-held dream. Clare can be contacted via clareconnelly.com or on her Facebook page.

Pamela Sadadi Yaye has a bachelor's degree in Christian Education and her love for African-American fiction prompted her to pursue a career in writing romance. When she's not working on her latest novel, this busy wife, mother and teacher is watching basketball, cooking or planning her next holiday. Pamela lives in Alberta, Canada with her gorgeous husband and adorable, but mischievous son and daughter.

In 2002 **Janice Maynard** left a career as a teacher to pursue writing full-time. Her first love is creating sexy, character-driven, contemporary romance. She has written for Kensington and NAL, and is very happy to be part of the Mills & Boon family – a lifelong dream. Janice and her husband live in the shadow of the Great Smoky Mountains. They love to hike and travel. Visit her at JaniceMaynard.com

One Night... Before Christmas

CLARE CONNELLY

PAMELA YAYE

JANICE MAYNARD

MILLS & BOON

First Published in Great Britain 2022
By Mills & Boon, an imprint of HarperCollins*Publishers* Ltd
1 London Bridge Street, London, SE1 9GF
www.harpercollins.co.uk

HarperCollins*Publishers*
1st Floor, Watermarque Building,
Ringsend Road, Dublin 4, Ireland

ONE NIGHT... BEFORE CHRISTMAS © 2022
Harlequin Enterprises ULC

The Season to Sin © 2018 Clare Connelly
A Los Angeles Rendezvous © 2018 Harlequin Enterprises ULC.
Blame It On Christmas © 2018 Janice Maynard

Special thanks and acknowledgement are given to Pamela Yaye for her contribution to the *Millionaire Moguls* series.

ISBN: 978-0-263-31791-6

MIX
Paper | Supporting
responsible forestry
FSC™ C007454

This book is produced from independently certified FSC™ paper to ensure responsible forest management.

For more information visit: www.harpercollins.co.uk/green

Printed and Bound in Spain using 100% Renewable electricity at CPI Black Print, Barcelona

THE SEASON TO SIN

CLARE CONNELLY

To the Romance Writers of Australia:

the best group of creative, talented and supportive writers in the whole wide world.

I'm so glad to be a part of the tribe.

PROLOGUE

I DREAMED OF her again last night. Of how she'd been on that last morning, her pale face blotchy from tears, her eyes holding apologies and lies, begging me to forgive her.

How could I, though?

She was leaving me. Just like everyone else.

I dreamed of my foster mother Julianne, and the dream was so real that in it I was able to reach out and hug her, to fall into her hug, to smile at her. To pull back through time and space and change the way the day had actually unfolded—to undo the way I had shouted at her and shoved her when she'd tried to draw me close.

In my dream I didn't swear at her.

In my dream I didn't refuse to go near.

It was just a dream, though: powerful enough to drag me from my fitful sleep, but futile in allowing me to change the past.

The past is a part of me and there is no escaping that.

CHAPTER ONE

THERE IS ONLY one word to describe the way he's looking at me. With disdain. There is a hint of boredom that curves his lips, lips that I have looked at far too often in the five minutes since Noah Moore walked into this bustling café, just around the corner from my office.

I've heard of him, of course. Who hasn't? Self-made billionaire, one half of the tech empire that's completely taken over the world as we know it. In the last ten or so years he's gone from strength to strength, his professional successes only outdone by his frequent outings in the society papers—for all the wrong reasons. Along with his business partner, he's renowned for his ruthless instincts and fast-paced lifestyle. Luxury. Glamour. Wealth. Success. Wild parties on yachts in the Mediterranean, the after-party they throw every year at the Cannes Film Festival that draws all the big-name celebrities. They might have made their money in the tech industry, but they're the epitome of Hollywood cool—the gritty, bad boy kind.

Yes, Noah Moore is a quintessential bad boy and, as if I needed any further proof of that, he arrived at our meeting in a leather jacket, black jeans, his dark hair a little longer than it should have been, stubble on his angular and symmetrical face, his brows thick, his lashes thicker, and with a hint of alcohol lingering around his very buff, very distracting frame. And it *is* distracting me. All six and a half feet of him, all muscled, *big* and tanned all over—or so I imagine—is making me forget that I am a professional.

'This isn't an appointment. I don't need a shrink. I just…want to talk.'

It had been a confusing declaration, given that he'd called me—a shrink—but I'd made the appointment with him regardless, despite my growing waiting list. Curiosity, you see, got the better of me.

I didn't get to be twenty-eight and divorced without learning that I have a predilection for bad boys. Specifically one—and he burned me, badly. Bad boys are my sinkhole, my quicksand. The longer Noah Moore looks at me with that scathing contempt, the more my pulse flutters at my wrist, hammering me in a way that makes me uncomfortably aware of the way he's sitting, his legs spread wide, one arm bent at the elbow supporting his head, the other resting close enough to his cock that I know I can't look anywhere near his hand. His gaze doesn't waver from my face. He has a magnetic quality. He's drawn the attention of most of the women in this place, and not because he's well-known. It's purely because of *him*.

I summon all my strength to hold his stare. 'Well, Mr Moore.' His lips flicker at the formal use of his name.

I can't help it. I feel I need every tool at my disposal to keep him at arm's length. 'We've covered the basics. Why don't you tell me why we're here?'

'Why we're here?' Noah Moore is Australian and, though his accent has been flattened by the years he's spent here in the UK, there's still that hint of lazy sunshine in his inflection, enough to warm me unconsciously. 'Isn't it obvious?' He lifts his brows, waiting for me to answer, turning the tables on me. His eyes, a green that would blend into the Mediterranean, narrow.

'Usually, my patients complete a pre-appointment form,' I say. 'You didn't email one back.'

His gaze doesn't shift. Curiosity sparks in my gut.

'You didn't complete it?'

'I'm *not* a patient.'

A frown pulls at my lips and I instantly wipe it from my face. I don't show emotion when meeting prospective clients. This process isn't about me and my feelings—it's about them. 'I see,' I say, nodding calmly. 'So why did you call me, then?'

He compresses his lips. 'To talk. To see what this is all about. I explained that on the phone.'

'Right.' I resist an impulse to respond sarcastically. 'I'd still like to have some of your details on file. Do you mind?'

'By all means.' He drags his fingers through his hair and then casts a glance at his wristwatch. It's not a fancy, expensive timepiece like you'd expect. It's a smart watch. Is that what they're called? You know, the ones that count your steps, forward your mail and lock your house.

I lift out my phone, opening the secure app I use to record confidential patient information. 'Here you are.' I hand it over to him, but he makes no move to take it.

'You fill it out,' he says with a shrug.

Rudeness has reached astronomical levels.

Now, I've been doing this a long time. I know I'm good at this. That's not ego speaking; it's the line of awards from the Guild of British Psychologists I've received; it's the magazine articles; it's the waiting list as long as your arm to get an appointment; it's the fact I can charge what I want—though rarely do. Because what I love most of all is to help people, and seeing my success in the way my patients' lives change—that's why I do my job.

It's why I agreed to see Noah for this 'audition', when I have far too much to do as it is. He sounded like someone who needed help. I want to help him.

Patients with trauma and severe trauma disorders, like PTSD, should be handled gently. Even the ones like Noah Moore, who seem as though they can handle anything, are only ever one distress away from bolting. From fleeing a therapy that is too hard to process.

Of course, I can only guess, at this stage, that he's affected by a trauma—he's not exactly giving me much to work with. Except for the 'tells', the small signs that indicate to someone like me that he's using every cell in his body to push me away, right down to insisting that this isn't a normal appointment, that he's not a 'patient'.

'If you'd like,' I say, with a soft nod and a smile that is my professional version of *But we both know you're being an asshole.*

Out of nowhere, I picture Ivy and warmth spreads through me. I work long hours, and God, I miss her so much. I have a picture of her on my desk, back in my office, because it helps to tether me to the other part of my life—the love of my daughter and the need to make her safe.

She looks just like I did as a child—like me as an adult, really. Our hair is the same shade of blonde, so fair it's almost white, though hers has been cut—at her request—into a bob whereas mine is long, halfway down my back, and I tend to wear it in a plait over one shoulder. We both have ice-blue eyes and our smiles are the same. She has her father's nose, straight and lean, whereas mine slants up at the end in a way that my dad used to call a 'ski jump' when I was a kid.

'Age?' I prompt, finger hovering over the appropriate box on the electronic form.

'Thirty-six.'

At least he's answering. I had expected him to prevaricate.

'Previous treatment history?'

His eyes narrow, and I know he's fighting an urge to tell me that this isn't 'treatment' either. 'None.'

'I see.' I tap 'nil' on the screen, then lift my attention to him once more. And freeze. He's watching me unapologetically, taking advantage of the fact I'm distracted by the form, and his eyes are roaming over me as though I'm a painting on display in a gallery.

My skin prickles with goosebumps.

Noah Moore is dangerous.

He has all the markers I have trained myself to avoid—he is rough and arrogant, ruthless and feral—and yet I stare at him for a moment, our eyes locked, and a surge of something forbidden rampages through my system. For the first time in five years, a slick of desire heats my blood, warming me from the inside out. I thought I'd never feel desire again after Aaron. I unmistakably feel it now.

'Can I get you something to drink, folks?' The waitress stands beside me and I flick my phone off automatically, discreetly hiding any information she might otherwise have seen.

'Piccolo latte,' I say.

'Nothing,' Noah says with a shake of his head. I frown. He suggested we meet for coffee and yet apparently has decided he won't drink one.

'Why are you here, Mr Moore?'

'Is that *you* asking, or your form?'

My smile is tight. 'Both. It will save us time if we cut to the chase.'

He makes a slow, drawled *tsk*ing sound. 'But where's the fun in that, Holly?'

He rolls his tongue around my name, making it sound like the sexiest word in the English language. 'Do you find this fun, Noah?' I return his challenge, inflecting his name with a hint of huskiness. I see it hit its mark.

His eyes widen slightly, his pupils heavy and dark, and speculation colours his features.

'No.' It's over, though. He's sullen and scathing once more.

'You didn't want anything to drink?' I say when the waitress returns with mine.

'Don't think this place serves my kind of drink,' he drawls, and I surmise he's referring to alcohol.

'Do you drink every day?'

'Some days,' he says with a lift of his broad shoulders. 'Some nights.'

'Is that why you asked to meet me?' I prompt. 'Do you think you have a drinking problem?'

His laugh is short and sharp. 'If I say yes, can we end this charade and both go home?'

'No one's forcing you to be here. It's just a "conversation", remember?'

He looks at me with barely concealed impatience and I am curious as to the reason for that.

'You work mainly with veterans,' he continues, and the knowledge that he's researched me does something strange to my gut.

It shouldn't. Most people research a doctor like me before making an appointment. There are myriad specialties amongst psychologists, countless ways to practise what we do. For Noah Moore to be here, he must know that I'm his best shot at help.

He's still researching me, though, in a way. Interviewing me before deciding if he wants to commit to a treatment protocol.

I think of the awards that line the walls of my office. They're just shiny statues, but to me they mean so much more. I can remember all my patients. The hurts in their eyes, the traumas of their souls. Those awards are the acknowledgement that I have helped some of them.

'I work with people who need me,' I say, returning my gaze to Noah's face. 'People who need help.'

'And you think I'm one of them?' There's fierce rejection in the very idea.

'You called me.'

He presses his lips together. 'This is a waste of fucking time.'

It takes more than a curse word to make me blush, though Noah Moore curses in a way that is uniquely interesting, drawing out the *U.*

I don't react as I want to. To be fair to myself, it's been a *long* time since I've felt anything for a guy and suddenly all of me is responding to all of him; my cells are reverberating on every level. 'You're free to leave.'

His anger is directed at me. Resentment too. It reminds me of the way he reacted minutes earlier when I told him no one was forcing him to be here and he simmered with that same angry rejection.

My mind ponders this as I sip my coffee. Our eyes are locked over the rim and my pulse ratchets up another notch. His eyes drop to my breasts and I feel an instantaneous zing of awareness. My nipples harden against the fabric of my bra and my stomach squeezes. I press my knees together under the table.

I'm used to this kind of attention. I've dealt with it

all my life. I'm on the short side, slim with breasts that are out of proportion to my small frame. They seemed to grow almost overnight when I was only twelve.

It's one of the reasons I wear dresses like this. Plain colour, dark, thick, demure. It falls to my knees and to my wrists, and the neckline is high. I'm not ashamed of my figure, but I don't want the nickname I had just out of university to catch on. 'The Sexy Shrink' is hardly the business pedigree I seek.

'I'm here now.' He shrugs as though he doesn't care, but I know otherwise. I know because it's my job to read people and I'm good at it, and I know because I have a sixth sense that's firing like crazy in my gut. 'Might as well let you sell yourself to me. Go on. Work your magic.'

I fight the urge to tell him there is no such thing as magic when it comes to trauma therapy. It takes hard work, long hours and dedication from both patient and physician. I'm willing to put in the hard yards, but is he?

I come back to the suspicion I have that he feels compelled to be meeting with me. *Obliged* might be a better word. Like he 'has' to go through with this appointment, not because he 'wants' to heal.

Usually, I would follow a more traditional form of approach to tease the answers out, but Noah Moore is not going to respond to traditional therapeutic means. It's why he insisted we meet here, in a coffee shop, rather than my office. I lace my fingers together, leaning forward slightly, elbows propped on the table. 'I get the feeling you're here against your will.'

'Yeah,' he grunts. 'Didn't you see the guy with the gun to my head when I walked in?' He laughs it off.

'You seem reluctant to accept my help,' I say softly. 'You keep stressing that this isn't an appointment, that we're just "talking". You refused to come to my office, because you feel safer in a neutral setting like this café. And yet while I've said you may leave, you're choosing to stay.'

There's a wariness that steals over him at having been called out. Good. Unsettling him is going to be crucial here. 'You think anyone could force me to do what I don't want?'

It's a good point. Noah Moore, even without the billions in the bank, is a man who would be impossible to intimidate. He is brawn, brains and beauty, all in one.

'You tell me.'

He expels a sigh. 'I contacted you, didn't I?'

'That doesn't mean someone wasn't holding a gun to your head.' I force another smile. 'Metaphorically speaking.'

He holds my eyes for a fraction too long and then reaches forward, wrapping his fingers around one of the water glasses the waitress brought and sipping from it. I wait while he swallows, impatience breeding frustration in my gut.

I'm not used to this degree of resistance. A little, sure. It comes with the territory. But generally there's some sense of apology for it. People know that my time is worth a lot of money. That usually encourages a compulsion to cooperate, even if only to a small degree.

'In a manner of speaking.'

It's an admission I don't expect and I can't suppress an outward display of surprise. My lips, painted a bright red, form an 'o'. I cover it as quickly as I can, but his grimace shows that he saw my response. Understands my surprise.

'Well, I'm glad.' Glad we are getting somewhere. 'In my experience, therapy works best when I have a willing participant on my hands.'

I swear I don't mean anything by it, but the speculation that grows on his handsome face shows he's analysing my words for a hidden meaning. For a sensual insinuation that should have stayed buried deep in the recesses of my brain.

Fortunately for me, he doesn't capitalise on the error, though he leans forward when he speaks so I catch a hint of his fragrance. Woody and alpine, masculine and strong. 'Are you saying you're not able to help me?'

A glimmer of disappointment pings in my chest cavity. Did I want him to volley back my unintentional double entendre? To tell me he'd be very willing to be in my hands?

He's looking at me, waiting for an answer. For almost the first time in my career, I'm struck mute. I run my eyes over his face, so handsome, and wonder at the secrets he's hiding. At the life he's lived that caused him to phone me. At the fact he's making me want to throw caution to the wind and make him mine.

'No,' I say finally. 'I think I can help you. If you want to be my patient.'

'I don't have time to be a patient,' he says, and it's so scathing that a shiver runs down my spine.

'Well, unfortunately, it takes time,' I point out firmly. 'There's no quick fix for whatever has led you to me.'

'You're confident saying that when you don't have the faintest idea why I organised this meeting?'

'Yes.' I glare at him. 'You know why, Noah?' God help me, the taste of his name on my lips is addictive. 'Because I do this all day, every day. People like you walk into my life, wearing your issues like a coat that only I can see.'

He narrows his eyes.

'It's in the set of your shoulders, the depths of your eyes. I see it.' I lean back and feel my heart pounding hard against my forearms. 'Trauma isn't something that can be drunk away. Nor is it something I can wave my magic wand and cure. The only way to get beyond it is to work through it. It's not a pleasant process, I won't lie to you. Sometimes the healing can feel worse than the original pain. But I can promise you that if you don't work through your problem you're going to come unstuck one day. I wonder if that hasn't already happened. Is that why you're here?'

'This is a load of bullshit.'

I can't help it. The woman might be hotter than Hades, but she's spouting psychobabble crap out of that beautiful red mouth of hers and it makes my skin crawl.

I hate this shit. I've heard it all before. If it hadn't been for Gabe's ultimatum, I'd never have arranged to meet her. But I'd do just about anything for Gabe, even without the threat to stand me down from the company while I *'sort myself the hell out'*—his words. I don't want to see a shrink, and I have no intention of seeing Dr Scott-Leigh—hell, I don't want to see anyone. I'm going through the motions, that's all. But I didn't come here expecting her to get under my skin like she is. I didn't expect to find her utterly fascinating.

'I'm sorry you feel that way,' she murmurs, and I wonder how *she'd* feel if I were to slip my hands under her dress, finding the softness of her thighs, the heat between her legs.

I drink the water again, thinking I really should have chosen a bar instead of this busy central London café. I replace the water glass and prop my elbows on the table, enjoying the way her eyes flare a little wider as my body looms closer, before she tamps down on the response and is all businesslike professionalism again.

Is there a Mr Dr Scott-Leigh?

No wedding ring, and you'd bet her husband would be smart enough to make sure she wore one. With a body like hers, she's no doubt got a never-ending queue of men at her door. Hell, if she were mine, I'd chain her to my bed. At least until the novelty wore off.

My lips twist at the missed opportunity. Yes, I definitely should have suggested a bar after-hours. Somewhere I could actually do something about the fantasies I've had about her since she walked in, aching to dispel all professionalism and aloofness.

I heave out a sigh, returning my attention to her face.

It's a face that is objectively beautiful. Huge blue eyes, a nose that can only be described as cute, with a neck that is elegant. Her hair is as fair as sunlight and it's plaited in a way that tells me she's trying to tame herself but, in contradiction to that, she's wearing little red earrings that I see now are Christmas gifts with glittering green ribbon.

She's what my nine-year-old self would have called *fancy.* All perfectly groomed and sweet-smelling, flawless and poised in a way that a ballerina would envy.

I know lots of women now, fancy and not. Fancy women tend to throw themselves at me, and it doesn't matter if their lingerie is high-end or from a supermarket, they're all just as eager to strip it off their bodies at the smallest encouragement.

They all scream with pleasure just the same.

She's watching me patiently, waiting for me to speak, and I can only guess it's a tactic taken from Therapy for Beginners. But it has little to no impact on me.

I watch back, my expression impassive, my lips curled with the derision I am famed for.

'Well.' She concedes defeat by speaking first. 'I suppose we can always talk about the weather.'

'Or we could talk about you.'

'Me?' I've surprised her. Again. Her lips open into a circle that is distractingly erotic. 'I'm not on the agenda. Sorry.'

Her manner tells me she's anything but apologetic.

'So I'm supposed to bare my soul and you give me nothing?'

Her smile is tight. She's pissed off. It's the first time I realise that I like riling her up; definitely not the last. 'Well, if you decide you want to undertake therapy, then I give you peace of mind in due course,' she murmurs.

But she's got no idea what ghosts run through me; what shadows fill my being. I am a wraith of my past's creation.

'Holly, I highly fucking doubt that.'

CHAPTER TWO

HER HAIR IS longer than I realised. And so much softer. Up close as I am, it smells like vanilla and honey.

I know it's a dream but, for the first time in a month, a woman has chased *her* from my mind and I am free from the cursed hauntings of my past. I clutch at the fine threads of this dream, refusing to let it slip from my mind.

'I love it when you kiss me,' Holly murmurs, her lips a perfect red. I reach for her, pulling her to me, my hands large against her fine frame, my fingers splayed wide on her hips.

Her body is pliant at my touch. Easy to control.

Surrendered completely to me, and what I can give her.

I yank her—hard—against my chest, enjoying the soft exhalation that brushes my jaw. Her breasts feel so much better than I imagined. They're firm and soft at the same time, so big and round. I lift a hand and palm one, my thumb brushing over her nipple, my fingers possessive and demanding.

She looks at me on a tidal wave of confusion and

uncertainty. This is new and different and she doesn't know how to respond.

She doesn't need to worry.

I know enough for both of us.

I lift her easily—she's light and I'm strong—and wrap her legs around my waist. I don't know how I want her but, God, I know I need her. Her dress is floaty, it moves easily over her hips, granting me the access I need. Even though it's my dream and I should be able to control this shit, she's wearing underwear—a barrier I don't want.

Her hands wrap around my neck, drawing my head closer to hers, and she's kissing me, her tongue seeking mine, duelling with me, her eyes swept closed against the assault of this passion.

But I don't want to kiss her.

Kissing is romance and reward—fucking is not. Fucking is passion and need—a primal, physical act that is over when it ends.

I break my mouth free and stride across the room. I don't know where we are. Dreams are funny like that. I push her back against a wall and, with her weight supported by the wall and my hips, I rip her dress open at the front. She's not wearing a bra—thank you, dream gods—and I crush my mouth to her breast, rolling my tongue over her nipple until she whimpers, and then I move to the other, this time pressing it with my teeth so her back arches forward and her fingernails dig into my shoulders.

I'm naked now—in a dream, clothes are capable of simply disappearing—and I slide her panties aside with my fingers, my eyes mocking her, teasing her, as I nudge my cock to her entrance, hitching myself at her seam, feeling her moist heat before sliding deep inside her.

She groans, a sound that comes from the base of her throat, and I laugh.

'This is just the beginning, baby,' I promise.

And because I'm pursued by demons that seek to punish me, I wake up at that moment, sweat beading my brow and a cock that's harder than stone. I drop my hand to it, rubbing my fingers up and down my length, curving my palm over my thickness.

It's no good.

Having dream-fucked Holly, I need the real thing.

I reach for my phone and check the time. It's midnight. I've been asleep only forty minutes. For Christ's sake.

I scroll through my calendar, going back to Tuesday last week when I met Dr Scott-Leigh in that café.

Her contact details are in the appointment file. I click on her email address:

Holly,
I need to see you again. Tomorrow.

I consult my calendar once more—these sleepless nights are playing havoc with my short-term memory.

Four p.m. is my only free time.
NM

I drop the phone to my bed and push up. I dress quickly, or as quickly as I can when my dick is like a tent pole, and throw back a tumbler of straight vodka, then call one of my drivers—there are four on rotation.

Graeme is on the roster.

He's probably the least able to hide his disapproval of my lifestyle, and that gives me a perverse sense of amusement.

'Where to, sir?' he asks without meeting my eyes. Did I wake him? Tough. It's his job, after all.

'Mon More,' I say, naming a club in Putney. Julianne has haunted my dreams for a month and now Holly is taking over. The only thing I know is I can escape them both in a loud bar with free-flowing booze.

It's not like I've been thinking of him since our appointment. At least, not only of him. I've had a lot else on my mind. Like working out how I'm going to make a Virgin Mary costume for Ivy before her Christmas concert and when I'll have time to help her with the gingerbread house she's determined to give her grandmother this year.

No, I've been far too busy to think only of Noah Moore.

Except at night, when my head hits the pillow and I shut my eyes. Then, all I can see is his face, his beautiful, exquisite, tortured face, his haunted eyes and sexy mouth, his body that I want to throw myself at, to curl up against, to be held and comforted by. He makes me want to surrender to his touch, to be safe within his arms.

I'm smart enough to know how absurd that is, but if I can't have the real thing, I should at least be able to satisfy myself with the fantasy. Right?

I've had plenty on my plate this week but, when I arrive at my office this morning, fate seems to have conspired to throw Noah Moore at my feet.

His email detonates in my consciousness like a charge. It's barely civil and it's sure as hell not how appointments are made. I can't even say for sure how he got my email address—it's not on my business cards and I don't routinely welcome patients to communicate with me directly.

There has to be a divide between my work and my home life. That's the way this works best.

Not for Noah Moore, though. I'm surprised to find a wry smile has rubbed across my lips when I scan my calendar for availability and none of the usual clinical detachment chills my emotions.

My day is full, and yet if I were to swap my one o'clock for twelve o'clock and miss lunch, I could move my four o'clock forward and make time for Noah.

I swallow past the doubts.

I can't say why, but I am compelled to answer, and I am driven by a desperate need to see him again.

I send a quick reply:

Noah,
I can meet with you again, but it will have to be in my office. Four p.m. works. Don't be late—I have another appointment directly after.
Dr Scott-Leigh

I send it, pleased with the fact I've kept it so formal, pleased with the way my email doesn't, in any way, shape or form, convey how utterly devastatingly sexy I think he is.

I'm proud and pleased as I load up the news browser I always read before starting work and Beatrice strides in with a coffee and bagel.

'Morning, Holly,' she says with a smile and leaves again without waiting for a response.

I love this woman so much.

She knows how desperately I need my sacred ten minutes without interruptions and I so appreciate her giving me that. Only now my brain is *full* of interruptions. Questions about Noah, his habits, his problems, his intentions, his needs.

I want to know him and I want to help him.

And I can't be at my most effective, therapeutically, if other issues, like my raging desire and the fact I haven't slept with a guy in over five years, take over my brainpower.

I employ mindfulness, breathing in deeply, exhaling slowly, counting beats and blanking my mind until I feel more like myself again.

But it's a godawful day.

I feel like I'm operating at half my usual capacity. I drag my brain through appointments, eat a muesli bar between my two and three o'clocks and then, after my three o'clock leaves, make a quick phone call to the hospital to check on a patient of mine.

When I disconnect the call, Beatrice buzzes through that Noah Moore has arrived.

My pulse leaps immediately, my heart thumps hard against my chest and my fingers begin to shake. I cast a quick glance at the compact I keep in my top drawer, run fingers over hair I have today left loose and stand to greet him.

I didn't know Noah Moore would book an appointment—it's not for him that I've worn this outfit but, the second he enters the room, his green eyes skim over me and I get a kick of satisfaction at the speculation I see in his eyes.

Holy hell.

What am I doing?

I have no business feeling all warm and tingly because he's staring at the way my leather skirt hugs my hips. It's high-waisted—it comes up to my belly button—and I'm wearing a gold cashmere sweater tucked into it. It's an outfit I would describe as perfectly professional but, the way his eyes light on my silhouette, I feel like a centrefold.

'Mr Moore.' My tone is cool. Good. Cool is good. 'Please, take a seat.'

He strides into the room, looking dishevelled in a way that is sexy but that I have every reason to believe is the result of a sleepless night.

He throws his large frame into one of the chairs, his legs spread wide, his hands resting on his powerful thighs. Today he's wearing blue jeans and a long-sleeved top.

'Holly—' his lips flicker into a smile, but it's over in a millisecond '—nice to see you again.'

I compress my lips. Normally, patients would express

gratitude at the fact I'd squeezed them in under short notice, but not Noah.

'Let's get started,' I clip. 'How are you?'

'Are you asking out of interest or as a doctor?'

My pulse ratchets up and I have to dig my fingernails into my palms to stop the guilty blush from creeping over my cheeks. 'As a doctor.' The words drip with ice.

His smile suggests he doesn't believe me. Crap.

'Then let me remind you; I haven't agreed to see you professionally.'

I frown. 'Haven't you? I would have thought that's just what you did when you asked for an appointment.'

'No.' It's cryptic. I leave it alone for now and reach for a pen. There will be time to discuss the semantics of how he wants to proceed.

'You were up late last night.' He arches a brow in silent enquiry, so I rush to explain. 'You emailed at midnight.'

He nods, dragging a hand through his hair, but says nothing. It's like pulling teeth!

'Are you always up so late?' I ask.

'Late? Midnight?'

I refuse to be embarrassed by him. 'Yes.'

'Yeah,' he grunts, and his eyes are wary. He's withdrawing from me, pulling back. Something about my line of questioning is hitting on an issue that is renewing his trauma.

It's nothing you would be able to tell, unless you had experience with this. Outwardly, Noah is every bit the charming, sexy bad boy he's renowned for.

I smile, lean back in my chair and drop the pen onto the notepad. 'It's cold today.'

A comment that surprises him. It makes him wary; his eyes skip to mine and a frown moves on his face. He doesn't say anything.

'Do you have plans for Christmas?'

'Christmas?' It's practically a sneer. 'Christmas is weeks away.'

I nod. 'It'll be here before you know it.' My eyes drift to the picture once more, a smiling Ivy, and I feel somewhat more centred.

'Do *you* have plans for Christmas?' he volleys back, his expression tight as he watches me with every fibre of his being.

I wouldn't normally answer—the question is too personal—and yet I hear myself say, a smile softening the words, 'Not really. Just a small family celebration this year.'

His eyes drop to my fingers. He's wondering what 'family' means to me. I don't elaborate on that score. That's common sense as well as training. Ivy is not a part of this world. She's mine—and she's all that is sweet and innocent.

'I make a pudding—my grandmother's recipe—we sing carols. The usual. Do you have any Christmas traditions?'

He knows I'm relaxing him and yet perhaps he also knows he has to give me at least something to justify the fact I've moved my schedule around to see him today. 'Yeah. Getting hammered.'

I arch a brow.

'It's just another day for me, Doc.'

'No family?' I prompt.

I get the strangest sense that he wants to say something. That the temptation to open up is pressing against his back, pushing him forward, but then he just shakes his head sideways once. A curt dismissal.

It's normal for patients to clam up around me, but I don't generally take it personally. Intense frustration zips through me now and, against my usual therapeutic practices, I say, 'Noah, I really want to help you and I think you want that too, but you're giving me nothing to work with.'

He stares at me belligerently and I stand up, hoping that will dispel some of the frustrated energy that's firing through me. I move towards the window, looking out at London, and I don't know if I'm imagining it but heat warms my spine as though he's still watching me.

I habitually deal with soldiers who've come back from war zones—men and women who've witnessed and perpetrated unimaginable crimes. People who have done what no human should ever have to do, who have seen first-hand the bleakness and despair of utter destruction. I understand their hauntedness and I know how to help with it, generally. Every patient is different, but at least I'm operating from the same wheelhouse. Not now, not with Noah. I need to tease information out of him gently. But I do need to get *some* information. Without it, I'm flying blind.

'When did you decide to seek help?'

He expels a harsh breath that has me turning slowly to face him. I was right. He's watching me. Blood jolts through my system as though each cell has been subjected to an electrical shock.

'Noah.' I say the word quietly but with a firmness that shows I'm serious. 'I moved my day around for this. Are you wasting my time?'

He seems to withdraw from me even further. Not in the way many of my patients do, by becoming visibly upset or distant. Now he is looking at me as though he wants to eat me—and my tummy is in knots.

He stands and moves towards me. Every single fibre of my being is vibrating on high alert, but I don't withdraw. Maintaining control of the session is vital. He is right beside me, at least a foot taller than me, and close enough that if either of us were to sway forward slightly we would be touching. Crazy thought! Where did that come from?

He looks down at me, so dominant, so strong and somehow so broken.

I stare at him for a long time, waiting for him to speak, determined not to break first.

Finally, his throat bobs as he swallows. 'I don't need therapy,' he says gruffly, as though I've dragged him here kicking and screaming.

'I see.' I nod, not wanting to mock his assertion, nor to question why he emailed at midnight if that's the case.

'I just…' He drags a hand through his hair and shakes his head. 'This is fucking ridiculous.'

'What is it?' I urge and, damn it, I step closer. Stupid, stupid move, because now there's barely a whisper between us and I can't surrender the strength of my position by pulling away. If I do, he'll know how he affects me, and that would be a disaster.

'I'm not sleeping.' He turns away from me and takes a step towards my desk, pressing his fingers against the wooden corner.

It is highly irregular for me to have people on this side of my office and I feel the invasion of Noah in every way. This is my space—my personal space. But the moment he's started to open up to me, I can't make him feel at fault. I move towards him and put a gentle yet professional hand on his elbow.

Tension is radiating from his bulky frame, as though this small admission of a perceived weakness has offended every iota of his hyper-masculinity. He flinches when I touch him and glares down at me.

Not with anger, though.

The desire that has me hostage is of a mutual kind. I feel him shift and it is all the confirmation I need that this crazy, dark lust surges through us both. My fingertips are still pressed lightly to his elbow. I nod towards the chair he'd been sitting in.

'Please, sit down.' It's a quiet murmur and for a moment I think he's not going to do as I say. He continues to stare at me and I find myself staring back, wondering what it would be like for those lips of his to drop to mine.

Temptation is thick in the air. I could push up onto the tips of my toes and kiss him… Would it really be so wrong? I step back just as he reaches for me, his fingers curling into my hair, wrapping it around his big masculine fist. 'Is this real?'

The question catches me utterly off guard. I take in a deep breath that barely reaches my lungs and stare at him with a sense of helplessness. I have a thing for bad boys, remember, yet I've never known anyone quite like Noah Moore.

I force myself to remember several things, and to remember them quickly. He is waging a battle against demons I don't yet comprehend; he has come to me for help.

And I don't do this.

I don't let men, no matter how sexy, make my pulse race and my knees knock.

That kind of thing was a million years ago for me.

'Is this real?'

The words are husky from his mouth and all my certainties and good intentions quiver inside me.

'What?'

Step away, step away! my brain is shouting at me, but I don't move. Instead, I swallow and his eyes drop to my mouth, then lower, to the column of my throat, watching the convulsive movement, before resuming their fascination with my lips.

Moist heat slicks between my legs and I clamp my lips together. My nipples press against the bra I'm wearing, little arrows darting through me from each hardened nub, radiating heat through my body. There is a fine tremble that passes over my spine.

'This. Your hair.' And his fist moves higher, towards my head, so his palm curves around my skull, his fingers still tight in the blonde lengths. He angles my head upwards and our eyes are locked. Our bodies are separated by inches and yet I feel the essence of him pulse into me, throbbing inside my gut. This is, hands down, the most intimacy I've ever felt with a man.

'Yes.' It's a word weakened by desire and my temptation to surrender to it completely. 'It's real.'

He nods but doesn't otherwise move. If I don't do something, anything, to grab control of this situation, I'm going to be in serious trouble.

'Noah.' I clear my throat and step away. For a second he doesn't relinquish his hold on my hair, and then he drops his hand to his side. His expression is knowing. As though he understands that I am now fleeing what we just shared.

'Please, sit down.' The words lack conviction and yet he complies, moving back to his seat and owning it with his body. I don't sit behind my desk, though. Instead, I cross to the other side of it and perch on the edge, crossing my legs at the ankle.

It's dangerous because I'm quite close to him, but I feel we need to maintain some of the connection he just established.

'You're not sleeping?' I prompt softly.

'No, Doc.'

'Not at all?' I frown, reaching around behind me for my pad and pen.

He shrugs, like it doesn't matter. 'I sleep a bit. Ten minutes. Twenty.'

'Then what?' I write *10...20* in the corner of my paper.

'I wake up.' The words are droll, bordering on sarcastic. My cheeks warm, but I dip my head forward to write a note.

'Do you have dreams?'

The wry sarcasm fades from his features. He focuses on a point behind me. 'No.'

Liar. I don't challenge him, though. It's too soon and, for the moment, he's made some admissions, which is a huge thing for a guy like Noah. I need him to trust me, and that's going to be a tough sell with him.

I scrawl *no dreams* and underscore it, which is my way of reminding myself that I suspect it's not the truth. 'Have there been any changes in your lifestyle recently?'

'Besides seeing you?' he says thoughtfully, his eyes shifting back to mine, all confident, charismatic, sexy bad boy again.

My heart leaps.

'I mean changes that could affect your sleep.'

'Oh, you sure affected my sleep last night.' The words are so far from what I expect that I lose my mask for a moment and show my surprise. I'm sure my face must pale visibly, that he must see the way I react. My stomach swoops and, briefly, I allow temptation to cloud my clarity.

But only briefly.

I'm a professional. I need to remember that.

'Perhaps we need to try something new,' I say, my smile an attempt at coolness that I suspect I don't pull off.

He lifts a brow, obviously teasing. 'I'm game if you are.'

CHAPTER THREE

'I SET ASIDE a full hour, but I can already tell there's no sense keeping you here that long.' She pushes off the edge of the desk and walks back towards the window. The afternoon light shimmers across her, backlighting her in a way that makes her look like an angel. A very sexy angel.

'Sick of me already, Holly?'

Her eyebrows knit together and I can see her cogs turning, analysing me. This is one of the many reasons I like to hook up with women who've got a drink or three under their belt. None of this psycho mind-reading bullshit.

And Holly Scott-Leigh is, I suspect, very good at this.

'You don't want to be here. And yet you came.'

'I was curious about where you worked,' I say lamely. Stupidly. She's too smart to fall for that kind of bullshit.

'So…' She lifts a hand to her thick blonde hair and scrapes it back from her brow. A sign of frustration? The action pulls her sweater across her breasts, and everything inside me jerks. She speaks as though I haven't. 'We're going to do five questions.'

'Five questions?' That's easy. Relief is palpable.

'But…' She lifts her finger, her lips twitching with barely suppressed amusement. 'You have to answer me honestly, and promptly. No faffing about trying to make something up and no dodging the questions.'

I can hear my blood throbbing in my ears like a fucking tsunami. There's a high-pitched noise too, like air from a balloon being pinched to release.

There was one summer I spent with a family who used to surf. They took me out with them, taught me how to ride a board. There is an art to keeping your balance; it's a constant seduction. Every tiny movement shifts your power and one wrong breath may mean you tumble into the ocean.

If I allow Holly to have this power over me, she will roll me into the sea.

I won't let that happen.

I stand, my eyes pinning her to the spot so I see the effect I have on her. She tries to cover it, but you can't hide desire. Not really. There are markers that I have seen often enough to recognise easily now. Her cheeks flush along the ridge of bone, her pupils swell to cover almost her whole eye and her breathing is rasped, her chest moving up and down, so that her round breasts push forward. Jesus, that shirt sweater thing looks soft. My fingertips itch to reach out and touch it. To scrunch it against her skin, to feel her through the fabric.

I stand just a couple of inches away from her and she keeps staring up at me, her big red lips parted, her eyes whispering seduction even when I know she's doing her best to hold the professional line.

I wonder how long she'll keep that up.

'On one condition.'

Her frown is infinitesimal. Her eyes drop to my lips and my gut jerks, wanting to pull me forward, begging me to kiss her.

Nah, not to kiss her, that's far too sweet a word for what I want to do. I want to pull her lower lip between my teeth, I want to push her back against that window, I want to fucking own her.

'What's that, Mr Moore?'

It's an attempt to put us back on a professional footing. Her own surfboard is tipping.

I lift a finger, touching her cheek lightly. She flinches with surprise and her eyes lift to mine slowly. She's in the water; it's threatening to consume her whole. 'For every one of your questions, you answer one of mine. Same rules.'

Her breath is soft, warm. I feel it on my inner wrist. Imagining it elsewhere on my body, I throb with heat and need.

'I told you last week.' The words are uneven. 'I'm not on the agenda.'

It's an intentional reproof. My smile shows amusement at her attempt to put up barriers. 'Oh, I think you are, Holly.' But I drop my hand and step backwards. 'Do we have a deal?'

She swallows, her throat bobbing. She's torn. Drowning and trying not to—drowning and asking me to save her all at once.

'I suppose it's fair,' she says after a beat.

Fuck, yeah, it's fair. If she expects me to pour out my heart, then she'd better believe I want my pound of flesh along with it.

She nods, as if to reaffirm to herself that she's going to go through with this. 'Shall I start?'

I ignore the twisting in my gut. I've agreed to this and I'm not afraid of much, least of all having a fucking conversation.

She is, though. She weighs her words carefully, studying me as she thinks. Her eyes are crazy beautiful. Huge and bright blue with a dark black rim around the iris and flecks of black close to the pupil. She has a tiny scar above one brow—like a line about half a centimetre long. I want to run my tongue along it—the certainty that one day I will fills me like cement.

'Did you have a favourite toy as a child?'

Of all the questions I expect, it's not this. I laugh—a dry sound that cracks from my throat.

'No. My turn. Did you think about me after I left last week?'

Her eyes widen and her throat jerks as she swallows. Her gaze darts to a space on the wall behind me. 'Of course I did,' she says, the words thready and soft. She darts her tongue out, licking her lower lip. 'You're my client.'

'No, I'm not. So far, I'm just some man you know.' My smile is wry and I lean closer, my words mocking. 'And you know that's not what I meant.'

'That's the question you asked,' she volleys back,

fire and spirit firing in her eyes. 'My turn. What's your favourite thing to do?'

I stare at her for a second, a sense of discontent rifling through me. A hobby? She wants to know what my hobby is? I drop my head close to hers, and when I whisper it's right in her ear, low and soft. 'Fuck beautiful women.'

I pull away so I can see her reaction. She's looking at me with something close to pity, though, and that fires me up. 'My turn.' I skim her face thoughtfully, then purposely drop my eyes to her rack. Jesus Christ, they're great breasts. 'When did you last get laid?'

Another swallow. 'Noah.' The word is half scold, half plea.

I shake my head, my eyes locking her to the spot and her intention. 'No lying.'

The room pulses heavily with silence.

'A long time ago.'

'That's not a precise answer,' I push, a thrill of something like triumph turning my blood to lava.

She expels a breath. An angry breath. 'Five years ago,' she snaps and then pulls herself together with effort.

'What's your mother's name?'

I don't bat an eyelid—not so much as a blink. 'Alison Parker.' She might have birthed me, but calling her a 'mother' is a step too far. I've spent thirty-six years wishing her name wasn't even in my mind, let alone her blood in my veins.

'Are you close to her?'

I shake my head. 'It's my turn, remember.'

A look of panic colours her spectacular eyes. She moves away to grab a glass of water from her desk. I follow her automatically and my eyes drop to the picture to the right of her. A little child, so exactly like Holly that it must surely be a relation, sits in a frame. 'Who's that?'

She looks at me and catches me looking at the frame. For a second I think she's not going to answer, or that she might lie, but then she shrugs. 'My daughter.' Her hand lifts betrayingly to a necklace she wears. A locket?

'Are you close to your mother?'

I was expecting this question. 'No.'

'You don't like her?'

I move my body closer—she braces her hands on the desk and looks up at me, and the air cracks like a whip as tension tightens between us.

'No.' Her expression flickers as she analyses this. 'Have you thought about me, other than professionally?'

Once more her eyes dart away from me. Such a give-away gesture for a woman as smart as she is. I would have expected her to have a better poker face. 'I...' A very faint peach colour spreads over her cheeks.

'It's a yes or no question, Doc.' I brace my hands on the outside of hers, bending my body forward so that I've effectively caged her on her desk. She closes her eyes and inhales deeply, drawing in a breath like she wants to draw me with it. When she speaks, it's with a courage I admire. A strength and determination—a fearlessness.

'Yes.'

I tighten all over and it takes every ounce of my

willpower not to push her back on the desk and rip that leather skirt off, to make her mine.

'You weren't raised by your parents, were you?'

She's still got her eyes closed, but the question is no less cutting or incisive for that.

If she were looking at me, she might have seen how off-kilter it momentarily knocks me. But I recover quickly. She has asked the right question but phrased it wrong. *Who raised you?* might have been better. That would have forced me to document the myriad foster homes I was passed through, or to explain that no one really took the time to raise me—that I was left to raise myself.

'No.' She looks at me now and, with her eyes fixed on mine, I move so close that my lips are almost brushing hers. 'Do you want to fuck me?'

She gasps and, before she answers, I do it. I do what I've wanted to do since I first saw that perfect Cupid's bow. I put my mouth to hers, lift my hand to the back of her head, wrap my fingers in her hair and invade her with my tongue. She makes a moaning noise and then she's kissing me back, her tongue clashing with mine; one leg lifts and hooks around my waist, holding me locked to her, my cock pressed hard against her cunt. She tilts her head back to give me all the access I want and I fucking plunder her. I kiss her to punish her for making me talk about my fucking mother. I kiss her because I can't not.

And she kisses me back.

But she hasn't answered my question and I want her to. It's not enough to feel her wants—I want her to own

them. To confess them to me. I have seen her courage,
her spirit—but still I want more. I want to hear her be
brave for me.

So I pull away but, before she can pretend she wasn't
affected by what we shared, I thrust my cock against
her, grinding my hips, and she moans, lifts her fingers
to my chest and digs them in. She tilts her head back
again.

Hell, if she hasn't been screwed in five years, I could
probably make her come right now. To test my theory, I
push against her again and she says my name, low and
soft, huskily, a beg, a plea.

'Noah...' Just a whisper, but so heavy with need and
desire. *'God, Noah...'*

I laugh low in my throat and she looks at me with
abject confusion, but then I drop my hand to her breast,
finding her nipple and flicking it.

She shakes all over, her body trembling near mine. I
can't tell you how much I want to finish this. To make
her beg for me right here, right now. She's so close. I
don't think she knows what day of the week it is.

Yeah, I want to fuck her, but here would be too
rushed. Such a waste of an opportunity to really make
her ache for me...

'Do.' I pull her earlobe between my teeth and roll
my tongue over it. She whimpers.

'You.' I scrunch her sweater in my fist and lift it out
of her skirt, feeling its softness in my palm before running my hands over her naked side. She makes a guttural noise of pleasure.

'Want.' I push it higher still, until my fingertips touch

the lace sides of her bra and then nudge beneath it so the ball of my thumb is on the underside of her sweet, rounded breast.

'Me.' Her leg that's wrapped around my waist jerks me closer, telling me not to keep her waiting. I laugh again, a sound of appreciation for a woman who knows what she wants.

'To.' I grip her ankle behind my back then run my hand along her calf. Holy shit, she feels so much better than I'd imagined. So soft and smooth and feminine. I pause in the hollow of her knee, watching her fevered face as her eyes darken and her cheeks glow. I run my fingers higher then, slowly, until I reach her inner thigh and she moans, once again digging her fingers into my shoulder and arching her back.

'Fuck…' I shove the elastic edge of her underpants aside and, with my eyes holding hers, mocking her for the fact she tried to pretend this wasn't happening between us, I nudge a finger inside her warm, throbbing heart. She's so goddamned wet I feel a drop of my own cum spill out, but I don't stop. I push deeper inside her and she whimpers, her fingers now scratching into me.

'You?'

She blinks, glaring at me for a second, and then she nods, just a simple tiny movement that is the release I crave.

Fuck, I needed that. I move my finger around and her breathing gets hotter. I pull my other hand away, but with no intention of ignoring that delicious breast.

I drop my mouth to it, taking her nipple into my mouth through the bra, and I use my free hand to jerk her skirt up higher and then one thumb rubs against her clit as my finger moves inside her.

She is mine within a minute.

She cries out so hard and loud that I have to give up her beautiful breast and claim her mouth instead, if only to silence her. I absorb her scream and cries as she orgasms around my finger. Her pleasure saturates the room, vibrating around us heavily—it's heavenly.

It's a start, but it's nowhere near enough…

'It needs to go higher, Mummy.'

'Up here?' I hook the ornament across and press it into the branch carefully.

'Nooo…' She sighs with exasperation that defies belief for a four-year-old. Ivy's mannerisms are captivating, except when they're frustrating. 'Way up there!'

I can still feel tingles in my body, unfamiliar and heavenly all at once, throbs of pleasure like little waves that rock me out of nowhere.

I blink and see the way he was *afterwards*. After he'd pulled his finger out of me and straightened my skirt with almost clinical detachment, stepping away from me and nodding, like I was an item on his 'to-do' list and he'd 'to-do-ed' the heck out of me.

'I'll come back tomorrow.' That was all. No 'What time suits?' or 'We should talk.' A directive rather than a question—a decision. A firm instruction.

And I'd nodded! What the hell had I been thinking?

I should have told him no. That we couldn't see one another again.

I should have told him how wrong we'd been to do... *that*. Oh, God. My insides are knotted. I know that when I slip away from Ivy and take a bath, my underwear will be wet with proof of my desire, that my body has been changed by Noah's possession and he didn't so much as show me his chest.

I can't see him again. I must see him again. I'm so torn. I draw in a deep breath. I know I can't see him *professionally*.

Our relationship isn't formalised—he hasn't filled anything out. I haven't billed him. I sweep my eyes shut. That's a technicality and I know it. But if I spell it out to him, making sure he understands that I can no longer have him in my office, no longer treat him as a patient, does that leave me ethically free to see him in other ways? And am I really okay with that?

'Mummy!' Ivy stamps her foot. 'You're just staring into space!'

'Sorry,' I mumble, turning my attention back to the job at hand.

I loop the ornament on the second-highest branch and, apparently satisfied, Ivy nods before reaching into the box and carefully unwrapping the next one along. Ivy has always been very careful. Even as a one-year-old she would take care when doing anything. She has always eaten neatly, used a napkin to wipe her fingers, placed her shoes side by side at the front door. She is the definition of particular.

In other words, the opposite to me.

And her father, come to think of it.

I have always thought certain areas were black and white, but this is one with many, many shades of grey. Noah came to me for help and, though our relationship isn't that of patient and doctor, I worry about how this development might affect him. And, yes, I worry about how it will affect me.

'What's this one?' She wrinkles her nose—so like Aaron's—and passes me the ornament.

I force myself back to Ivy, the tree, and try to ignore the fuzzy worries on the periphery of my brain. 'Ah. I made this when I was ten years old.' I stare at the little decoration, the small foam ball that I painstakingly stuck fabric to, then dotted with sequins. I remember sitting on the floor of my parents' lounge, my knees covered in a blanket, my hair long around my shoulders, determined to make the decoration according to the instructions. 'It took quite a long time.'

'Really?' Ivy probably doesn't mean to sound so scathing and I can't help but laugh.

'Yes, dearest.' I push the ornament into the branches and wait for another decoration.

'Ebony James says it's too early to put up the tree,' she says, her eyes darting to mine and then flicking away, as if afraid of the sacrilegious assertion she's just repeated.

My smile is kind. 'Everyone has different traditions. Perhaps in Ebony James's house they put their tree up later.'

'Do most people put their tree up now?'

I shrug. 'They're up in shops, aren't they?'

Ivy nods but looks far from convinced.

'Why shouldn't we enjoy the tree for a month? Christmas only comes around once a year and it's such a waste not to enjoy it fully. Don't you think?'

'I suppose so.' Her smile is more genuine now.

She goes back to unboxing ornaments and I go back to hanging them, but my mind keeps threatening to drag me back to Noah, my desk, my office and that pleasure.

Decorating the tree is one of my favourite pastimes. We have a real tree, but of course it's too early to have a chopped tree, so ours is potted. I water it every few days to keep it fresh and then, after Christmas, once it's denuded of decorations once more, I put it on a trolley and push it back into our small courtyard garden. There it remains all year round, dormant and hibernating, waiting for its time to shine—literally—with the strings of lights we weave through its greenery.

I love doing this, and even more so now that Ivy is old enough to join in with me, but I'm barely in the moment.

By the time Ivy is in bed, and I have had dinner, I am itching to crawl between my sheets and surrender to the dreams of him that I know will follow.

I check my emails quickly first—a habit I've fallen into since having Ivy and needing to do some of my work from home—and his name is the first I see.

Noah Moore—Bright Spark Inc

I click into it faster than I can believe.

It's a short email. Just a few words. But they rob me of breath and make my knees sag.

I can smell you on my hand. Tomorrow I want to taste you.

CHAPTER FOUR

HIS EMAIL SPINS through my mind all day. I hear the words he'd written, voiced in his inimitable accent. Australian with a dash of arrogance and a bucketload of don't-give-a-fuck. I guess having squillions of pounds could give someone that attitude, but I don't think that's the beginning and end of it.

I'd put money on Noah having been like this for a long time—before having money and commercial success. I think his arrogance is stitched into his being; every cell of his body is made up of the same.

But my lines of deduction are now very blurry. As a therapist, I would have the ability to look beneath that arrogance and see what he's trying to hide—to guess at what makes him tick. As a woman, I see only the arrogance and it's sexy as all hell. I don't want to push at it. I don't want to guess what's beneath him.

Professionally, that makes me redundant.

I make a soft groaning noise and dip my head forward, catching it in my hands.

'I'm heading off. You need anything before I go?' Beatrice steps into my office. 'Are you okay?'

I nod, masking my doubts with ease for her. It's only Noah who seems to have unstitched my defences, to have robbed me of my stock-in-trade ability to conceal my feelings and thoughts.

'I'm fine. Thank you, Bea.'

My smile feels wooden, but hers is natural, as though nothing is wrong. As though everything is fine. She leaves and a moment later I hear the clicking of the outer door.

It's Friday and that means I'm alone—no need to rush home. Ivy is spending the night with her grandmother—Aaron's mother, not mine. It's part of our agreement, one I didn't have to enter into but felt would be best for Ivy. Aaron might be an A-grade asswipe, but that doesn't mean his mother is. And it doesn't mean Ivy should lose all connection with that side of the family—just because I never want to see him again.

I can smell you on my hand. Tomorrow I want to taste you.

My stomach swoops and I fix my gaze to the screen, forcing myself to skim through my patient notes as though I'm not falling apart at the seams.

An hour later and I can't ignore the fact I'm disappointed.

Because he's my kryptonite. I barely know Noah, but there's something so indefinable about him. His cockiness and the haunted vulnerabilities I have glimpsed flash for a second before they are once again concealed beneath the surface. Far beneath the surface, out of my prying hands' way.

He makes me raw and exposed with just a look. Should I run a mile? Away from him? Or to him? Should I pursue this? Do I dare?

'You know, you frown when you're concentrating.'

Jesus Christ! My heart slams into my ribs and the hairs on the back of my neck stand on edge. Survival skills I had thought long since discarded leap to the fore, making my body tremble with its adrenal response, my eyes naturally darting to the door for an escape.

But it's not Aaron.

It's okay. I'm safe.

No, I'm not safe. I'm in more danger than I'd realised because Noah Moore is in the sanctuary of my office, staring at me like he has every right, and I am speechless.

'What are you doing here?' Slowly my heart finds a different rhythm. Still far faster than it should beat, but for a different reason.

He's wearing a *suit*.

A suit. All tailored and professional and smart-looking, but it's *Noah Moore* and he's as hot as ever. No, more so like this. The perfect contradiction.

He strolls towards me and places his hands on the edge of the desk, his body once more invading my personal space, his scent inviting me to breathe deeply. I do just that and see the quirk of his lips, like he knows what motivates me. It sobers me and I swallow, turning my gaze downwards.

'What do *you* think I'm doing here?' The words are

drawled out slowly and they pour over my flesh like sun-warmed butter.

My heart skips a beat. 'I don't know,' I hear myself murmur, wondering at the fact I'm still able to speak at all. 'But, Noah, I have to talk to you. If you're here for therapy, I need to tell you that I absolutely cannot see you again. Professionally, I mean—' my cheeks flushing '—not after what happened. I'm a professional and I can't treat someone who's…who I've…'

'Yes?' he drawls.

'I just can't be your therapist, okay? I have to say that to you now, loud and clear. It's a line I'm not prepared to cross.'

'That's good. Because I don't want fucking therapy.'

There's a dark edge to the words. They are honest and plainly spoken. I cannot misunderstand him, and yet I ask: 'So what do you want?'

'You.'

There is only the sound of my own breathing. Fast and sharp. He is watching me, waiting for me to speak, and I can't. I fear I'm my own worst enemy. I cannot give in to this desire—*not again!* I don't do this kind of thing. Do I?

'Yesterday was a mistake.' I say the words bluntly, hoping to avoid his perception that there's any wriggle room. 'As you obviously know, it's been a long time since I was intimate with anyone and I…obviously… feel attracted to you.' Heat simmers in my blood; embarrassment clips at my heels.

'Why was it a mistake?'

I swallow. 'Where to begin?' I'm going for humour,

but there's nothing lighthearted in the way he's looking at me. I stand up, reaching for my handbag, hiding
the way my fingertips are shaking.

'You're… Look.' I shake my head.

'Yes?' He's intense.

'You're *you*,' I say, shaking my head. 'Billionaire,
famous, and I think you live in a very different world
to me.' My smile is an attempt to soften the rejection.

'I'm not talking about marrying you,' he says with a
slow, purposeful wink. 'I'm talking about you, me and
all this chemistry…'

There's something like relief in the admission—that
he feels as I do. That our chemistry is mutual.

'Chemistry isn't a good enough excuse for me,' I
say, moving towards the door to my office as every
single bone in my body wants me to throw myself at
his chest.

My fingers curl around the doorknob and he's there,
a hand pressing to the wood panelling on one side of
me, then the other, caging me, so that when I turn I'm
imprisoned by his beautiful body. He's so broad and
tall, so strong and masculine. 'Let me tell you something, Holly.'

My name on his lips is pure, sensual heat. I swallow,
not sure if I'm capable of speaking.

'You know what I think?'

I shake my head slightly. He catches my cheek in
the palm of his hand, holding me still. His touch is like
wildfire; it spreads flame through me.

'You're lonely. You want me. And I want you. So?'

There is truth in all those statements. Still, I can't bring myself to admit that.

'Noah.' His name is a moan. 'It's clear that we're attracted to one another. I'm not going to bother lying to you, or trying to hide it.'

His laugh is an arrogant agreement. 'I'm glad to hear you say that.'

'But you came to me for therapy…and I can't ignore that.'

His eyes narrow. 'You just told me you won't take me on as a patient.'

I nod. 'I meant that.'

'So help me in this way,' he demands.

My eyes sweep shut because it's exactly what I want.

'I need you to see someone else. I know a good doctor, Dr Chesser. I can make an appointment for you. I can help you in that way. Because I'm not going to be the reason you didn't get the therapy you need. Got it?'

Anger flashes in his face.

I lift a hand to his chest. 'I mean it, Noah.'

'I don't need fucking therapy.'

'That's your decision. But if you want me…then you'll agree to this. You'll agree to let Dr Chesser help you instead of me.'

His eyes lock on mine. I can see that he's waging a war, a battle that is ancient and primal and all-important. Finally, he leans closer and his breath glances across my cheek. 'And then you'll be mine?'

I nod slowly, a frisson of awareness travelling the length of my body. 'Yes.' And I mean it, from deep within my heart.

* * *

It's freezing cold when we emerge onto the street. My office is just around the corner from London Bridge. I've been here for the last three years; prior to that, I was in Mayfair. This is a far better commute, though— our home is a twenty-minute walk from the office and on days when Ivy is with her grandmother I prefer to walk. No matter the weather, I find it clears my mind. I walked this morning, though my mind isn't feeling particularly clear right now.

He is right beside me. Not touching, but I feel everything. His breath, his thoughts—I feel all of him.

'Here.' He reaches onto the back of a motorbike and pulls off a helmet. My chest thumps.

'This is yours?' I nod towards the bike. It's big, matte black and like nothing I've ever seen. It's like a stallion, all sleek and strong and somehow beautiful despite the fact I hate motorbikes. Their noise, their speed, their inherent danger.

'Nah. I just thought we'd steal it for the night.' He grins as he lifts the helmet onto my head.

All arguments are silenced as I am lost to the effect of his proximity. His fingers are surprisingly gentle as they graze my jaw, locking the helmet into place. And his concern for my safety is somehow pleasing, reassuring, like what we're about to do meets some criteria of a 'normal' relationship when there is *nothing* normal about this.

He turns back to the bike and climbs on, his haunches so powerful in his suit, his expression holding a silent challenge as he looks at me. 'Well? Aren't you going to climb on?'

The double entendre is intentional this time. My cheeks flame.

'On that?' I point at the rear end of the bike dubiously.

'Jesus. You're afraid of this too?'

'I'm not afraid of...' I close my lips and look around guiltily. 'Do you enjoy teasing me?'

'Yes. Get on the bike, Holly.'

My name on his lips kicks confidence into me. Thanking the heavens I wore pants today, I lift my leg over the side of the bike and settle myself behind him. There are little divots that are the natural resting place for my feet and so I place them there. My hands are another story.

Despite the fact I've twice now begged this man to fuck me, I am shy about holding him intimately.

He looks at me in the rear-vision mirror—he can't see my eyes through the helmet, but he wears none and his look is mocking. So much mocking from this man and it doesn't occur to me to mind.

'Hold on, Doc.'

I should ask him to call me something else but, now that I've spelled out the boundaries of our relationship, I have to admit that hearing him call me by my professional title is so damned hot.

I nod, figuring touching him is better than falling off the back of the bike and being roadkill.

I wrap my arms around his waist and wriggle forward so our bodies are melded together. His eyes burn into me and, despite the fact he can't see me, my soul sears at the eye contact; it melts at the physical contact. My body is on fire.

The engine throbs to life, a powerful reverberation beneath me, and I have to bite down on my lower lip to stop from groaning. My body is over-sensitised and every single nerve ending jumps in response to this stimulus.

He pulls out into the traffic and hunches down a little—I stay curved around his back, my head pressed to the side, watching London in a blur as we tear through the city.

Despite what Ebony James might think, London is already wearing her festive finery. Lights twinkle overhead and Christmas trees mark the public spaces. It's hard not to be caught up in the beauty of it as we pass— but I'm only partially aware of the sights. Same with wherever we're going.

Noah Moore between my legs feels amazing. I know this is crazy and out of character, but when did I last do anything like that?

I've never been into the casual sex thing. Aaron was my first boyfriend, my high school sweetheart. And before I knew what a controlling bastard he was, I'd lost my heart and my virginity to him.

Still, I've never been with anyone else. I don't know if I can make love to someone and then move on, if I can be Noah's drug of choice.

By the time he pulls up out the front of a bar—and I have no idea where—my buzz is at risk of disappearing.

Despite that, I'm reluctant to walk away from him. Danger signals are everywhere and yet I loosen the helmet and place it on the handlebars, then step off the bike and put my hand in his, our fingers interlaced as though we are already intimate lovers, used to weaving our bodies together like this.

'Let's go, Doc.'

Pushing my doubts aside, I admit to myself that I want this with all of me. For once in my life, I'm going to do something selfish and stupid and to hell with the consequences. I suspect Noah Moore will be worth it.

CHAPTER FIVE

HE SHOULDERS THE door in—my stomach swoops because the small, meaningless gesture seems metaphorical. Like I've cracked open a wardrobe and I'm slipping into Narnia. One night, one decision and I already know my life will never be the same again.

The place is pumping. It's a Friday night, and though I prefer to be at home catching up on period dramas, apparently the rest of the world still does *this*.

I like it. No, I more than like it. I love it. I feel like an entirely different woman as I walk in beside Noah Moore. People turn to look at him, then me and, unlike my usually reserved self, I don't care. I like being seen with him. Confidence straightens my back.

It's probably almost loud enough to drown out my thoughts and doubts. He's known here. The woman behind the bar—Jesus, I thought I had big breasts—winks at him and now the jealousy is unmistakable. I go to pull my hand free, but his fingers squeeze mine. He looks down at me and, for a millisecond, it's like no one else exists. There is just the throb of heat between us, a bright, burning, existentialist need that I will have to face or conquer—and soon.

'Hungry?' It's so loud that he has to lean down and whisper into my ear. Just the feel of his breath on my skin spreads goosebumps across me. My tummy drops as though I've just crested over the high point of a roller coaster—I'm in freefall.

I nod, just a jerk of my head. It's all I'm capable of.

'What do you want?' His lips twitch, like he knows what I *really* want. And of course he does. He's forced me to admit that—to him, and myself.

'Whatever.' I shrug. It's definitely not my usual style. I'm more of an Italian-at-six kind of diner.

He grins and weaves through the people until we reach the bar, where he's immediately served by she-of-the-big-breasts-and-low-cut-top. He speaks quietly to her too, so I don't hear what he orders, and I think my tummy is too twisted into knots to manage food anyway.

His eyes pierce me then and he jerks his head to his left. I follow the direction of the gesture and see only more people. But Noah leads me that way, his fingers still tight on mine, guiding me through the throng of revellers and, behind them, to a table in the back. It's a high table with two stools.

'Something you reserved?' I ask as we sit down.

It's so loud I have to raise my voice and I'm still not sure he hears. That suspicion is confirmed a minute later when he shakes his head and then stands, coming to my side and propping his elbow on the table. Once again, I have the sense that I'm imprisoned by him, by his big body and strong arms. And I realise how much I like that feeling.

It is a dangerous impulse—remember? I like bad boys. And the sense of being protected is almost always a lie. Men like Noah break your heart. Men like Aaron nearly kill you. The only protection comes from within. I am my own strength now.

'You come here often?' I say instead, wishing I had a drink to swallow the sudden dryness in my throat. As if my thoughts could convert to deed, a waitress—not Big Breasts, someone else—saunters over and places an ice bucket with champagne in the middle of the table. Two glasses are hooked into it, but she also has a pint of beer. She pushes it towards Noah with yet another wink—is that how they communicate here?—then swishes her hips as she walks away.

I'm way happier than I should be when his eyes stay trained on my face instead of following her curvaceous departure.

He's staring at me, in fact, and the longer his eyes roam my face, the faster my pulse throbs in my body, the hotter my blood becomes. I don't look away; nor does he. When I swallow, in an attempt to bring moisture to my desert-dry mouth, his eyes drop—briefly—to my throat, and then my lips. My stomach twists.

'Do I have something on my face?' I arch a brow, trying to sound a little sarcastic when I desperately don't want him to stop looking at me.

But I should have known better than to stir Noah Moore. He reaches for my chin, gripping me lightly between his thumb and forefinger, holding me for examination. Holding me under the beam of his gaze, staring at me in a way that makes my skin goose all over. Staring at me like I am the only person in the room—no, the world. He moves closer, within the triangle of my legs. Our body heat is volcanic.

'Nah. Your face is pretty perfect.'

Pleasure pumps my heart.

He grins and drops his hand from my face—the absence of contact sears me—turning to lift the champagne flutes and bottle from the ice bucket. He pops the cork with ease, like a man who's done so often, and fills only one of the glasses before sliding it across the table to me.

In university, I used to drink vodka, lime and soda. And more than I should have. Now I don't drink often, and almost only drink champagne. Noah's chosen my favourite bottle. I lift the glass to my lips, savouring the first hint of bubbles as they pop against my flesh and breathing in its crisp, fruit-driven aroma.

He watches me with that intense way he has, as I take a sip and swallow, and heat is simmering through me. He's so close, just an inch or so from my knees. Doubts are somewhere deep in the back of my mind, but I cannot grasp them now. I don't want to grasp them. Instead, I smile at him and he smiles back. A slow, considered smile that makes me ache to know everything about him.

He draws a sip of his beer and then places his glass on the table, right beside my champagne flute. His hand drops to my knee. It's a casual touch, but it's possessive too, like he's staking his claim, and I like it. Oh, I like it so much.

'So, you have a daughter,' he prompts, his Australian accent sounding thicker here.

I nod, and my lips twist with a smile as I think of Ivy.

'How old?'

'She's four and a half. She'd want me to say the half—it's very important to her. She's already planning her fifth birthday extravaganza.' I'm babbling. His fingers have crept higher, to my hip, which brings his body right back to mine, so close.

'She looks a lot like you.'

'I know.'

'Who's the father?'

The question is surprising, and not. I mean, it's a natural thing to wonder about, isn't it? If I weren't wildly attracted to him, would it strike me as a strange thing to ask? Would I be hesitating like this?

Or is it just that I haven't spoken to anyone about Aaron for a really long time? Even within my family, he is a taboo subject. My parents' shame is a complex emotion—their shame at my divorce, at the situation I was in and at their inability to be there for me when I needed them.

'My ex,' I say.

Noah laughs. Just a short sound that mixes derision with amusement. *'Obviously.'* He drawls the word in his best, most mocking tone. Why do I find even that sexy?

Because I like bad guys. Shouldn't I have learned my lesson by now?

'When'd you break up?'

These are normal questions. And yet ice is taking over the flames within me, cooling me, reminding me of the fear that dogged my every step for many years. 'We... grew apart.' I reach for my champagne and take several sips, my eyes focused on a point over his shoulder.

'I call bullshit.'

He's right. I jerk my head in a small nod. 'We were together a long time. Right from school... We dated while I was at university and then when I opened my practice.' My eyes meet his for a moment and I'm comforted by whatever it is I see in their depths. He tops up my champagne and murmurs something I don't catch, but words I take as encouragement to continue.

To my surprise, I do just that. 'He's a musician,' I say, rolling my eyes at my innocent naivety. 'A guitarist.' As though that explains everything. 'Very, profoundly talented. But a tortured artistic soul.' I'm making light of the situation. My parents aren't the only ones with shame coursing through their veins.

He nods, his eyes drilling into me. 'What aren't you saying?'

I'm surprised. It must show on my face. I'm the one who reads people and yet he's summarised me with ease. And though this isn't a therapy session and he's not my patient, I add his perceptiveness to what I know about him. It is not uncommon in people who have experienced lengthy trauma—trauma like mine. I became adept at analysing every single flicker of emotion that passed over someone's face; I suppose that was my flight or fight instincts.

'Why do you think there's anything I'm not saying?'

He shrugs. 'Because it's the truth.'

'You think you know me so well?'

'Well? Am I wrong?'

Our eyes are locked; it is a battle of wills that is making my knees tremble. I reach for my champagne and realise he's hardly touched his beer.

'No,' I say, once I've had a sip. 'It's just not a subject I like to talk about.'

'There's an irony in that.' He grins.

'I'm a therapist,' I tack on. 'It's my job to ask the questions, not answer them.'

'Whereas you just want to fuck me?'

My cheeks burn at the directness of his question. 'I...'

'How long were you together?' He lobs the question back, his directness reminding me that he is a very successful businessman. That beneath the bad boy stubble and the loud, growling motorbike and the fact he swears and drinks like a sailor, he is smart and incisive, ruthless and intelligent.

'Six years.'

'And were you happy together?'

'What do you think?' I deflect. 'We split up.'

'That might mean he cheated or you did...'

'I didn't cheat,' I say firmly. 'And I don't think he did either.'

'So?' He shrugs. 'What happened?'

It's highly likely the glass and a half of champagne I've consumed on a near-empty stomach have loosened my tongue, or maybe it's the five years of not speaking to anyone except my lawyer and the judge, but I hear myself say, 'When I was four months pregnant with Ivy, he strangled me until I passed out.' I can't look at him. The shame that runs through me is hard to ignore. I trace invisible circles around the base of my champagne flute. 'I kept thinking he'd change, you know? It wasn't like he was abusive—that's what I used to tell myself. He was just stressed. His recording contract was dissolved, or he felt inferior to me because I earned five times what he did.' I shrug. The excuses sound so ridiculous to me now. 'And it was nothing—in the beginning. You know? Like he'd grab my arm too tight, but he was always so apologetic. And I'd known him and loved him for so long.' Tears clog the back of my throat. I thought I was done crying for him!

'Anyway. I kept waiting for things to calm down, for him to go back to "normal", but that became the new normal.'

'He beat you?' The question is asked softly, but I hear it loud and clear, despite the background noise of the busy bar.

Another waitress appears, placing a platter down on the edge of the table. Neither of us look at her or it; I'm simply aware of it in the periphery of my vision.

'Beat me? Yeah, I guess you could call it that. He controlled me. Manipulated me. Pulled my hair. Broke my wrist. Locked me in our bedroom for two days straight and refused to let me eat or drink anything.' I lift my eyes to Noah's face now, finding the whip of strength that compelled me—finally—to leave Aaron. The look on his face robs me of breath.

There is such understanding there. Such a look of

empathy that I feel I am speaking to someone who understands. 'I never thought that could happen to me. I'm strong and smart and I come from a close-knit family. They all adored Aaron. From the outside, we had the perfect life.' I grimace. 'Such a cliché.'

'Fucking bastard,' he says after a moment.

'Yeah. Anyway, once I was pregnant, I knew I couldn't take the risk any more. I'd let him treat me like a punchbag for years, but what if he did that to our baby? I'd tried to help him. I'm a therapist, for Christ's sake, surely I should have known what to say or do…'

'You can't help some people,' Noah says with authority, and I wonder if he's speaking about himself or someone he knows.

'I learned that lesson,' I admit.

'Do you ever see him?'

I shake my head. 'I have a restraining order. Not that I need it. He's in prison. A week after leaving me, he strangled a prostitute. Put her in a coma for six months.' I swallow. 'Attempted murder—fifteen years.'

'Jesus.' Noah doesn't touch me and he doesn't offer me platitudes, both of which I appreciate. I need to absorb the fact that I've just told someone my deepest secret. And that I'm still standing.

Well, sitting, technically.

He doesn't say anything for a really long time and I wonder if I've spooked him. There's a reason I usually keep this stuff to myself.

'I don't know why I told you that,' I say, shaking my head so that my hair fluffs against my cheeks. 'I don't generally…'

He lifts a single finger to my lips, holding it there to silence me.

'I asked.'

I swallow. I don't know why but the simple explanation is somehow important.

His finger lifts higher, running over my cheek, and I instinctively blink my eyes shut as he moves his finger higher, to the ridge of my brow. To the scar that is roughly six years old.

'His handiwork?'

I forget about the scar, most of the time. It is just a part of me now. One of the many bumps and indents that have formed on my body over time. Some from ageing, many from Aaron.

I nod slowly and Noah swears harshly under his breath. 'I want to kill the fucker.'

A frisson of something like danger rolls over my spine because I don't for a second doubt he means it. That he would—and could. His virile strength is a huge part of his appeal, but I want him to use that strength for pleasure, not pain.

As if sensing the surge of fear and adrenaline that rushes over me, he smiles, a smile that is sexy and charming and draws me back to the moment. I reach for my champagne and sip it, no longer self-conscious or nervous—no longer analysing the faults of my fate. I am simply surrendered to it.

'Sometimes you sound very Australian.'

He arches a brow, reading my comment for what it is: a distraction.

'I am Australian,' he says dismissively and surprises

me then by leaning forward and pressing a kiss to my eyebrow, to the scar that marks my flesh.

My heart turns over in my chest and my danger sensors flare.

With a sixth sense that perhaps my emotional health depends on it, I smile thickly and continue, 'When did you move here?'

'To London?' He pulls back, reaching for his beer and sipping it before topping up my champagne. 'About five years ago.'

'To England,' I clarify.

I sense his desire to pull away from me, but he doesn't. I'm unbelievably pleased. 'A week after I turned eighteen.' His smile is a very masculine version of the Mona Lisa's, every inch as enigmatic and mysterious. I wonder at the secret memories he's holding on to, and why he keeps them wrapped to his chest.

'But not straight to London?'

'No.'

Closed answers. In a therapy session I would let him get away with it, being ever-careful not to spook him, to antagonise and alienate him. Here, in a packed bar, with his beautiful body between my legs and the temptation of a night together on the periphery of my mind, I make free to push him.

'Where did you go?'

He looks as though I'm the dentist and he's terrified of needles. Odd, when I think Noah Moore isn't afraid of much at all. 'Oxford.'

'Oxford? As in university?'

'Would that surprise you?'

I frown. It does, and I can't say why.

'My…business partner and I did a coding course there,' he says. 'It was just a summer school—not really affiliated with the university, just using the campus.'

'That's where you started Bright Spark?'

He nods again. 'At least, where we started on the path towards it. It was another few years before we launched.'

'And then it all happened very fast,' I say, noting the admiration that softens my words.

He dips his head forward in concession and I sip my champagne. Is that my second or third glass? I don't know, but it's delicious.

I am buzzing all over. In my abdomen and my soul, my mind and my mouth. I am a lightning storm and he is the ocean, drawing all of my electricity down, causing me to spark and flash.

I look at him and a bolt of awareness lights up, hard and fast. I shiver—a good shiver. One of anticipation and indulgence; one of reward.

I don't realise how affected by the champagne she is until she stands, looking for the ladies' room. She presses a hand against my chest to steady herself and my cock surges forward, thinking his moment is nigh.

Only, she sways and her eyes blink, like she's confused in some way. Shit. She's had almost the whole bottle and eaten very little. I've been demolishing the platters as we've talked, satiating one hunger before turning my attention to another.

Her eyes scan the bar, but her frown gathers, like she barely knows where she is.

'This way.' My voice is gruff. I put an arm around her waist, offering more support than guidance, and lead her to the restrooms at the back. I fight the urge to take her in myself—but wince as she walks down the hallway and has to hold the wall for support.

Five minutes pass. Six minutes. I'm on the brink of storming into the restroom myself when she comes out, looking a little more in control, though still resting her hand on the wall as she walks towards me.

Her smile is bright as she approaches. 'Let's go home.'

The words are slurred, but her meaning is clear. My heart slams against my ribs as I imagine the doc in my home.

'Your place?' I prompt.

'No.' She shakes her head emphatically and then winces once more. She presses a finger to my chest. '*Your* place.' She runs her finger down the centre of my chest, all the way to my abdomen, lingering there as her eyes lock on mine and her teeth pull her full lower lip in.

I fight an urge to push her back against the wall. I fight many urges, in fact, in this moment. I'm as shocked as anyone could be to discover that I have some ancient decency within me that makes the idea of taking advantage of her violently abhorrent.

That makes me more concerned for her than I am aroused—which is really saying something as my body is like a fucking grenade about to go off.

'This way.' The words are unintentionally short, as though I'm angry with her, and I see hurt flash in her eyes.

She reads me like a damned book and I hate that. I smile—it's tight on my face, but I hope it placates her. At the entrance to the bar, I look outside. I can't see any photographers and this is hardly the kind of place that anyone of note frequents—one of the reasons I like to come here and unwind. Blow off steam. Be unknown. I prop Holly just inside the door and stride out, retrieving my bike helmet and then returning to her.

Her eyes are shut, but she's standing.

'Here.' It's a hoarse directive. I fasten the helmet and then scrutinise her. 'Are you going to be able to hang on?'

'Yeah.' She nods. 'Let's go.'

I put an arm around her waist, guiding her from the bar, then seat myself on the bike. I keep a hand on her as she gets on behind me, relieved when I feel the press of her legs on my thighs, her arms around my waist, her head heavy against my back.

My place is only a ten-minute drive from the bar, but I practically hold my breath the whole time, needing to get her home, needing to get her off the back of my bike before she falls off.

She didn't seem at all affected by the champagne. She was talking, asking her fucking questions, eyeing me like she couldn't wait to get in my pants. And then she was…paralytic.

My face is a grimace as I pull the bike to a stop, the sludgy Thames issuing a steady, throbbing noise from its bowel as it bleeds a retreat to the sea.

'You okay?'

She's quiet for a moment before nodding, her eyes

so beautifully, distractingly hooded that I have to bite
back a curse. 'Yeah. I'm fine.'

She gets off the bike somewhat unsteadily, so I move
fast, kicking the stand down and then covering the distance between us in one motion. She sways again and I
swear under my breath, lifting her up over my shoulder
and stalking towards my front door.

'Hey!' Her laugh is breathless. 'What are you doing?'

'Getting you inside before you fall down.'

'I'm fine,' she insists, slapping her hand to my back
before sliding it lower, and lower, until her fingertips
find the bottom of my suit jacket and pull it up. Jesus. I
fumble with the key—this place is a hundred and fifty
years old and the keys must be almost as ancient. Big
and brass. That should be an advantage, but with all the
blood rushing to my dick I'm finding it cumbersome as
hell. Finally, I get the door open, right around the time
Holly triumphs over my shirt-slash-pants scenario and
finds the bare flesh of my back. Her fingers run over
me with a curiosity that is sensual and distracting.

I flick the lights to my left and she swears softly.
'That's so bright.'

'You're still wearing a helmet.' I laugh roughly, carrying her into my apartment and dropping her onto the
sofa. She falls elegantly—how can she do that when
she's drunk as all hell and wearing a helmet?

Her fingers fumble with the straps to no avail and,
suppressing a smile, I reach down and unclip it for her.

Shit. I'd forgotten her face. How distracting it is—
how fascinating. I'd forgotten the fucking scar too. A

surge of protective anger flashes through me so fast and shocks me to my core.

I'm not a protector.

Not even close.

At least, I've never felt that kind of instinct for anyone other than Gabe—probably the only person who needs protecting even less than I do.

But I feel it now. I feel an inexplicable fury that anyone could damage Holly. And because I understand the way scars work, I know the formation of the external scars is nothing compared to what she must carry inside. A heart that is scratched all over from repeated lashings and torment, a soul that is part withered from neglect and terror.

I'm lost in this moment of contemplation and so don't realise that she's pushing up to stand. Not until her sweet body presses against mine, her eyes hooded by desire and drunkenness. 'I.' She lifts unsteady fingers to the buttons on her shirt and undoes the top one. 'Want.' She works quickly for someone who's so clearly affected by alcohol. I see the lace swirls of her bra. Shit. 'You.'

I swallow hard as she removes the shirt altogether, revealing creamy skin and breasts I could weep for. It's perfect. 'To.'

Her hands move to the button of her pants and I know that I need to put an end to this. That I need this woman, who is already scarred and hurting, to be better than I am.

'Fuck.' She says the word as she pushes her pants down over her hips, revealing a tiny white thong that matches her bra. My body is tighter than a spring.

She steps out of her pants and then reaches around, unclipping her bra, dropping it at my feet while keeping her eyes locked to mine. 'Me.'

Holy shit.

I take several steps backwards, not running away from what she said so much as needing to get a better view of her. My throat is drier than the Strzelecki Track; my abdomen tightens with an ancient, primal need to possess.

'Holly.' I hear the pleading tone in the way I say her name, my desperation so very obvious. She sways unsteadily as she steps towards me; it would be callous of me not to catch her. But fuck, I wasn't prepared for how her skin would feel beneath my palm. My hand drops, curving around her arse, feeling her sweet roundness, holding her against the answering hardness of my aching cock.

She moans, her sweet cherry-red lips parting as her eyes find mine. Her throat is exposed and I want to run my mouth over it, to taste every single inch of her—all of her.

'Please,' she whispers and pushes up on tiptoe, trying to kiss me, looking for more of me.

I have about half a second to make my decision and it is so far from being easy. Because I want to fuck her. I want to fuck her hard, to make her all mine, to make her beg and make her scream, but she's drunk and, as I said, I have discovered I am a better man than I knew. A fact that is borne out by the way I once more lift her, this time cradling her to my chest, holding her against me and taking her up the exposed stairs that dangle from wires in the ceiling, leading to the mezzanine bedroom. I am gentle when I place her on the bed. She reaches for me and I kiss her gently, tasting the champagne and need on the tip of her tongue. I press my body over hers and I swear I could come. There is something within her that calls to me and I am desperate to answer it.

But not now. Not like this.

CHAPTER SIX

'WHAT TIME IS IT?'

I lift my eyes to the clock in the kitchen. 'Three.'

'You're still not sleeping.' Gabe's disapproval is obvious. I grip my neck, massaging it hard as my eyes lift, without my permission, to the mezzanine. She is almost completely silent, but for the occasional rustling of bed linen as she turns her near-naked body in my bed.

For three hours I have grappled with the fact that I have Holly Scott-Leigh in my bed and that I am down here, staring at a pixelated screen rather than being up there with her. Holding her. Kissing her. Worshipping her body.

'I take it you didn't keep your appointment to see the therapist?'

It's useless. I stand, walking into the kitchen and grabbing a bottle of rum down from above the fridge. 'I wouldn't say that.'

There's a pause. 'Really?'

I can understand Gabe's surprise. I love him like a brother—hell, we *are* brothers, courtesy of the foster system that birthed us both—but I nearly flattened him

when he gave me the ultimatum. When he told me I'd
lost my grip and needed help.

'So you're going to see her?'

'I saw her this afternoon,' I say, pleased I can be so
frankly honest with him. I don't add that she's flat-out
refused to see me as a patient. That her sense of ethics
has made that impossible. She's now just a woman I'm
going to fuck—no, more than that, but I can't express
that to Gabe.

I don't tell him that I've spent tonight with her. That
I've felt her sweet, soft skin and tasted her delicious lips.
That professionally I don't want a bar of Holly Scott-
Leigh, but in my bed I want all of her; all that she's got
to offer I'll take.

'Good.' I feel like a lying bastard when I hear the
relief in Gabe's voice. 'I know how hard it was to lose
Julianne...'

A familiar chasm in the region of my heart opens
wide. My fingers shake a little as I half fill the tumbler,
staring at the beautiful golden liquid. I lift it to my nose,
inhaling its intoxicating aroma gratefully.

'I'm fine,' I lie. 'What's happening in New York?'

There's a longer than normal pause and then Gabe
expels a breath. 'Nothing new.'

A frown tugs at my brows. I know Gabe better than
anyone, and I know when he's lying. He *doesn't* lie. He's
the most outrageously honest to a fault person I've ever
met, even when being honest causes him to come off
as an out-and-out bastard. He doesn't care. The truth
is his thing.

'Gabe?'

'*Sì?*'

My lips twist at the way he slips into his native tongue. He had six years in Italy before his mother stole him away, dragging him to her native Australia before abandoning him into the foster system. I didn't know him until much later, but he's told me that he spoke not a word of English. That he spent the first year in Australia being bullied for his accent and called 'dumb' despite the fact he is, and always has been, incredibly intelligent and focused.

Now he spends much of his time in Italy, and sometimes that language is at the fore of his brain more than English. Particularly when he's stressed.

'What the fuck's going on?' I demand, cutting to the chase.

'*Niente.* It does not matter.'

'But something *is* wrong? Is it the Calypso?' Calypso is the code name for the smartphone we have under development. It's incredibly confidential—one team of thirty-seven engineers has been working on it for fourteen months—but it's obsessed Gabe and me much longer than that and we're close to launch.

'No. It's…nothing. You need to go to sleep.'

I grunt. 'Fat fucking chance.'

'Noah.' Gabe says my name quietly. 'If you don't think she can help, I will find you someone else. I am… concerned for you.'

I expel a harsh breath. I know he's worried. I've gone off the rails lately—even for me. I can see it from his perspective and I can see it's not fair to him. I hate that I'm doing anything that might cause him pain but,

Jesus, this all just happened a month ago and I'm still dealing with it. That's normal, right?

'Don't be.' Once again, I lift my eyes towards the mezzanine. 'I'm coping fine.'

What the hell is that? Why are there blades slicing across my brain? What is that beating of tiny little drums against my nerve endings, making my temples throb with an unbearable pain? Oh, my God, my throat is stinging and… Oh hell. I'm naked.

In a bed that I would put money on belonging to Noah Moore.

Oh, my God.

Did we…? I stare down at my body, my naked body, except I'm still wearing underpants, which surely means…what? What does it mean? I think back to the way he kissed me and touched me in my office, on my desk, and I have no certainty about what has happened here. How can I?

I turn bleary eyes towards the bedside—there is no clock there and I have no idea where my bag and phone are. The best I can do to estimate the time is look out of the window. I reach for the thin, soft blanket at the foot of the bed and wrap it around my shoulders like a cape, planting my feet over the side of the bed and standing gingerly for a moment while I wait for the tectonic plates of my brain to shift back into alignment.

I'm never drinking again.

I tiptoe across the room—I have no idea why I'm being so stealthy—towards the window that's behind the bed.

London is still dark, the sky a velvet black, the moon a pearlescent glimmer hidden behind leaden clouds. I look back towards the bedroom, needing to take stock of my surroundings.

The bed is a mess, but that doesn't indicate that Noah was in it with me. I mean, I'm a flippy-floppy sleeper from way back. When Ivy was little, we used to co-sleep, but when she was two she asked to go into her own room because I woke her up so often. With the blanket wrapped firmly around my shoulders and desperately wishing I had some clothes I could put on instead, I take the first step down and then another. My head is throbbing.

No, it's cracking apart at the seams—emphatically, angrily.

I pause halfway down the stairs and study the apartment below.

It's less an apartment and more a loft, completely open and barely furnished.

A sofa—flashes of memory return, cemented by the sight of his motorbike helmet discarded carelessly on the floor beside it. A table. An armchair. There's no TV. No photographs or paintings on the walls, just one big whiteboard down the end with lots of writing on it, and another table in front of it that has several laptops all cabled together.

I have no idea where we are, what part of London, only that we're near the Thames. I can hear its lifeblood humming close by.

A noise calls my attention and I swivel my head—far too fast, *ouch*—towards it. Noah is emerging from around the corner, a glass of something that looks like alcohol in his hand. My stomach convulses at the very idea.

Please, please, *don't throw up.*

As if he hears my presence, his eyes lift to the mezzanine, landing on me almost instantly, and the tug of desire that swirls through me overtakes almost everything else. Almost, but not quite.

I hold the blanket tighter around me and resume my slow walk of shame, moving downstairs until I'm on the same level as Noah, albeit across the room.

He doesn't speak, but his face says everything. His face that is part-mocking, part-amusement and with a dash of concern.

'I…' What? What can I say to explain the way I wrote myself off? Hardly sophisticated. I wish I could remember what we did when we got back, but alas, my mind is an utter blank. 'What happened last night?'

It's still the same night, but he doesn't correct me. He throws back a glug of whatever he's drinking, keeping his eyes pinned to me.

'You don't remember?'

Oh, God. Did we sleep together? Did I waste my chance of being with Noah by being too drunk to remember it? Did he sleep with me when I was in that state?

'No.' I shake my head and then wince—he winces in response, apparently understanding my pain.

'Sit down, Holly, before you throw up.'

I glare at him, like this is all his fault. 'I'm fine,' I lie. 'Where are my clothes?'

He places his drink down on the table and prowls towards me, heat burning me with his proximity.

'I like you naked,' he says, his eyes dropping to the opening revealed by the blanket.

I can't meet his eyes. Instead, I stare at the floor, keeping my hands clasped around the blanket. 'Did we…? I can't remember.'

'Did we what?' He's enjoying my discomfort. Bastard.

'Did we sleep together?'

'I don't sleep, remember?'

And I realise that it's the middle of the night and he's wide awake, still wearing his suit, though he's shed the jacket and rolled his shirtsleeves up to his elbows, revealing tanned forearms that are works of art.

'Did we…have sex?'

'No, Holly.'

That jerks my eyes up to his, and I think it's relief that's swirling through me. But only because I have no memory of the night, not because I'm glad we didn't. I still want him in a way that robs me of air.

'We didn't?'

He shakes his head.

'Oh. Good.' I nod brusquely. 'Then why am I hardly wearing anything?'

He walks towards me, closing the gap completely, his fingers curling around the fabric of my blanket cape. He pulls at it and drops it to the ground easily, his eyes challenging me to say something. I don't. I don't know why, but being undressed in front of Noah doesn't feel as weird as I'd thought.

When his eyes drop hungrily to my body, as though he is starving and I am his feast, it feels pretty damned good.

'Because you…' He presses a finger to the space between my breasts and I inhale a tortured breath. 'Wanted…' His eyes hold mine as he draws a line outwards to my left nipple, running a circle around it that makes me moan softly. 'Me…' His hand runs lower, to the soft flesh on the underside of my breast. He cups me and then drops his head forward, taking my nipple in his mouth and torturing me with his beautiful tongue until my knees are so weak I feel like I might fall. I barely hear the 'to' as he says it right against me, against my desperate, tortured nerve endings, against my body that is quivering for him.

He lifts his mouth to mine then and kisses me far harder than I would have thought I could manage, given my pounding head and scratchy brain. He kisses me like we are lovers who have been parted a decade, a kiss that sears my flesh.

'Fuuuuck…'

He pushes the word into my mouth, rolling it around with his tongue before lifting his head an inch and staring into my eyes. His hand that held my breast has roamed to my butt and is pushing me against him so I feel the thickness of his arousal on my stomach. 'You.' The last word is a hoarse, whispered admission.

I am lost, floating in an ocean of indeterminate swell and destination, simply being pulled whichever way it wants me to go.

If I wanted him to fuck me, why didn't he? I know he wants this as much as I do… 'But…you didn't?'

'No.'

'Why not?'

'When I fuck you, Doc, you're going to be screaming my name, not slurring it.'

'I was *not* slurring,' I say defensively, though of course I can't actually remember that for sure.

'You were drunk.' He lifts a hand to my brow. 'How do you feel now?'

'Fine,' I say, not intending to tell him my head's about to blow apart. And you know why? Because I want him—and I don't want him to have an excuse for not sleeping with me. All this build-up, all the flirtation, all the seduction—I can't bear it if it doesn't go anywhere. In fact, I'm not going to let that happen. I'm going to reach out and grab him with both hands.

Having opened the floodgates to desire when I have sought to ignore its existence for five years, I am unwilling to ignore it a moment longer.

'I still want you to fuck me,' I say boldly and catch the speculation in his eyes, the look of interest.

'I know.'

'So?' I lift my hands to his chest, tentatively at first, lifting my fingers to his buttons and unbuttoning the top two. He watches me without a word as I move painstakingly down his shirt, separating it finally from the waistband of his trousers and revealing his broad, muscled chest. He has a tattoo on his left pectoral muscle, a muscle that is strong and firm. I lift a quivering fingertip to it and trace the letters: *MCMXCIX*

Roman numerals? I wish I could remember how to decode them, but it feels like for ever ago that I learned the symbolism, that I was taught to translate the *M*s and *C*s and *X*s and turn them into relatable digits.

'What is this?' I murmur, wishing I were brave enough to lean forward and kiss him, to taste his flesh, to kiss him gently, firmly, desperately.

'Numbers.'

I roll my eyes. 'Yeah, obviously. But what number?'

'Nineteen ninety-nine.'

He catches my wrist and pulls it away, but I lift my other one, running my hand over his chest and feeling every dip and swoop, every muscle and sinew. His skin is smooth to touch, roughened by hairs down the middle. I swallow, taking a step to his side, where I see more tattoos at the top of his shoulder and across the blade of his bone. Tattoos that are somehow frightening, yet I don't know why. One is of a wraithlike creature, eyes that are sunken and knees that look to be made of stone. I shiver when I look at it.

'What's this?'

His jaw clenches and I wonder if he's not going to answer. But then he speaks, slowly, his accent thick and a lingering aroma of alcohol on his breath that should make me queasy but doesn't.

'Malingee,' he says, the word inflected with sounds that are foreign and new.

'Malingee?' I repeat, hoping for the same accent and missing.

His smile shows that I haven't pronounced it correctly. 'It's an Aboriginal spirit.'

'Really? What's its significance?'

He looks at me then and my breath catches in my throat for his nearness and beauty overtake me. 'I like it.'

I nod slowly, tracing around his back. It is blanked of ink but ripples with muscles beneath sinew and flesh. I can hear my blood pounding in my ears, heavy and demanding, torrid and fast. I reach his other arm; there is a simple dark scrawl that runs over his round shoulder. My eyes meet his and perhaps he senses my doubt, for he lifts a brow and watches me, his own breath seemingly held.

I lean forward, emboldened by him, me, us, this. My tongue finds the swirling edge of the tattoo and tastes it and him; his saltiness makes my stomach roll with instant need. Suddenly, having sex with Noah Moore has become the most important thing in my world and I will do whatever I can to make that happen.

No longer do I hear a single doubt from within my mind; I am conviction and certainty. As if to underscore my commitment to this, I run my hands around his back and slip my fingers into the waistband of his pants, finding the inch of flesh at the top of his butt. I hear his sharp exhalation of breath, feel it rustle the hair at my temple.

My body no longer aches with the after-effects of overconsumption; I am alive with anticipation for what will be.

'I haven't slept with anyone since him,' I say, knowing Noah understands. 'I haven't slept with anyone *but* him. Ever.' I don't know why but my smile is apologetic, as though my lack of experience might offend him in some way. And indeed, I see the shift of emotions crossing his face, the charge of wariness that makes him tighten and stiffen.

'I don't want him to be my only lover,' I say honestly, shrugging my shoulders, forcing myself to hold his gaze. 'I don't want him to be that.'

'You want me to fuck you to erase him?'

'No,' I say quickly, surprised at the way that sounds, about how it cheapens Noah—who should mean nothing to me and doesn't. 'I mean yes, but not just because of that,' I say honestly. Uncertainty is creeping back inside me. 'I thought you wanted this too.'

He looks at me with a hint of the mockery that defined our first and second meetings, a look that makes my doubts surge and makes me feel like maybe he really doesn't want me at all.

Did I say something wrong? Do something wrong?

Heat tingles through me—regret is my bedfellow. I hate drinking to the point I am drunk. I never do it.

Aaron used to drink. Aaron used to be drunk, often.

I pull away from Noah, stepping backwards, wishing desperately I were fully clothed. 'I…' I lift a hand to my temple, pressing my fingers into it uncertainly. 'I'm sorry.'

He doesn't react. 'What for?'

Good question. Maybe I'm still a bit drunk, because I don't seem able to think clearly. Or maybe that's just the proximity to this guy, his naked chest, his… All of him. 'I guess just…drinking so much.'

He laughs, the sound filling the apartment. 'Doc, I don't care. You think I'm offended by that?'

I shake my head slowly, wishing I could regain the confidence of moments earlier.

'I should go.'

He's quiet and watchful. 'Is that what you want?' he says after several long beats have passed.

I don't know what I want. Rather, I do, but I don't know now if I *should* and my indecision is driving me crazy.

'Where's your daughter?'

'Huh?' I spin around, Ivy the last thing on my mind at that moment.

'I presume she's not home alone?' he prompts, skimming his eyes over my face thoughtfully.

'Oh…no.' I shake my head. 'She's…with Aaron's mother. Ivy stays with her every Friday night and most of Saturday. Sometimes Saturday nights too. They're close…' I'm babbling. I don't realise until he crosses to me and lifts a finger, pressing it to my lips.

'So here's what's going to happen,' he says, speaking quietly. 'You're going to go back to my bed and sleep off the rest of your hangover. Naked, like this, so I can watch you if I want to, so I can see the way your breasts move as you breathe and your skin flushes as you dream of me. And then I'm going to wake you by kissing you here…' He touches my breast lightly and drags his finger down my body, lower and lower. 'And here.'

He touches the front of my underpants. 'And I'm going to kiss you here until you are falling apart and you are begging for me and then, Doc, I'm going to blow every other man from your mind. Sound like a plan?'

She is a restless sleeper, like me. When I do fucking sleep, which isn't often these days. She throws an arm over her head and her face scrunches up. I will myself not to wake her, not yet. I am testing myself—my strength and resolve—seeing if I can delay the inevitable. I am a man who enjoys instant gratification rather than delayed. I am a man who values instant pleasure.

And yet, with the Doc, I am savouring the anticipation of being with her, like I know the real thing won't live up to what I hope, what I need. Like I know she can't possibly feel and taste as good as she has so far.

But what if she does?

What if her body answers mine in every way? What if I feel a connection with her that is new and inherently dangerous for its impermanence? What if I get addicted to the way she feels and tastes and smells, to the small noises she makes in my arms. What if I become addicted to her smiles and her words, and her soft way of speaking?

Addiction is dangerous, so too the illusion of permanence, for nothing lasts for ever, and nor will this.

CHAPTER SEVEN

I DON'T KNOW what time it is when I wake. It is brighter; the sun has chased away the darkness, though the day is grey and gloomy. For a moment I forget where I am, stretching my arms over my head and expecting to connect with the familiar smooth wood of my bedhead and finding instead padded fabric.

A small frown as I consider this difference and then a noise, just a slight shift in body weight, and I look to the wall and see Noah. Noah Moore.

I'm in his apartment.

Memories of last night and earlier this morning shoot through me like flashes of lightning, spiking my blood.

He is reclining against the wall with a natural-born indolence, watching me. Staring at me. Devouring me with his eyes.

I sit up, the sheet tucked under my chin, my eyes doing their own hungry inspection of him. At some point since I last saw him, he has changed. Showered? His hair is damp. He's wearing a pair of jeans with the button undone, and nothing else.

My throat thickens with lust and hunger. 'Have you slept?'

He pushes off the wall but doesn't smile. He has two smiles—mocking and charming. I think I prefer the former for its honesty. The latter I suspect is simply a shield. A defensive mechanism developed to beguile and charm out of necessity rather than pleasure.

It is an insight that comes from nowhere and that cannot be explained nor substantiated.

'No.' For a second I forget what I've asked him, and what he's answering.

But then I see the hint of grey smudged across the skin beneath his eyes and something inside me flips over. 'You haven't slept at all?'

He shrugs, like it doesn't matter. 'I shut my eyes a few times.'

I trained as a psychologist but, beyond that, it's who I am. All thoughts of my own nakedness are forgotten. I drop the sheet and lean forward, concern etched on my face. 'You have to sleep,' I say urgently. 'It's important.'

He shrugs again. 'I will.'

'When?'

'When I do.' There's a hint of impatience zipping through the answer, but I refuse to be cowed.

'What is it?' I ask, bringing my knees up under my chin and looking at him seriously.

'Maybe it was the fact you were lying in my bed like this.' His smile is a ghost of a smile. 'Hard to sleep with a raging hard-on.'

I snatch a breath, holding it inside me, unable to exhale, unable to swallow. But I take the threads of our conversation and chase after them. 'When did you last sleep? For more than ten minutes,' I add before he can fob me off once more.

'Does it matter?' He strides towards the bed.

'Yes. There are loads of things that can happen if you're not sleeping properly. It's dangerous and...' He climbs in front of me and, as with last night—no, this morning, earlier—he presses a finger to my lips. I have no choice but to cease speaking.

'How do you feel?' His voice is gruff as he asks the question and my heart thumps.

'I'm serious, Noah. We need to talk about this.'

'Doc?'

I blink.

'I thought you said you didn't want to treat me.'

'I don't. I mean, not officially. But this is serious.'

'I really don't want you to be a therapist right now.'

I sink my teeth into my lower lip. 'No?'

'No.'

And he kisses me, hard, hard enough to press me back onto the bed, hard enough to make my head swim and my eyes close. His weight on top of me is the answer to a craving I didn't realise I felt. The feeling of him, pressing me against the mattress, makes all my nerves tingle.

'How do you feel?' He asks the question as his fingers slide into the waistband of my underpants, finding my thong and loosening it, pushing it down my thighs.

My arms lift and wrap around his neck, my fingers tangling in the thick dark hair at his nape.

'Doc?' He drags his mouth down to my breast, rolling his tongue over my nipple, drawing me into his mouth so that I arch my back and cry out all at once. I feel his smile against me and have no way of verifying that my feeling is correct because my eyes are squeezed shut, allowing the deluge of sensations to ransack my body.

'How do you feel?'

'Good,' I groan into the room, digging my fingernails into the sheets. How long has it been since a man has kissed me like this? Longer than five years. Five years since perfunctory, horrible, terrifying lovemaking with Aaron—so much longer since my body has been feted in this manner. He touches me as though I am made of porcelain and might break, and yet his kisses are savage and wild, thrilling me with their intensity and desperate need.

'No headache?'

'No!' And I no longer want him to treat me like porcelain. 'I'm fine!' I say the words loudly and push at his chest, wrapping my legs around him as I topple him backwards. On top of him, I have a thrill of something like power and pleasure and it dances through my system, fascinating my nerve endings.

I need him, need him so badly I cannot think straight. I find his jeans and push them down, just low enough to expose his dick. It's so hard and bloody huge that I have a momentary burst of doubt about what we're about to do. I try not to make comparisons to Aaron—it wouldn't be fair. No comparison to Noah seems fair, for any man.

I am so desperate for him, I ache to feel him between my legs, hot and strong inside me. He's disposed of my underwear and I hover over him, my fingers finding his cock and circling it tentatively at first and then more confidently as he groans. 'Fuuuuck…' The word is long and slow, the vowel extended, the tone dark.

'That's my plan.' I grin, lifting up and taking him inside me. Just his tip at first, and then he thrusts into me. It's been so long and he's so big that I feel almost as though it's my first time. I have forgotten how it feels to be so completely joined with someone. Have I ever felt this?

He holds my hips and anchors me so that I am on top while he is still somehow in control. He draws me down his length, my wetness slicking him, and then he holds me still while he thrusts into me, powerful and perfect. I am a bundle of feelings.

I tilt my head back, cresting along the wave of pleasure that his body offers, and when his hands run over my stomach, towards my breasts, his fingertips finding my nipples, I cry out—it's more pleasure than I have ever known. I am frightened and empowered all at once.

'It's so good,' I moan, lifting my hips now and trying to make him feel what I am, but he grips my hips tight and tumbles me back onto the bed, his eyes clashing with mine, daring me to argue.

His removal is an agony of extreme proportions. He pulls away from me and I push up onto my elbows, prepared to chase him—prepared to chase him to the ends of the earth if necessary.

He strides to his bedside table and pulls something small and metallic out and it is the first time I recognise that I haven't even thought of a condom. I would have had sex with him; I would have welcomed his release if he had offered it, without hesitation.

It is frightening enough to draw me out of the moment. 'Oh, my God.'

'What?' He's worried for me. It colours his expression and a drum bangs somewhere near my heart. 'Are you hurt?'

'No, I just can't believe I didn't think of protection.'

His smile is my crack cocaine. 'I guess you really wanted this.' And he pushes back inside me, now with him on top, and it feels new and different all over again. Doubts have no space in the field of pleasure; I am simply a ball of nerve endings and they are delighting in his nearness.

I realise that he was holding back before; perhaps worried about the complications of being in me without a barrier. Now he thrusts hard, possessing me as though it is his path to happiness and joy, as though I am his anchor point.

The wave collects me and every thrust brings me higher upon it, taking me to its peak, rolling me in its crest and dumping me onto the next wave, dragging me higher and higher until I am so close to the stars I swear I could reach out and touch them. My fingers drag over the sheets, but I feel celestial magic within my grasp and then I hear a noise, a sharp, loud, agonised cry—it takes me a moment to realise it is the sound of my own ecstasy, wrapping around us both. It takes me a moment to realise that an orgasm is wrenching me apart, one delightful sob at a time.

And then he is with me, his fingers laced through

mine, his body racked with the same grip of release, our cries combined, our breath fast, our bodies coated in sweat despite the coolness of the morning. He drops on top of me afterwards and I wrap my arms around him instinctively; my legs too. As though I am afraid he will withdraw and I will lose him—and this—even when I know that I must. That it is the natural conclusion to what we are and what we've done.

I can't think about that yet.

His breath is heavy and his body heavier still. I stay there, my arms wrapped around him, until he is unbearably heavy and then I shift a little, sliding sideways at the same moment I realise that he has fallen asleep. I wriggle out completely, my eyes searching his face, seeing the beauty in his sleep and recognising that it is, nonetheless, a tortured, unsettled repose. No rest for Noah. Not really.

What demons drive his tormented nights? What devils demand this fractured sleep of him? I want to know—not only because I want to help but because I *need* to understand. He is a puzzle that I suddenly, desperately ache to complete. He is an answer to a question I don't know how to pose.

I watch him sleep for a long time. At least ten minutes. I wait for him to wake, as he says he does, but his eyelids are flickering like moths near a flame and I suppose then that he is fast asleep. Knowing what a rare commodity this is for him, I dismiss the very idea of waking him.

Besides, I need space and time to process what I've done. To acknowledge this development and allow it into my being—to allow this to make up a part of my truth now.

I step out of the bed silently. There is nothing to remove from the mezzanine but myself. All my clothes and personal items remain where I left them, or where he left them—I'm still so foggy on the details of last night.

I creep down the stairs like a burglar post-heist, and it is only once I discover my shirt and trousers, neatly folded on the kitchen bench, that I realise I've left my underpants in his bed somewhere.

I look guiltily towards the mezzanine but think better of retrieving them. I plan to take a cab straight home—better that I don't wake him for a pair of briefs.

I dress quickly and, at the door, take one last look in the direction of where he's sleeping. I can hear his breathing, steady and rhythmic. I close my eyes, inhale and allow myself to imagine that I am still there with him, his arm perhaps casually thrown over my body, his hair flopping onto the pillow.

With a shake of my head to clear the seductive image, I take the irreversible step of leaving his home, of pulling the door shut firmly behind me. I am now on this side of Noah's world and he on the other.

We are worlds apart.

I wake as the door clicks shut, but I don't move. I know instinctively what the door signals and I fight every residual sensation of having left. I feel every single closed door. And Holly is now a part of that.

I stretch my arms and roll over, keeping my eyes

shut. Not in the futile pursuit of sleep so much as an attempt to replay what we've just shared. I can smell her in my bed; I can hear her in my bed. Her fervent, vocal pleasure. Her surprise at the orgasm.

It was painfully obvious that she hadn't felt like that before and I am glad for my sake, and sorry for hers.

Good sex is a gift; everyone should experience it. Is there anything that is more natural and more important in life than the body's ability to pleasure another?

I see her face again as she fell apart, her eyes rolled back in her head, her mouth clamped shut, her nipples hard beads thrust forward, her skin goosed all over... and an animalistic surge of power throbs through me.

I did that to her.

And I'm going to do it again.

I don't know if I expected to hear from him. I know he knows how to email me. I know he has my number. And as Sunday bleeds into Monday, which gives way to Tuesday, I have to face the fact that perhaps he is choosing not to contact me.

I have always been analytical, perhaps too much so, and in the last three days I have found myself going over every single detail of our time together, reliving his words, touch, mood. I wonder at the way we came together, at the euphoric sense of heaven that overtook me, and the way I stole out of his home.

By Thursday, I am contemplating calling him. Worrying for him. Wondering if he is okay. It is absurd and stupid and I have learned not to let a man weaken me—I am not who I was five, six, seven years ago.

If Noah doesn't want to call me, if all he wanted was one night with me, then it is better to learn that truth now than in a year's time. Right?

I tell myself I am grateful that it only got this far, and I congratulate myself for the escape from possible disaster. I focus on what is right in front of me, and what matters. I concentrate on Christmas and Ivy and the fact she's asked me about her father for the first time in her life—this is a day I have dreaded. I have no ready-made answer to respond to her question. I don't know how to discuss Aaron with her.

Old-fashioned platitudes, like *We both love you very much, but we were better living apart*, don't seem to apply here, seeing as he tried to kill me when I was pregnant with her.

Instead, I focus on the fact her father is a beautiful musician and put on one of his CDs for her to listen to, even though it sends shivers of panic rioting through my body.

I hate his music.

I hate him.

On Friday afternoon, it has been a week since I saw Noah Moore. My heart drops at the thought that it's simply the first of many weeks I must tick off in this fashion. I know from experience that it will get easier—that I will become more adept at sidestepping this ache of need.

Besides, I took a step out of my comfort zone and I'm glad for that. I'm glad to have slept with him. I walked into it with my eyes wide open and I got what I wanted.

As if on cue, heat floods my body and my nipples tingle with remembered pleasure. I smile.

It was an incredible night. Morning. Whatever.

I tidy my desk, sort my files, answer emails and, near seven o'clock, I go to close my computer down. Out of nowhere, in my mind I see Noah. I see him as he was—so beautiful, so strong, so handsome, so mysterious. I remember the tattoo on his shoulder, the one that frightened me and weakened my knees and stirred my gut all at once.

What had he called it?

Malingee?

I can't do justice to the way he pronounced it, but it was something like that.

I open a browser and type *Malernguy* into the computer. I get a Danish computer company. That's not right. I try three more variations on spelling before I hit on something that sounds close enough.

Malingee: an Australian Aboriginal spirit, both nocturnal and malignant, that terrified humans. While it didn't seek to engage them, it would ruthlessly slay any who crossed its path, using its stone dagger to kill. A terrifying spectre.

A frisson starts at the base of my skull, tingling and pulsing and running down my spine like wildfire, spreading unease and doubts anew.

Why would Noah have this tattoo on his shoulder?

Dozens of new questions open up inside me. There is so much about him I don't know—so much I will never know, if last week was the end for us.

The thought is like a detonation and it fires me to

stand. I shut my computer down and grab my bag, locking up my office.

I am reminded then of closing Noah's door as I left his apartment—and I wish I could go back in time and stay, as I had contemplated. I wish I hadn't left.

I want him—all the more because I have felt him move inside me and the reality outstripped every single one of my fantasies.

Once, surely, just wasn't enough.

CHAPTER EIGHT

I SEE HER the moment she steps out onto the street, her hair pulled into a bun that I instantly imagine loosening with my fingers, pulling free and tangling around her shoulders. She's wearing a cream trench coat belted at the waist and, from this distance, it looks like dark pants that hug her slim legs. Legs that have wrapped around me; legs that I haven't yet tasted—remiss of me. I have been fantasising about running my tongue down her calves, finding all her sweetest spots and tormenting her with them.

Her head is bent; she doesn't see me. I wonder where she's going?

Has she been thinking of me?

She hasn't called. She hasn't emailed. Did I expect her to? Has she been waiting to hear from me? I don't chase women. I don't chase anyone. But damn it if I didn't want to turn up at Holly's office Monday evening and drag her back to my bed. Ditto Tuesday, Wednesday, Thursday and, finally, here I am. Telling myself that having waited a week I have proved to myself that she is as disposable as everyone else in my life.

A familiar sense of distance calms my pulse. It doesn't matter what she's been thinking or wanting; I don't care.

This isn't about anything except the present—and the present we can give each other. I have no expectations of her and she sure as hell doesn't of me, or she would have tried to contact me.

That's perfect. There's no need for my chest to be feeling like this—Holly Scott-Leigh *is* different to my usual lovers, but she's the same in many ways. I can manage her, this, us, whatever the hell I'm doing.

And I did sleep better after she'd left. For the first time since Julianne died, I was able to get several hours of sleep in a row. Perhaps Holly did that. Maybe fucking her worked magic on parts of me distinct from my cock.

She looks towards me as she crosses the street, but it is a cursory inspection, only to make sure she is safe to go, and she doesn't look towards me long enough to recognise me. She drops her head down and surges forward. As she reaches the footpath, I step off my bike.

A thrill of anticipation is unmistakable, and when I step forward the thrill trebles in intensity.

She has been abused and she is wary—perhaps it's a wariness she'll always feel? The idea of that rubs me completely the wrong way, but I shelve my reaction to better observe hers. She looks at me, her expression confused and hurt and then angry and, finally, cold, colder than ice, as she lifts an elegant brow and crosses her arms.

'Noah.' My name is a dismissal, not a hello.

She's pissed with me.

Fascinating.

'Holly.' I grin, enjoying the way my cavalier response needles her. I told you, I like needling her and the more I do it, the more I realise that.

She doesn't know what to say. She's looking at me as though she's trying to find words and I offer none; I simply watch the play of emotions as they constrict her face.

'What are you doing here?' she asks finally. Unmistakably cold now.

'What do you think?' I reach behind me for a helmet and hold it out to her. She makes no effort to take it. Something like iron wraps around my chest.

'A booty call?' She is outraged at that, angling her face away from me, showing only her cold profile.

'Are you okay?' The question is surprising to me. I think it's the first time I've evinced concern for anyone's emotional state, besides Gabe's perhaps. I'm not into dating; I don't do it often. If I see a woman, it's a light, casual affair. A few nights. A bit of fun.

I don't ask them if they're 'okay'. I don't hold my breath while waiting for the answer, as I am now, desperately needing to hear that she is.

'Fine.' The crisp answer shows she doesn't care that it's a first for me. She draws in a breath and turns back to face me; I feel as though I've been slammed in the chest with a stack of knives. She's so beautiful and somehow I'd forgotten, even in the thirty seconds since she spun her face away from me. 'Anyway—' I hear the finality in the word '—I was just about to head home.'

I narrow my eyes and nod. 'I'll give you a lift.'

'Noah…'

A car goes by, Christmas carols playing loudly, and she waits until it has passed.

'I don't know what you want from me.' It's simple and complicated. Terrifying and empowering.

The problem is, I don't know what I want from her either. Besides the fact that she's an addiction that's spilled into my bloodstream, I know only that I need her now. Here. Not here, because she deserves better than that, but the first place we can get to with a modicum of privacy.

'Don't you?' It's a gruff reply that has her tilting her head forward.

There's a look of defiance in her eyes. Surrender too. 'I guess it's exactly what I want from you.'

We didn't have the 'your place or mine' conversation, but I'm glad he's taking us back to his apartment. I was drunk when he brought me here before, but in the morning I realised we were in Bermondsey and his home was actually a converted wharf building right on the river. Completely hollowed out at some point, leaving the open-plan design he obviously prefers.

It's not far from my office and he rides quickly—as eager as I am, obviously, to renew our bodies' acquaintance with one another. And I am *so* desperate for that, but other things are knotting through me.

Noah Moore is a mystery and the part of me that likes to find order in chaos needs to understand him. Despite the fact he isn't my patient, and never can be, the therapist I trained to become and have spent years working as *needs* to dig through his issues, to understand what brought him to me in the first instance. It's a compulsion.

I need more than just to understand him, though; I need him.

He pulls his bike up in front of the building and I step off before he does, removing my helmet, not giving him a reason to touch me—yet.

I wait by his front door and he takes only a moment to join me, unlocking it and pushing it inwards, staying on the outside, his arm outstretched to allow me entry. I move past him but, once inside, all the memories of last week slam into me and I am sucked back in time.

'Are you hungry?' He is maintaining a distance that is interesting.

'Yeah.' I think I might be, though it's hard to read beyond the desire that's swarming me.

I follow him into the kitchen, where he disappears into the fridge—it's a huge fridge, two, actually, side by side. I wonder at the kind of entertaining he does to necessitate that.

He pulls out a couple of cardboard boxes, each the size of a laptop, and places them on the bench, then reaches in for a bottle of wine. He pours me a glass and grabs a beer for himself.

'So, did you rationalise what we did last week?'

I think about lying to him, but don't. 'You want me. I want you. It's a simple equation. Apparently desire outweighs common sense.'

He nods. 'I like that. Mathematical sex.'

'Sure.' I bite down on my lip. 'I never thought I'd do anything like this.'

'Why not?' he asks curiously.

'Isn't that obvious?'

'Obviously,' he teases. 'Not.'

I force myself to meet his eyes. 'My whole life is dedicated to helping people.' I swallow. 'You came to me for help. And I can't be that person. But, beyond that, what if I do something that hurts you…?'

'Do you think I'm that fragile?' he prompts with disbelief.

I shrug my shoulders. 'Why did you come to see me? Why do you think you need therapy?'

He is instantly wary, just like in our first session. He tries to cover it, out of deference to what we've shared, but I see it. I see the wall he throws up between us.

'Don't hide from me,' I say softly. 'Tell me.'

His jaw clenches and a muscle moves at the base of his throat. 'Tell you what?'

'Why you came to me!' I shouldn't be annoyed—in my office I wouldn't be. With my patients I can control my emotions completely, but Noah isn't my patient. And here, with him so close and my body flaming with liquid heat, I am just a woman, not a doctor; I'm a woman who is full of desire and little else right now.

'I've told you. I'm not sleeping.'

'And have you ruled out any physiological cause for that?' I push, watching as he steps away from me and grabs his beer, throwing back at least half of it in one long draught.

'Such as?' He has slipped into a combative mindset.

He looks at me as though I am his enemy and I don't want that—I am pushing him too hard and I know it won't achieve results. Not with anyone and least of all Noah Moore.

There's more than one way to skin a cat, though. I've always hated that expression! Perhaps I can circumnavigate Noah's situation and find his pains all on my own.

With an effort I smile, but it is fake. A forgery. An imitation of what I think a smile should be. 'Alcohol in the evening can actually disturb your sleep. Perhaps that's it?'

We both know it isn't. He smiles and, just like mine, it rings with falseness.

'Could be.' He takes another sip from his beer, though, his eyes holding mine over the rim and there is a challenge in them. *Back off.* He doesn't want me to have my therapist hat on. I promised him I wouldn't, didn't I? Wasn't that the trade-off I made, to sleep with him?

But I can't *not*. It's hard to draw the line between what I do for a living and how I live my life. Particularly with people I care about.

Yes, I care about Noah Moore, and not just because we've slept together. I care about all of him, including his health, his happiness. I want to help him, but not as a therapist. As…what? As the woman he's sleeping with? That's normal, isn't it?

'What's for dinner?' I prompt, desperate to return our mood to its previous lightness. He hesitates only a moment before reaching for the cardboard boxes and flipping the lids. One is filled with oysters and scampi, the other with sushi.

I adore all three and my tummy gives a little groan of appreciation. Now when he smiles, it is genuine.

'What would you like?'

'Um…oysters.'

He lifts a brow, but neither of us says what we're thinking—the rumoured effects of oysters as an aphrodisiac. I've never found that to be the case anyway; then again, until meeting Noah Moore, I had thought myself to be somewhat disinterested in sex. I reach for my wine. Before he takes a plate from the cupboard, he washes his hands at the sink. It's a normal gesture, just a small one, but it seems almost incongruous. He dries his fingers slowly and then turns to face me.

He catches me watching him and smiles. My heart lurches.

'Have you ever been to Rivière?' I ask the first thing that pops into my head.

'The oyster bar?'

'Yeah.' I nod. 'It's one of my favourite places. I used to go there all the time when I was younger, and get a half-dozen oysters and have a glass of champagne.'

'Before you had your child?'

'Ivy,' I supply.

His smile lifts to me. 'Ivy?'

I nod.

'Like Holly and Ivy.'

Used to being teased about my love of Christmas by all and sundry, I'm more sensitive than perhaps I should be. 'Yes.'

'Like the Christmas carol?'

'Like the Christmas carol,' I confirm with a defiant nod.

'That's pretty fucking cute.'

My pulse throbs. 'Really?'

'Sure.' He takes a plate down and begins to arrange oysters onto it for me. 'Lemon?'

I nod.

'So I take it your asshole of an ex didn't mind you going to your oyster dates solo?'

'He didn't know.'

'Really?' Noah passes me a plate and then begins to arrange his own. I stay sitting on the countertop and he perches his arse opposite, watching me as he swallows his first oyster. It's strangely erotic to see it go down his throat. I look away.

'I used to leave work early on Friday,' I say. 'I'd go there and have a quiet hour all to myself.'

'With the oysters,' he says, the jocular comment undermined by the ice-cold determination in his eyes.

'Right, with the oysters.'

'You said you met him in high school?'

Do I want to speak about Aaron? Not really. Yet I find myself nodding. 'He's two years older than me. You know what it's like when you're a kid—there's something so...cool...about older guys.' I roll my eyes. Before he can ask another question, I reach for an oyster. It is ice-cold and so salty that I moan as I eat it.

'Jesus. Maybe that's why they're supposed to be sexy.'

I laugh self-consciously. 'What about you? Any

sexy school girlfriends in your past? Big, romantic love affairs?'

'Nah.' Another word that makes him sound so Australian.

'Nah?' I try to imitate it and fail. He grins.

I like his grin.

'Nah. Nope. Nada.' He takes another oyster and eats it. I look away, sip my wine. My face is warm.

'Nothing?'

'Nothing,' he says with a shrug.

'You mean you've literally never been in a relationship?'

'You going to psychoanalyse that?'

I reach for another oyster, buying time. 'I can't switch off my brain just because you don't want to talk about your past.'

He arches a brow. 'So what do you read into it, then?'

'I thought we agreed I wasn't going to do this.'

'I'm just curious,' he prompts.

'Well—' I choose my words with attention '—I suppose I'd say that it's…interesting.'

'Why?'

'It's unusual,' I continue. 'To be your age and not have someone in your past.'

'I haven't been living a monk's life,' he points out.

'Things you probably don't need to discuss with me.' It's unexpectedly haughty.

He laughs, a sound that runs like smooth caramel over my back. 'Jealous?'

I don't answer. I am—it's no doubt very apparent. My silence seems to sober him.

As if realising that he's crossed a line I don't like very much, he sighs. 'I'm a busy man, Holly. Gabe and I have been like hamsters on a wheel since things took off. Ten years later, I look around and I'm thirty-six. I haven't exactly had time for anyone else in my life.'

'So you're saying you want a relationship, to get married, grow old with someone, but you just haven't had time to find the right person?'

'Better than marrying an abusive shit like you did.'

Silence follows his statement. I'm hurt, of course, and the depth of that emotion is unexpected. But I have slipped back into my therapeutic headspace and I am used to having patients throw insults and cross reprimands at me—usually, it is a sign that I am close to finding a wound they don't want reopened.

'I'm…sorry.' Noah frowns. 'That was fucking rude.'

I laugh, because only Noah could apologise for rudeness and include a curse with it. 'Yeah, but you're right.' I smile reassuringly, not wanting him to think I'm upset. Not wanting him to shut down. 'I'd do anything to not…'

I freeze, surprised at the admission I'd been about to make. It goes against the determination I have to see the positives in my relationship with Aaron.

'Yes?' he prompts, finishing off his oysters and moving back towards me.

'I mean, I'd do it all again in a heartbeat to get Ivy, but it was…a dark phase of my life.'

He lifts a brow. 'Is that therapy-speak for it sucked balls?'

I laugh. 'Something like that.' He watches me as I sip my wine; his eyes on my face make my skin flush. 'What about family?'

He doesn't welcome the question. He visibly bristles and his shoulders tense. 'What about them?'

'Well—' I shrug my shoulders '—you have one, I presume?'

'Everyone has family, right?' He moves towards me, placing a hand possessively on my thigh. 'Did you miss me this week?'

The question is out of left field. He's trying to change the subject and I let him, but I make a mental note, determined to return to this later, determined to find out *something* about him that he doesn't necessarily want to share.

'Did you think about me?' I'm wearing a silk blouse and he undoes it slowly, his eyes hooked onto mine. My breath is forced, my pulse frantic.

'I...'

His smile is just a mocking twist of his lips. 'No lies, Doc.'

'Of course I thought about you,' I say, knowing on some level that he needs to hear that. He is tough and appears confident, but I sense his insecurities and this is one of them. There is no sense in obfuscating. I don't want to be the kind of woman who sleeps with someone like Noah and doesn't think about him, anyway.

For this reason I don't ask the question back. I know he thought about me. I don't need to surrender to my insecurities and beg him to admit it.

But, without prompting, he says, 'I wanted you so fucking bad.'

'When?'

'Every day.' He pushes the shirt down and I lift my arms out, mesmerised by him, distracted by him, owned by him.

'I thought about these.' He cups my breasts, pushing them out from under the bra before reaching around to unhook it. 'A lot.'

'Did you?' A whisper. I don't need to speak, though, my body is speaking for me. I push myself forward, nudging my breasts closer to him, needing him to touch me, to kiss me.

His smile shows that he knows. 'I thought about the way I touched you in your office, and how ready you were for me. How wet and sweet. How quick to come.'

A gargled whimper dies in my throat. I'm all that again, already. Oysters and wine are forgotten.

'Noah…'

He runs his mouth along my jaw, not touching me, just close enough that I feel the warmth of his breath. I shiver. He pushes his lips against my throat and kisses me, sucks on me, and a whirl of feeling starts in my gut. His touch is like flame; my body burns in response.

When he finally drops his mouth to an aching, hard nipple and sucks it deep in his mouth, I am beyond rational thought. I make a bubbling cry and wrap my legs around his waist, just like on that first day in my office, holding him close to me.

I feel his hard cock through his clothes and mine and

I grind myself against him, needing to feel him inside me, but for the moment making do with this. Feeling his firm length against my pulsing heart is heaven.

'Are you wet now?' he asks, the words breathed against my flesh, reverberating through me.

I nod, though I think his question is rhetorical.

'Let's see.' His fingers find the waistband of my pants, loosening them, and I wiggle my bottom so he can slide them down lower. I am naked in his kitchen and it doesn't even occur to me to be embarrassed or to think it's weird. It's not. It's perfect.

The only sound is my breath, loud and rasping, as though I've run a marathon when, in fact, it is anticipation, not exhaustion, that fires the sound.

'Noah.' A whimper, a need.

He knows. 'Lie back.'

I don't, not straight away, so he grabs my knees and pulls on them a little, sliding my butt forward. I drop back onto my elbows; the kitchen counter is marble and ice-cold beneath me.

I don't have time to process that discomfort, though, because suddenly his mouth is on me. On my seam, his tongue running across me, his hands holding my legs wide.

I have *never* been kissed there.

'You're kidding.'

I must have said that aloud—I didn't mean to. But, seriously, I have never been kissed there and I've never even really been interested in it. I mean, it seems almost gross. Or it did. Noah's mouth on me is the best thing I've ever felt—just about. I am breathing harder and faster, louder, arching my back on the marble slab, reaching for him, for something, for sanity, but there is nothing.

Just me and my abandonment to this beautiful rightness.

'You taste so fucking good,' he groans, and the words tip me over, spreading through me like a whip of desire.

I curl my toes around the scalloped edge of the bench and cry out as I come, hard, fast, impossibly inevitable.

It is like being doused in warm water, so beautiful and perfect and relaxing despite the fevered racing of my heart. I need to take stock, to feel this, to let it permeate my being, but Noah doesn't allow that. He grabs for me, pulling my hips, and I don't realise he's undone his trousers until he's lifted me around his waist, away from the bench. We don't go far; he pushes me against the fridge, my back used to cold surfaces and not minding the shock of that when answering heat is promised.

And it is.

He thrusts into me, hard, and his mouth reclaims a nipple, and my body zips with feelings, still processing my first orgasm, as he drives me towards another. I hear something, a voice, keening over and over, and realise it is me. I'm crying out in a fevered state, the words shaking with intensity.

His hands on my hips are splayed and his possession of me feels so unbelievably natural that I don't stop to think about the fact that he's possessing me so completely, that I have fallen under his spell and would do anything he asked of me. Anything. I am addicted to this and him.

The pain I've endured this week, the wondering, the loneliness—these things don't matter. It is just Noah, and now.

And, for now, this is enough.

CHAPTER NINE

HER BODY IS sheened in perspiration and her cheeks are pink. Her eyes moist—not with tears but with heightened pleasure. I stand above her, watching her, my arms crossed, the thrill of power unmistakable.

I have done this to her. And I am pretty sure it's the first time she's ever known this kind of drugging desire. A thrill spreads through me.

Her ex was a bastard; I shouldn't feel any kind of competition with him. I have seen his marks on her body now. Little marks, small scars, but I know without asking how she came to wear them.

He isn't worthy of competing with, and yet the knowledge that I have given her so much pleasure, that he certainly didn't, does something inside me.

Then again, at what cost?

Holly Scott-Leigh is dangerous for me—there is risk here, with her. She has entered my bloodstream and I don't even bother trying to pretend otherwise. She's not like any other woman I've ever known. If I make her feel new different pleasures, she does exactly the same to me.

Losing myself in her body has become my latest addiction, and not just because it seems to give me a reprieve from my dark thoughts—if only for a while.

Her chest, and those beautiful breasts, are shifting with each of her breaths, slowing down now, and I wonder if she is tired? If she would like to sleep?

I swallow past a throat that is constricted by pleasure and reach into my bed, lifting her. I've lost count of how many times she's come. In the kitchen downstairs, on the bench, against my fridge, and then in my bed, when I used my fingers to drive her to the edge… I scoop her against my chest and her eyes lock onto mine.

Something shifts in my chest. Desire, surely, rampant and uncontainable. I look straight ahead, needing her as an addict needs their next fix.

My en suite bathroom is big—the kind of place I could never have imagined, growing up as I did. It's at least twice the size of most bedrooms I knew as a kid and it's covered in marble tiles. A spa bath is at its centre and to the side, with frosted windows that overlook the Thames, there is a shower. I like to shower. I like the feel of water on my skin and I have an overhead nozzle as well as one from either wall.

Holly lifts a brow with amusement. 'You don't think this is kind of overkill?'

It's impossible for someone like her to understand. You grow up with nothing and it does things to you. Trust me, I know about this stuff.

'You haven't felt the shower.' I grin, making light of it, not wanting to open the door to my reasons for living as I do. My bathroom is a palace and the rest of my home is like a loft—there's nothing luxurious nor expensive, nothing particularly personal, anywhere in this place. As though I'm expecting to pick up a rucksack at any point and walk right out that door. Like I've done so many times. I guess old habits really do die hard.

'I don't know if my feelings can take anything else wonderful tonight…' she says, teasing me, reaching out and curling her fingers in my hair in a gesture of such simple intimacy that my heart stalls with ice and rejection immediately.

Intimacy—other than physical—is a lie. A lie people tell themselves, a benign lie, but one with the power to rip your soul out.

'Let's test that theory.'

I designed a home app that runs this place—I can control everything from my watch or phone, or from within my car, where I have an audio transceiver hooked up. I programmed the shower with seventeen settings. I go for number five now. All the jets turn on and the water is warm, just warm.

I don't put Holly down, though. Instead, I lower her onto my cock—my ever-hard cock, right now, thanks to her—and she moans as I do so, her body covered in water, her hair slicked back, her eyes almost panicked when they meet mine. As though she can't quite believe how good it is between us. How much she wants me.

She tips her head back, her eyes on the ceiling, a cascade of water dousing her.

I'm not wearing a condom. I just want to feel her like that first time, when she climbed on top of me and took

me without a single thought for anything other than as-
suaging her needs, for slaking this desire.

'I'm on the Pill,' she says, the words higher in pitch,
which I now know means she's close. Her words drill
into me. Is she saying what I think she is? 'Are you...'
Her eyes drop to mine for a moment and, despite the
pink in her cheeks, the tautness of her nipples, she
seems to find sanity for a moment. 'I mean, I presume
you're...safe?'

As it happens, I had to get a full raft of tests a couple of weeks ago—my life insurance is worth enough
to buy a country and they like to keep an eye on me. I
suppose I'm one of their higher risk clients.

She nods. 'I don't want you to use a condom.' She
tilts her head back again and the way she said that,
what she's giving me, is just about the biggest turn-on
I can imagine.

I make a primal sound of assent and pull her away
from me. She's so small, I seem to have forgotten she
has free will and I'm moving her according to my own
desires. One look at her face, though, and I see that she
doesn't mind. That she wants this. That she feels all the
good feels right here with me.

I spin her around, facing her towards the windows
that overlook the river, bracing her hands on the window ledge.

'It's a nice view, but I kind of liked what we were
doing,' she says.

I don't answer. Not verbally. I push into her from behind and her legs spread wider for me, her body tilting

forward so I have complete access to everything I want and need. *This!* This is how I need to feel her.

I cup her breasts possessively as I push into her and my mouth drops to her shoulder, my teeth pressing against her flesh. She whimpers, her body throbbing around me already. But I'm not going to give her time to absorb each orgasm; I'm going to deluge her with them. I drop one hand to her clit, finding the sensitive cluster of nerves and teasing them with my fingers as my cock moves hard within her. I torment her nipple, rolling it between my thumb and forefinger, plucking it, pulling it until she's crying out and I am addicted to the sound of that, her raspy, broken moans of surrender.

I know what Holly has been through and from the moment she told me I have felt protective towards her, have thought I should treat her with kid gloves. But what I want, and what I am realising she wants, is for me to simply fuck her, hard.

I do that now, pushing into her as deep as she'll take me, and the harder I move the more she cries out, begging me over and over, 'Please, Noah, please.'

My name on her lips is heaven. I will never stop, so long as she keeps calling to me like that. 'No—ahhhhh…' She pushes backwards, giving me better access, and I grip her hips with both my hands, holding her hard against me as I slam into her. Her body shakes and quivers and her voice is a primal, feral cry that reverberates around the bathroom as she comes.

I hold her still, steadying her, reassuring her, and my dick throbs inside her as Holly's warm, wet muscles squeeze me tight, whispering at me to join her, to find my own ecstatic release. But I don't want this to end yet. I am high on what I can do to her, what she can do to me.

I am high on this feeling.

It takes all my willpower, but I stay hard inside her, refusing to give in to the waves of euphoria that are running through me.

She stays as she is, staring out of the window, or perhaps not seeing, I don't know. She is shaking all over, her body physically changed by what we just did. I remember then that I didn't want to give her time to recover.

I run my hand around to her beautiful pussy, brushing against the base of my cock in my quest to touch her. I rub my fingers against her and she moans; I feel her muscles clench anew, wrapping around my cock. Hell, I feel my own ministrations as I massage her into another climax and grit my teeth together, holding off, wanting her to come again, needing her to.

'What are you doing to me?' she whimpers, right before she explodes and now I hold her breasts tight, cupping her with both hands, thinking they are the most perfect breasts I've ever felt. Thinking she is perfect.

It's a stray thought and I dismiss it, but then Holly does what I could never have expected. She pulls away from me, a moan of emptiness escapes her as she removes my cock. She turns around to face me and she looks just what she is—a woman who has been fucked. Thoroughly.

I wonder what she'll say or do. My dick is hard and huge between us and her eyes drop to it. I see her swallow as she takes in my length, perhaps wondering how the hell I fit inside her in the first place.

And then, slowly, fatalistically, she drops to her knees, right in front of me, her hair a wet pelt against her head, her eyes locked to mine.

Is she going to do what I think? What I am now hoping against hope?

Her lips, always painted a bright red, have been kissed free of cosmetics and are simply pale pink, full and perfect. My fingers find their way to her hair, stroking it gently at first.

Then she opens her mouth and takes my tip—just my tip—inside, encircling me with her tongue, testing herself and me, and I find my fingers curling tighter, fisting around her hair, and I'm trying not to hold her still and push myself farther forward. It should be at her pace; she's tentative and I gather this is new for her too, that she hasn't done this often, maybe never. Power is an aphrodisiac.

I want to roll my hips and claim her mouth; I want to feel the back of her throat, hitch myself in deep and far. I don't, but I do hold her hair tightly, as though it alone will save me. I am drowning in this—in her.

And then, out of nowhere, she moves her mouth along my shaft, and my tip hits the softness at the back of her mouth. I cry out, a hoarse sound that might be her name or might be a curse, and I throw my head back for a second, letting my body feel everything. But only for a second because I want to watch her. Her on her knees, her hair drenched by the shower, her body pale and creamy except for the pale pink patches I've left with my stubble and my touch.

She draws back, rocking on her knees a little, and then swallows me again, making a little sucking noise that is hotter than I can say.

My breath hitches in my throat and she pulls away, looking up at me, removing her mouth. 'Show me what you want,' she says.

'You're doing it,' I promise throatily.

'No—' And she knows me so well, knows what I want. 'Show me.' She lifts a finger to my hands that are curled in her hair, her eyes challenging me. 'I'm not made of glass,' she whispers.

God, she's in my head. She hears my thoughts. It terrifies me. But she's right. I am treating her more gently than I want to, and she doesn't want that.

'Show me,' she says again.

'Because you haven't done this before?' I ask, needing to hear it. Getting off on the admission.

She shakes her head. 'Never.'

Fuck. I'm done for. I'm fucking done for.

The darkness within me consumes me then, the need to possess her and own her and fill her up with me takes over. Almost against my will, my hands push her head forward, bringing her back to my cock. A thread of concern runs through me and I hear myself say, 'Tell me if I'm too much for you…'

'You're definitely too much for me,' she says, a small laugh on her face that is taken away when I throb into her. I push her head all the way forward; my cock fills her mouth and I jerk my hips back and forth, fucking her lips, my fingers digging into her scalp. Her eyes hold mine and then, as I move her, she drops a hand between her legs and touches herself.

It's the most erotic thing I've ever done.

Her mouth is so moist and I'm so far back, her tongue flattened by me. I know I need to look after her, and I pull back out to let her recover before taking her mouth once more.

She makes a moaning noise and I see that she's climaxing again, her body quivering.

And I can hold off no longer. 'I'm coming,' I grunt, letting go of her hair, giving her a chance to pull away, but she catches my wrist and lifts it back, her eyes warring with mine.

Fuck.

I hold her right against me, so deep her lips encircle the base of my cock, and I thrust twice more into her mouth, releasing myself with a guttural oath, giving her my seed and holding her there while I shake with the power of my release.

I am weakened and strengthened by this. I reach down for her, grabbing her under her arms and lifting her, her wet body sliding along mine as I cradle her against me. I step out of the shower, using the voice command to turn it off. I have a stack of freshly laundered towels on the bench—not my work, obviously, so much as the cleaners who come and look after this place—and I wrap one around her as best I can, without relinquishing our bodies' contact. Her eyes are heavy, dropping shut as though weighted with cement.

But as we reach the bed and I lay her down gently

she smiles at me, her lips curving upwards and her eyes holding mine. There is a silent question we each pose the other: *Are you okay?* She smiles and I return it.

We're better than okay.

She is asleep almost the second her head hits the pillow. I towel her dry gently, squeezing water out of her hair so that she doesn't feel uncomfortable, and then I pull a sheet up around her.

She smiles in her sleep and rolls onto her side, facing the emptiness of the bed. I look at her for a moment and think of going downstairs, of having a Scotch or a coffee or a fucking sandwich. But instead I peel back the sheet and lie in bed beside her, staring at her, watching her sleep, envying the ease with which she's found peace.

I watch her and, the next thing I know, she is watching me and it's morning.

The sun is reaching in through the windows, though it is wintry and weak.

'Hi.' She smiles at me and my gut twists, like her hands have reached inside me and toyed with my organs.

'Hi.' My voice is gruff.

'You slept.' She reaches a finger out and touches my lip, tracing it in a way that tickles.

I frown. She's right. I *did* sleep, and the whole night through. When was the last time that happened? Before she died. But I don't want to think about Julianne now.

I don't want to think about the way I treated her. About the impossibility of making amends, changing my actions, mending her heart.

Holly has this thing she does, when she's trying to

work out what to say to me. She bites on her lip and pinches her eyes together, just a little, just enough to make me know she's worried she's going to offend me or push me away.

It gives me enough time to prepare for whatever is coming. How long has she been watching me? And what has she been thinking about? An unfamiliar—no, not unfamiliar—a long-forgotten vulnerability creeps along my spine. A sense of being exposed and weak.

I swallow. Ignoring the feeling. Telling myself it doesn't apply here.

'Why don't you talk about your family?'

Jesus. I wasn't prepared for *that*. We were talking about this last night, though. In the kitchen. Before. Before everything.

'Why do we have to?'

Her frown is infinitesimal…and instantly unpalatable. I don't want to make Holly frown. I want to make her smile and laugh, to make her face contort with pleasure in a way that is evidence of her mind being blown.

'We don't *have* to. I'm just curious…'

Of course she is. A normal woman would be curious by now and Holly is no normal woman. 'It's *family*,' I say with a roll of my eyes. It's an act I've perfected over the years. A pretence that I'm long-suffering, like everyone else. Like I have a raft of aunts and uncles and siblings and cousins who drive me crazy instead of the paralyzing loneliness I have known almost my entire life. 'Do you want to talk about *your* family?'

She frowns. 'My family is…nothing special.'

I sense a reprieve, and also curiosity sparks inside me. Both push me to ask, 'They must be to have made you.'

The compliment shivers across her flesh, goose-bumps spreading before my eyes. Power thrills in my gut. 'Tell me about them.' I drag the sheet down, exposing her nakedness to me, my gesture possessive and unapologetically so.

'I thought you didn't want to talk about family.'

'My family.' Or lack thereof.

She rolls her eyes. 'That's not fair.'

'Isn't it?' I grin, my fingers finding the curve of her hip and drawing invisible circles there, running figures of eight over her silky flesh until she exhales softly.

'My parents are very conservative, both in the armed forces. My mother has an administrative role—it's how they met. My brothers signed up as soon as they were eighteen. I don't think my dad's ever forgiven me for not doing the same.'

'He must be proud of what you do.'

'He hates shrinks,' she says with a shrug.

'Why?'

'Does he need a reason?'

'In my experience, there's usually a reason.'

'Like with you?' she prompts.

'Nice try, Doc, but I asked first.'

She rolls her eyes, such a sexy gesture that I want to pin her back against the bed and kiss her until she whimpers. My dick jerks.

'Let's just say there's a reason I specialise in PTSD. Particularly with returned military personnel.'

'Your dad?'

'My dad *and* my older brother. But I was already practising by the time Logan came back from Iraq.' She sighs. 'My dad was in the first Gulf War. He was... changed by it. Irrevocably. Not so you'd notice if you didn't know him well. It was just...little things around the house. A temper that would come out of nowhere, whereas he'd never been like that. Paralysing panic attacks that made it impossible for him to go out, and a weird anger whenever Mum tried to organise normal stuff, like family holidays.'

'How old were you?'

'Young. Seven...eight. I saw the way he'd changed and I wanted to fix him.'

'And did you?'

'Not me, but he did get help.' Her lips form a lopsided smile.

'And now you help other people.'

She looks at me meaningfully for a long moment. 'Yeah, if they'll let me.'

CHAPTER TEN

'YOU TOLD ME you're not close to your mother.'

Noah looks like I'm digging into his flesh with a knife. He is recalcitrant, closed off and apparently kicking himself for agreeing to this. But he *did* agree to it. I reach for a slice of cheese and taste it, waiting with the appearance of patience for him to speak.

Finally, his voice gruff, he says, 'I did.'

'And that you weren't raised by your parents. So, who did you grow up with?'

A muscle flexes in his jaw as he grinds his teeth. He doesn't want to have this conversation, but I'm done waiting for him to open up to me. This is for both our sakes. This is important.

'Noah?' I lean forward, pressing my hand over his. 'I want to help you. Not as a doctor but as a...' I search for a word that encompasses all that we are. 'A friend.' It's manifestly unsuitable, but it's the best I can do.

His eyes hold mine and there is hopelessness and pain in them, like he wants, so badly, to believe me. I ache for him then, and I swear I will make him whole again, no matter what.

'I was a foster kid,' he says slowly, standing, walking towards the enormous windows that overlook the Thames. His back is to me and I allow that; perhaps he finds it easier to speak without looking at me. That's not unusual. His shoulders are tense, his back ramrod-straight. 'From when I was three.'

So little!

'But my mum still had visitation rights—I saw her every second week. When she wasn't high or stoned or pissed.'

He says the words as though it's a joke, but I hear the pain scored deep in his voice.

'Do you…remember your life? Before foster care?'

'No.' I suspect it's a lie, but I don't want to push the point now.

'And what about your foster family?'

'Foster family?' He angles his head so I see his profile. 'I lived in seventeen homes, Holly. I didn't have a *family*. I had a revolving door of bedrooms and people and new schools and new rules.'

It starts to make sense to me now, and my heart throbs in sympathy for the little boy he was. 'Which foster home did you spend the most time at?'

There is a pause, and I don't know if it's significant or if he simply can't recall. 'The Morrows,' he says after a moment. 'Julianne and Paul.'

There is no malice in his tone. 'You liked them?'

He shrugs. 'It was a long time ago. I was with them when I was eight years old.'

'And what happened?'

'What do you mean?' He's impatient now.

'Why did you leave them?'

'They left me,' he says matter-of-factly. 'Paul got transferred interstate. A big job in Melbourne and my biological mother wouldn't give permission for me to leave the state. I had to stay in Sydney.'

I nod. 'I imagine the foster system is similar to here—your mother's wishes had to be respected.'

'My mother was a drugged-out whore,' he says bitterly. 'Her wishes should have been irrelevant.'

'You wanted to go with the Morrows,' I surmise.

'At the time,' he says coldly, 'I didn't want to have to move into a new home, a new school, find new friends. I wanted to stay with the Morrows because it was easier.'

'But you would have had to meet new friends and go to a new school if you'd gone to Melbourne,' I point out logically.

'I was eight. I didn't think it through like that.' There's rich frustration in his tone now.

'So they left,' I say quietly. 'That must have been hard for you.'

'Not really,' he says, and again I feel he is lying. Hiding something. 'I was used to it by then. They were my seventh family already.'

'So many,' I say with a shake of my head. 'Did you keep in contact with them?'

'No.' A terse word. I make a mental note to ask him about this again later. Another time.

'Do you keep in contact with any of them?'

'Any of who?' Belligerence is back.

'The people you knew through foster care?'

'Yes.'

Closed book. 'Such as?' I prompt.

'Gabe.' The word is very quiet; at first I almost don't catch it. And it's not immediately meaningful to me. But then I recall something I've read about Noah at some point, and I recall his business partner is a man named Gabriele Arantini.

'Your business partner?' I prompt.

'Friend, business partner, foster brother. Take your pick.' He turns to face me and his face is pale. There is a hint of perspiration on his brow.

His response is classic for someone with PTSD; I've pushed him too far. I still don't know what exactly provokes this reaction in him, but somewhere within these questions is the key.

'You know,' I say thoughtfully, tilting my head to the side, 'Ivy would love to stay another night with her grandmother. Why don't I organise it and you and I can do something…fun?'

'Fun?'

He repeats the word, his eyes clouded, still pained by his recollections. I must remove that hurt for him. Now with a sticking plaster, and in time with conversation and understanding.

'Yes. Dinner? Movie? You know. Fun.'

He says nothing for a moment and I wonder if he wants to be alone. If perhaps I'm moving him too fast.

But then his eyes lock onto mine. 'I have a better idea.'

Noah's better idea is something I would never have predicted. Standing at City Airport, staring at a sleek white jet with the Bright Sparks logo on the tail, I have the sense that I'm falling down a rabbit hole with no end in sight. How far does it go? When will I land?

He grips my hand, intertwining our fingers in that intimate way, and grins at me as we walk towards the jet, leaving his driver and his limo—so he *doesn't* always use the racehorse bike—on the tarmac.

'I suppose you think this is all very impressive,' I say with a small laugh, being purposely ironic.

'I already know you're impressed by me.' He winks and reaches up to my cheek with his spare hand, touching me lightly.

My heart squeezes. I turn back to the jet. It's small, as in not like a passenger jet, but when we step inside and are greeted by two women in smart navy blue uniforms, I see it's bigger than I realised. There are seats at the front, bigger than first class, in rows of two. Behind them, there's a large table and, beyond that, some sofas and armchairs all angled towards a movie screen.

'Jesus.' I blink as I study the obvious glamour and luxury. 'This is how you travel?'

He shrugs. 'Something wrong?'

'Are you kidding? It's amazing. I just don't want to go back to the real world afterwards.' It's a throwaway comment, but it could so easily apply to our personal relationship as well as his aeroplane. 'It's beautiful,' I say, to cover up any misunderstanding.

He shrugs. 'You get used to it.'

It's not yet lunchtime and the prospect of the twenty-four hours ahead fills me with excitement.

'You're smiling,' he says, his eyes latched on to my face.

I nod. 'I was just thinking how nice it is to be doing something like this. Something just for me. It's been a long time since I've…had fun. It's…kind of nice.'

'Nice?' He arches a brow, but his smile is broad, like I've said something that's making his heart glow too.

'Better than nice.' He leads us to the sofas and waits for me to settle down. There's a seat belt low down in the cushions; I slip it around my waist.

'You've done it tough the last few years?'

I shake my head. 'Not as tough as most. I'm lucky to have such good support with Ivy. And she's an incredible kid. Smart and funny, and sweet, and so easy. She's always been a good sleeper, great eater, well behaved. But, yeah, there have been times when it's been hard. I mean, just having someone to laugh with about her silly games, or whinge to when I'm exhausted and she's not listening, or have a glass of wine with and watch a movie, someone to rub my feet when I'm tired.' I lift my shoulders. 'But I love my job and it keeps me busy and, other than wishing, sometimes, that Ivy had a dad in her life, I don't regret the way I'm doing it.'

He is quiet for a moment, letting my words sink in. 'I'll bet you're a great mum.'

'I'm the best mum I can be. Some days great, other days not so much. But that's parenthood.' I eye him thoughtfully. 'What about you and kids?'

He grimaces exaggeratedly. 'As in having kids of my own?' Another grimace. 'No, thanks.'

He's making light of the question, so I laugh, just

a small laugh, but something the exact opposite of amusement courses through me. I tell myself it's just surprise—surprise he can be so adamant about not wanting children when the experience is so rewarding. If *I* can say that—when I've borne a child to a person I hate, when I've raised that child on my own—then surely anyone can.

'You don't like kids?'

'From a distance? If I can't hear them or smell them? I like them okay.'

I roll my eyes. 'They're not that bad.'

'Sure. They're just not for me.' He's grinning, like he doesn't realise the significance of this conversation. Like he doesn't comprehend that it is an admission that immediately restricts our relationship. I mean, it was probably already limited by who we are, but I don't know. There's something so different about Noah and the way I feel with him that, without overthinking this, I would have said it was impossible to define what we are and where this will end up.

But an unnegotiable aversion to kids is a deal-breaker. I mean, I have one. But I'd like to have another one day. Holly would be a great sister and I've always clung to the hope that some day in the future I'd have what I so badly coveted as a single mother. A real family.

A loud family.

A family who talked and laughed and shared ideas and went on holidays together.

'Excuse me, Mr Moore?' A stewardess approaches

us with an efficient click of her shoes. 'Can I get you a drink before take-off?' Her smile encompasses us both.

Noah flicks a glance at his watch. 'Yeah. A beer. Holly? Champagne?'

I shake my head. 'Just a water, thank you.'

He nods. 'And something to eat. I'm starving.'

'Of course, sir.'

She departs quickly, leaving us alone. There is a whirr, though, as the engines fire to life.

I push aside my misgivings with regard to Noah's desire not to have children. After all, this is all new and different for both of us. I'm not naïve enough to think I can change his mind, but I do feel like there might be a hundred reasons for this thing to run out of steam. Maybe we'll just wake up and decide we don't want each other any more. Maybe this is just an itch I'm scratching. I mean, five years, come on.

I smile brightly at him, refusing to let my tendency to analyse the heck out of everything tarnish this wonderful break from normality. When was the last time I did anything even remotely like this? The answer to that is simple.

Never.

'So, Mr Moore,' I purr. 'Where are we going?'

'That, Miss Scott-Leigh, awaits to be seen.'

The stewardess appears with a tray. She places our drinks down, then reaches between us to arrange a little armrest-cum-table. She places a bowl of fries and a fruit platter on it, then smiles brusquely and walks away.

'Is this how you like to wine and dine women, Noah?' I watch him thoughtfully, pleased that I can ask such a sensible question without sounding jealous or possessive.

'I don't wine and dine women,' he responds seriously.

'Then what do you call this?' I gesture to the food.

'Lunch.' He grins, reaching for a chip. I watch him eat it, not realising that I'm frowning. He scans my face, though, and I make an effort to relax.

'Well, I'm starving,' I say, just to fill the silence.

'You had an active night,' he points out, his voice deep.

My cheeks flush pink.

'And you're fucking adorable when you blush like that.'

'I didn't know I blushed until I met you,' I say seriously.

He laughs. 'I'm glad I can bring your blood to the boil.'

'In more ways than one.'

His phone rings and he lifts it out of his pocket, frowning. 'I have to take this.' He unbuckles his seat belt, standing and moving away from me.

Despite the fact he's on his phone and standing in the middle of the plane, we begin to taxi. Apparently the rules are vastly different for private planes versus commercial, or perhaps Noah Moore was just born to disobey rules.

I think about the conversation we had this morning— about the information he reluctantly gave me. His upbringing was far from conventional, and that would have a huge effect on his development.

As children, we need to feel safe and secure, to have a healthy attachment to someone or something. It governs all our relationships for the rest of our lives—the ability to form natural relationships, relationships that rely on trust and respect. It's a problem with a lot of kids who come from abusive homes or, yes, end up in foster care.

As children we are taught that, no matter what we do, our parents will still love us.

Noah never had that.

Noah doesn't do relationships, even now, except his friendship with Gabe Arantini. The roadblocks that were put in place during his childhood continue to shape his personality, his ability to attach.

But there's something more.

His sleeping issues suggest a deeper trauma—a trauma that has re-emerged in recent weeks. I'm not treating him; he's not my patient. And yet I know I will find out what's happened to him, because I can't not.

Because I care.

I care about his problems and I'm terrified that I'm starting to care about *him*. All of him.

We are in Paris. Of all the places I thought Noah would bring me, Paris wasn't on the list. And I don't know why. Maybe because it's so classically romantic and he's insisted that he doesn't 'wine and dine' women, and this ancient city is quintessentially romantic, especially at this time of year. Right now, it has fairy lights sparkling and Christmas wreaths hanging from the ornate lamp posts and snow drifting down on the glorious buildings.

I am in love with Paris. It's a new love affair, just a

couple of hours old, but it feels like the best place on earth to me.

When he slips the key into the lock of the penthouse suite of the Ciel Étoilé and pushes the door open, I am instantly hit by the view. The Eiffel Tower is perfectly framed by enormous windows, hung on either side by burgundy velvet curtains. The whole apartment is more sumptuous than I knew hotels could ever be. Gorgeous white leather sofas, a grand piano, hallways that are tiled in marble, a Christmas tree decorated with sumptuous gold baubles, and a Juliet balcony that has views towards the Seine.

'Wow.'

'You like?' he asks, unbuttoning the top of his shirt to reveal the column of his neck.

'It's beautiful, Noah.' I smile at him, and then something catches my eye through an open door. I move towards it on autopilot, aware he's following just behind me.

The bed is huge. King-size, covered in cream bed linen and enormous European pillows. There's another floor-to-ceiling window scenario in here, offering yet another breathtaking view of this glorious city. But that's not what caught my eye. A dress is draped over the bed—a stunning dress, designer for sure. I frown, moving towards it. My first thought is there's been a mistake. I run my fingers over it and look to Noah. He's casually reclined against the door jamb, watching me, a small smile curving his lips.

A knowing smile.

'Is that...?' I ask him, confused.

'A dress.'

I frown. 'For…me?'

His nod is slow.

'Noah…' I lift it up and hold it against my body, moving towards the mirror. It's a beautiful dark blue with spaghetti straps and a demure neckline, but at the back it scoops right down—I imagine that when I wear it, it will show almost my whole spine. The skirt falls to my knees. It is soft and silky.

'It's…beautiful,' I say, my breath hitching in my throat. It's so far removed from the kind of clothes I usually wear—my mum clothes or my work clothes— and a thrill of pleasure runs through me at that. All of this is unusual for me—wonderfully so.

He walks into the room then and looks at the dressing table. He opens a drawer and pulls out a box. A velvet box, about the size of a small sheet of paper. He walks towards me, holding it flat in his hand. 'And for this beautiful neck…' He watches me intently as he opens the box.

I don't look at it, though. I'm frowning at him, my heart racing. He doesn't wine and dine women and yet there's no other way to say how I'm feeling. I am spoiled and I am adored and I am happy.

'I saw this and thought of you.' His voice is thick with emotion—emotions I can't comprehend.

I look down then and I can't help the sound of confusion that escapes my throat. It's a huge pink gemstone, so sparkly it's almost blinding, and it's surrounded by crisp white diamonds.

'What is this?'

'A necklace.'

I can't help but roll my eyes. 'I see that. Why?'

'Because—' he lifts it out of the box, his fingers distracting as they find the dainty chain and hold it '—I want you to have it.' He comes to stand behind me so that he can clasp it behind my neck. The gemstone falls to the base of my throat, resting in the hollow there. It's heavy and cool. I turn towards the mirror, lowering the dress now to stare at the image I make.

The necklace is distracting in its size and beauty. 'Is it a…a pink diamond?'

I'm guessing. I have no knowledge of jewellery. My mother never wears anything but her wedding ring, and it's not something I've ever bought myself. Nothing more than costume jewellery, anyway.

'It's Poudretteite,' he says, though I barely catch the word. 'Very rare.' His eyes meet mine in the mirror and my heart stutters. 'This gem once belonged to Marie Antoinette.'

'Noah—' I say his name softly '—it's too much. Way too much. This must have cost a fortune.'

He shrugs. 'I have a fortune.'

Like it's nothing. Unimportant. Irrelevant. It's strangely disconcerting when I'm sure he meant to assuage my concerns.

'Well,' I say quietly, 'you didn't have to do that.'

'I wanted to,' he reiterates. 'You deserve beautiful things, Holly. I want you to wear this tonight and then, when we get back here, I want to take you to bed wearing only the necklace.'

CHAPTER ELEVEN

'I COULDN'T EAT another thing.'

His eyes find mine, laughing and scorching, reminding me of the way I took him into my mouth.

'I'm sorry to hear it,' he drawls, his accent thick, his words seductive.

I grin. We are sitting beside one another, looking out of the window at the street beyond. I lean over a little so that my breath warms his cheek. 'At least, not for a while.'

His eyes meet mine and I see anticipation heat them. Beneath the table, his hand curls over my thigh, his fingers resting there as though that is natural and normal.

And it feels it; it feels wonderful.

We are in a tiny bistro somewhere in the Latin Quarter. We passed the Sorbonne as we came to dinner, our taxi moving quickly, with scant regard for my desire to take everything in. Then again, perhaps if he'd slowed down, I would have been overwhelmed. Not just by the beauty of Paris in the lead up to Christmas, all twinkling and magical, but by the feelings throbbing between Noah and me. By the way my heart, mind and body all seem to be bursting with something warm and huge, something I can't define but that I am greedy to feel more of.

We've feasted on baked Camembert, scampi, steak and frites, oysters; we've sipped wine and shared a crème brûlée for dessert. I am full, satisfied and fuzzy around the edges in the nicest possible way. His hand on my thigh is the cherry on top of a night that is already one of the best of my life.

I place my hand over his, lacing our fingers, no longer feeling it to be an odd intimacy. I've known him for weeks, slept with him, and I glimpse in him something that I didn't even know was missing in my life. I feel a strange completeness when we are together. If you'd asked me a month ago if my life was missing anything, I would have denied it. I've worked hard to build a great life for Ivy and me. I never considered letting anyone else into the fold. How could I risk it after what Aaron was? How could I trust my judgement?

Strange then that I know Noah is keeping so much of himself closed off from me and yet I still feel like I could trust him with my life. Some things, some instincts, go beyond what is said. This is a feeling, and I like it.

'Do you come here often?' I rub the pad of my thumb over his hand gently. His eyes fall to our fingers, his expression inscrutable.

'We have an office here.' He nods. 'And a factory in the south. Gabe and I split the responsibilities.'

He hasn't spoken of his friend much. I go gently,

careful not to scare him off. 'Do you do basically the same thing in the company?'

Noah's smile is rich with amusement. 'No.' I wait for him to expand and he does, taking a sip of his beer before continuing. 'I'm the coding side. I love programming. I don't do it so much now, except for fun—'

'Like the shower you talk to?' I tease.

He nods. 'Exactly. Gabe was never into computers. He's the business side. He got our first bank loan that floated the company, that allowed us to launch; he runs all that stuff. I've got no interest in that.'

'What is it about programming you like?' I wrinkle my nose and he leans over and places a light kiss on its tip. My heart twists.

'Everything.' There is an intensity in the word.

'Elaborate.'

He laughs. 'Are you ordering me, Doc?'

'Yep.' I smile to soften the command. 'I'm curious. It's very foreign to me. I wouldn't know where to start.'

He shifts his body weight and his hand on my thigh moves higher. Sparks of desire shift inside my gut. 'I used to do it to get into my own head,' he says, the words almost dragged from him. His eyes are stormy, filled with past pains. I hold my breath, aching for him and needing him to tell me more. 'I was twelve when I first started. I got a book from the library and devoured it, cover to cover. I was in a boys' home at the time,' he says, so casually, as though that's not devastating in and of itself. 'And they had good facilities.' He laughs awkwardly. *'At the time*, I thought they were good facilities. Now I see it was just a couple of old PCs, but for me, being able to load them up and practise what I'd read was what saved me.'

He has a faraway look in his eyes, like he's in the past. There is a haunting pain. Holly who is his lover wants to kiss it away. Holly who is a professional therapist wants to dig into the wound and expose it, knowing it gets worse before it can ever get better.

'Saved you from what?' I ask, hoping to strike a middle ground by smiling brightly.

He expels a sigh. 'You're going to drill me until I bare my soul, huh?'

But it's said almost with wry humour, and so I reply in kind. 'You betcha. But I'll make it up to you later.' My wink is a promise we both know we'll fulfil. Heat simmers in my blood; I ignore it. My brain is demanding more of me. I want to know him. I want to understand him.

'I was heading for a different kind of future,' he says stiffly. 'The boys' home was like a last chance for kids like me. Most of the guys I was in with had juvie records. I was there because no one else would take me. I'd been in and out of foster homes—sixteen times. I'd developed some...not good habits.'

My heart squeezes for him. 'You were just a kid.'

'A kid who torched cars, stole from my families, got into fights over nothing. I was always bigger than everyone else. Stronger. I was glad for that.'

'You're not violent, though,' I say.

'How do you know?' His eyes pin me to my seat.

I speak slowly, calming a heart that is racing. 'Because I've known violence. I've seen it, remember? I know the lure of it, the control of it, the temptation it holds for those who respond to it. You might have lashed out because you were angry and scared, because you didn't know how to handle your emotions differently. That's not the same thing.'

His eyes widen at my comment. I see something strange in his face. Relief? As though I have said exactly what he needs to hear?

'Did you ever get a rush from hitting someone? Did you ever crave that?'

'Fuck, no. Jesus, Holly. Never.' It's like he's remembered where we are and who he's talking to. He lifts his hand from my thigh, cupping my cheek, locking us together. 'I would *never* hit anyone, ever. I would never hurt you. I'm not that kid I was. And I'm not Aaron.'

Something like tears clog my throat. I haven't cried in a really long time. I can't believe I feel that emotion now! But his assurance pulls at something deep inside me. Something that aches to be told I am safe.

'You're so right,' he says, moving closer. It's just us in the restaurant—or that's the way it feels. 'I didn't *want* to be like that. It felt, sometimes, like the only way I could be heard.'

'What happened? After the boys' home?'

He frowns.

'You told me you had seventeen homes. And just now you said sixteen. So? Where did you go next?'

'You're astute,' he says, the words almost panicked. 'I pay attention. It's my job.'

His eyes skim my face thoughtfully. 'I was taken in

by a couple who had four grown children still living at home. It's where I met Gabe.'

'He's one of their kids?'

'He was fostered by them. They needed *"strong young men"*.' He says those words differently, like he's impersonating someone. 'To help around the house. We were basically slaves.' The words are said with derision. 'Gabe had been there years before I came along.'

'Were you happy there?'

He is thoughtful for a moment. 'I was safe there. They fed us. The house was clean. Gabe and I shared a room, but it was big, and they were worried enough about appearances to buy us new shoes each season and dress us good. It was one of the better homes I was taken in by.'

In all ways but one, Holly thought sadly, her heart breaking for both Gabe and Noah. To have never known love, to have never known the security and peace of mind it offers…

'I didn't like him at first.' Noah's smile is loaded with memories. 'He's a good guy. Always has been. Smart. Loyal. Intelligent. He drove me crazy. But, once I got to know him, I understood he was just like me. He'd learned to cope with the foster system by flying under the radar. I coped by railing against it. We were apples and oranges.'

'And peas in a pod,' I say, striving to lighten the mood.

He nods. 'Yeah.' But he's lost in thought. I watch him, the flicker of emotions on his face, each transition seeming to carry weight and meaning. 'He's the reason I came to you. It was his idea.'

And the crumbs he'd dropped in our first meeting come back to me. 'He wanted you to get therapy.'

He shrugs, like it doesn't matter.

'Why? Why did he decide you need help now?'

'You know why,' he says with a shrug, pulling away from me, putting distance between us.

'Because you're not sleeping. But he must know more. He must know there's something at the root of it. Something that has hurt you. Something new.'

'He's not a fucking psychic, Holly. I sought therapy because Gabe begged me to. Because I'd do anything not to worry him. I've done enough of that in my time. Besides, it was no hardship to come to you, believe me.' His eyes linger on my face for a moment before dropping to the necklace at my throat and then the swell of my cleavage.

A torrent of emotions swirls through me, frustration chief amongst them. 'I don't believe you,' I say softly. 'I think you were terrified of therapy. I think you still are. I think your idea of hell would be submitting to me for a full hour, letting me pull you apart, piece by piece.'

'I don't know. If you were naked...'

'You make jokes to keep me at a distance.'

He doesn't say anything.

'You throw up barriers every opportunity you get. You clam up when I ask you too much about your past. You are sitting on feelings and emotions that are like ticking bombs inside you. You're not violent, but you are hurting. I'd guess that something happened recently, something that hurt you. And it reopened all the wounds of your childhood. Things you thought you'd dealt with.

Feelings you didn't even know you still carried. Until you process that, you're not going to sleep. You're not going to be able to breathe properly until you find a way to comprehend what you're feeling.'

'This is bullshit,' he snaps, but he puts a hand over mine, almost apologetically. 'I know it's your job and your reputation is impressive, but you're wrong here, Holly.'

'No, I'm not.' There's sadness in my tone, because I grieve for him and for myself. He will never have a meaningful relationship until he faces these demons. There will only ever be sex for us. Sex, Paris and a beautiful necklace.

'Fine. What do I have to do, Doc? What's your prescription?'

'Like I told you the day we met, there's no easy fix. No one-size-fits-all counselling approach. You have to face whatever you're running from.'

His eyes give nothing away when they meet mine. 'And what are you running from?' he prompts, turning the tables on me with ease.

'Me?' My lips tug downwards as I frown thoughtfully. 'What do you mean?'

'I mean—' his hand grazes my thigh beneath the table; the intimacy is very welcome '—your dickhead ex has been in jail a long time. Why haven't you been with anyone else?'

My heart rolls over. 'I've been busy. Raising Ivy. Running my practice. It's not an easy juggle.'

'And you're proud of yourself,' he prompts, hearing the lines I haven't spoken.

'Yes.' My chin juts forward. 'There have been times in the last few years when I could have surrendered to a feeling of hopelessness. Of grief and shame. There have been times when each day has seemed insurmountable and I've wanted to curl up into a ball and refuse to go outside, to refuse to parent, to refuse to be anyone to anything because it's all so damned hard. There have been times when I have berated and blamed myself and been so *angry* with the choices I made. But none of this was my fault. I fell in love with the wrong man. That's all. And I loved him even when most people would have been long gone. I loved him until that love threatened the only person I loved more. Ivy saved my life, you know.'

'*You* saved your life,' he says seriously. 'She might have been the catalyst, but the hard work was all you.'

I half smile in acknowledgement. 'Had it not been for her, I probably wouldn't still be here.'

A muscle jerks in his cheek. He's pushing his teeth together. 'So you never met anyone else that made you want to get back out there?'

I feel a dangerous lure in this conversation. A tug towards swirling undercurrents of an ever-darkening ocean; a riptide that will suck us under before we realise it. Because neither of us is ready to discuss what we are, what we're doing, and defining this so prematurely might be disastrous.

'No.' I shut the conversation down with a bright smile. 'Shall we go for a walk?'

He looks at me for a long moment and then lifts his hand in silent agreement, signalling for the bill. It is brought swiftly but, before Noah can brandish his credit card, I've pulled mine from my bag.

'You got the flight and the hotel, not to mention the necklace and the dress. Let me get dinner.'

His eyes show surprise; he covers it quickly, removing my credit card from the small silver tray and sliding it towards me. His own credit card replaces it—a type I haven't seen before. It's matt black with a gold stripe at the top and his name is written in white cursive letters. 'I thought you wanted to be wined and dined.' The statement is droll and my tummy flip-flops.

A waiter removes the card and we are alone once more.

'I thought you didn't do that,' I volley back.

'So did I.'

It is snowing when we emerge onto the near-deserted streets of Paris. Just a few people walking in the distance and a swirl of white in the air that ruffles my hair. I reach for Noah's hand, lacing our fingers together, and my pulse pounds through my body.

How perfect this moment is!

'Thank you for dinner,' I say, looking up at him. My breath catches in my throat. He's so handsome, so rugged and primal and masculine and hot. It takes effort to remember to put one foot in front of the other.

'No problem.' He is distracted, but when he looks at me he smiles. 'What are you doing for Christmas?'

It's such a normal question. I wonder what he was like a few weeks ago. Before whatever happened to re-ignite childhood traumas. Still, essentially, the same man, sure, but more socially functional. More able to perform as people expected. Without this huge chip on his broad, muscled shoulder.

'My parents, brothers and Aaron's mum will come over. Ivy is at an age where she wants to help with everything, so we'll cook together.' I lift my shoulders in a shrug. 'What about you?'

'Will it be a big traditional lunch?' he asks, ignoring my own question.

'Yeah.' I smile but squeeze his hand because I want to know about him too. 'Turkey, stuffing, potatoes, greens, pudding, mince pies—*everything*. You?'

'Sounds delicious.' He drops my hand but only so he can put an arm around my shoulders and hold me to him. I breathe in his masculine fragrance and something in the region of my heart pings.

I know all the dangers here and yet I feel myself sinking. I feel my heart cutting itself in two, leaping into another person's body, offering half of itself to a man who will undoubtedly break it. Not because he's an awful bastard like Aaron but because he won't be able to help himself.

'Do you spend Christmas with Gabe?'

'We both hate Christmas,' he says. 'We have an unspoken agreement not to speak of it.'

'Wait. What?'

'We hate it.' His eyes shift to mine and they are swirling with emotions that are dark and resentful. His eyes warn me not to push this.

I don't listen. 'How can anyone hate Christmas?'

'How can anyone love it? It has no significance to me. I'm not spiritual, religious. It's not my holiday.'

I can't imagine feeling as he does and yet I understand. With what he's told me about his upbringing, I imagine Christmas was a time of great sadness. 'Did you ever have a good Christmas? With presents and food and something that made you happy?'

His fingers stroking my shoulder pause, stilling as I speak. Then, as if he doesn't want to, he says slowly, 'Yes. Once.'

I am fascinated. 'When?'

He clears his throat, tilts his head away from me. We continue walking through the snow with no destination in mind. We are moving nearer to the Eiffel Tower.

'Years ago.' A rebuff.

I won't let him put me off, though. 'How many years ago?' The words are patient yet firm.

'I was eight,' he says.

Eight. My head jerks to his. 'The Morrows?'

His answering smile is tight. Pained. The feeling that I am close to finding what has upset him settles around me. There is something in his manner that speaks of fresh hurt, not old ones. I must uncover it. And I will. But slowly, gently.

Cautiously.

'How did you…?'

'You told me about them,' I say quietly. 'Remember?'

He nods, but it's as though he's trapped, imprisoned, and he doesn't want to be.

'What did you do with them that Christmas?' It's a

question designed to relax him. To take him back to a more pleasant time.

But Noah isn't like anyone I've ever spoken to; he's not my patient and he doesn't act like a man who wants help. 'It was twenty-eight years ago. Before you were born. I barely remember.'

'Liar,' I say, half joking. 'Did they give you a present?'

He is stiff at my side and then he lifts a hand and points at the Eiffel Tower. It is midnight and it's sparkling like the stars from heaven have drifted across it. It's a subject change I don't want to allow, but it's breathtakingly beautiful.

And, as if he needs extra insurance, a guarantee that the matter is closed, he spins my body in the circle of his arms and kisses me—kisses me to silence me and distract me and remind me of how much we need *this*, both of us for different reasons.

'Spend Christmas with me.' I breathe the invitation into his mouth, my tongue whispering it to his.

He stiffens again, frozen, still, rejecting.

It only serves to heighten my determination. I pull away from him slightly. It was an impulsive suggestion, but now that it's out there I realise how *right* it is.

'I mean it, Noah. Why not come over?'

'Jesus, Holly, you don't ever give up. I've told you, I don't want to fucking celebrate Christmas, okay?'

CHAPTER TWELVE

I DON'T WANT to hurt Holly but Christ, if she won't back off, that's what's going to happen. Not physically—never, ever physically—the very idea of her being wounded wounds me. But her emotions are far too invested in this, and I don't want her emotions.

Emotions are untrustworthy and dangerous.

But when she frowns, blinks as if she's misheard me, my gut rolls and I think maybe her emotional wounds wound me as well.

'I'm sorry.' I mutter the apology, shoving my hands into my pockets and turning to stare at the Eiffel Tower. 'But I think us spending Christmas together would be a bad idea.'

To her credit, she rallies. Holly's not like anyone I've ever known. She is sensible and confident even in the face of outright rejection. 'Why? Why is it a bad idea?'

'Because, Holly! I just told you, I hate Christmas, and you're like a fucking elf. I bet you've got a big tree up and decorations and presents all wrapped with matching paper...'

I don't look at her, but I know I'm right. I don't need confirmation.

'You have a daughter! Have you even thought about what it would mean to her to wake up and see the man you're sleeping with on Christmas morning?'

Her cheeks flush and her jaw drops; I can tell that she hasn't. Worse, I can see that she's anguished by that realisation. I soften my voice, but it is no less intense for that.

'And because I don't need you to take pity on me. To include me in a family celebration because you feel sad about how I'm spending my day.'

'And how will you spend your day?'

'I don't know. It's a few weeks away. I guess I'll shower, eat, work, drink.'

She makes a noise of disapproval.

'And then, if I'm really good, maybe Santa will send you over at night.' I turn to face her then, my eyes holding a warning, hers ignoring it.

'To sleep with you.'

'Not to sleep with you.' I lift a finger to the thick lapel of her coat, pushing it aside so I can touch the soft skin of her décolletage. 'To fuck you.'

She blinks up at me and again I feel her hurt rolling over me. 'You're trying to push me away,' she says simply. 'That's what you do when you start to feel something for someone, isn't it?'

'For fuck's sake. Do we have to do this?'

'You want my help? Then yes.'

'I *don't* want your help!' My voice is raised and I lower it with effort. 'I never did. I don't need help.'

'Gabe apparently disagrees.'

My eyes narrow. 'Don't bring him into this like you know him. You don't know anything about him, or me, or why he wants to force me into bullshit therapy. No offence,' I tack on—the most useless phrase in history because obviously I've offended her.

'If you think therapy's so bullshit,' she says, defiance in her eyes, 'then submit to it and see.'

My breath burns in my lungs. 'What?'

'It's simple. If therapy is bullshit, as you claim, then go and see the guy I've found. He's good. He'll help you.'

It incenses me. 'No.'

'Why not?'

'It's just…not necessary.'

'So? You lose an hour.'

'I'm not going to go and tell some man my inner secrets, okay?'

'Then see me,' she says, and I see wariness in her expression. 'Let me help you, Noah. Give me one hour to work on you. If it's just a load of *crap*, as you seem to think, you've only lost time—and not much. But if you're wrong, that hour could change your life. For the better.'

'You're the one who said you can't be my therapist,' I point out, knowing I'm clutching at straws.

'And I still think that. I still think you should see someone else.'

'Then what are you saying?'

'That the most important thing to me is helping you.' She pauses, her eyes skimming my face. 'I wouldn't really be your therapist. It would just be you and me, just like we are now, but we'd be in my office.'

I don't say anything because I don't know what to say.

But she looks at me with her big eyes and a hopeful expression. Inwardly I groan.

'Come on,' she says softly. 'Please?'

It's stupid, and yet I've hurt her and I don't want to have, and so I find myself nodding. Smiling. A smile that is tight and wrong, angry and resentful.

'Fine.' I lean down and press a kiss to her nose. 'I'm not afraid of you.'

I'm nervous. Despite the fact I've been doing this a really long time, I've never felt like a therapy session is as high-stakes as this. Even a weird one-off therapy session with the man I'm sleeping with. I know how important this is, though. If I can't help him, then we have no future, and I realise that this isn't a temporary thing for me. I want more. I want all of Noah, and I want him for all time.

'Please have a seat.' I gesture towards the chair opposite my desk, the seat he occupied the second time we met. Everything feels different now. Off-kilter.

He's wearing black jeans and a white long-sleeved tee shirt that makes the tan of his skin pop. He seems relaxed and calm, but I know it's a veneer, because I know him.

'Sure. Why don't you come join me?' He gestures to his lap. To his powerful thighs. Thighs that have straddled me, pinned me to walls, wedged my legs apart. My mouth goes dry.

His smile shows that he knows it. He stands, slowly, purposefully, moving towards me, coming around to my side of the desk. He stands above me, then bends forward, dropping his hands to the armrests of my chair, imprisoning me.

'Don't I at least get a kiss?'

It's been three days since we got back from Paris and to say I've been craving his touch is an understatement. I've been busy as all hell—I finally organised Ivy's nativity costume and the pudding has been made—but, no matter how much I have on in my days, all I want is to see Noah. To hear his voice. To touch him. For him to touch me.

It takes an intense amount of willpower to shake my head now. 'You're my patient today.'

'Not your lover?' He lifts a hand to my shirt, his fingers finding an erect nipple through the lace of my bra and the silk of my shirt.

I shiver involuntarily. 'Not now.'

But I groan and my legs spread, so he moves forwards into the triangle I've created. 'God, Noah—' my eyes meet his '—I've never felt like this.'

There's a look of satisfaction on his face. A look of triumph that is primal and masculine and thrilling.

'Like what?' he prompts, crouching down in front of me and sliding his hands along my thighs. He finds my underpants and I groan again as he drags them lower.

I want to talk to him. We have an hour and time is

precious. But he pulls my pants down my legs and I bite down on my lip to stop from moaning.

As if he understands, he lifts a finger to his own lips, urging me to be silent.

I need to stop this. He's doing this to waste time—to avoid therapy. But God, I need him.

'Don't think this gets you out of our session,' I say.

His eyes mock me as he takes my hands in his and pulls me to standing. My underpants are discarded on the floor at my feet. He takes my seat, unbuttoning his jeans as he does so, pushing his cock out of his boxers.

Hell.

'Sit on my lap,' he demands, the words throaty, his expression dark.

'I…'

'I'll pretend to be Santa if that helps.'

It's so ridiculous I laugh, but my eyes drop to his dick and its throbbing arousal. I lick my lower lip so that now it's Noah who moans. 'Now, Holly.'

I nod, my need as primal and demanding as his. I hike my skirt around my hips and position myself over him, clenching my lips together as I take him inside me, needing not to scream even when a roar bursts through my insides.

His fingers dig into my hips as I drop over his length. I am on top but he's in control, lifting me and pulling me down, moving me as I need to be moved. Flames spike in my blood. I am dying and immortal all at once. I dig my nails into his shoulders and bite down on my lip, hard. He thrusts harder and I come apart, silently but with an intensity that terrifies me.

He watches me and the look of primal possession on his features robs me of breath.

But I'm not a possession and Noah doesn't own me.

Before he has enjoyed his own release, I stand, my legs wobbly but my expression determined.

'Thanks. I needed that.'

Surprise whips across his features.

'Get back here.' The growl is demanding and seriously hot.

I eye him thoughtfully, my hand on my hip, my breath not at all steady.

'Not yet,' I say softly. 'Not until we've done this.'

His cock jerks, drawing my eyes downwards for a moment. There's triumph in Noah's face. Like he understands that I want more of him, that I'm forcing myself to be strong when I desperately want to just give in and take what he's offering.

But I'll never get him back in my office. Not willingly. This is my one shot to help.

'Answer my questions and you can have me.'

He shakes his head. 'All night.'

I frown. 'It's a Wednesday.'

He nods slowly. 'I don't care.'

And I feel his burning need. Not for me sexually, but for me personally in the aftermath of whatever will happen here.

I think of Ivy and my heart turns over. I can arrange a sleepover for her with Diane easily enough.

And I *do* want to see this through with Noah…

'Let's see how…compliant…you are first.' And, unable to suppress the regret from my voice, I say, 'Zip up, Noah. Let's get down to business.'

'I thought we were.'

I shake my head, repressing a smile. 'You can stay in my chair if that helps.' I can't sit down. My blood is zipping; my insides are quivering. I stalk towards the window and look out at the view. The sky is grey today, reminding me a little of the morning we left Paris. Snow had turned to sludge on the ground, stained brown by feet and time.

'Tell me about the tattoo.'

'Tattoo?' He almost laughs. 'Which tattoo?'

'Nineteen ninety-nine.'

His eyes narrow. 'What about it?'

'What does it mean?'

'Why do you think it means anything?'

I roll my eyes. 'You just got a random number burned into your skin?'

'Inked, not burned.'

'Whatever. What's the deal?'

He presses his lips together and I force myself to stare at him, not his cock, which is still exposed to my view and hard as anything.

'It's the year I met Gabe,' he admits finally.

I feel like I've cracked a hard nut. Success fires through my blood. It's small. Inconsequential.

'He has one too.'

Any other time, I might have disarmed him with a quip about friendship bracelets, but not this time. Not now. I nod seriously and change tack.

'Let's talk about your childhood.'

He stands and I watch him for a moment, but he's simply zipping his jeans up. He doesn't sit down again, though. He comes to stand opposite me, his shoulder pressed against the window jamb, his eyes resting on the same view as mine.

'What do you want to know?'

I hear the terror and displeasure in his voice, but he's here. Answering me.

'Were you ever hit?'

'No.'

'Abused physically in any way?'

'No.'

'Sexually?'

'No.'

'Were you happy?'

A slight pause. 'No.'

'Were you afraid?'

'Sometimes.'

'Did you have friends?'

'No.'

'Did you read books?'

'No.'

'What were you afraid of?'

Another pause. 'The dark.'

'Really? Anything else?'

A muscle throbs in his jaw. 'The bogeyman?'

He's not being serious. Fine.

'Tell me about the Morrows.'

Just like that, his eyes whip to mine. Anguish. Anger.

'Why?'

'Because I want to know about them.'

'They were a nice couple. Full stop.'

'What did they do with you?'

'Nothing.'

'On weekends, for example. How did you spend them?'

His eyes assume a faraway look. 'I can't remember.'

'Don't lie to me,' I say, barely able to keep the frustration from my voice.

'I'm not lying to you.'

'Did you play sports with them?'

'No.'

'Watch television together?'

His eyes are haunted. 'We rode bikes,' he says thickly, the words dragged from him, hurting him, aching in his mouth. 'Julianne taught me. She was so patient.' He shakes his head. 'I'd never known patience. I didn't know it was called that then. It was more just an absence of criticism when I didn't do something wrong.' He lifts his broad, powerful shoulders.

'How long did it take you to learn?'

His eyes clash with mine, then look away again. 'A while. I'd never had a bike before.'

'And she bought you one?'

He nods. A slight dip of his head in concession. 'It was red. With a black stripe down one side. And a horn that sounded like a dying frog.' His laugh is brittle. 'Once I got the hang of it, I'd ride it all afternoon, around and around in circles until my legs hurt. And even then I wouldn't want to come in, but eventually Julianne would make me.'

'How long were you with them?'

He looks at me, anger unmistakable now. 'Is this really necessary, Holly?'

'Don't you think?'

'No. I don't. Everyone has a childhood. A past.'

'Yes, but not everyone's past torments their present. How long did you live with them?'

'Almost a year.'

'And after them you went…'

'Somewhere else,' he says, like it doesn't matter.

'Where?'

He glares at me. It is a battle of wills and we are both too stubborn to back down. 'The Adams family. Two parents, three fosters.'

'Were you happy there?'

'No.'

'Why not?'

'They were assholes, Holly.'

'In what way?'

'If you want me to define the faults of every single foster home I lived in, we'll be here all night.'

'I'm game if you are.'

'This is bullshit,' he says wearily, dragging a hand through his hair. 'You want to help me and I'm telling you there's nothing fucking wrong.'

But there is, and I think I know. I'm trying to prod around the edges of his life, but he's making it difficult. 'How did Julianne tell you they were leaving?'

His head whips around to face mine as though I've asked him to jump out of the window.

'What?'

'When Paul was transferred, how did she tell you?'

His throat bobs, like he's swallowing hard. 'She just told me. I don't remember.'

'Did you wonder why he didn't turn the job down? I mean, once they knew you couldn't go?'

'It was a much better opportunity. They needed the money.'

'More than they needed you,' I say softly. 'They wanted money, not you.'

His expression is closed off. 'No. It wasn't like that.'

'Yes, it was. They could have stayed in Sydney with you, but they ran away. They left you. Like everyone leaves you. Because you're not worth staying for. Right?'

He opens his mouth to say something—something that I suspect would have been a curse-laden tirade, but then he clams up, eyeing me warily.

'You're not worth loving,' I push on, hating saying these words but needing him to admit his wounds, to find them, hold them and weave through them.

'They left—' he grinds the words out '—because they had to. My biological mother, fucking bitch that she was, is the only reason they didn't keep me.'

'No, that's not true, Noah. Lots of people get offered jobs interstate and decide not to go.'

'Fine.' He shrugs, like it doesn't matter. He's so good at this—this pain is one he has obviously ignored for a very long time. 'They didn't want me. That was nothing new. It wasn't the first nor the last time I'd been kicked out of a home.'

'But it was the only time it hurt,' I say. 'It was the only time you let yourself fall in love with your foster parents.'

'Jesus, Holly. What do you know?'

'I know that the day they left you something happened deep inside you that you still can't change. You were heartbroken and ever since then you've kept your heart locked up in case you're rejected again. I know you were set on a destructive path until you found programming and Gabe. That you found it easier to screw things up and be unlovable before anyone could reject you.'

His eyes narrow. 'Thank you so much for the elucidating character sketch.'

I feel like the ground is tipping beneath my feet. It occurs to me that helping him like this might be ruining everything we share, but *not* helping him isn't an option. I want him to be better. To be happy. To be capable of accepting love, to open his heart to trust and relationships.

'Did Julianne stay in contact with you?'

'She wasn't allowed,' he says, his expression rock-hard. 'The foster system is very "protective" of its kids. Once I moved on, I was assigned to a new guardian. She wasn't allowed to have my details.'

'So you never heard from her again?'

A muscle jerks in his cheek, but he is quiet. Quiet for so long that I contemplate a new line of questioning. 'When I turned eighteen,' he says quietly, 'she was able to get my contact information from the foster system then.'

My heart warms. This woman cares for him. Loves him. To have contacted him after so long shows she never forgot him. 'What did she say?'

'Does it matter?' There is a bleak pain in his voice.
'I think it does.'

His jaw tightens. 'She said she thought about me
every day since they left. That she wondered about me
and hoped and prayed that I was happy. That I was with
someone who loved me as much as she did. She said
she wanted to see me again.'

Tears clog my throat, but I can't give in to them. I am
trying to be professional, and to treat him as I would
any other patient. 'How did that make you feel?'

I expect him to say *happy* or *relieved*. Instead, I get
'Fucking livid.'

'Livid?'

'Yeah, Doc. I mean, for fuck's sake, I didn't want to
see her. She was in my past.'

'You were still angry with her. For leaving you.'

'No! I just didn't want to know her.'

'When did you last hear from her?'

He scowls at me. 'Two months ago.'

'What did she say?'

'I don't want to do this.'

'I know.'

'I mean it, Holly. I'm done. This is shit.'

He stalks towards my desk, bracing his hands on its
edge. I know I'm close. So close to whatever has brought
him here, whatever brought us together.

'Are you afraid?'

'No!' He whips around angrily and his face is pure
emotion. Handsome but scarred by the wounds he carries. 'I'm not fucking afraid. I'm bored. Sick of this.
Over it.' His nostrils flare as he draws in a deep breath,

so deep his chest puffs with it. 'Two months ago she wrote to me to say she had cancer. That she needed me to know how much she loved me and how god-damned proud she was of what I'd achieved.' His chest falls as he exhales. 'Two weeks after that, she died.' He pauses, his eyes spearing mine like blades. 'There you go: the answer you've been looking for this whole fucking time. She died, I went to the funeral and since then I haven't been able to sleep. Ta-da! It's no deeply held secret—it's life, and it's *my* life, and I want you to butt the hell out of it.'

I've had patients shout at me before, but only one man I loved has ever done so. I have endured so much worse from Aaron, but it never hurt like this. I brace my back against the wall because I'm not sure I can stand any more.

'You think you know what makes me tick?' he says, moving closer towards me, his body a contortion of rage. I am not afraid, not like I would be if this was Aaron. I am afraid *for him*, for the emotions that are coursing through him. For the pain he feels and how it controls him.

'I'm trying to,' I say softly. 'I want to.' A muscle near my heart throbs and I know then what I need to admit to him and myself. 'I want to love you, Noah. I want you to let me love you. I know that's not going to be easy for you, but I'm falling in love with you and I need you to be brave enough to own that. I want to help you deal with this so we can be together. Properly.'

He stares at me like I've started speaking a foreign

language. 'Are you fucking kidding me?' he whispers, haunted and cross.

'Fight your instinct to push me away. Isn't that what bothers you? That you pushed away Julianne? That you pushed away her love when you wanted it so badly?'

'You don't know shit about me, Doc.' He stalks towards me, close but not touching me. 'You think this is love? This is sex. I like fucking you. I decided I'd fuck you the first moment I saw you to prove that I could. That's who I am and that's what this is. You think I have issues with love? Maybe you're right. But they're nothing compared to your issues. You have a sick need—you *want* to love someone who's going to hurt you. You were hurt by your parents—you could never win their approval. You weren't what they wanted. So you look for that hurt now—you found it in Aaron and you're looking for it again in me. You know this is a disaster waiting to happen—we both do—but at least I'm smart enough to walk away before it explodes. *Fucking* bloody love!'

I am shivering and hurting and shocked in equal measure. 'Noah…' I lift a hand to his chest. His heart is beating slowly, like he's not even bothered by what he's just said. But I take a punt. 'You're angry. Maybe I've pushed you too hard. Let's…just…let this go for now.'

'You don't get it,' he says condescendingly. 'That's what I'm doing. I'm letting it go. I'm letting you go.'

'Wait a second.' I shake my head, trying to see things clearly with a heart that's breaking. 'You're doing what you always do. You're pushing me away before I can push you away. I'm not going to hurt you, Noah.'

'Oh, for God's sake, Holly. I don't think you're going to hurt me. You don't hold that power over me. I don't love you.'

I pull in a breath, shocked. Hurting. Aching.

'I'm not single because I'm damaged or running from love. I'm single because I want to be. I like being on my own. I like fucking a variety of women. You must know that about me. Surely you've heard the rumours? Well, Doc, they're all true.'

My heart shreds. I stay standing, somehow.

He straightens and turns away from me.

He's pushing me away, that's all. But he's doing a damned good job of it.

No one's ever loved Noah enough to fight for him through his bullshit. But I'm going to. 'You're angry,' I say calmly, even when my insides are on fire. 'You're trying to hurt me because I've hurt you. I understand.'

He laughs. 'Your optimism is a marvel.' He grabs his leather jacket from the back of the chair. 'How can I put this more simply? I'm walking out that door and I don't want you to follow me. I don't want you to call me. I don't want to see you again. You and your so-called love can go fuck themselves.'

He doesn't even slam the door when he leaves. I stay, staring at the door, exactly where I was, pressed against the wall, my body trembling, my heart cracking, my mind spinning. What the fuck?

That did *not* go as I planned. I walk towards my desk... My underpants are still where they were dropped. I bend down to pick them up and a single tear falls onto my wrist.

I am almost certain that I'm right. That he's just pushing me away however he can, terrified by what he's revealed and what I've offered him. Terrified of losing him.

I reach for my phone. My fingers are trembling, but I type a quick message to Diane, asking her to keep Ivy for the night.

Something's come up with a client, sorry.

I'd love to have her! We're learning The Night Before Christmas.

I smile at that, slipping my phone into my handbag. I have three patients to get through before I can go to Noah, but I'm going to fix this for him, for us, because I love him, and I'm going to show him that love means fighting. Love is lasting. Love is permanent and he is worthy of all of those things.

CHAPTER THIRTEEN

SHE'S WEARING THE same perfume as Holly. It smells like chocolate and flowers. It's why I approach her, because I catch a hint of the fragrance as I pass the bar on my way back from the john and the smell draws me in, like a man who needs an urgent fix of a drug he can't have, so he settles for something—anything—to ease the pain.

This woman is nothing like Holly, though. This woman has a body like a fashion model, all skin and bone, draped in a black leather dress. Her hair is black, pulled into a silky ponytail. Once upon a time, I would have fantasised about wrapping my fingers around the ponytail and pulling her head back, kissing her lips, taking her against the bar.

Instead, I take the seat next to her and order two Scotches. 'Join me.'

It's a gruff command. She doesn't seem to mind. Her eyes are brown; I'm glad they're not blue. Holly's eyes are like ice.

Out of nowhere, I see them as they'd been that afternoon. I was right, in Paris. I feel Holly's pains as if they were my own. Her emotional hurts haunt me.

But fuck her.

What did she expect?

Making me talk about Julianne and whether or not she could have kept me? Should have stayed in Sydney? Then telling me she, Holly, loved me? Jesus. I've known her only a few weeks. It's just sex!

And sex is something I'm good at, I remind myself, wishing I felt a stirring of desire for the very beautiful woman I'm sitting next to. I don't, though, but I've done this enough times to fake it.

'Nice…dress,' I say, dropping my eyes to her cleavage.

When I look at her face, her lips are parted and then she smiles at me. Her fingers run across the dipped neckline and she leans forward, purring, 'You should see what's underneath.'

'I'd like that, sweetheart. Have a drink with me first, though.'

I slide the Scotch across to her and throw my own back, signalling the barman for another. It's busy for a Wednesday night. I guess that's this fucking Christmas time of the year, though.

'You drink like you're trying to forget,' she says smoothly, a hand creeping over to my thigh.

'Do I?'

She tilts her head to the side, her feline eyes appraising me. 'There are other ways to forget. Better ways.'

She's right. Holly used me to fuck Aaron out of her body and now I see the logic of that. Of being able to devalue what you had with someone by having exactly that with someone else.

'What's your name?' I ask the woman.

'Do we need to swap names?'

My chest lifts with relief. What a pleasure it is to talk to a woman who doesn't want to psychoanalyse everything I say and do. I tell myself this is good. This is healthy. It's an added bonus that she doesn't recognise me. I'm not exactly famous, but I find I get recognised often enough to dislike it.

'I'll tell you what I want, sweetheart. I want to get drunk. And then we're going to...'

The words die on my lips. I see Holly. Not here, just in my mind. But I see her as she'd been that first night: in my bed, so beautiful, so willing, so gentle, so kind.

I see her as she'd be if she knew I was planning to fuck this other woman. I see her hurt and my heart cranks in my chest.

Fuck it.

Holly was an aberration. A break from my usual rules. That doesn't mean I'm bound to her for ever. I don't owe her anything, just like she doesn't owe me anything. She could be with someone else and I wouldn't care.

That's a lie. The very idea fills me with bile. The thought of another man's hands on her body makes me want to vomit.

But that's wrong. Because Holly deserves a nice man. A nice man who won't hurt her. A nice man who smiles when she says she loves him, and buys her roses as a sign of his love. All that romantic shit I don't have any time for.

'Yes?' the woman opposite asks, running her palm

higher so her fingertips graze my cock. I fight an impulse to dash her hand away.

I've been in this bar for the better part of the night. I have no concept of what time it is. But another Scotch doesn't feel like the answer.

'Let's go,' I say, standing up, reaching for her hand and holding it as though it is the talisman that will save me from the nightmare I've woken up in. 'Now.'

The air is frigid against me as we step out of the cab. My place is just down the street a little way. Whatever-Her-Name-Is is slightly uneven on high heels and with a shitload of alcohol in her system. Drunk messy sex is going to get Holly and her fucking therapy session out of my head.

This is the therapy I need!

'So,' the woman purrs, snuggling up beside me, so I wrap an arm around her waist, holding her there, refusing to compare her slim, hard figure to Holly's beautiful, soft undulations. 'You're rich.'

I laugh. 'Am I?'

'You have, like, two thousand pounds in your wallet and you live here,' she says, shrugging her shoulders.

She must have seen my cash when I paid for the cab. And, as for where I live, I suppose it is a sign of wealth. I look towards the steps; it is dark, but a light from just down the street highlights the outline of a figure on my steps, hunched over.

A tramp?

I am already reaching for my wallet, happy to throw a few hundred quid his way, when the figure straightens and I stop walking, my heart jerking frantically inside me.

Holly.

She is as surprised as I am, her face pale, her eyes frantic, her lips parted.

She was waiting for me and instead she got us. Me and a woman whose name I don't know, who is practically drooling at the thought of being in my bed.

What we are about to do is impossible to misinterpret. So I don't bother insulting Holly's intelligence by pretending. By apologising. I meant what I said in her office. We're done.

'Noah.' The word is tortured from her, a groan that reaches inside me and snaps what little self-control I have left. I turn to the woman beside me, the woman who doesn't even want to know my name, and smile.

'Go inside, sweetheart. I'll be in soon.'

'Don't keep me waiting,' she murmurs, standing up on tiptoe and nipping my earlobe.

Holly gasps as though she's been stabbed. My gut responds accordingly.

I unlock my door and hold it inwards while Skinny Model Girl teeters in. I pull the door shut afterwards, giving Holly my full attention.

'What are you doing?' she whispers, her knuckles white as she grips the railing behind her.

'Isn't that obvious?'

Her eyes are huge. 'You don't… You don't want to do this, Noah.'

'Oh, believe me, I do.' And maybe it's seeing Holly, maybe it's a reaction to the panic inside me, but my cock is hard. I grab Holly's hand and palm her across my front.

Tears sparkle in her eyes. Fuck. Not tears. I can't handle that, and nor can I handle her.

'What do you want?' I ask bleakly, my buzz disappearing. I am stone-cold sober now.

'I… Noah…' She swallows, lost for words. She hadn't prepared for this. 'I can't do this while she's here.'

'Do what?' I demand. 'I told you today, we're done. I meant it. This is who I am, Holly. This guy. Not the man you think you can make me.'

'I don't want to change you…'

'You just want to "heal" me,' I say.

'Is that so wrong?' she whispers.

'Yes. I don't need to be healed. Now kindly fuck off.'

She draws in a harsh breath, but determination is stoked anew in her gaze. 'No.'

'Well, I hate to break it to you, Holly, but I've got plans and, unless you're into threesomes, you're not invited.'

More tears. 'You're such a bastard,' she says.

'Yes. But that's your thing, right?'

'Apparently.' Her face is pinched. 'Fine. Go and… and fuck her. See if I care.'

'You don't care, Holly, not really. That's the whole damned point.'

I stare at her for a long second and then turn away, my blood gushing through my body and my chest feeling like it's been split in half.

When I go inside, I lean against the door, my back

pressed to it for several moments while I come to terms with what's just happened.

That afternoon I had Holly in her office and she was so sassy and confident, bribing me with sex for therapy, and I loved seeing that she knows how many cards she holds with me. For using them to her advantage. I loved her confidence.

And then it all unravelled.

The night I thought we'd share had become this.

I feel like I'm halfway down a river, there's a waterfall at the end and the current is going too fast to turn back. I am at the whim of the tide and it's definitely turned against me.

I can't breathe. I stare at the front door, and it's as though my body has been tortured, or silenced, as though I am withering from the inside.

I squeeze my eyes shut, trying to breathe, trying to think.

Noah is going to have sex with that woman. And I'm what? Going to let him? I can't. I have to do something.

But what?

Barge in there? Pull him off her? What good is fidelity if it's achieved through such measures? I grip the railing and move down the steps slowly, my body feeling bruised all over.

I knew he was broken when I first met him; I saw the pain in his eyes and still I went and fell in love with him. Maybe Noah's right. Maybe that's my thing. Maybe I like men who are closed off. Maybe I'm addicted to healing and fixing.

I reach the bottom of the steps and turn to face the door. No. It's more than that. Aaron wasn't broken when we fell in love. At least, not in any of the ways I could have recognised. His wounds were buried deep inside him.

And I love Noah despite his hurts, not because of them. I love him anyway. I love all of him, body and soul, mind and magic, and that means accepting him as he is.

But this? How can I possibly accept this?

I swear under my breath, wrapping my arms around myself. There is a bar somewhere nearby and it's playing Christmas music. I move in that direction without thinking, my feet going one in front of the other. The crooning sound of Diana Krall is instantly familiar to me. 'What Are You Doing New Year's Eve?' makes my stomach drop.

Because I know that whatever I'm doing, it won't be with Noah.

My life suddenly drags before my eyes—everything I've been, everything I've done and now this. The absence of him.

I've acknowledged that I love him, but it's only now, right here, that I understand what that really means. It's a complete infiltration of my life. He has found a space in my being, in my home life, despite the fact he's never been there, in my family life, even though he's never met Ivy. I have *imagined* him there, I have *foreseen* a time when he would be with me all the time, by my side.

I dash at hot tears that are clinging to my lashes. What a foolish, idiotic woman I've been!

To let him so deep into my soul when he's insisted all along that he doesn't want that.

Hurt morphs to fury, carrying me farther down the pavement, away from the bar. I step out onto the road without looking and might have been hit by a black taxi cab had it not blared its horn loudly and swerved to avoid me.

My heart beats a frantic tattoo in my chest, and I support my weight against a thick tree trunk. I stare at the road and, beyond it, the Thames, and I curse. I curse Noah, I curse Gabe, I curse Julianne, and everything that conspired to bring him into my life. How dare he do this to me.

How dare he think we were ever just about sex.

Fuck him!

I glare back in the direction from which I've come and I begin to walk that way, my back straight, my eyes unwavering from Noah's door. He thinks he can do this to me? No way.

He's going to hear exactly what I think of this decision—to hell with his pains and hurts. This is about me now.

The girl from the bar has helped herself to a drink and is looking around my place.

I'm bored of her. I want her to go. I feel invaded and angry that she's here.

But I don't want to admit that, even to myself.

'So, sweetheart. What do you do?'

'Do?' She lifts a brow. 'You mean sexually?'

I laugh, but it's a sound of despair. Frustration. Confusion. What's happening? Is this a dream? Can I shake myself awake from it? I look down at my hands. They're real enough. Shaking slightly.

'I mean professionally.'

'Oh. I'm a model.'

'Of course you are.' I can't help—and don't bother trying to hide—the derision that curls my words.

'I'll take that as a compliment.' Her fingers find the straps of her dress, toying with them.

My body doesn't respond. Not even a little bit.

'What do you do?'

'Software development,' I say, somewhat disingenuously. It's been a long time since I've coded for more than fun.

'That explains all this.' She waves a hand around.

I don't want to sleep with her. I want to get rid of her. Holly's eyes are in my mind again. Filled with tears. Her lips parted. Her face pale.

Fuckety-fuck.

'Look, sweetheart, you're very attractive, but you're not really my type.'

Her eyes narrow. 'You don't like models?' she prompts, sashaying towards me, her skinny hips jerking from side to side. I would have gone for her a month ago. Three weeks ago. Pre-Holly I'd be stripping that dress from her body and pulling her against me.

'I've never been with a model.'

She pauses in front of me, locking her hands behind my back. Still my body doesn't respond. I am impatient to be alone now. 'And I don't intend to be now.'

She lifts up on her toes, dragging her lips against my cheek. I step back.

'I think you should go.'

'What the hell? You invited me back here.'

'I changed my mind.'

'Well,' she snaps, but steps away from me, 'you could at least let me finish my drink.'

She throws it back in one go. I remember Holly on that first night, when a few glasses of champagne knocked her sideways, and my gut clenches.

I call the model a cab, and when I hear it beep out the front I open the door, intending to make sure she at least gets safely inside, feeling somewhat responsible for her fully drunk state.

Holly is standing at the bottom of the steps when I open the door. Our eyes lock and my body squirms, my heart throbs, my blood stills.

Holly.

She looks away almost instantly, her arms crossed. She's bundled up in a huge coat, wrapped tight against the weather. She's pale, her face pinched, her eyes firing into mine.

I press my lips together, walking Model to the waiting cab and holding the door open for her. She smiles at me as she slips in and I slam the door shut with more force than intended.

Holly.

I turn back to my steps and walk towards her, my expression guarded.

'What are you still doing here?'

She opens her mouth to speak, but she can't. She's

gaping like a fish out of water and then she shakes her head, digging her fingertips into her chest and staring at me like she's drowning and only I can save her.

'I…I don't know. I just… I'm so angry at you! I had to tell you…' But she doesn't sound angry. She sounds like someone who's deflating slowly before my eyes.

'And I guess… I guess I had to know. I had to know, without a doubt, that you'd… I had to know that you'd slept with her,' she says thickly, gripping the railing again, needing its stability.

Thinking I'd fucked the model is killing Holly and I don't want to do that, not even a little bit. I'm angry with her and she's angry with me, and I know I can't see her again, but I don't want her to hurt because of me. Not because of this. There are enough things I've genuinely screwed up without adding a phantom lay into the mix.

'I didn't sleep with her.'

She nods. 'Fucked her, I should have said.'

'I didn't do that either.'

'I don't believe you.'

'I'm not lying.'

Her eyes narrow. But she shakes her head. 'It doesn't matter.'

'Doesn't it?'

'No. If I hadn't been here, would you have slept with her?'

I open my mouth to deny it but can't. 'Yes. Probably.'

She sweeps her eyes closed, the pain on her face unmistakable. 'God, Noah. You're seriously messed up.'

'No shit.' And suddenly I want Holly. I want Holly

so damned bad. I need her. I take a step towards her, but she shakes her head, lifting a hand to hold me at bay.

'Don't. Don't you dare touch me.'

Had my intent been so obvious?

'You don't get to touch me,' she says, as though the idea is repugnant to her when I know otherwise.

'Why are you here?'

'Because I love you.' She says the words as though they offend her. 'I can't be with you, Noah, and God, you make me madder than hell.' I see then that she's been crying and my chest heaves. I ache for her. 'Maybe you were right about everything in my office today.' It's just a whisper, an admission that I am desperate to rebut. 'But that doesn't mean I don't care about you.'

It's the last thing I expect her to say.

'It doesn't mean I don't still want to help you.'

'Come inside,' I say gruffly, but she shakes her head.

'No. I don't… I don't ever want to go into your house again.' She swallows, her beautiful throat bobbing with the action. 'But I'm going to make an appointment for you with Dr Chesser.'

'No.' I'm emphatic. 'No more doctors.'

'He's great at what he does. You won't be able to pull your crap with him.'

'I said *no*.' The words are forceful. 'If you're not going to come inside, Holly, then go home. This conversation is over.'

I give her a second to agree, to join me, and when she doesn't I storm into my home and shut the door. As before, I lean against it, waiting for my breathing to return to normal, waiting to feel like myself.

I don't. I don't know how long passes with me standing like that, but eventually I straighten. I wrench the door inwards, wondering if she's still there, not knowing what I'll say if she is.

She's not, but a carrier bag is on the top step. I hadn't noticed it before.

I reach for it automatically. It has the Rivière logo on it. I peer inside. A dozen oysters and a small bottle of champagne, as well as a little box. My heart races as I open it. There's a single ornament inside. A turtle dove made of silver, with a red velvet ribbon and a bell at its base. It twinkles as I shove it back in the bag and then my fingers curl around a piece of card. A business card, as it turns out. Her name is on the front, and on the back...

This isn't over, Noah.

She obviously wrote it before tonight. Before this.

And maybe she believed it when she wrote it. But I'd sure shown her. She walked away from me like everyone else—but only after I made it impossible for her not to.

I had Christmas lunch around the corner from her house.

I had Christmas lunch surrounded by happy families, couples, people drinking and eating turkey, ham and pudding, and now I am here, half-cut, staring at her door with a belligerent rage. A rage at how beautiful her house is. At how picture-perfect, like all those houses I coveted as a child. A big, fluffy green wreath on her door, made of holly and ivy, and more strung down the steps that lead to it.

The windows are glowing now, the light from within warm, and my heart achingly cold, like the rest of me.

I nurse the bottle of beer against my gut, leaning on a fence across the street from Holly's perfect house, biding my time.

It underscores how bad I am for her. How wrong. Wrong in *every* way. Holly is beautiful, smart, with a daughter just like her. Holly has suffered enough. Holly has a great job and a beautiful home and she deserves to be with someone who will slide into this lovely life of hers. Who'll sit by her side and eat roast turkey and sing carols and laugh with her.

My stomach has a stitch deep in its lining. It's not me. That will never be me.

Eventually, another couple leaves and I'm sure this must be the last of them. I stare at her house, waiting to catch a glimpse of Holly, just a glimpse.

She is my kryptonite and I am hers. She talks of love, but that's not how it's meant to be, is it? Love is meant to strengthen people, not weaken them, and Holly has unpicked me to the end.

Or is it the absence of Holly?

My needing Holly?

I grimace and cross the street unsteadily, waiting on her doorstep to see if I hear noises within but catching only the faint rasp of Christmas carols.

I lift my hand, thumping it loudly on the door, then step back, arms crossed, waiting.

She answers quickly enough, but it feels like an eternity. Her surprise is obvious.

'Noah?' She grips the door jamb. 'What are you doing here?'

'You invited me. Remember?'

Her eyes narrow and a pulse point jerks at her throat. 'I invited you to Christmas lunch. It's almost eight o'clock.' She shakes her head. 'And that was a long time ago.'

It wasn't. Just over a week. But a lot's happened in that time.

'I don't want Christmas lunch,' I say simply. 'I want you.'

Her eyes sweep closed and she swallows. I feel her weakness. I feel her swaying towards me.

'I… This is my *home*. My *daughter* is asleep upstairs…'

'I'll be quiet,' I say, and now I push past her, into her house. It is so picture-postcard perfect that I almost groan. Everything is cosy and pretty and normal and so very fucking Holly that I feel like I'm at my wits' end. I spin around as she closes the door, latching it in place.

It is a home. The kind of home I've only known once before—at the Morrows'. Love and happiness is visible in every corner; every knick-knack is chosen for its rightness and significance to Holly.

'Noah.' Her brow is drawn lower, her expression wary. 'You said you didn't want to see me again.'

'True.' I shrug, like it doesn't matter, when it matters

so damned much. The idea of not seeing Holly again fills me with a strange drowning sensation.

I step towards her; she holds her ground.

'I thought I meant it. But I've been thinking about that session in your office.' Her eyes lift hopefully to mine, as though I'm here to fucking talk, to let her 'fix' me in the ways she thinks most valid. With therapy.

I need to dispel that notion. I wrap an arm around her back and pull her towards me, holding her tight against my body, pushing my arousal forward so she feels it for herself.

'I've been thinking how we need to finish what we started.'

And I step forward, pushing her back against the wall, supporting her body there while I kiss her, hard, desperately, hungrily. I taste her tears in the kiss and still I don't stop.

She is my kryptonite.

'Noah.' She says my name into my mouth. 'You're drunk.'

'So what? Who cares? I want to fuck you, Holly. Drunk, sober—what does it matter?'

She sobs, her hands pressing against my chest. 'No.'

'No?' I hadn't expected this, and I don't know what to do with it. No means no, always, without exception, and yet I know Holly and I know what she wants. Or do I? Maybe she doesn't want me as much as I want her. Isn't that what I've been fearing all this time?

'This isn't the answer,' she says, her fingers relaxing, dropping to the bottom of my shirt, finding my skin, running over it hungrily.

'Maybe not, but it's something.'

Her eyes hold mine and a shiver runs the length of my spine.

'It's another mistake,' she says quietly, and now she pushes at me—pushes me away. 'We're not having sex.'

My cock jerks hard in my pants, its rampant needs unwilling to be quashed.

But Holly is strong—stronger than I've ever known myself to be. She offers me a smile, but it's tight and it's sad. 'You can stay and have coffee, sober up, before you go. You can stay and talk to me about the Morrows and the boys' home and Gabe Arantini. You can stay and sleep this off—in the guest room—but you don't get to touch me any more.'

'I thought you loved me,' I respond sarcastically, even as her words are doing weird shit to my gut.

'I do love you,' she admits softly. 'But I can't sleep with you.'

'That's not love, then.'

She responds with a calmness that is somehow terrifying. 'Believe me, Noah, it is. If I loved you less, I'd sleep with you now, but we both know it's just letting you run from what you really need to sort out. I won't be a party to your denial any longer. I never should have been.'

'You're saying you regret this? What we did?'

She bites down on her lip, stares at me, and then she nods. 'Yes, Noah. I regret it. But we can't change the past. You and I both know that through personal experience.'

Of all the things we've said and done to each other

these last few weeks, her admission now is what breaks me apart fully. Her desire to undo everything we've shared, her fervent wish to go back in time and not sleep with me. Maybe to not even meet me.

I stare at her for a long minute and then turn away.

'I was wrong to come. Forget I was here.'

'Noah—' she follows me '—you can't go home like this. Have a coffee...'

'I don't want a fucking coffee.'

I slam the door behind me and don't look back.

'You said this was urgent?'

God, he is so like Noah my heart stutters in my chest. I know they're not related by blood, yet there is something in them that is instantly familiar. In looks, they are similar, both bigger than the average man, strong-looking, with a raw sort of animalism tangible. Gabe Arantini is wearing a suit, though, and a top-quality watch. He looks every bit the expensive banker, and he speaks with an accent that is tinged with Italian and Australian.

He's looking at me with barely concealed impatience, and I know it's impatience to hear what I have to say, not to be away from me. Because he cares about Noah. And I am happy—so happy Noah has someone in his life who will fly internationally on the day after Christmas because a woman he's never met called him.

'Yes. Please, take a seat.'

'I'm fine standing.'

So like Noah, a tired smile slides across my face. 'As you wish. This won't take long.'

My penance is the smallest part of my concerns. Confessing to what I did weighs on me like a ton of bricks, yet it is just the beginning of what I need to tell Gabe.

'I don't want to talk about what Noah has told me. I consider that confidential.'

Gabe crosses his arms over his chest, staring at me as if he can see into my mind with just that look. 'But I can imagine.'

'Yes. You know him better than anyone.' It hurts to admit that. I thought I knew him, but if I did, then I wouldn't have pushed him so hard he'd run away. I wouldn't have hurt him like I did. 'Gabe,' I say slowly, knowing perhaps I should employ formality, refer to him as Mr Arantini, but I can't. This man I have heard so much about I now feel I know him too.

'*Si?*'

He's worried. I must do this better. Faster.

'There's no easy way to say this.' I stand up, needing to be more on a level with the handsome tycoon. 'Noah and I...became involved. Personally involved.'

He stares at me for a long moment, angry colour slashing his cheeks. 'You're a *psychologist*,' he snaps, gesturing to the wall that is adorned with my degrees and awards.

'I know.' I shake my head with frustration, knowing there's no point explaining the shade of grey that our relationship inhabited, knowing that it won't matter to Gabe that I'd outright refused to see Noah as a patient, just so I could sleep with him. That's a pretty unprofessional thing to do anyway. 'It shouldn't have happened.'

'You think?' His sarcasm is scathing. 'I sent him to you because you help people! People like him! You were supposed to talk to him, not go to his bed.'

It strikes the error of my decision into my heart, more firmly than before. Because he's right. I chose my own sexual satisfaction over Noah's welfare. I'm so ashamed. 'I know, believe me, how much I've messed up. I know how much I've let him down.'

'So what? You're dumping him on me? You don't want to deal with this mess, so I have to?'

It's not far from the truth. 'I *can't* deal with the mess. I've tried. I…love him, Gabe.' Admitting it to someone else helps. 'And Noah being Noah, he's determined to push me away. He's so angry with me. And he's… It's all wrong. I…I have my own reasons for needing it to be over. But yes, I'm worried about him, and I know you care about him, and that you'll speak to him and stay with him until he gets help.'

'Another doctor who'll seduce him?' he snarls.

'It wasn't like that, believe me,' I say, but wearily, because it doesn't matter who seduced whom, nor how we defined and justified our situation. 'I know a doctor who will be perfect for Noah, but he… I suspect he's on a downwards spiral. I think he's going to need to be dragged, kicking and screaming, into therapy.'

'And whose fault is that?' The words are said with haughty derision.

'Mine. I know that. Believe me, Gabe, you're wasting your energy trying to make me feel bad about this. I couldn't feel worse than I do.'

'Oh, I doubt that.' He glares at me for several seconds and then crosses his arms. 'He deserved better than this.'

CHAPTER FOURTEEN

'Fuck off!' I shout the words, but the sound makes my head bang. Screw this hangover. Where am I? I lift my head up and stare across the room. I'm on my sofa. Wearing jeans and nothing else. I push up to sitting as the banging at the door continues.

What time is it?

I stand. A wave of nausea surges through me. I grip the sofa back.

The banging continues.

The clock on the wall tells me it's almost four o'clock. What time did I go to bed? Was I alone?

Holly.

My chest squeezes and I taste her tears in my mouth. I remember going to her home and practically demanding she fuck me. Jesus Christ. As if on cue, I see the discarded beer bottles littering my home.

Is it Holly at my door? Has she come to see me?

I stumble forward, lurching as fast as I can go in my probably still drunk state, and wrench the door open.

'Cristo.'

Gabe's lips compress. I haven't seen him in a couple of months, since Julianne died.

'You look like shit.'

'Thanks.' I step back, not bothering to invite him in. There's no need. Gabe knows he has a standing invitation to my home.

'So it's true. You're just going to drink yourself into oblivion? That's your plan?'

'It was Christmas,' I say defensively, my head splitting in two. 'I have it on good authority it's okay to over-imbibe.'

'You don't celebrate Christmas.'

'I did this year.'

'Alone?' He is looking at me with sympathy. I don't want it.

'So?'

His eyes lift to the mezzanine bedroom. 'You got hammered here, by yourself?'

'What's wrong with that?' It's not as though Gabe leads the life of a saint.

A muscle jerks in his jaw. 'You *know* what's wrong with that. What the hell is going on with you?'

I am so angry in that moment. So angry—angry enough to shove Gabe out my door.

'Nothing's wrong.'

'I saw your girlfriend,' he says scathingly, and because I don't think of Holly in that way it takes me a second to understand his meaning—and to unpack the consequences.

'Holly?'

'Yes, Holly. How many doctors are you sleeping with?'

Jesus. 'She told you about us?'

'*Si.*'

Immediately I see it from Gabe's perspective. Gabe with his black and white morality. Everything is right and wrong with him; there is no middle ground. It won't matter to him that Holly refused to take me on as a patient. All Gabe will see is that he found me a doctor, the best doctor for men like me, and she screwed me.

'It's not her fault,' I hear myself say, my head ripping itself apart. Fine beads of sweat have broken out on my forehead. I collapse onto the sofa, lying back and throwing a forearm over my eyes.

'She chose to sleep with you, did she not? After you went to her for therapy?'

'I wanted her,' I say. Annoyed to be talking about this with Gabe. Annoyed to be talking about Holly as though she's erred in any way. 'You know how persuasive I can be.'

'She's a psychologist. She should have known better.'

'She did. I didn't consult her professionally. From the first moment I saw her, it was just about sex.' Saying that hollows me out completely. About sex? Holly? It was so much more than that, but I can't define how and why.

'Jesus, man. You can sleep with anyone you want. Why the doctor I found to help you?'

'I told you, I wanted her…'

Gabe grimaces, grinding his teeth together. 'She should have known better.'

'She did! She knew it was wrong…'

'But still acted on her feelings,' Gabe says scath-ingly. 'Anyway. I don't give a shit about your sex life. I care about your head. What's going on with you, man?'

'Nothing.' I'm sullen. Angry. Hungover as hell.

'Liar.' Gabe spins away from me, stalking to the other side of the room. 'You need help. I can't help you. She can't help you. No one can until you decide you want that.'

He stalks to the door of my apartment, staring at me angrily. 'You owe it to yourself, and me, to see the guy she suggested. Until you sort your shit out, don't bother coming in to work.'

I stand up, my head spinning, ready to fight him, ready to fight anyone.

'Don't.' Gabe lifts a finger. 'Don't give in to that im-pulse. You know I'm right.'

But he doesn't leave. He stares at me for a moment, long and hard, and then he walks back to me and wraps me in a hug. I can't remember the last time we did this. It's been years. But he hugs me and a strange lurching grief spasms in my chest.

I pull away from him, shoving my hands into my pockets.

'How was she?'

He doesn't immediately answer. 'You can't think of her. There'll be plenty of women once you get your-self sorted.'

'How was she?' I repeat more emphatically.

He sighs. 'I don't know her well enough to say. She was quiet. Obviously concerned for you.'

That fills me with guilt. I'm pretty sure I don't deserve Holly's concern.

'Sleeping with a patient is seriously deplorable. Talk about questionable ethics.'

'It was very mutual,' I say wearily. Defensively.

I blink and see Holly. Holly in all her guises. Loving. Laughing. High on the drugging need of sex. Crying. My gut twists.

'I really fucked up.' My statement is bleak.

My blood is screeching through my body, begging me to do something, enraging me, enlivening me and, yes, enlightening me. Holly loves me. She loves me and she fought for me. She isn't pushing me away, even now, after all I've done. She called Gabe.

My stomach is on a bad acid trip, lurching and squeezing. I grip the back of the sofa and swear. 'I fucked up.'

'Noah—' Gabe sighs '—you need help. You don't know which way is up right now.' He pauses, dragging a hand through his hair, his eyes full of emotion. 'We both carry the scars of our childhood. I understand you, Noah, because I've been there. We are birds of a feather, my friend.'

'Yeah?' I stare right back at him. 'Then how come you never go off the rails? How come you seem fine with everything?'

Gabe's eyes lance me; something in the coldness in his gaze makes *me* worried about *him*. 'Because I don't have a heart like yours, Noah. You feel everything deeply. You need help to process your feelings, whereas I have none.'

I laugh because it's such an absurd thing to say, that he must, surely, be joking.

'I do feel deeply,' I mutter after a while, and I look at Gabe, completely lost, and uncertain as to what to do. 'I fell in love with her. With Holly. I thought... I don't know. She was different from the start, but I didn't realise...' It is a strange thing to recognise love, an emotion that should be filled with hope, and to simultaneously understand how utterly hopeless it is.

There is no going back from the errors I've made. I love Holly because she is smart, strong and fearless—qualities that will stop her from ever forgiving me for how I've acted.

It is four weeks since I last saw Noah. Four weeks.

I know that doesn't sound like long—a lot can happen in four weeks. But my God. I have felt every second that has made up each long, barren day. I have never known such a soul-deep hurt as this.

I've worked hard. I've spent extra time with Ivy, holding her close, knowing that it will be her and me for the rest of my life. How can I love again? How will I ever?

I walk slowly, barely feeling the January chill that is thick in the air. Ivy is staying over with Diane, and I'm glad. On these nights, these rare nights when I am on my own, I can accept my grief, and I do.

I plan to soak in the bath and then watch a depressing movie. *Schindler's List* or *The Piano*. Something that will allow me to cry all these tears, to hang my grief on something inherently sad.

I unlock my door without looking down the street, pushing it shut and sliding the chain in place.

Our breakfast bowls are still on the table. On the mornings when I have to go to work and Ivy has school, we are often rushed like this. I dump my handbag to the floor, stretch my back and then scoop up the bowls, carrying them through to the kitchen. The fridge is covered with Ivy's artwork—pictures of her, me, the cat she desperately wants and sometimes pretends we have.

My smile tastes metallic on my lips. I open the fridge door and retrieve a bottle of sparkling water, cracking it and drinking several sips before placing it on the counter.

I'm almost out of food and, though I'm barely hungry, I know I should take advantage of the fact Ivy's not here to go to the supermarket.

It's the last thing I feel like doing. Then again, that's true of everything now.

I stack the dishwasher and then retrieve my handbag, pulling it over my shoulder and wrenching the door inwards.

The last thing I expect to see is Noah Moore, handsome as hell in a dark grey suit with a crisp white shirt, his expression sombre, his body tight.

My handbag slips from my shoulder, falling to the floor, but otherwise I don't move.

'Holly.' He says my name softly, as though I'm an animal about to bolt. I must look like I feel. So full of emotions that I'm terrified.

'Don't shut the door.' The statement is throaty, and

I realise I'm clutching the wood with that exact intention. 'I just…need a minute.'

I shake my head, my eyes filling with tears. 'No.'

He nods, as if he understands. But how can he? How can he realise how impossible I'm finding it to function? How can he know that his being here is undoing four weeks of hard, hard work?

'I'm sorry it's been a month.'

A month? It feels like so much longer.

'I'm sorry about what I said in your office. I'm sorry about the night at my place. I'm just so sorry.'

I squeeze my eyes shut, shaking my head, locking him out. But I can't do that, not completely. 'How are you?' He touches me. Just a light touch against my cheek, but I pull away.

'Don't.' It's a gasp. A gasp of fear, because I am so close to wrapping my arms around his waist.

He nods, a muscle jerking in his jaw. 'I didn't mean to.' He jams his hands into his pockets, as if to physically keep himself away from me. 'Will you give me five minutes?'

Five minutes? I've given him my whole life, whether he knows it or not. 'Fine.' But my grip tightens on the door. 'But out here.'

I can't say why, but it's important to me to keep him out of my house, as if symbolically that will stop further incursions into my heart.

'Okay.' He nods, and I'm relieved. Relieved he doesn't push this. 'You were right about me.'

My heart tingles. 'In what way?'

'About Julianne. About you. About why I wasn't

sleeping.' He hesitates, his eyes locked to mine. 'I've been seeing Dr Chesser. He's helping me.'

I sob, a sob that comes out of nowhere. 'I'm so glad.'

Something sparks between us and he moves closer, just a fraction of an inch. 'It's hard work, like you said. I still fucking hate therapy, Holly.'

'I told you, there's no magic cure…'

'Damn right,' he grunts, but his lips are soft, as though he wants to smile, or cry, I don't know.

'I haven't had a drink in a month,' he continues.

I close my eyes because I don't know what to say, and looking at him is hurting me.

'I didn't want to need you, I didn't want to need anyone. But, fuck it, I can't live like that. Not any more. Not now I've met you. I want you in my life, Holly.'

My heart is being blown up like a balloon. It hurts so much.

'And I know I'm messed up and that I've messed this up. I know I need to work out my own shit, but I'm asking… I'm here today, asking if you'll wait for me. If you'll wait for me while I become the man you deserve. I don't want to lose you, and I know you should go, that you have to think of yourself, and Ivy, but God, Holly, I don't want to lose you and I know I can be what you need.'

It takes all my willpower not to show how much his words mean to me. Because he's right. He's messed this up. 'You're not the only one with baggage, Noah. I have every reason to stay away from you. I don't want to be with another man who makes me miserable.'

'Your happiness is my life's mission,' he says with such honesty that my heart lurches.

Trust is a force at my back, but I'm stronger than I used to be and I ignore the emotion. 'I'm glad you're getting help. I really am. I want you to be happy and well. But I don't for one second think I can trust you again.'

'Then let me show you.'

I open my eyes, looking at him, trying to understand, and I'm shaking my head.

'I'm not talking about what we were,' he says softly. 'I know we'll never be that again. I can't undo how I was. I wish, I wish beyond any words I can offer, that I had listened to you. That I'd got help at the beginning. But I'm doing it now, and I'm doing it because it's important, and I want to not feel like this. And because I want a future with you, and I know I'm going to have to work my arse off to deserve you.'

I bite down on my lip and taste tears; I hadn't realised I'd let them fall.

'I just… I'll never forget the sight of you with her.' I shiver and push away from the door so I can support my back on the wall just inside. 'I'll never forget the things you said. And I know it's because you're messed up and you needed to push me away, but… Don't you get it, Noah? You were my pleasure. You were everything I'd been waiting for and I loved you so hard and I gave you my whole heart, all of it.'

'And I didn't even act like I cared,' he admits thickly, coming inside so he can cup my cheeks. 'I cared. Believe me, Holly, I cared. I loved you then and I love you now, and I'm going to prove it to you.'

He presses a kiss to my forehead, his eyes holding mine with an intensity that can't fail to make my chest throb, and then he smiles.

'I'll be seeing you.'

I watch him go with a frown and yet a lightness is living in me for the first time in a month. Hope is beating its tired, broken wings…

A week later Noah is waiting for me outside my office when I leave. I wasn't expecting him and the sight of him in jeans and a leather jacket bowls me over.

I stand still, staring at him as he crosses the street, my heart in my throat.

'I came to walk you home,' he says, lifting his hands in a gesture of surrender. 'We don't have to talk. I won't ask to come in. I just…want to be in your airspace for a bit. Is that…okay?'

And hope beats again, little wings seeking light.

'It doesn't mean anything,' I say coldly, locking my gaze straight ahead, refusing to look into eyes that have always enchanted me.

'I know.'

We walk in silence. At the bottom of my steps I turn to him and he's just watching me, as though trying to memorise everything.

I don't smile. I turn away from him and walk inside. I dream of him that night and for the first time in a long time I don't wake up feeling like a devastating cyclone has rushed over me.

* * *

He is waiting for me the next week, this time on the
same side of the street as my office. We walk as before,
with no conversation, no contact. But I feel him beside
me, I hear his breathing and his heart calls to mine.
When we reach my home, I leave him on the footpath
without a goodbye.

For four more weeks we do this. But on the fifth week
he has something. A gift in a bag. I frown but take it
from him.

'I don't want presents from you.' I think of the necklace he gave me in Paris that I've stuffed into a shoebox
in the bottom of my wardrobe.

'It was your birthday on Tuesday,' he says softly.

My eyes jerk to his and my breath escapes in a
ragged noise.

'I wanted to call, to see you, but I wasn't sure…'
His uncertainty breaks something inside me, but it's a
good breaking. It's like the bursting of something tight
and painful.

'What is it?' I lift the bag.

'Have a look.'

I peek inside, but whatever he's chosen is wrapped
in tissue paper. I open it carefully, the precious ornament the most beautiful thing I've ever seen. It's the
most delicate glass, and it's been etched with a nativity scene, the intricacy incredible. It hangs from a red
velvet ribbon and a dainty bell is inside.

'Do you like it?' The question is soft.

I nod. 'It's beautiful.'

'They're very rare. Gabe…collects them.' His smile is wry. 'I had this one made for you.'

My chest heaves. 'Thank you.' I wrap it and place it gently into the bag. We walk, side by side, in silence. But at the steps, I turn to him.

'I'll see you next week?'

Triumph glows in those beautiful eyes. 'You can count on it.'

I start to count on it. On him. Every week he is waiting for me without fail.

Sometimes he brings hot chocolates for us to drink on the walk, other times small gifts. Never anything extravagant. A book he thinks I'd like. A scarf he saw and knew I'd love. Occasionally, he goes overseas for business, but he's always back by Friday, and when he's been somewhere exotic he brings me something from that country. Bookmarks from Japan, magnets from Australia and then a set of princess merchandise from Disney for Ivy.

It is four months before I ask him to come inside, and even then only for a cup of tea.

I curl my fingers around the mug and look across my dining table at this man I have loved since we first met and I smile. A natural smile. A smile without reservation, a smile that is stretched by my hopes and the certainties that have slowly been re-forming.

'How is therapy?'

His eyes hold mine and I don't see even a hint of hesitation. 'I still go every week.'

My heart turns over.

'I still haven't had a drink, Holly.'

I swallow and look over his shoulder, not knowing what to say to that. He understands. He doesn't want to pressure me.

'I love you,' he says simply and then stands, pushing his tea aside. He comes to my side of the table. 'And I'm not going anywhere.' He brushes a kiss against my hair and then lets himself out.

I sit there for a long time, staring at his mug, his empty seat. Strange that I think of that seat as his even though he's occupied it for only a brief period of time. Perhaps I long ago allocated it for his use, when I was painting fantasies in my mind about what my future would look like.

Five more weeks of walking home together and sharing a quiet cup of tea, and then I hear myself say as he stands to leave, 'Can you come next Thursday instead?'

His eyes meet mine, a silent enquiry in their depths.

'Are you busy Friday?'

There is pain in the question. Pain, like he thinks maybe I'm seeing someone else. I can't bear to hurt him. I shake my head.

'It's just…' I suck in a deep breath. 'Ivy will be here,' I say. 'I thought we could have dinner.'

His smile is everything I have ever wanted in life. It

is bright and beautiful, bold and so full of every single shred of joy that surges inside me. He nods. 'Thursday.'

He's nervous as we walk home, and I remember then that he doesn't want children. That this is a stumbling block distinct from all others. I ask him about it, and he looks at me slowly. 'Dr Chesser has helped me understand that I'm afraid of becoming a father. Because I never had one. I don't know if I'd be any good…that's all. It's not that I don't want that…'

I let him leave the sentence unfinished because I understand.

And by the end of the night I know what he perhaps doesn't. He will be an excellent father, one day.

We continue to walk home together on Thursdays but also on Fridays, and three Fridays after he first met Ivy I ask him to stay for dinner—with me. Not just a hot drink. The weather is warm now and we have a salad in my courtyard.

He leaves after he's stacked the dishwasher, and my heart drops. I contemplate asking him to spend the night, but something—a shyness born out of how new all this is—holds me silent. The old rules don't apply. It's as though we haven't been together yet.

Two weeks later, I find my courage. 'I want you to stay,' I say simply.

His eyes shine with triumph and gladness, but he shakes his head. 'Not yet.'

I don't know what he's waiting for.

* * *

A month later is Ivy's birthday, and Noah is at the party. He is an important part of it, for Ivy now adores him as much as I do. He sings 'Happy Birthday' loudly, and I know then how much I love him.

Autumn nights morph into winter and we no longer see each other only twice a week. He comes over most nights for dinner, sometimes a movie. Sometimes he picks Ivy up from school when I have to work late, and stays with her until I'm back.

He is with me every day, but in a way that exists outside of our relationship. I feel like I have been holding the world on my shoulders for a very long time, and now someone is doing it with me.

Christmas approaches, and I remember this time last year, when I first met Noah. I remember the way sexuality formed so much of our relationship and now our love is full of so much more. Though God, if we don't make love soon, I am going to combust, because I still want him as though he is the salvation to all my ills.

Ivy performs in her school concert; this year she's a Wise Man. Noah comes with me, sits beside me, laughs with me and holds my hand. When I get tears of pride over Ivy's performance, he lifts my hand to his lips and kisses my inner wrist. My heart soars.

It is Christmas Eve and Noah is with us. I didn't invite him, but it makes no sense that he'd be anywhere else. My family come too; they are all familiar with Noah by now. And while they don't understand our relationship, they like him. Even Aaron's mum seems to find him charming. I serve turkey with all the trimmings, and Ivy has made custard for dessert. It's late when everyone leaves.

Noah doesn't.

It's a long time since we met, and a long time since my heart was ripped apart. A long time since hurt and pain dogged my steps and life seemed like an impossible journey.

I'm happy.

I shower, butterflies in my stomach, because I know that tonight is special. I know that he's staying over, and that tomorrow it will be Christmas, and that beautiful morning will be all the more special because he'll be with me. With Ivy. With us.

When I emerge into the lounge, everything is spotless. Noah has done the dishes, tidied the table and put out some mince pies. There is a little gift bag beside them.

'Just a small trinket,' he says with a shrug.

'Oh, Noah.' My heart churns. 'Shouldn't I save it for tomorrow?'

He shakes his head. 'There's more for tomorrow.'

And I look towards the tree and draw in a shocked breath. He's right! The tree is groaning under the weight of gifts.

'They're mostly for Ivy,' he admits with a self-conscious grimace. 'I hope that's okay.'

God. He's so perfect. I nod and close the distance

between us. The bag is simple white and inside there's a small box. I open it, my confusion growing when I see a ring inside. A ring with an enormous sparkling diamond in the centre and several more surrounding it.

I turn to Noah to ask him what it means, but he answers me silently, for he's knelt to the floor and his expression is loaded with feeling.

There is no long, flowery speech. What can he possibly say that will mean more than these last eleven months? He has shown me every week, every day, every minute we've been together that he loves me.

'Will you marry me?'

He need say no more.

I nod. 'Yes.'

Our hearts, though, are full and they communicate for us, and when he stands and kisses me everything we've been, everything we are, explodes around us. I cry, but they're happy tears. The Christmas tree shines, my ring sparkles and hope no longer beats its wings only within my chest: it is everywhere around us, and I know we deserve that.

* * * * *

A LOS ANGELES RENDEZVOUS

PAMELA YAYE

Chapter 1

"Good afternoon, Millennium Talent Agency," Jada Allen chirped, pressing the headset closer to her ear so she could hear the caller over the noise in the reception area. She'd worked at the agency for two years, as an administrative assistant to Maximillian "Max" Moore—one of the most successful Hollywood talent agents in the business—and the only thing the twenty-seven-year-old Inglewood native loved more than her job was cheesecake. "How may I help you?"

"Is Max in? I've been texting him all day, but he hasn't responded, and I'm worried…"

Jada recognized the high-pitched voice with the Spanish accent. She couldn't believe the actress was calling again—the third time in thirty minutes. Max didn't want a serious relationship with the Mexican beauty, and had broken things off with the TV sitcom star days earlier. Jada should know. She'd sent the "breakup" flowers to the actress's Beverly Hills condo, with a Hallmark card, but every time the brunette called the office she sounded more upset, almost hysterical. Jada adored Max and was proud to be his assistant, but his favorite hobby seemed to be breaking hearts, and she worried one day he'd mess with the wrong woman and pay the price.

A chilling thought came to mind. What if the Mexican beauty came after Max? Sought revenge? What if he got hurt? Max was all about the chase, but once he slept with the object of his affection he lost interest, every single time. Jada only hoped his womanizing ways wouldn't get him in trouble.

"I need to talk to him… It's important…"

"I'm sorry, but Mr. Moore isn't available right now. He stepped out," Jada lied. The truth was, Max was in his office, alone, but Jada didn't want the actress to show up at the agency unannounced and cause a scene.

"Tell him Josefina Acosta called. I need to speak to him ASAP. It's an emergency…"

It always is, Jada thought, adjusting her oval-shaped eyeglasses. Hanging up, she turned back to her computer screen. Logging on to the internet, she checked the Outlook calendar for Monday's meeting, appointments and conference calls. Jada made a mental note to confirm Max's travel plans for his business trip to New York before she left for the day.

The desk phone rang. A female was on the line, demanding to speak to Max, but Jada took a message and hung up. All day, she'd been fielding phone calls from women who were eager to speak to Max, but it didn't surprise her. It was Friday, and his "girlfriends" were busy making plans for the weekend. They wanted to spend their free time with him, and it was evident by the desperation in their voices that they were willing to do anything to make it happen.

Of course they were desperate for him. Everyone was—including Jada. It was hard to find something about him she didn't like. Max was the kind of man people gravitated toward and instantly hit it off with. Charismatic and drop-dead handsome, he had dozens of A-list clients, knew everyone who mattered in LA and was invited to the hottest parties in town. He was a well-known, highly respected agent, who negotiated multimillion-dollar contracts for his clients. And not only did Max have a remarkable eye for talent, he had a knack for pitching ideas to television and movie executives. Was so good at it he had a production deal with an LA studio. Max pushed himself to be the best, and everyone who mattered thought he was.

For the second time in minutes, Jada admired the framed photographs hanging on the vibrant blue walls in the reception area. In every picture, the twenty-eight-year-old talent agent looked confident, and was grinning from ear to ear. Max lived for his work. He schmoozed. He networked. He wheeled and dealed. He charmed and seduced. He was known for being a ruthless negotiator, and his keen deal-making skills had helped make him—and his clients—filthy rich. Millennium Talent Agency was a prestigious boutique agency, and the business awards prominently displayed on the glass shelf proved how hard Max worked.

Jada picked up her mug and tasted her peppermint tea. It was her favorite time of year, and everything about the holiday season made her smile. Christmas was several weeks away, and Jada was looking forward to the holiday festivities in LA. There was the Christmas Ball at the Sheraton Hotel, Cocktails under the Mistletoe at a popular jazz lounge in Santa Monica and several exclusive Prescott George events, as well. Prescott George was a national organization for African-American millionaires, founded in the 1940s, and Max was a proud, card-carrying member. The club was as discreet as it was powerful; members couldn't buy their way in— they had to be invited. The Moguls were more than just wealthy businessmen with yachts, mansions and private planes: they did good work. For decades, they'd provided college scholarships to needy students, funding to inner-city organizations and million-dollar donations to local charities. Every year, Max invited his staff to the Prescott George charity bash on Christmas Eve, and Jada wouldn't miss the celebrity-filled party for anything in the world.

Jada's ears perked up. Leaning forward in her chair, she listened to the college interns as they strode through the lobby, praising the chic holiday decor throughout the main floor. Beaming, she watched the trio snap selfies in front of the ten-foot evergreen tree positioned in the corner of the room. To make the reception area look festive, she'd hung up velvet stockings and mistletoe around the room, sprinkled garland on the leafy potted plants and taped oversize red ribbons to the windows. All week, several female staff had tried to get Max under the mistletoe, but he was always on the move and would rather hang out in his office, making calls and reading scripts, than in the reception area.

"I asked you to make me look good, and you delivered…"

Peppermint tea sloshed over the side of Jada's mug and splashed onto her gray pencil skirt, creating a damp spot. At the sound of Max's voice, lust filled her body. His silky-smooth baritone was the sexiest thing her ears had ever heard, and when Jada glanced away from her computer screen and spotted Max standing in the doorway of his office, her mouth watered. Her boss was one of the most eligible and desirable bachelors in LA, and for good reason. Six feet tall, with buttery brown skin, soulful eyes and a body that was pure perfection, he was every woman's dream. If Hollywood had a Sexiest Man award, Max Moore would win it every year. Jada had been working for the UCLA graduate for years, but every time he looked at her she felt light-headed, out of it, as if she suddenly had no control over her body.

It was a miracle he even hired me, she thought, cringing at the memory that flashed in her mind. She'd been so nervous during their thirty-minute interview that she'd stuttered and stumbled over her words. If not for her stellar résumé and references, Max probably would have shown her the door, and she would have missed out on working at the popular talent agency. Located only a few blocks from the iconic Kodak Theater on a busy, tree-lined street, Millennium Talent Agency was filled with plush furniture, exotic plants, contemporary artwork and a marble wet bar. Sophisticated and überposh, the office had a tranquil ambience, and Jada made sure everyone who walked through the front doors—whether it was an aspiring actress, a D-list actor or an up-and-coming boy band—received VIP service.

"Good job sending those personalized gift baskets to Brielle and Felicity," Max praised, his voice filled with awe. "Both ladies called me this afternoon, gushing about how sweet and thoughtful I am, and it's all thanks to you."

"It's no biggie, Max. I was just doing my job."

"No, as usual, you went above and beyond the call

of duty, and it's greatly appreciated. You're a godsend, Jada. I don't know what I'd do without you."

Jada returned his smile. She took a moment to admire his chiseled facial features and his stylish gray suit. A self-proclaimed ladies' man with a penchant for European models, Max was working his way through the Victoria's Secret catalog, and often joked about eloping with a centerfold. Every time he did, Jada felt a profound sense of sadness. Max was the kind of guy her father had warned her to stay away from, but Jada couldn't stop crushing on her dreamy boss. She was attracted to scholarly types, men who loved to discuss literature and world history, but everything about Max appealed to her—his lopsided grin, his devil-may-care attitude, the thousand-dollar Cuban cigars he smoked in his office at the end of the workday—and over the years her feelings for him had grown.

"You're leaving?" she asked, noticing the brown leather satchel he was holding in his right hand. "Another hot date with *Sports Illustrated*'s Swimsuit Model of the Year?"

"I wish. Nothing beats spending the night with a beautiful, curvaceous woman."

He flashed a wicked grin, and desire rippled across Jada's flesh. Dimples pinched his cheeks, and if that wasn't bad enough, he smelled of expensive cologne, a scent that was so strong and masculine it was wreaking havoc on her body. Then Max licked his lips and a tingle shot down her spine. The moment she'd laid eyes on him it had been lust at first sight, and over the years nothing had changed. It was hard to find something about Max she didn't like, and despite his womanizing ways, Jada still wanted him. She couldn't imagine a better Christmas gift than making love to the eligible bachelor from Santa Monica with the killer physique.

"I'm going to visit my dad at his estate," he explained. "My brothers called an emergency family meeting tonight, so I canceled my business dinner with Big Ticket Movies executives and rescheduled it for first thing Monday morning."

Jada wore a sympathetic expression on her face. "How is Reginald doing?"

"As well as can be expected. Despite his prognosis, he's in good spirits."

"That's great, Max. I'm glad to hear that. Is he doing chemotherapy?"

"No, he can't…" His voice broke, and seconds passed before he could finish his sentence. "It's too late. His doctors said it won't help, and suggested he get his will in order."

The phone buzzed in her headset, cuing Jada she had an incoming call, but she ignored it. Wanted Max to know she cared about him, and his family. Standing, Jada took off her headset, dropped it on the desk and approached him.

"Dr. Petrov said there isn't anything more they can do for him, but I'm not giving up hope. Hope is all I have left."

Jada smiled sadly. Five years ago, his mother had died from cancer, and now his father was battling the debilitating disease. Despite everything happening in his personal life, Max hadn't lost his sense of humor and was always joking around with his staff in the break room. But yesterday, when Jada walked into his office with the day's mail, she'd found him sitting behind his executive desk with tears streaming down his cheeks. He'd laughed it off, saying he had something in his eyes, but Jada didn't believe him. Knew he was lying. She'd seen the anguished expression on his face, sensed his pain and couldn't resist giving him a hug. Holding Max in her arms had been amazing, and now Jada felt closer to him than ever before. "I can't imagine what you're going through, Max, but I'm here for you. Anything you need. Just ask, and it's done."

"Thanks, Jada. It's great knowing I can always count on you."

I wish I could do more. Like kiss you—

"Hey, did you check out that vlog I sent you?"

Jada cleared her mind. "Yeah, but I didn't think Kid Quentin was funny. Sorry."

"Are you kidding me? His celebrity impersonations are spot-on, his comedic timing is remarkable, and I almost died laughing when he flipped his skateboard in front of Times Square and chipped his front tooth." His face lit up as he chuckled, and his mood seemed to brighten. "Mark my words—the kid's going to be a famous child star!"

"I believe you," Jada said, fervently nodding her head. "You're the one with the eye for talent, Max, not me. I'm just your lowly assistant."

Max spoke in a stern tone of voice. "Don't talk like that. You're not a lowly assistant. You're my right-hand girl…"

Her breath caught in her throat, and for the first time in Jada's life she was speechless. Every morning, when she arrived at the office at seven o'clock, Max was already hard at work in his office, answering emails, reading contracts and scheduling meetings, so his words surprised her. Made her head spin and her skin warm. *Max thinks I'm special? I'm important to him? I'm the best administrative assistant he's ever had?*

Jada resisted the urge to dance around the room. Pride filled her and made her heart light. A smile teased her lips. *Not bad for a girl from Inglewood*, Jada thought, as bitter memories of her childhood overwhelmed her mind. Her parents, Colette and Ezekiel Allen, had split up after fifteen years of marriage, and when her mom had relocated to New York to chase her dreams of stardom on Broadway, custody of Jada and her three younger siblings had been awarded to her dad. Money had been tight, and juggling three custodian jobs left Ezekiel little time for his children, so Jada had picked up the slack in his absence. Now her family was thriving and closer than ever. Jada talked to her mom several times a year, and that was more than enough. They weren't close, and she didn't miss her. As a child, she'd always feared her mother's temper and found solace in her dad's arms. Ezekiel had been her mother *and* father, and Jada loved him dearly.

"I better get going. I have to pick up Taylor by six o'clock, or my ex will kill me."

"Wow, two weekends in a row with your beautiful daughter. That's awesome!" she exclaimed.

"Taylor's grandmother, Shay's mom, had surgery, and she'll need a lot of help once she's discharged, so I offered to take Taylor for the weekend." He shrugged a shoulder. "It was the right thing to do."

"You're a great dad, Max."

"Tell that to Taylor. She hates me!"

Jada scoffed. "No, she doesn't. Don't say that."

"It's the craziest thing. I can manage the careers of dozens of clients, but I can't manage a successful relationship with my ten-year-old daughter. If we're butting heads now, what's life going to be like when she's sixteen?" Max shivered. "It's a chilling thought."

"Taylor's going through a phase. Don't sweat it. It's perfectly normal, Max."

"I hope so, but I still wish she was my sweet little girl who used to think the world of me." Releasing a deep sigh, he retrieved his iPhone from his jacket pocket and swiped a finger across the screen. "Have a good weekend, Jada. See you on Monday."

Max put on his sunglasses and marched through the front door, whistling a tune.

Slumping against the desk, Jada fanned her face. Her attraction to Max was so powerful and intense she needed a moment to catch her breath. Her mouth was wet and her pulse pounded in her ears, making it impossible for her to think straight. She had memos to write and emails to answer, but Jada couldn't stop fantasizing about Max and all the delicious things she'd like to do to him—on his expensive executive desk.

Chapter 2

Max strode into the lavish great room of his childhood home in Malibu, took one look at his ailing father sitting on the couch and willed the tears in his eyes not to fall. Reginald used to be a tall, imposing figure with a toothy grin and dynamic personality, but now he was a shadow of his former self. His reputation destroyed after the scandal in San Diego and his longtime friends casting him aside, he found little these days to be cheerful about, and Max missed his father's hearty laughter. Reginald's membership in Prescott George—one of his greatest pleasures in his life—was revoked because an internal investigation had uncovered solid evidence against him in the sabotage case. Less than a week later, he'd received devastating news. He was diagnosed with stage four prostate cancer and his doctors didn't think he'd live past the New Year. No one did, but Max was holding out hope for a Christmas miracle and believed with all his heart that Reginald would beat the odds. If anyone could, it was his gutsy fifty-nine-year-old dad.

Life is so unfair. Why me? Why my *family?* Max thought, taking off his sunglasses and dropping them on the coffee table covered in business magazines. *First my mom gets cancer, and now my dad. Haven't I suffered enough?* Burying his pain, he marched confidently through the living room toward his dad, sporting a smile.

Bathed in natural light, the mansion had a chef's kitchen, an in-home movie theater, an art studio and three master bedrooms. The glass walls provided picturesque views of the lush green landscape, but the tranquil scenery did nothing to soothe Max's troubled mind.

The mansion held great memories for Max, and seeing his mother's oil paintings displayed on the fireplace mantel made sadness prick his heart. Constance Moore hadn't been just his mom; she'd been his best friend. She'd quit her high-powered managerial job at the Getty Center to raise him and his older stepsister, Bianca, and when his mom wasn't volunteering at their private school or baking cookies for his soccer team, she was chauffeuring him around to his extracurricular activities. Growing up, his friends had loved coming to his house, and Constance was the reason why. She had a warm, caring nature and made everyone who visited their home feel welcome. Not a day went by that Max didn't think about his mom, and his only regret in life was that he hadn't been at her bedside when she took her last breath.

"What's up, fam?" Max greeted his half brothers with a fist bump. Lean, with close-cropped hair, intense eyes and stylish designer eyeglasses, Trey looked more like an actor than a Hollywood screenwriter at the top of his game. He'd fallen hard for Kiara Woods, the owner of *the* preschool for the children of Hollywood's elite, and stunned everyone who knew him when he'd proposed. She'd said yes, and the couple was busy planning their spring wedding.

"I thought you'd never get here. What took you so long?" Derek asked, glancing at his gold wristwatch. Tall, toned and athletic, Derek was a successful real-estate mogul who collected properties the way rap stars collected luxury cars. Last month, he'd reconnected with his first love, model Alexis Armstrong, and after a passionate night together they'd discovered they were pregnant. He'd popped the question on Thanksgiving Day, and the parents-to-be were overjoyed about the impending birth of their child and their upcoming fairy-tale wedding.

Max had never been close to his brothers, but they'd been working together for weeks to clear Reginald's name, and now he respected and admired them. "It's good to see you, Dad. How are things?"

"Can't complain. Had a massage this afternoon, and Tanesha sang my favorite Christmas song. It was amazing. Hours later, I can still hear her angelic voice in my ears." Closing his eyes, he snapped his fingers and hummed a tune. "You should sign her to your agency, son. She's talented, and cute as a button."

Max nodded as his dad spoke, even though he had no intention of meeting the singing masseuse from Brentwood.

Observing his dad, Max found it hard to believe Reginald used to be two hundred pounds of steel-hard muscle. He was thin and frail now, the disease having ravaged his body. It took everything in Max not to cry as he stared at his dad. He couldn't imagine his life without him and struggled to control his emotions. Without Reginald, his life would be empty, and it pained him that Taylor wouldn't have any more Sunday afternoon "dates" with her grandfather. He'd never take her for ice cream again, or teach her how to play spades, or how to drive a stick shift.

"Son, if you sign her to your talent agency, do I get a finder's fee?" Reginald joked, arching an eyebrow. "I think fifty percent is fair. After all, *I* discovered her."

Max wore a wry smile, chuckling when his dad called him a cheapskate. In spite of everything Reginald had been through—his wife's sudden death, losing his membership to Prescott George, the groundless accusations against him and his heartbreaking diagnosis—he'd never lost his smile, and it gave Max hope, the strength to get out of bed and face the world every day even though he was broken inside.

"I hate to interrupt this touching Hallmark moment, but we need to discuss Demetrius."

There was a note of bitterness in Derek's tone, but Max didn't say anything. Wisely held his tongue. He didn't want to argue with his brother in front of Reginald. That was the last thing their father needed, and Max didn't want to say or do anything to stress him out. "What about him? Did you uncover more information linking Demetrius to the sabotage case? Are we any closer to clearing Dad's name?"

"No, not yet, but I'm working hard on it."

"Then what's on your mind, D? Why do you look so stressed?"

"Because nothing makes sense," he complained. "Why would Demetrius want to frame you? You've been his oldest and dearest friend for decades."

Reginald dropped his gaze to his lap. "I, ah, have no idea."

"Of course you do," Trey snapped, his tone matter-of-fact. "You're not fooling anyone, Dad. It's obvious you're lying, and it's time to come clean."

His brothers grilled Reginald until sweat dripped from his brow.

"Why are you blaming me? What makes you think I did something wrong?"

"Because before you got kicked out of Prescott George, you were a jerk," Derek said. "You didn't think of anyone but yourself, and it was infuriating."

"It's true, I was, but I've changed for the better."

Derck and Trey shared a "Yeah, right" look, and Max knew they didn't believe their father. Was this why his brothers had called an emergency family meeting? Because they wanted him to grill Reginald? Well, it wasn't going to happen. His brothers always made him feel guilty for having a close relationship with their father, but he wasn't going to stand by and let them bash Reginald. Not now. Their dad was sick, physically and emotionally spent, and Max didn't want his brothers ganging up on him. No one truly understood what Reginald was going through, and he wanted him to feel supported, not insulted. "Guys, ease up. Dad's had a rough few weeks, so quit badgering him about Demetrius. He'll confide in us when he's ready."

"How long are we supposed to wait? Time is of the essence," Trey pointed out. "Dad, if you want us to help you, you have to be honest with us about everything."

"We'll never get to the bottom of things if you keep coddling him," Derek said, addressing Max, his gaze dark and narrowed. "Reginald needs to be straight up with us, so we can clear his name and put this mess behind us."

Reginald coughed into his fist. "I… I—I can't. I don't want you boys to think less of me."

Derek scoffed. "Too late for *that*. We know who you are and what you're capable of, and to be honest, there's nothing you can say or do to surprise me…"

Derek trailed off when Max silenced him with a look. Reginald wasn't perfect; he'd screwed up and made mistakes—mistakes Trey and Derek liked throwing in his face over and over again. His brothers hadn't grown up with Reginald, but Max had a very different relationship with his father and saw him as a loving, loyal family man. When Reginald was married to Trey's mother, he'd cheated on her with Derek's mother, refused to acknowledge Derek as his kid until a court-ordered DNA test proved it, then found his soul mate in Max's mother. Reginald was so in love with Constance that he'd never had another adulterous affair and had remained faithful until her death. It saddened him that his brothers had such a negative opinion of Reginald. He'd been a father to Max in every sense of the word, and he had enough memories of his dad to fill a hundred scrapbooks. Reginald had taught him to ride a bike, taken him to his first NBA game, and attended his school events, even if it meant leaving work early. "'He who's without sin cast the first stone,'" Max said, quoting the well-known Bible verse. "Dad isn't perfect, and neither are you. Hell, no one is, so cut him some slack, would ya?"

Derek took his car keys out of his pocket. "This is a waste of time. I'm out of here."

"Me, too." Trey got up. "Dad, when you're ready to have an honest conversation about your past and explain the real reason behind your beef with Demetrius, let me know."

Trey and Derek strode through the great room, speaking in hushed tones.

"I slept with Ellen," Reginald blurted out.

Trey and Derek stopped and turned. All three men faced their dad, eyes wide, jaws slack. They'd asked him outright a couple weeks ago if he'd had an affair with Demetrius's wife, and Reginald had denied it.

"You did what?" Derek shouted.

Max cursed. He couldn't wrap his head around his father's confession. All this time, he'd thought that his dad was grieving the loss of his mom, so he was shocked to hear about his father's tryst with Demetrius Davis's former trophy wife, Ellen Davis. "Dad, how could you? Demetrius is your best friend, and he's always been like a second father to us."

Trey closed his gaping mouth. "Are you insane? What were you thinking?"

"I-i-it was an accident," Reginald stammered, in a shaky voice.

Throwing his hands in the air, Derek rolled his eyes to the ceiling. "An accident? How do you accidentally sleep with your best friend's wife? Explain that to me. I'm dying to know."

"I was lonely, and she was upset about Demetrius neglecting her and came on to me one afternoon when I stopped by the house. It only happened once. I swear on my life."

Only once? Yeah, right, Dad, and I'm a born-again virgin! Max knew Reginald was lying, but didn't expose him. It would only make things worse, and he didn't want his brothers to go off on their dad. He remembered seeing Reginald and Ellen at an expensive

French restaurant last summer, but Max had been at a business meeting and never had an opportunity to speak to them. And old friends of Reginald and Demetrius had also mentioned seeing the pair together a few times. Wow, they'd had an affair? Demetrius must have found out about it and thought he could kill two birds with one stone: hurt the San Diego chapter's chances of winning Chapter of the Year *and* frame his "best friend" as payback.

Max didn't want to believe it, felt guilty for even thinking such a horrible thing about the successful businessman, but the truth was staring him in the face.

"No wonder Demetrius hates you," Trey said, shaking his head. "You're lucky he didn't strangle you for messing with his wife. I would."

"I don't understand how he found out. No one knew about our affair. Unless…" Reginald straightened in his seat. "It had to be Ellen. She promised to take our secret to the grave, but threw me under the bus. I can't believe this shit."

Max shrugged. "Never trust a big butt and a smile."

Reginald chuckled so hard his shoulders shook. Max felt a rush of pride. It had been weeks since he'd heard his father's hearty laugh, and the sound was music to his ears. As he thought about Reginald's shocking confession, Max weighed his options. He didn't want to make waves in Prescott George, but he had to act. Had to prove to everyone in the organization that his dad wasn't the cunning, conniving snake Demetrius said he was.

Guilt tormented his conscience. It killed Max that Demetrius had framed his dad. But everything pointed to it. Which made Max feel even worse: his father had been telling the truth all along, but he'd doubted him. The evidence had been indisputable—until it wasn't.

But no one had believed Reginald. Because his father hadn't lived an upstanding life, Prescott George members had rushed to judgment. Deep down, Max had had a hard time believing Reginald had done the things he'd been accused of, but he'd sided with the organization instead of standing by his father, and his earlier position filled him with remorse.

Max rested his hands on his dad's shoulders, wanted him to feel loved and supported. Now that he knew why Demetrius hated Reginald, he could finally clear his dad's name. And he would. By any means necessary. Even if it meant raising hell. No one messed with his family and got away with it—not even a man he used to admire. Demetrius was going down, and when Trey and Derek nodded their heads, Max knew they shared the same thought.

Chapter 3

Max parked his orange Ferrari 458 on the driveway of his ex-wife's Tudor-style home, jumped out of the car and activated the alarm. Still reeling from what Reginald had said at the family meeting, Max struggled to put one foot in front of the other. He couldn't stop thinking about the sabotage case, or the heartless things Demetrius had done to his father.

Glancing down at his cell phone, he wondered if it was too late to call Jada at the office. He wanted to vent about his frustrations and knew she'd understand what he was going through. She always did. The truth was, Jada knew him better than anyone—even his siblings— and he trusted her explicitly. Petite, with a soft voice and shy demeanor, she was so darn likable everyone in the office adored her. At times, Jada got flustered when one of his male clients flirted with her, but she had a dazzling smile and the cutest laugh he'd ever heard. She was wise beyond her years, and Max valued her opinion. Most important, Jada wasn't afraid to disagree with him, or tell it like it was, especially when it came to his daughter, and he loved her for it.

To clear his mind, Max took a deep breath. He had to get a hold of himself, had to stop fretting about his problems. He was spending the weekend with Taylor, and he didn't want her to know he was upset. His daughter was ten years old, but these days it seemed as if she was speaking a different language. Even though Max saw his daughter for dinner three times a week, they barely communicated. Lately, everything he said and did was wrong. They used to be close, used to laugh and joke around, but ever since Taylor turned ten it had been hard to connect with her.

Before Max could ring the buzzer the front door opened, and Shay appeared with a scowl on her face and a hand on her hip. Even though she was glaring at him, she looked youthful and pretty in a striped off-the-shoulder sweater, skinny jeans and suede boots.

"Hey, Shay. How are things?"

"Max, what are you doing here? You're supposed to pick up Taylor tomorrow."

"No," he corrected her, shaking his head to underscore his point. "On Monday we agreed that I'd come get her today after work, so here I am."

"Oh, really? It must have slipped my empty little mind." Leaning against the door frame, Shay folded her arms across her chest and rolled her eyes skyward. "*Or* you changed the plans at the last minute, which you have a habit of doing whenever it suits you."

Max said nothing, knew if he did they'd end up arguing, and he didn't want to butt heads with his ex-wife. They'd been divorced for years, but nothing had changed: Shay still looked at him with disgust, as if she couldn't stand to be in his presence, and it annoyed the hell out of him. He'd never been "Husband of the Year," but he'd been a great provider, and because of his tenacity, hard work and ambition—and his generous alimony payments—she could afford to live in the most desirable neighborhood in Santa Monica.

How had things gone so bad so quick? Max wondered for the umpteenth time. He'd met Shay Wilcox his freshman year of high school and fallen hard for the voluptuous student-body president. To his shock and amazement, they'd gotten pregnant on prom night despite using a condom. Max, who'd been raised in a happy home with two parents who were madly in love, proposed, figuring they'd repeat his parents' success, even though they were teenagers. But by the time Taylor was born they were bickering nonstop. Max thought providing a great life for his family was everything. Being a workaholic had caused a rift between him and Shay; he was so busy going to university, trying to be a good father to their daughter and interning at a hot new talent agency that he was neglecting his wife without even realizing it. Shay had wanted a more hands-on partner instead of a husband who was always on the phone—making deals, soothing upset clients, and reading contracts and movie scripts at the dinner table. Being young parents took its toll on their relationship and it didn't survive, despite them both trying hard to make things work. After seven years of marriage, Shay had filed for divorce, and now Max's focus was on keeping the peace in his family and improving his relationship with Taylor.

"How is your mother feeling? Has she finally been discharged from the hospital?"

"Don't worry about my mom. She's fine."

Fine? Really? But she had major surgery yesterday!
It was obvious Shay didn't want to talk to him about her mother's health, or anything else, so Max peered inside the house in search of his spunky daughter. "Can you let Taylor know I'm here?"

Shay gestured to the gate with a nod of her head, and her ponytail swished back and forth. "Taylor's in the backyard with her friends. Good luck getting her to leave."

"I'm her dad. Of course she'll want to go with me. I have big plans for us tonight."

"If you say so," Shay quipped, wearing a doubtful expression on her face. "See ya!"

Hearing his cell phone ring, Max took it out of his back pocket and read his newest text message. Strolling along the stone walkway, he could hear singing and laughing, and knew his daughter was having the time of her life with the neighborhood kids. For a moment, he considered leaving so she could hang out with her friends, but changed his mind. How were things supposed to get better if they didn't spend quality time together? If he didn't show Taylor that he loved her and valued their father-daughter weekends? These days, Max couldn't seem to connect with her, but he wasn't going to give up.

Max opened the gate, spotted Taylor in the outdoor living room with her friends and froze like one of the marble statues decorating the flower garden. An upbeat pop song was playing on the stereo system, but his daughter was slow-dancing with a tall, lanky boy who wore an Adidas sweat suit and sported a Mohawk hairstyle. Max couldn't believe his eyes.

Gazing up at her dance partner, Taylor draped her arms around the boy's scrawny neck.

His jaw dropped. Max wanted to pummel the kid in the ground when he kissed Taylor on the cheek, but exercised self-control. *Good God! Is Taylor wearing makeup?* Scrutinizing her appearance, Max cursed under his breath. Her cheeks were rosy, and her lips were glossy and pink. Diamond stud earrings twinkled in her ears, colorful bracelets filled her arms, and long, thin braids hung loosely over her shoulders. Taylor looked adorable in her Zendaya-themed sweatshirt, leggings and high-top gold sneakers, and his anger abated when he noticed she was wearing the heart-shaped silver necklace he'd bought her weeks earlier at the mall.

"What's going on here?" Max shouted, jogging across the manicured grass.

Taylor dropped her hands to her sides and stepped away from her dance partner. "Dad, what are you doing here? Shouldn't you be at work?"

"Say goodbye to your friends," Max said. "You're spending the weekend with me, so go inside and grab your stuff. You have five minutes."

Her face fell, and her shoulders sagged. "But I want to stay here. Do I have to?"

Max felt a twinge of disappointment, but he smiled. He didn't want Taylor or her friends to know that her response hurt his feelings. There was a time when he couldn't go anywhere without Taylor nipping at his heels, and it saddened him that his only daughter would rather hang out with her friends than have a father-daughter date with him. "I have a fun weekend planned for us, and I know you're going to love it, so let's get out of here."

"Where are we going?"

"That's for me to know and for you to find out."

Giving Taylor a one-arm hug, he kissed her forehead. He didn't care that her friends were watching them. He wanted his daughter to know that she was special to him, and that nothing mattered more to him than making her smile. "I will say this. There's a butt-kicking at Monster Mini Golf with your name on it, and I can't *wait* to beat you! You're going down, Taylor Moore."

"Okay, okay, I'm coming. Let me just say 'bye to my friends. I'll meet you out front."

Marching back through the yard, Max unbuttoned his suit jacket and loosened the knot in his tie. He couldn't help wondering what would have happened if he hadn't shown up when he did, and made a mental note to speak to Shay about supervising Taylor and her friends outside.

Minutes later, Taylor opened the passenger-side door of the Ferrari, clutching her purple backpack in one hand and her shiny gold iPod in the other. Sunshine rained down on them through the open sunroof, and the cool evening breeze flooded the car with a refreshing scent. "Ready to go down?" Max put on his seat belt.

"Ha! Dad, you couldn't beat me at mini golf if I was blindfolded!"

It felt good joking around with Taylor, made Max feel as if he'd done something right, for once. Cruising down the street, he noticed teenagers playing basketball, joggers breezing through the park and moms pushing designer baby strollers.

"Looks like *someone* loves her new iPod," Max said, gesturing to the electronic device in his daughter's hands. To make her laugh, he wiggled his eyebrows, then winked. Taylor giggled, and the sound brought a wide smile to his lips.

"I don't like it. I *love* it! It's the best birthday present

I've ever gotten, and my friends are totally jealous that I have the newest version." Taylor plugged the device into the Bluetooth system, selected the song she wanted to hear and faced him, her eyes round and bright. "Can you set the date and the time on my iPod? I tried to do it last night, Mom, too, but we couldn't do it."

"I don't know anything about iPods. I'll call Jada. She'll help us—"

Taylor bolted upright in her seat, as if she'd been pricked with a pin, and Max broke off speaking.

"What's wrong?"

"Y-y-you didn't buy my iPod?" she stammered.

Shame burned his cheeks, and perspiration wet his pin-striped dress shirt. "Taylor, honey, I'm sorry. I didn't mean to upset you," he said, patting her leg. "Jada bought your birthday present because I asked her to. I knew you'd love it, and I was right."

"What about the card? And all the nice things you wrote about me? You said the day I was born was the happiest day of your life, and that being my dad was your greatest joy..."

Max coughed to clear the lump in his throat. *Oh, snap! I shouldn't have said anything about Jada's involvement!* Damn. He'd messed up. Now Taylor's lips were pursed, her arms were folded across her chest, and she was glaring at him with more intensity than Shay did. It was at times like these that Max wished he could hit the rewind button and cram the words back into his mouth. Of course, Jada had bought the iPod and loaded it with his daughter's favorite music. His assistant always picked the right thing; it was why she was his right-hand woman. His best employee. Jada chose all the gifts for the people in his life, including Taylor, his girlfriends and his celebrity clients. Not to mention she made everything run smoothly at the office and went above and beyond her job description.

"Did you write the note inside my birthday card, or did Ms. Jada do it for you?"

His mouth was so dry he couldn't speak.

"I should have known you didn't buy it," Taylor said, staring out the windshield. "You're too busy working twelve-hour days and chasing thots to do anything nice for me."

Staring at Taylor in disbelief, Max gripped the steering wheel so hard his knuckles cracked. Did his tween daughter just say what he *thought* she said? He was glad they were stopped at the intersection, because if he'd been driving he probably would have driven off the road and crashed into a palm tree. Her words stung, and he didn't appreciate her tone. Taylor sounded like Shay—cold, bitter and angry—and he feared that his ex-wife was bad-mouthing him in front of their young, impressionable daughter. And he wasn't going to stand for it. But before he could get to the bottom of things, he had to make things right with Taylor. He couldn't risk losing her respect. "Baby girl, I messed up, but I'm going to make it up to you in a big way. I promise."

"Yeah, right, whatever," she drawled, wiping her eyes with the sleeve of her sweatshirt.

"Taylor, don't talk to me like that. I'm your father, and I love you—"

"Actions speak louder than words."

"I'm here, aren't I? There's nowhere else I'd rather be."

"Well, I don't want to be with you," Taylor shot back. "Just take me home."

"No. You're spending the weekend with me, and that's final."

"This is so unfair. You *never* listen to me. You only care about yourself."

"Honey, that isn't true," he said, hoping to get through to her. "You mean the world to me, and I'll do anything to make you happy."

Taylor snorted. "Yeah, right. If that was true, you wouldn't be forcing me to go to your boring bachelor pad. I hate that place."

There was a long, painful silence, and even the popular rap song playing on the car stereo couldn't cheer Max up. He felt dejected, like a failure as a father. And when Taylor put in her earbuds and closed her eyes, his heart sank to the bottom of his shoes. He needed help with his daughter and knew just whom to call.

Chapter 4

"I really outdid myself this time," Aubree Allen announced, with a proud smile. "I hate to toot my own horn, but I nailed Grandma Loretta's sugar cookie recipe!"

Skeptical, Jada dipped a spoon into the bowl of cookie batter, licked it and puckered her lips. "It's bitter." She grabbed her metal water bottle off the granite countertop inside her cousin's spacious kitchen and drank some ice-cold water. "I think you used too much lemon zest."

"Then I'll add a dash of wine to sweeten the recipe." Aubree opened the cupboard above the stove and rummaged around inside for several seconds. Raising an arm triumphantly in the air, she waved around the bottle. "A splash of zinfandel should do the trick."

Delilah Allen-Fayed, another cousin of Jada's, wrestled the bottle out of Aubree's hands and put it on the table. "We'll do no such thing," she hissed, an incredulous look on her face. "These Christmas cookies are for the Los Angeles Mission, not for dessert with the Book Club Divas, and I don't want us to get in trouble with Father Joseph."

"There's nothing wrong with a little wine. It's good for the heart *and* our sex drive."

"Then we're definitely not doing it," Jada said. "Kids are going to be eating these cookies, too, and I don't want them to get drunk."

"Gosh, Jada, you're such a killjoy!" Aubree complained, rolling her eyes to the ceiling. "Must you take the fun out of everything?"

"You're a fine one to talk," Jada shot back. "You're scared of heights and horror movies, and the last time you were on a plane Clinton was president!"

Erupting in laughter, Delilah gave Jada a high five. "Good one, cousin! *You* told her!"

Jada grabbed the wine bottle, marched into the pantry and put it on the top shelf. "Add some more milk to the batter," she advised Aubree, slamming the door shut. "And if that doesn't work put lots of icing on the cookies. No one will even notice they're sour."

Keeping an eye on what her wine-loving cousin was doing, Jada wiped the metal pan with butter. She grabbed a handful of dough, rolled it into a circle and dropped it onto the cookie sheet. That morning, after breakfast, she'd driven to Aubree's swank two-bedroom Malibu townhome to help bake holiday treats for the homeless shelter. While her cousins rolled the cinnamon buns, they discussed their plans for the Christmas holidays, their respective careers and relationships. Jada didn't have much to add to the conversation, but she enjoyed hearing about Aubree's dating woes and Delilah's storybook marriage. The stay-at-home mom had been married to an aircraft mechanic for a decade, and Delilah was so madly in love with her husband her face lit up every time she said his name.

Aubree, on the other hand, was single and actively looking for Mr. Right. The bold, brash graphic designer never left the house without makeup—not even to walk across the street to the community mailbox—and when it came to fashion, the thirty-year-old beauty never made a mistake. She looked chic in her printed silk headscarf, cashmere sweater and black, studded leggings, and Jada envied her cousin's effortless style.

Lightning lit up the dark, cloud-filled sky. Rain pelted the windows, and a strong breeze whipped tree branches in the air. From where she stood in the kitchen, Jada looked around at Aubree's living room. Adorned with pendant lamps, fuzzy pillows on velvet chairs and couches, and dozens of scented candles, the town house looked expensive and modern.

Working alongside, Aubree and Delilah reminded Jada of all the summers they'd spent together—watching MTV, pigging out on junk food, gossiping about their crushes and practicing the latest dance moves. In high school, Aubree had been voted most likely to succeed—and she had—and Delilah was the most loving wife and mother Jada knew.

"I went for a consultation at Malibu Fertility Center yesterday," Aubree announced.

Delilah snorted a laugh, dismissing the comment with a wave of her hand. "Sure you did, and on the weekends I moonlight as an exotic dancer at a gentlemen's club!"

"Why would I lie? One of my colleagues used the clinic last year and said it was the best decision she's ever made. Now she's six months pregnant and positively glowing."

"You want to be a mother?" Jada asked, flabbergasted by her cousin's words.

"Yes, of course. Why do you sound so surprised? You know me. We grew up together."

Eyes wide, Delilah wiped her hands on her apron. "*Exactly*—that's why we're stunned. No offense, coz, but you're the least maternal woman I know. You rarely babysit your nephews, and when you do you fuss and complain about every spill, runny nose and dirty diaper."

Aubree picked up the bowl now empty of cookie dough and chucked it in the sink. "That was then, and this is now."

"Girl, please," Delilah drawled. "That was a week ago, and if I didn't throw you out of my house you'd still be bitching and complaining about my amazing kids!"

"Talk to us. What's going on?" Jada asked, eager to get to the bottom of things. "Is this about Grayson's new girlfriend?"

An anguished expression pinched Aubree's face, but she shook her head. "No, of course not. Grayson's old news, and his fake-ass engagement has nothing to do with my decision."

"Okay," Delilah trilled. "But babies aren't puppies. When you change your mind, which you inevitably will, you can't take it back to the hospital. It doesn't work like that, Aubree."

Smirking, Aubree tilted her head to the right and fluttered her fake, extra-long eyelashes. "I know—don't worry. If I change my mind I'll just drop Aubree Junior off at your house!"

"You wish! You better give your kid to Jada, and

leave me be!" Delilah said, hitching a hand to her hips. "Gosh, you're worse than Ibrahim. He wants another baby and won't let up about it. I'm just not ready to get pregnant again, and I don't know if I'll ever be."

Aubree set the timer on the oven, then filled the mixing bowl with soapy water. "Really? But for as long as I can remember you've always wanted a big family, at least four or five kids."

"That was *before* I had two kids in three years."

Surprised by her cousin's harsh tone, Jada studied her closely. Her ponytail was crooked, dark circles lined her eyes, and there was a stain on her white scoopneck top.

"Don't get me wrong," Delilah said with a sheepish smile. "I love my children, and wouldn't trade them for anything in the world, but motherhood isn't as fun as celebrity moms make it look. It's stressful, taxing and damn hard, if you ask me."

"I bet, and you didn't even get a push gift after giving birth to baby Hakeem." Aubree grabbed the coffeepot, filled three mugs and plopped down on one of the wooden stools at the breakfast bar. "It's not too late. Tell hubby you're not having another kid until he buys you diamond earrings and the new Hermès Birkin bag."

"As if! With me not working, it's hard to make ends meet, and I don't want Ibrahim to feel bad about our financial troubles. He's a good guy, and despite everything we've been through, he's my everything."

Delilah wrapped her hands around the ceramic mug. Her smile returned, shone brighter than the lights in the bronze chandelier hanging from the ceiling. Listening to her cousin gush about her husband made Jada think about Max and their nonexistent romantic relationship. An image of him popped into her mind, and her heart jolted inside her body. Jada knew she was out of Max's league, that he'd never settle down with a plain Jane from Inglewood who loved crossword puzzles, science fiction books and baking, but she couldn't stop herself from lusting after him. Having been Max's assistant for years, Jada knew him better than anyone, and it was obvious he had a penchant for actresses and models. Still, she couldn't stop fantasizing about him no matter how hard she tried.

"You guys, I need your help," Jada blurted out, desperate for her cousins' advice. "My feelings for Max have gotten stronger the last few months, and I don't know what to do to get his attention. I want him to notice me, but I'm fresh out of ideas."

Aubree and Delilah arched their eyebrows, and Jada wished she'd kept her thoughts to herself. Wished she hadn't confided in her cousins about her crush on her suave, debonair boss, because the skeptical expressions on their faces said they didn't believe in her.

"I'm not surprised. We've been telling you for *years* you need to update your look, but you won't listen to us," Delilah reminded her. "No makeover, no Max. It's just that simple."

"Those dowdy glasses? Get contacts. Your do-nothing hair? Extensions, girl, or get a chic, new cut! Those shapeless cardigans and ballet flats? Wear pencil skirts and stilettos!" Aubree advised. "Coz, you're hiding an amazing body under boring, frumpy clothes, and it's a damn shame, if you ask me."

Unconvinced, Jada vehemently disagreed with her cousins. She loved Aubree and Delilah, and valued their opinion, but she didn't want to change who she was to snag a guy—not even one she was crushing on.

"It's high time you got some." Delilah inclined her

head to the right and wiggled her eyebrows. "And if you revamp your look, men will be falling at your feet, including Max."

Jada had to admit she liked the sound of that. Just the thought of kissing Max made her skin tingle and her temperature rise. He was a force, the kind of man who could weaken a woman's resolve with just one smile, and his charming personality and go-getter attitude was a turn-on. And it didn't hurt that his hard, chiseled body was pure perfection.

"Jada, you need a makeover ASAP," Aubree stated in a curt, no-nonsense voice. "After the cookies are done we're going to Envy Beauty Salon to get your hair done, then shopping for some trendy, skintight clothes…"

Dread filled her body and pooled in the pit of her stomach. Shopping with her cousins was an all-day event—one that Jada didn't enjoy. They'd spend hours going in and out of high-end boutiques, trying on dresses and shoes they couldn't afford, despite her protests. Jada preferred going into Bloomingdale's, buying what she needed and going home. Not Aubree and Delilah. They treated shopping as if it was a professional sport, and Jada wanted no part of their Saturday afternoon outing to Rodeo Drive. "No way. I'm not going. I'm fine just the way I am—"

"Like hell you are," Aubree interrupted, her tone filled with attitude and sass. "You're going, even if we have to drag you out of here, kicking and screaming."

Delilah fervently nodded her head. "You need our help, and with the holidays right around the corner, it's the perfect time to unveil a sexy, new you, and we'll show you how."

Jada wanted to argue, but it was true; she didn't know anything about fashion trends. How could she? Helping to raise her siblings had left her no time to experiment with hairstyles, makeup or clothes. Hence her decision to keep her look simple—lip gloss, a cardigan, dress pants and ballet flats. Jada never deviated from the script, and even though Aubree and Delilah had been criticizing her wardrobe for years, she was scared to change her appearance.

Conflicted thoughts crowded her mind. What if she looked ridiculous? What if she hated her makeover, and Max did, too? She'd never be able to show her face at the office, and she didn't want to put her job in jeopardy. Jada loved being Max's administrative assistant, and wanted to work at Millennium Talent Agency for many more years to come. "I hate the idea of snaring Max through a dramatic, over-the-top holiday makeover," she confessed. "Shouldn't he fall for me because of who I am, not my hairstyle or clothes?"

Aubree scoffed. "In what world? Need I remind you that Max Moore is one of the hottest bachelors in LA? He's a sharp dresser with a handsome face and a rockhard body."

"Is he frumpy?" Delilah asked, tossing an arm around Jada's shoulder. "No, so get with the times, girl. If you don't, someone will swoop in and steal him right from under your nose."

The thought of Max falling for another woman frightened Jada, and as much as she didn't want to admit it, her cousins were right. She had to act. Now. Before it was too late, and she lost Max forever. The problem was, Jada didn't know anything about making the first move, and wasn't confident enough to bare her soul to him. What if he rejected her? What if her confession ruined their relationship? Jada didn't know what to do, and struggled with following her heart. *Should I risk my career for love, or keep my mouth shut?*

"Jada, there's nothing wrong with having natural hair if you style it, but you never do." Delilah raised her mug to her mouth, blew in it, then took a sip. "I love you, girl, but you've been rocking the same, tired look for years, and you need to try something different."

"Or you'll remain a single, lonely virgin forever," Aubree warned.

Jade winced. She couldn't believe her loved ones could be so mean. She wanted to remind her know-it-all cousin that she was single, too, but before she could speak, the timer buzzed. Aubree hopped off her stool and rushed over to the stainless-steel stove.

Humming "Silent Night," Aubree slipped on silicone mitts, opened the oven and took out the cookie sheets one at a time. She put the racks on the stove, then helped herself to a cookie. "These are *so* good," she gushed, slowly licking her lips.

Jada's cell phone rang, and she picked it up from the counter. Frowning, she stared at the number on the screen. She didn't understand why Max was calling on her day off. Unless... Fear gripped her heart. Had his father passed away? Did he need her support?

Clearing her throat, she put her cell to her ear and spoke in a confident tone of voice, even though her mouth was bone-dry. "Hey, Max, how are you? Everything okay?"

"No. Taylor got mad at me yesterday, and twenty-four hours later she's still giving me the silent treatment," he explained in a somber tone of voice. "Needless to say, it sucks."

Relief flowed through Jada's body, and a sigh fell from her lips.

"I apologized, and even ordered pizza for dinner, but she's still in a miserable funk."

"I'm sorry to hear that," she said, unsure of what else to say. "That's rough."

"Tell me about it. I feel like a visitor in my own home, and the silence is killing me."

"Is there anything I can do to help?"

"I'm glad you asked. I'm taking Taylor to FunZone Galaxy this afternoon, and I'd love if you could join us. My daughter enjoys your company, and so do I. Please say you'll come."

His words warmed her heart, and a smile curled her lips. "I… I—I'd love to," Jada stammered. Thrilled Max had asked her out, she wanted to dance around her cousin's apartment. Sure, it wasn't an official date, but he'd never included her in a family outing before, and his invitation made Jada feel special.

"Great! Thanks, Jada. I knew I could count on you. You're a lifesaver…"

And you're the dreamiest man I've ever met.

"We'll pick you up from your condo at two o'clock. How does that sound?"

"I'll be waiting," Jada said, surging to her feet. "See you then!"

Ending the call, she grabbed her purse off the couch, waved goodbye to her cousins and made a beeline for the door. They followed her through the living room, asking a million questions about her mysterious phone call, but Jada was so hyped about seeing Max on her day off, nothing could spoil her good mood. "I'll give you guys a ring later."

"Where do you think you're going?" Aubree asked, thwarting Jada's escape by positioning herself in front of the door. "You can't bail on us. We're supposed to drop the cookies off at the homeless shelter, then get our hair and nails done."

"I know, but I have to go. Max needs me. It's important."

Delilah sucked her teeth. "Oh, so Max calls and you go running?"

Yeah, pretty much. He's my boss, and I'll do anything for him!

"I'll make it up to you guys, I promise," Jada vowed. "Give my love to Father Joseph, take tons of pictures with the kids we mentor at Tween Connection and enjoy your day of beauty!"

Aubree opened the closet, grabbed an umbrella off the top shelf and handed it to Jada. "Here, use this. We don't want you to look a mess when you meet up with your fine-ass boss."

Jada giggled. "Thanks, girl. I owe you one."

"Call us later." Aubree unlocked the door. "We want to know how your date went."

"It's not a date," Jada said, pulling up the collar on her denim jacket. "His daughter is coming with us to the arcade."

"Then be creative," Delilah advised, her eyes bright with mischief. "Go home with them, and help him put his daughter to bed. After she falls asleep, lure Max into the master bedroom, lock the door and handcuff him to the headboard…"

"Now I know why Ibrahim popped the question after dating you for only three months," Jada joked, swatting her cousin playfully on the shoulder. "You're a freak!"

Taking a deep breath, Jada threw open the screen door. She sprinted down the walkway, careful to avoid the mud puddles dotting the sidewalk. Running full speed toward her black Nissan parked across the street,

Jada could feel water in her shoes. The strong wind ripped the umbrella from her hands, and rain pelted her cold, quivering body.

Reaching the car, Jada got in and collapsed against the seat. She stared at her reflection in the rearview mirror and groaned. Water was dripping down her face, her hair was sticking to her cheeks and neck, and her sweatshirt clung to her skin.

Wanting to freshen up before Max and Taylor arrived, Jada put on her seat belt, started the car and drove slowly through the apartment complex. Like her hair, her shoes were soaking wet, but hanging out with Max was worth every inconvenience. And if Jada had her way, this would be the first of many Saturday afternoon dates with her boss and his adorable daughter.

Considering what her cousins said, Jada decided it was time to make her move. To tell Max the truth. To bare her soul to him. She smacked the gas pedal with her foot and sped through the intersection, anxious to see the man she loved. Jada only hoped that when she told Max how she felt about him he wouldn't reject her. Or worse, laugh in her face.

Chapter 5

The buzzer on top of the arcade game Half Court Hoops sounded and Max sprang to action. Grabbing one of the small orange basketballs in the cage, he arched his arms and shot at the miniature net. It fell in, and his confidence soared. Determined to win, Max focused on making every bucket, even though his limbs were still sore from playing dodgeball with Taylor and Jada earlier.

FunZone Galaxy was a family-friendly establishment, with a bowling alley, gymnasium, go-kart racing, a snack shop and a small restaurant. It was a paradise on earth for entertainment lovers, and the striking black-and-gold decor gave the space a unique look. They'd been at FunZone for hours, and Max was so hungry his stomach was moaning and groaning. The arcade smelled of popcorn and cotton candy, and his mouth watered at the delicious aromas in the air. Filled with teenagers, birthday party guests and children racing from one game to the next, the place was noisy and crowded, but Max was having a great time with his daughter and wasn't ready to leave.

Moving at lightning-quick speed, he made one basket after another. He watched Jada on the sly, noticed her careful, precise movements. She wasn't wearing makeup, her eyeglasses were perched on the tip of her nose, and her thick black hair was pulled back in its trademark bun. Her polka-dot sweater and capri pants gave her a serious, mature appearance, but she had a fierce expression on her pretty, heart-shaped face. "Jada, give up while you still have a chance, because there's no way in hell I'm letting you beat me…"

Max tried to rattle Jada by cracking jokes, but she never took her eyes off the basketball net, focused in on it like a laser beam. Playing against his assistant was fun, and listening to Taylor's colorful commentary made Max laugh out loud. His daughter was a character, hands down the funniest kid he knew, and he loved her sense of humor.

Down five points, Max hurried to catch up. Jada had easily won the first round, and he had to redeem himself. He couldn't let his perky, petite assistant beat him twice. If she did, Taylor would tease him mercilessly for the rest of the weekend, and Max couldn't think of anything worse than his tween daughter poking fun at him. "Jada, you're toast," he shouted over the loud pop song playing on the stereo system. "You're going down."

"You wish!" she shot back. "I beat you once, and I'll do it again. Just watch."

Taylor cupped her hands around her mouth. "You can do it, Ms. Jada! I believe in you!"

Max glanced over his shoulder, caught his daughter's eye and faked a scowl. It was hard not to crack up when

Taylor was jumping around the arcade like a kangaroo, but he wore a straight face. "Traitor. Keep it up, and I'm not buying you dinner."

"Sweetie, don't worry," Jada said with a wink and a smile. "I got you. Pizza's on me."

"Thanks, Ms. Jada. You're the best! Not like my dad. He's *so* sensitive."

The buzzer sounded, the score flashed on the screen and Max plucked the collar of his navy button-down shirt. "I *told* you guys I'd win," he said.

Jada shrugged a shoulder. "Lucky shot. It could happen to anyone."

"You're just mad because I won. Better luck next time, Brown Eyes!"

Taylor linked arms with Max and Jada, and gestured with her head to the other side of the arcade. "Let's play *Dance Dance Revolution* and *Guitar Hero*. They're my favorite games."

"*After* we eat." Max walked into the restaurant, dropped down at one of the vinyl booths and grabbed a menu. "You've been dragging us around this place all afternoon, and if I don't eat something soon, I'm going to get hangry, and it'll be all your fault."

Taylor didn't laugh at his joke. "Fine, Dad, you can eat, but we're going to dance."

"I'm going to take a break, too," Jada said. "I'm starving."

"But I want to play more games," Taylor argued.

"Fine, don't eat," Max said, perusing the menu. "Sit down and keep us company."

Breathless, Jada collapsed in the seat. "We'll take a short break, and as soon as I'm finished eating I'm all yours. We can play *DDR* a million times if you want."

Wearing a long face, Taylor sat down beside Jada and crossed her arms.

Max swallowed the words on the tip of his tongue. His daughter was pouting, acting like a spoiled brat because she didn't get her way, but he ignored her behavior. Pretended not to notice her pursed lips and rigid posture. They'd had a great afternoon, and he didn't want anything to ruin their outing. He rarely hung out with Jada socially, and he enjoyed learning more about her. As usual, she'd come to his rescue, and for the first time since Max learned of his father's illness, he could breathe. He didn't feel as if a boulder was sitting on his chest, slowly suffocating him.

Max studied Jada from behind his menu. All afternoon, she'd been sympathetic and supportive, there for him when he'd needed it most. While watching Taylor play *Donkey Kong*—a game he'd played hundreds of times with his mom in their home media room when he was a kid—he'd found himself thinking about Constance. As if reading his thoughts, Jada had leaned in close and patted his forearm. "You must miss your mom," she'd said, in a soft, quiet tone of voice. "Cherish your memories, and honor her legacy by being the man and father she'd want you to be." Comforted by her words, he'd given her a one-arm hug. Max thanked his lucky stars that she was his ace assistant. Over the years, she'd changed from a shy, insecure woman to a confident beauty, and he valued her opinion above everyone else's at the agency. She thought for herself instead of relying on other people's opinions, and her candor was refreshing. Max liked having her around and looked forward to seeing her every morning. Jada made his life easier, calmed him down when he was upset, and best of all, she had a terrific relationship with his daughter.

"I don't know what to order," Jada said, studying the laminated menu with a furrowed brow. "Taylor, what do you recommend?"

Dropping her hands in her lap, the tween moved closer to Jada in the booth, chattering excitedly about her favorite drinks and appetizers from the snack bar.

Anxious to eat, Max signaled to the waiter wiping tables nearby. He ordered appetizers, pitchers of soda, three Caesar salads, and the pizzas Taylor and Jada wanted.

Using his iPhone discreetly under the table, Max checked his email. He tried not to work when Taylor was around, but he had dozens of messages, and he didn't want his celebrity clients to think he was ignoring them. His job was never-ending and consumed every area of his life. When he wasn't negotiating deals, fielding offers or meeting with clients for lunch and dinner, he was answering phone calls and text messages by the hundreds.

"I'm so pumped about Christmas it's all I can think about," Taylor confessed, giggling.

Max kept his head down, listened with half an ear as his daughter shared about upcoming events at her school and her three-page Christmas list. Settling back comfortably into his seat, he crossed his legs at the ankles and read a movie script on his cell phone.

His mind wandered, and the words blurred on the screen. It was hard to concentrate on work when all he could think about was his dad. That morning, he'd talked to his stepsister, Bianca, and found himself tearing up as they reminisced about their favorite childhood memories. They'd always been close, and Max wished

Bianca was around to help him with Reginald. An Ivy League graduate, Bianca was a successful software developer in New Hampshire, and Max was proud of everything she'd accomplished. His stepsister was coming to town for the holidays, and Max couldn't wait to see the look on Reginald's face when Bianca arrived at the Prescott George charity gala on Christmas Eve.

A waitress with tanned skin and wavy hair arrived with the drinks and appetizers, but the script was so intriguing Max didn't want to stop to eat. The waitress batted her eyelashes, but he pretended not to notice her coy smile. He was with his daughter, and he didn't want to encourage the waitress's advances. Though he enjoyed flirting with the opposite sex, it wasn't the time or the place. Playing the field would never get old, and although he envied his brothers for finding smart, captivating women with model good looks, Max had no desire to settle down. Romantic relationships were damn hard, and he didn't have the temperament for them. Couldn't see himself ever getting married again. Once was more than enough.

Thankful that Jada was keeping Taylor occupied, he read the second page of the script and made several comments in the margin. Blown away by how interesting the characters were, he made a mental note to call the up-and-coming screenwriter after Taylor went to bed. Would do everything in his power to sign her to his agency. He'd fulfilled, many times over, his hopes and dreams for his company, but it was never enough. A self-proclaimed workaholic, Max was always looking for the next big thing, the next blockbuster movie or breakout star, and was never satisfied with his success. Always wanted more. Millennium Talent Agency was one of the fastest-growing agencies in LA, but he wanted to increase company revenue next year and prove to his critics that it was a varied and versatile agency. To do that, he'd have to sign talent in all areas of entertainment, including publishing, theater, sports and advertising. It was going to be tough, but Max was up for the challenge. More than anything, he wanted to cement his place in Hollywood as a powerhouse who made things happen. And he would, even if it meant outwitting the competition.

"How are things going at school?" Jada asked. "Still loving the fifth grade?"

"Oh, yes," Taylor gushed, in a high-pitched voice. "I *love* school. My crush sits next to me now, and we talk and laugh all the time. To be honest, he's the best thing about school…"

Max glanced up from his cell phone. In his haste to speak, he tripped over his tongue, and his daughter stared at him as if he'd lost his mind.

"Max, are you okay?" Jada wore a concerned expression on her face. "You look upset."

"Damn right, I'm upset." Pocketing his cell phone, he spoke in a stern tone of voice. "Taylor, you're too young to have a crush. You're only ten years old. Furthermore, your mom and I send you to school to get an education, not drool over boys."

"TaVonte is wonderful." Stars twinkled in her eyes, and a lopsided smile curled her lips. "He's the smartest kid in my class, and the nicest, too—"

"TaVonte?" Max repeated, cutting her off. "What kind of name is that?"

Taylor picked up a mozzarella stick and took a bite. "Dad, you don't know him, so stop throwing shade. I think it's a cute name. Just like TaVonte."

"I think I'm going to be sick," he grumbled, feeling

an ache in his stomach. "I *knew* we should have enrolled you in the Malibu Girls Academy, but your mom wouldn't listen to me."

"I'm glad she didn't. If I was at a private school, I wouldn't have met TaVonte…"

Taylor sighed in relief, infuriating him, and it took everything in Max not to curse.

The waitress returned with the salads and pizza but he'd lost his appetite. Jada encouraged him to try her honey barbecue wings, but eating was the last thing on his mind. All he could think about was getting through to his daughter. And he would, because he didn't want history to repeat itself. Shay had gotten pregnant on prom night, at just eighteen years old, and even though Max didn't regret having Taylor, he didn't want her to make the same mistake. He wanted her to go to university, travel the world and work in her desired field, without anything ever holding her back.

"Everyone at school calls us T and T, even our homeroom teacher. Adorable, right?"

"No," Max snapped, leaning forward in his seat. "You need to focus on your studies, not boys. You're only ten, for goodness' sake! A baby!"

"Dad, I'm ten and a half. Get it right," she scolded, reaching for her glass.

An Arab girl wearing a pink hijab, a cropped hoodie and high-waist jeans stopped in front of their table. "Hi, Taylor! Want to play flag tag in the gym with me and my cousins?"

"Dad, I'm finished eating. Can I go?" Taylor wiped her hands with a napkin. "Please?"

Max hesitated. He didn't want his daughter hanging out with teenagers, or making friends with the high school boys playing basketball in the gym. "Sure, but stay with your friend. No wandering off," he said, glancing at his Rolex wristwatch. "Be back at six o'clock."

Taylor cocked her head. "That's not enough time for us to hang out."

Annoyed, Max stared intently at his daughter. *Is this kid for real?*

"You guys can leave when you're ready. I'll just ask Nawal's parents to drop me home later." Standing, she slung her beanbag purse over her shoulder. "I'm sure Mr. and Mrs. Almasi won't mind. Nawal and I are practically besties."

"No, you'll be back in an hour, or you can stay here."

Taylor started to argue, but Max silenced her with a look, and she closed her open mouth.

"Fine, I'll be back at six."

Whispering to each other, the tweens left.

"Do you see what I'm talking about?" Max asked, unable to conceal his frustration, his anger finally bubbling to the surface. "Taylor used to be a sweet girl who listened to her parents, but now she's argumentative, disrespectful and obsessed with boys."

"Max, calm down. You're shouting, and people are staring at us—"

"Of course I'm shouting! My ten-year-old daughter is out of control. 'Everyone at school calls us T and T,'" he mimicked, adopting a high-pitched female voice. "What kind of nonsense is that? I have half a mind to call the school and complain."

Jada set aside her plate, took a sip of her soda, then clasped her hands in front of her. "Max, I know your relationship with your daughter is none of my business, and it doesn't matter what I think, but can I be honest with you?"

"Please. That's why I invited you here. I need your help to get through to Taylor."

"But Taylor isn't the problem," Jada said, looking him in the eye. "You are."

Chapter 6

"Come again?" Max asked, pointing a finger at his chest. "You think *I'm* the problem? How do you figure? I'm not the one with the bad attitude."

Jada swallowed hard. Pretended not to notice the peeved expression on Max's face. He was glaring at her as if they were enemies. Had she said too much? Overstepped her bounds? They'd spent the afternoon playing games and goofing around in the gym, and the last thing Jada wanted to do was ruin his good mood.

Jada could feel her heart beating in double time, and her pulse throbbing in her ears, but she said, "Let me explain."

"Please do because I'm dying to know what I'm doing wrong."

"Max, it's obvious you love your daughter more than anything, but you treat her like she's five years old, and she's not a little girl anymore. She's a tween who's changing in many different ways, and it's perfectly normal."

He was quick to say, "I don't have a problem with Taylor growing up. I have a problem with her chasing boys instead of doing her schoolwork."

"You overreacted about Taylor having a crush, and it hurt her feelings."

"What was I supposed to do? Tell her to invite the kid over for dinner?"

"That's a start. Taylor's going to be a teenager before you know it, and it would be wise to get to know the kids she hangs out with."

Inclining his head, Max wore a thoughtful expression on his face.

"When Taylor confides in you and you shut her down, you're damaging your relationship," Jada pointed out, feeling compelled to speak her mind. All afternoon, she'd fantasized about them being her family—her gorgeous husband, Max, and her precocious stepdaughter, Taylor—and wanted to help out any way she could. The truth was, Jada wanted her own family, wanted it all with Max. She'd been secretly in love with him for a long time, and spending quality time with her humorous, fun-loving boss made her desire him even more. He wasn't perfect, but he was perfect for her, and no one else could ever take his place in her heart.

"What do you suggest I do?"

"Be transparent," she advised. "The next time Taylor opens up to you about a problem she's having with a friend, or about someone she has a crush on, just listen. Don't react. If you lose your temper every time she confides in you, you'll never have a healthy relationship."

Max took a breadstick out of the plastic basket and broke it in half. "Taylor shouldn't be obsessing over boys. She should be riding her bike and playing with dolls…"

Memories flooded Jada's mind. As a child, she'd always wished she could do fun things with her dad, like going bowling or to the movies, but he'd never had the time or money to take her. "You're getting worked up over nothing. It's a harmless crush, and nothing more."

"That's easy for you to say. You don't have kids."

"Oh, so because I don't have kids I can't have an opinion about a healthy parent-child relationship?" Jada asked, irked by his flippant remark.

Max shrugged a shoulder. "Yeah, pretty much."

"That's ridiculous. I've always had a great relationship with my dad—"

"I believe you, but you're a pretty, young woman who knows nothing about kids."

His words gave her a rush. *You think I'm pretty?*

"Normally, you're bang on about Taylor, but this time you're dead wrong."

Jada swiped a napkin off the table, scrunched it into a ball and tossed it at Max.

Chuckling, he swatted it to the floor. "What? Don't get mad. I'm just keeping it real."

"No," she argued, fighting the urge to laugh. "You're terrible, that's what you are."

Max picked up a slice of pizza, took a bite and chewed slowly, as if he was savoring the taste. "I know you mean well, and I appreciate your advice, but Taylor isn't going to date until she's thirty, and that's final," he said, with an arch grin.

As they ate, Max opened up to Jada about his family meeting the day before at his father's estate. He held nothing back, confided in her about his father's declining health, his fears of losing Reginald during the holidays, and his improved relationship with his brothers.

Jada propped her chin in her hand. It was hard not to admire his handsome face and his broad shoulders. Her hands were itching to squeeze them, but Jada exercised self-control. Forgetting everyone else in the room, she blocked out the boisterous chatter, laughter and music around her and concentrated on what he was saying. Jada could listen to Max talk all night. Couldn't take her eyes off him. Captivated by the sound of his voice, Jada imagined herself leaning across the table and kissing him. She could see it now—their lips mating, their tongues teasing and exploring, their hands caressing each other—and trembled at the thought. Her nipples hardened under her blouse, yearned for his touch, and it took everything in Jada not to pounce on him. She'd never felt such intense feelings for a man and hoped she didn't do anything to embarrass herself.

"Did you hear back from the event planner? Can she plan the office Christmas party, or do we have to hire someone else?"

Jada was so busy fantasizing about Max she didn't hear what he'd said, and felt like an idiot when he waved his hands in front of her face and repeated the question. Meeting his gaze to assure him she hadn't taken leave of her senses, Jada nodded in response. "Everything's been taken care of," she said brightly, remembering the conversation she'd had with the celebrity event planner yesterday afternoon. "We're good to go."

"Awesome. I invited my brothers and their fiancées and several of my business associates to the party as well, so make sure you touch base with the caterer on Monday to confirm the number of guests. I'd hate for us to run out of food or drinks at the office party."

On the outside, Jada was smiling, but on the inside dread pooled inside her stomach. Jada had no interest in attending the office Christmas party, and considered faking an injury. Her colleagues were bringing their significant others to the event, and she'd be the only one without a date. Thankfully, she'd had strep throat last year and couldn't attend the party, but she'd heard from the staff how Max's pop-star girlfriend had stolen the show in her cut-out dress and seductive dance moves. Jada would rather eat broken glass than watch Max make out with his date, and made up her mind to stay home next Friday.

"I look forward to meeting the special man in your life." Max took another slice of pizza, folded it in half and took a bite. "Tell me more about your boyfriend."

Jada felt her mouth drop open and quickly slammed it shut. She wasn't used to having his undivided attention, couldn't recall him ever asking her about her love life in the two years she'd been his assistant. He was always on his cell, texting, talking and Tweeting, and her colleagues often joked about him being obsessed with his iPhone. Jada relished their newfound friendship. They were closer than they'd ever been, and even though she was nervous about baring her soul to Max, it was time to come clean. "I'm not seeing anyone right now," she blurted out. "I'd rather read than peruse cheesy dating apps."

"That's a shame. A beautiful woman like you should be going out on the weekends, exploring the incredible LA nightlife, not sitting at home twiddling her thumbs."

I agree! But the only *man I want to spend my evenings with is you!* For several seconds, Jada mentally rehearsed what she wanted to say. Choosing her words carefully, she met his gaze and forced the truth out of her mouth. "I've been interested in someone for a long time, but up until now I was too afraid to say anything—"

Max peered over her shoulder, and Jada lost her train of thought. She was so distracted by his wandering eye that her confidence deserted her, and she broke off speaking. Max straightened in his chair, and Jada knew there was an attractive woman standing behind her. Had to be. Why else would he be straining his neck?

Frustrated that he wasn't listening to her, Jada glanced over her shoulder to see who the object of his attention was and widened her eyes. Max wasn't lusting after a female; he was watching a tender, heartwarming scene. A silver-haired man was holding a toddler in his arms, laughing uncontrollably. Singing a nursery rhyme at the top of her lungs, the blue-eyed girl smacked his cheeks with her chubby hands, then pinched his crooked nose.

Turning back around, Jada noticed the pensive expression on Max's face and instinctively reached for his hand. A soft sigh escaped her lips. *This is heaven on earth!* Jada liked feeling his skin against hers, enjoyed stroking his soft, smooth flesh with her fingertips. It was obvious Max was thinking about when Taylor was a toddler, and it saddened her that he was in pain. Jada didn't know what to say to make him feel better and searched her heart for the right words. Her confession would have to wait. Max wasn't in the right frame of mind to have an open and honest conversation about their relationship, and Jada wanted them to talk when he was in a good mood, not when he was stressed out.

Her gaze dropped from his eyes to his mouth, and a shiver shot down her spine. The desire to kiss him was so overwhelming, Jada couldn't think of anything else. She'd wanted him from the day she'd first laid eyes on him, and didn't know how much longer she could resist the needs of her flesh.

Get a hold of yourself, woman! chided her inner voice, in a stern, no-nonsense tone. *Max needs to be comforted right now, not seduced, so back off!*

The waitress returned to clear the dishes and wipe down the dirty table.

"Thanks," Max said. "Everything was great tonight, especially the service."

"It was my pleasure," the redhead cooed, sticking out her chest. "Anything else?"

"No, thanks. Just the bill."

The waitress didn't move and continued to stare at Max with lust in her eyes. Jada didn't blame her for flirting with him. It happened all the time. His clean-cut good looks and boyish smile drove women wild, and Max couldn't go anywhere without attracting female attention. It didn't help that he was Mr. Personality, and when his business associates teased him for being a ladies' man he'd wink and chuckle, as if every salacious rumor about him was true.

Max's cell phone buzzed, and he scooped it up off the table. A slow smile crept across his lips, and Jada suspected he was reading a text message from one of his girlfriends.

"Derek and Alexis are the most," he joked with an amused expression on his face. "Alexis is only in her first trimester, but they've already finished decorating the Disney-themed nursery at my brother's Malibu estate."

Max held up his iPhone, and Jada stared at the image on the screen. The bright, spacious room had stuffed animals, jumbo alphabet letters, colored blocks and wooden shelves lined with toys, picture books and family photographs. "Talk about efficient," Jada said in an awe-filled voice. "If I ever have a baby, I want Derek and Alexis to decorate the nursery!"

The grin slid off his mouth, and he raised an eyebrow. "I hope you're not thinking of settling down and having kids anytime soon. Are you?"

Something told her not to speak, so she didn't respond to the question.

"I hope not, because I need you at Millennium Talent Agency. You do a kick-ass job at the office, and I couldn't survive a day without you, let alone three months."

"I absolutely want to be a wife and mother, and the sooner, the better, but don't worry, Max. I'll give you plenty of notice before I run off to the suburbs and set up house."

"Can I give you some advice?"

Before Jada could respond, Max gave her his take on relationships. And what he said shattered her hope of them ever being a couple. Heartbroken, her head bent, she stared down at her hands. Jada was so disappointed she couldn't look at Max. She feared if she did she'd burst into tears. Based on comments she'd overheard him make in the past, Jada knew his views about love and relationships were tainted by his divorce, but she didn't realize he was anti-commitment, anti-marriage and dead set against having more children. *I've been fooling myself all this time*, Jada thought, wanting to flee the restaurant. *How could I have been so stupid? Max doesn't want me, and he never will.*

"I'm not trying to burst your bubble, Jada, but relationships are a waste of time."

Staring off into space, he seemed to be in another world, and his anger was evident by his tone.

"Happily-ever-after is a myth, a fallacy used to sell movies, books and engagement rings, and if you don't abandon the ridiculous notion of finding your soul mate and riding off into the sunset, you'll wind up being miserable and disappointed."

Too late for that. I already am, she thought sourly, a bitter taste filling her mouth. Jada felt low, as if someone had ripped her heart out of her chest and stomped all over it, but she found the courage to ask the question in her mind. "Do you plan to spend the rest of your life alone?"

"Maybe one day, when I'm old and gray, I'll find love again. Never say never, right?" His laugh was hollow. "Settling down is the last thing on my mind right now. I like my life just the way it is, and I have my hands full with Taylor, work, my family and Prescott George."

"Humor me," she said, curious to know more about the man behind the dashing, larger-than-life persona. "What kind of woman could take you off the market permanently?"

Max didn't speak for a long moment, then surprised her by answering the question.

"Someone humble, loyal and sincere," he began. "I want to be with a woman who enjoys the simple things in life, like breakfast in bed, long scenic drives, picnics in the park and afternoons binge-watching classic TV shows."

Max, I love all those things, and I love— Jada stopped herself from finishing the thought. He didn't want her, never would. Their mutual attraction had been nothing more than a figment of her imagination, and it was time to quit pining over him. Now that it was clear they'd never be a couple, or have the relationship Jada had always dreamed of, she had to move on. It was going to be hard, especially after the heartfelt conversation they'd had during dinner, but Jada wasn't going to waste another second of her life on a man who obviously didn't want her.

"Look what I won at Treasure Quest!" Taylor sidled up to the table with a bright smile, clutching a brown teddy bear. "I named him TaVonte Jr. Isn't he cute?"

Jada saw the color drain from Max's face and hoped he didn't lose his temper again. "Did you have fun with your friends in the gym?" she asked, cleaning her sticky hands with a napkin.

"Yeah, Nawal and I creamed her cousins at dodgeball. One of the guys nicknamed me *La Bestia*, which means 'The Beast' in Spanish, because of my strong right arm."

Max stood and gave Taylor a one-arm hug. "That's my girl! Show no mercy!"

"Dad, you'd be so proud of me. I knocked out most of the players by myself."

"Way to go, Taylor. Your opponent's right. You *are* a beast."

Max retrieved his leather wallet from his back pocket, took out three twenty-dollar bills and put them on the plastic bill tray. "Are we ready to go?"

"Dad, can we stop at Creams and Dreams on the way home?" Closing her eyes, Taylor licked her lips and rubbed her stomach. "I'm craving cookies-and-cream ice cream."

The waitress returned, scooped up the bill and thanked Max for his generous tip. Heading for the exit, Max took his car keys out of his pocket. The rain had stopped, but the cold, blustery wind was still battering trees along Lincoln Boulevard.

"Jada, is it okay with you if we make a quick detour

for dessert?" Max asked, opening the passenger-side door. "*La Bestia* wants a sweet treat, and if I say no she'll give me a beatdown."

Taylor giggled, and the sound of her girlish laughter warmed Jada's heart. She glanced at Max and could tell by the light in his eyes that he felt the same way. Father and daughter were both in a playful mood, but Jada didn't feel like joking around, was ready to call it a night. She wanted to return to her condo, climb into bed and sleep until she forgot what Max had said about relationships.

As she replayed their conversation in her mind, her disappointment was so profound she couldn't look at Max. She wondered if she'd ever get over him. She'd spent months obsessing over a man who'd never give her the time of day, but enough was enough. No more fantasizing about him, doodling his name inside her journal or staring at pictures of him online.

A troubling thought came to mind, one Jada didn't have an answer to. *How am I supposed to overcome my feelings for Max when all I can think about is kissing him?* Tears pricked the backs of her eyes. She hadn't been this upset since Braydon dumped her, but she had to maintain her composure. Didn't want Max to know anything was wrong. Jada loved her job and it didn't matter how much she was hurting inside; she'd never do anything to embarrass him or jeopardize her position at Millennium Talent Agency.

"Please, Ms. Jada?" Taylor begged, clasping her hands together. "I promise to be good."

"Sweetie, don't be silly. You're *always* good. I'm just tired, that's all."

"Then we should definitely go to Creams and Dreams,"

Taylor said in a matter-of-fact tone of voice, wiggling her eyebrows. "Ice cream makes everything better!"

To make Taylor happy she agreed to join them at the ice-cream parlor, but as Jada put on her seat belt, she decided this would be her last outing with the Moore family. There'd be no more dates at the arcade or for ice cream, and even though Jada wanted to spend more time with the lovable father-daughter duo, her heart couldn't take it. It was going to hurt like hell, but she'd rather be alone than chase a man who didn't want her.

Chapter 7

Speed-walking along Hollywood Boulevard on Wednesday afternoon with Max's dry cleaning in one hand and her cell phone in the other, Jada mentally reviewed everything she had to do when she returned to the office. She had to order stationery and other supplies, organize the slide show for the conference Max was speaking at in San Francisco tomorrow, and touch base with the party planner about some last-minute details for the office Christmas party on Friday.

As she sweated profusely in her cashmere sweater and pleated skirt, perspiration drenched her skin, causing her eyeglasses to slide down her nose. Pushing them back in place, she narrowly avoided colliding with the teenagers dancing in front of the Palace Theater Building and hurried up the block. It had been a long, stressful week, and all Jada wanted to do was go home, kick off her shoes and stretch out on the couch to watch her favorite reality show, *Extreme Dating*. She had no plans, no dates, and even though Aubree claimed to have the "perfect" guy for her, Jada didn't want to meet her cousin's friend at a local bar. She couldn't think of anything more depressing than going on a blind date, and no matter how much Aubree badgered her about it, she wasn't having drinks with the Sacramento-based construction worker. Not because he had a blue-collar job, but because her heart belonged to Max, and even though she'd vowed to quit pining over him, he still dominated her thoughts.

Jada stopped at the intersection and waited impatiently for the traffic light to change. The air smelled of flowers and pine, and everywhere Jada looked, there were Christmas-themed signs and decorations. Lamp-posts were swathed in garland, trees were decorated with jumbo ornaments, and red satin ribbons hung in store windows. Christmas was three weeks away, but Jada could hear the distant sound of bells and saw a man of Asian descent dressed in a velvet Santa Claus costume standing on the street corner begging for change as he sang an off-key rendition of "We Wish You a Merry Christmas."

Her thoughts wandered, filled with images of her tall, dark and sexy boss. For the past five days, she'd replayed her conversation with Max at the arcade in her mind a million times, but it was time to let it go. Needed to find someone who shared her hopes and dreams. A man who'd be proud to claim her as his girl and show her off to his family and friends. Jada wanted it all—a loving marriage, a large family, a house with a white picket fence in the suburbs—and she refused to settle for anything else. And that was why she had to forget about Max.

Her cell phone buzzed, the screen lit up, and a smile filled her lips as she read her cousin's newest text message. Their hour-long conversation that morning had lifted Jada's spirits. During her commute to the office, she'd called Delilah, and listening to her cousin gush about her husband had made Jada envious. Made her wish she had a special man who brought her breakfast in bed, too. Delilah had advised her to forget about Max and have a Christmas fling, and Jada had to admit it sounded like a good idea. She had to get him out of her system. She'd never had a one-night stand, but Jada had to do something drastic to get over Max. *Yes*, she decided, fervently nodding her head. *A Christmas fling is* just *what the doctor ordered.*

A shiny black SUV with tinted windows and chrome wheels sped up to the curb. Afraid it would splash in the puddles and ruin her outfit, Jada jumped back and put the garment bag behind her. Doing personal errands for Max during her lunch break wasn't part of her official duties, but he was stuck in meetings all afternoon, and Jada didn't mind helping out. Without looking up from his iPhone, he'd handed her his platinum credit card, asked her to pick up his dry cleaning and requested Vietnamese food for lunch. His fingers had brushed against hers, arousing her flesh with just one touch. Electricity had shot through her veins, leaving her dizzy and weak. And when Max flashed a smile of thanks, she had to fight the urge to climb onto his lap and rip his suit from his body. Max was so fine he made *People* magazine's Sexiest Man Alive look homely, and if Jada didn't love her job—and her salary—she'd kiss him until she was breathless.

"Are you following me? First, I run into you at the dry cleaners, and now you're standing across the street from my favorite coffee shop, staring at me with lust in your eyes."

Am not! The deep, boisterous voice belonged to Shazir Toussiant, and as the talent agent climbed out of the SUV, her heart thumped inside her chest. She'd met Shazir last year at the Prescott George Christmas Eve charity fund-raiser, and since his office was only blocks away from Millennium Talent Agency, she bumped into him on a regular basis.

"Jada, you don't have to follow me around town," Shazir said smoothly. "If you want my number all you have to do is ask for it."

"I don't have time to follow you around. I'm a very busy woman," she quipped, trying not to notice how attractive he looked in his navy suit. "I have several more errands to run, so if you'll excuse me, I have to go."

Shazir slid in front of Jada, blocking her path, his boyish smile on full blast. "Not so fast, pretty lady. I have a weakness for women in cardigans, so you're not going anywhere until you agree to have dinner with me."

Amused, Jada stared at the pretty-boy bachelor with growing interest. With his soulful brown eyes, high cheekbones and dimpled chin, Shazir could easily have a career as a Disney prince. Admiring his striking facial features, Jada wondered if everything the talent scouts at Millennium had said was true. Did Shazir have a bad reputation? Did he hook up with his female employees? Did he play mind games with the opposite sex?

Jada broke free of her thoughts, told herself it didn't matter. She wasn't inviting Shazir back to her place for a passionate afternoon of lovemaking. They were just flirting, and Jada enjoyed their fun, playful banter. She sensed his interest in her and was flattered by his attention. Jada couldn't remember the last time she'd been on a date, and liked the idea of hanging out with the successful talent agent. Why not? She had nothing else to do on the weekend and hoped Shazir would give her some insight about Max. After all, they were members of the same exclusive club and had known each other for more than a decade. "Shouldn't you be off somewhere searching for the next big child star?"

"It can wait. Gotta get your digits first."

Jada smirked. She couldn't resist teasing the businessman who was thirteen years her senior. "Digits? What is it? Nineteen ninety-nine? Do you moonlight as a rapper, too?"

"Baby girl, I'll be anything you want me to be." Chuckling, Shazir unbuttoned his suit jacket, then slid his hands into his pockets, as if he was posing for a photograph. "When are you going to let me take you out? I like a woman who plays hard to get, but don't you think this cat-and-mouse game between us has gone on long enough?"

Conflicted emotions battled inside her. Max would be pissed if he found out they were dating. Jada frowned. Or would he? Chances were he wouldn't care. He had a bevy of beauties to keep him busy, and probably never gave a second thought to what she did in her free time or whom she did it with.

"Stop playing hard to get," he admonished, checking himself out in a store window. "I'm a great guy who knows how to treat a woman right, and I guarantee we'll have fun together..."

Tempted, Jada considered his offer. She needed something to take her mind off Max, so why *not* hang out with Shazir? He was a catch, but they'd never work as a couple. He was too cocky, obviously obsessed with his physical appearance, and she suspected he spent hours in front of the mirror admiring himself. *Sure, he's not my type*, Jada conceded. *But I'm not marrying the guy; we're just having dinner!*

"Are you free tonight?"

Jada shook her head. "No, sorry. I have other plans."

It was a lie. The only plans she had were with her sofa, but Shazir didn't need to know the truth. If she accepted his last-minute invitation, he'd think she was desperate, or worse, crushing on him, and that couldn't be farther from the truth. Jada liked his personality, but she had no desire to be his girlfriend.

"Fine, then we'll hook up tomorrow after work."

Jada surprised herself by saying, "We will? What do you have in mind?"

"Dinner at Ryan Gosling's Moroccan-themed restaurant, front-row seats to see *The Nutcracker* at the Los Angeles Ballet, then cocktails at a chic lounge in Malibu."

Intrigued, Jada listened closely. Liked what he said and how he said it. She had to admit Shazir certainly had a way with words, and since Jada was a huge fan of the Los Angeles Ballet, she accepted his invitation. At his urging, she saved her number in his cell phone under the Contacts app and promised to text him later with her home address.

A car horn blared, drawing her attention to the street, and Jada spotted an elderly couple cuddling on the wooden bench in front of the bus stop. The sight gave her hope. *That's what I want, someone to grow old with who loves me for me.*

"I'll pick you up from the office. I'm working late tomorrow, so it makes more sense for me to swing by Millennium after my meeting. Can you be ready to go at five o'clock?"

Her ears perked up. She wondered how Max would feel about Shazir showing up at the office, but remembered he was going out of town tomorrow and wouldn't be back until the holiday party on Friday night. Not that it mattered. Max didn't want her, and she had to quit hoping he'd come to his senses and declare his undying love. It wasn't going to happen. Ever since the arcade, Jada had realized she'd been fooling herself. Her instincts had been wrong: they weren't a perfect match. Max wasn't attracted to her and would never be her man.

"This date is long overdue, but I hope it'll be the first of many…"

His cell phone lit up, and he trailed off speaking, staring at the device intently. Every few seconds it buzzed, and the incessant noise grated on her nerves. Jada hoped Shazir wouldn't be glued to his iPhone during dinner tomorrow night, because if he was he'd be seeing *The Nutcracker* alone. "I better go. I'll talk to you later." Eager to return to the office, Jada waved goodbye, slung her purse over her shoulder and dashed into the Vietnamese restaurant on the corner.

Minutes later, Jada left the establishment with a take-out order for Max and crossed the street. Glancing at her bracelet-style watch, she realized she'd been running errands for over an hour, and chastised herself for wasting time. If not for stopping to chitchat with Shazir, she would've already been back at the office, hard at work tackling her to-do list.

Hearing her cell ring, she glanced at the screen, hoping Max wasn't calling to check up on her. With everything going on with his dad, his clients and his employees, Max had a lot on his plate, and Jada didn't want to do anything to add to his stress. Thankful it was Taylor calling, Jada sighed in relief. She pressed the answer button, and the moment she heard the tween's voice, she knew something was wrong.

"Hi, sweetie," she greeted her, curious why Taylor was calling her in the middle of the school day. It was lunchtime, and Jada worried there was a problem at school and Taylor had been unable to reach Max at the office. "How are you? Is everything okay?"

"I need a favor."

Her voice was a whisper, so quiet that Jada strained to hear what she was saying.

"Sure, sweetie. What do you need?"

"My mom's going to Sacramento to help take care of my grandmother, which means I'm stuck going to my dad's place again this weekend."

"Taylor, that's great. Your dad loves having you around, and he always plans something fun for you guys to do, so I know you'll have a blast."

"I doubt it," she complained. "He'll be glued to his phone, working as usual, or watching football, and I'll be upstairs in my room, bored out of my mind."

Troubled by what Taylor said, Jada decided to speak to Max about his daughter's upcoming visit when she returned to the office. Taylor was changing in many different ways, and she needed her father's guidance and support now more than ever.

"I need help getting ready for the Christmas dance on Saturday night. My dad doesn't know anything about hair and makeup and I need to bring it…"

Frowning, Jada stared down at her cell. *Bring what? It's an elementary school dance!*

"Guess what? TaVonte asked me to be his date for the dance, and I said yes!" Taylor continued in a giddy, high-pitched voice. "This is my first real date, and I don't want to look like a little girl. I want to look better than T-Swift!"

Jada laughed at the tween's joke. Taylor was the spitting image of her mom, but she had her dad's sense of humor and fun-loving disposition. A bell sounded, and animated voices filled the line. Worried Taylor was going to be late for her next class and suffer her father's wrath when he found out, Jada said, "Sweetie, you should go. I'll text you later."

"Ms. Jada, can you do my hair and makeup on Saturday for the dance?"

Jada had no words, didn't know what to say in response. She didn't want to lie to Taylor, but Jada didn't think it was a good idea to hang out with the tween on the weekend, not after the conversation she'd had with Max at FunZone Galaxy. As hard as it was going to be, she had to avoid seeing her boss socially and distance herself from Taylor. If she didn't, she'd never get over Max, and would always think she had a chance with him—even though she didn't. Jada wished things could be different, but she had to protect her heart.

"Please, Ms. Jada. I won't give you any trouble. I'll be on my best behavior. I promise."

Jada adored Taylor and loved the idea of them having a girls' day, but she worried about going to her boss's estate on the weekend. What if Max was there with one of his girlfriends? How would she feel when he introduced her to his lover?

"TaVonte is the most popular boy in school, and he asked *me* to be his date for the dance. Me? Can you believe it? I know it probably doesn't seem like a big deal to you, because you probably go on dates all the time, but I'm only ten and a half, so this is *huge*."

Memories of her first school dance came to mind.

It was a disaster, one of the worst days of her life, and Jada wanted Taylor to feel confident on Saturday night, not insecure.

"Ms. Jada, are you free on Saturday?"

Stopping at the intersection, Jada leaned against the lamppost to catch her breath. She couldn't bring herself to say no to Taylor, and hoped she wouldn't regret her decision later.

"I am now!" she said with a laugh. "I'll talk to your dad first, and if it's okay with him, I'll make the necessary arrangements. We'll go shopping at the Third Street Promenade, and get our hair and nails done at one of the trendy salons. How does that sound?"

"Thank you, Ms. Jada. That would be awesome!"

"A girl never forgets her first date," she said, injecting happiness into her voice even though she felt a twinge of sadness. "It's going to be a memorable night, and I want you to look and feel your best at the Christmas dance."

"Was your first date memorable?"

Jada winced as if she had an infected tooth. "Yeah, but for all the wrong reasons."

"What happened?"

"Don't you have a class to go to?"

"Duh, it's lunchtime." Taylor giggled. "Tell me what happened at your first date."

Heat flooded Jada's skin at the thought of Valentine's Day from hell, but instead of changing the subject, she told Taylor the truth about her first school dance. "My crush was standing at the concession stand, and I was so anxious to talk to him I tripped over my feet and fell flat on my face. Everyone in the gym laughed, including my crush, and I was so embarrassed I hid out in the bathroom for the rest of the night."

The light changed, but Jada didn't move. She was

busy thinking about the worst day of her life. To this day, she couldn't look at a Valentine's Day card or heart-shaped chocolates without cringing. It had been over a decade since she'd graduated from high school, but she never forgot how her peers had made her feel inferior, as if she didn't measure up to them because of her secondhand clothes and kinky, unruly hair. Her dad never failed to tell her how beautiful she was, even when she'd had a terrible bout of acne her sophomore year, but she'd never had close friends or a boyfriend, and had always longed for a romantic relationship.

"Wow, that's savage. If that happened to me I'd have to transfer to Malibu Girls Academy, because I'd never be able to show my face at school again."

"Believe me, I tried to switch schools, but my dad wouldn't let me." Her mind transported her back to the night of the dance, and remembering how her dad had picked her up from school and taken her for ice cream made her smile. Her father meant the world to her— her siblings, too—and she'd do anything for him. "My dad told me not to let one bad day ruin my year. He was right, of course, but at the time I was crushed, and if I didn't have to help my siblings I wouldn't have left my bedroom for the rest of the year!"

Crossing the street, Jada spotted Christina North exiting Millennium Talent Agency and watched as the petite fashionista hopped into her silver SUV, then sped off. They'd met through Max, and Jada enjoyed chatting with the gregarious personal assistant to Prescott George board member Demetrius Davis. Everyone liked Christina, and handling the day-to-day bookings for the organization's Rent-a-Bachelor fund-raiser had increased her popularity.

"I found the perfect dress for the dance!" Taylor said,

changing the topic. "It's a frilly, strapless dress, with lace trim along the sides, and a…"

Listening to the tween with half an ear, Jada recalled the last telephone conversation she'd had with Christina, and still couldn't believe the scandalous things the assistant had told her about Prescott George's upper-class members. Jada had considered "booking" Max for Christmas Eve, but when she found out the staggering cost of the service she'd changed her mind. Jada couldn't think of anything better than spending the holidays with Max, but if she used all of her savings to fulfill her Christmas wish, she'd regret it when she needed emergency cash. Sure, she made great money working for Max, but she didn't have an extra five thousand dollars lying around to make her Christmas dreams come true. Her siblings needed bus passes to get to and from school, money for tuition and textbooks, and Jada wanted to help her dad with his monthly expenses.

"That sounds like a lovely dress."

"TaVonte says I look pretty in pink, and he's right. I do," she said, giggling.

Arriving at the agency, Jada said, "Sweetie, I have to go, but once I talk to your dad about Saturday I'll text you the details."

"Thanks again, Ms. Jada. You're a saint!"

Laughing at the tween's joke, she ended the call and marched into Max's spacious corner office. It was larger than her condo, and the cream furniture, polished marble floors, glass sculptures and pendant lamps gave the space a luxurious feel.

Moving quickly, Jada hung up the dry cleaning in the walk-in closet and opened the window blinds. The office had everything Max needed at his disposal—a private shower, closet and cabinet space, a mini fridge stocked with fruits, vegetables and protein shakes, and a state-of-the-art treadmill—and Max often called the office his home away from home.

Jade wiped the table and set it with silverware and napkins. Max would be back from his meeting soon, and Jada wanted everything ready and waiting by the time he returned to his office for lunch. All week, he'd been working around the clock, and Jada—

Hearing a loud, angry voice in the reception area, Jada peered through the office door, curious to see who was shouting. Millennium Talent Agency was an upscale agency that gave their celebrity clientele VIP service, and Max would be pissed if he heard one of his employees yelling and cursing in the reception area. Someone was being a nuisance, and if they didn't stop, there'd be hell to pay when the boss found out.

Jada cranked her head to the right, and her mouth dropped. She couldn't believe what she was seeing. *Max* was the nuisance, the person who was creating a scene in the reception area, and Jada feared he was having a nervous breakdown. Was he losing it? Had he finally cracked from the pressures at work, the stress of his dad's illness, the problems at Prescott George and his ongoing issues with Taylor?

Jada deliberated over what to do. Should she call 911? Or reach out to his brothers? This wasn't Max. He didn't yell or shout or curse. Ever. He was the King of Cool, the person everyone at the agency looked to during a crisis. His calm, unflappable demeanor put others at ease, especially the opposite sex, and in all the years Jada had worked for him, she'd never seen Max lose his temper.

"That no-good son of a bitch!" Huffing and puffing, Max stalked into the office and slammed the door with such force the windows rattled. "I'm going to kill him!"

Jada knew it was none of her business, and that she should return to her desk, but she was worried about Max and wanted to help. He was so handsome in a slim-fitted charcoal-gray suit that she found it hard not to stare at him. His earthy cologne was a scrumptious mix of musk, saffron and sandalwood, and her mouth watered at the scent in the air.

Max paced the length of the office. His eyebrows were furrowed, his jaw was tense, and his designer leather shoes smacked against the floor as he marched back and forth. "I have half a mind to go down to his office and kick his ass."

His gaze was wild with anger. Jada worried that if he didn't regain control he'd have a heart attack, and she couldn't imagine anything worse than seeing the man she loved collapse to the floor. "Max, what's wrong?" Hoping he'd mirror her actions, she spoke in a quiet tone of voice and remained perfectly still. "Why are you shouting?"

Balling his hands into fists, Max spoke through clenched teeth. "Because that snake Shazir Toussiant stole Kid Quentin from me!"

Chapter 8

Words didn't come. Dumbfounded, Jada stared at Max with wide eyes. She didn't understand why he was bad-mouthing his fellow Prescott George member—a man he'd known ever since he'd joined the prestigious club ten years earlier. "How is that possible?" she asked, reclaiming her voice. "Kid Quentin agreed to sign with us last week and his agent promised to fax the signed contracts back to us by Monday. It's a done deal."

"I thought so, too, but Shazir befriended the teen sensation online, then invited him to a party at his estate last night that included some of the biggest names in entertainment," Max explained, kicking the chocolate-brown ottoman with his foot. "The next thing I know, Kid Quentin signed with my rival, and Shazir's been bragging about it on social media."

Her temples pounded and her throat dried up. Jada couldn't speak. Didn't know what to say to make things better. She knew the two businessmen didn't like each other, but she'd never dreamed Shazir would double-cross another Prescott George member. For the second time that day, Jada had doubts about having dinner with the talent agent, and when Max cursed in Spanish she decided to text Shazir later to cancel their plans for tomorrow night. Dating him wouldn't be right. Not after what she'd learned about him. If she went out with Shazir she'd feel as if she was betraying Max, and Jada didn't want to do anything to upset her boss or jeopardize her job.

"If not for everything going on with my dad and the problems with Demetrius, I'd tell the board members at Prescott George about Shazir's dirty business practices," he said, scowling.

"Max, I'm sorry that you lost Kid Quentin."

"Me, too, and if I had a pistol I'd use it."

Surprise must have shown on her face, because Max wore an apologetic smile.

"Kid Quentin is special, and I had big plans for him." His voice was resigned, and his shoulders were hunched in defeat. "I could have mentored him and taught him the ropes about the entertainment business. He's a great kid, and we really bonded, you know?"

Moved by his confession, Jada wanted to hug him, but stayed put. Knew if she acted on her impulse it would ruin their relationship. Or worse, she'd get fired. Max spoke openly, didn't hold back how he was feeling. He wasn't upset about losing Kid Quentin as a client because of the potential financial gain; he was upset because he genuinely liked the teen and wanted to help him achieve even greater success in his career. To cheer him up, Jada wore a bright smile and spoke with confidence.

"Don't sweat it. You'll sign someone bigger and better in no time," she said, fervently nodding her head. "You're

Max Moore, talent scout extraordinaire. You don't sit around waiting for things to happen. *You* make things happen, and I have complete faith in you."

He raised his shoulders and puffed his chest out, stood taller, straighter. "Thanks, Jada. You always know just what to say to make me feel better."

His long, lingering gaze aroused her body. She could hear the phone ringing on her desk in the reception area, but Jada didn't move. How could she, when Max—her dreamy, delicious crush—was staring deep into her eyes? Her knees were knocking together like two blocks of wood, but they didn't buckle.

"You're a sweetheart, Jada, not to mention thoughtful and sincere and…"

Stepping forward, he slowly wet his lips with his tongue.

Excitement welled up inside her. *He's* finally *going to kiss me!* she thought, overcome with happiness. *Jeez, it's about time! What took him so long?*

Jada moved toward him. She closed the gap between them before she lost her nerve. She wanted Max to know she desired him more than anything, that he was the one and only man for her. The thought came out of nowhere, shocking her. Jada didn't know what was wrong with her. One minute she was determined to forget Max, and the next minute she was willing him to kiss her—and more.

It felt as if the walls were closing in around her, pushing her even closer to him, right into his arms. His lips were moving, but Jada didn't hear what he was saying, couldn't concentrate. As usual, she was too busy staring at his mouth.

Swallowing hard, Jada discreetly wiped her palms along the side of her pencil skirt. She wished she had a mint or a stick of gum to freshen her breath. She could taste a hint of garlic inside her mouth and hoped Max didn't notice. *If I'd known we were going to have our first kiss today, I wouldn't have had a vegetarian omelet for breakfast!*

Jada closed her eyes, leaned in close and waited.

And waited.

And waited.

But nothing happened. She heard the distant sound of voices, the incessant ringing of the telephone at the front desk and footsteps— Footsteps? Jada frowned. Peeling open one eye, she spotted Max sitting at his desk in his leather executive chair, and snapped to attention. He was staring at her with concern, as if he was worried about her mental state, and the expression on his face made Jada realize how stupid she'd been, how foolish. When was she going to get it through her head that he didn't want her? That she wasn't his type? The sooner she came to terms with the truth, the better off she'd be, but getting over Max was easier said than done.

"Jada, are you okay? You're not coming down with the flu, are you?" he asked, peering at her as if she was a specimen under a microscope. "I hope not, because I need you to hold down the fort when I'm in San Francisco tomorrow."

Disappointed about the kiss that wasn't, Jada forced a smile. "I will. I should get back to my desk. You still have to eat lunch, and I have tons of work to do."

Jada spun around on her heels and marched toward the door. Her feelings were all over the place, as confusing as a Shakespearean play, and it saddened her that the man she loved considered her an employee and nothing more.

"Jada, I need you to…"

His iPhone chimed, and he broke off speaking.

Facing him, she felt an overwhelming rush of emotion. On the outside, Jada was smiling, but on the inside she was struggling to keep it together. As she watched him type on his cell phone, her heart ached with sadness. He was texting a woman. Had to be. A grin covered his mouth and he looked relaxed, confident, as if he could have anything—or anyone—he wanted. And Jada didn't doubt it. Like her, most women found him irresistible.

Max erupted in laughter. "This girl," he said, typing on his cell for several seconds more.

"You were saying?" Jada prompted, scared she'd be stuck in his office for the rest of the day, forced to watch Max flirt with other women via text. "What is it you need me to do?"

He lowered his cell from his face and smiled apologetically. "Sorry about that, Jada. Taylor sent me a hilarious golf meme, and I wanted her to know I liked it. That kid. She reminds me of myself when I was that age, but *way* cooler."

"Speaking of Taylor," she began, remembering the conversation she'd had with the tween minutes earlier. "She asked if I could help her get ready for the Christmas dance on Saturday, and if it's okay with you, I was thinking we could have a girls' day out. We'll go shopping, get our hair and nails done, and have lunch at one of the trendy cafés—"

"What school dance? Taylor never mentioned it to me, and we've been texting all day."

"Then act surprised when she tells you about it," Jada said with a wry smile. "Don't spoil this for her, Max. It's a big deal, and she's over the moon about her first real date."

Jada watched the color drain from Max's face. She recognized her error, but before she could smooth things over, he complained about the planning committee at his daughter's elementary school and vowed to call the superintendent about his concerns. "Ten-year-olds shouldn't be thinking about dating. They should be thinking about their grades."

"Max, they're kids. They should have fun during the holidays, just like everyone else."

"I guess, but things were very different when I was a kid, and I'm scared my baby girl's growing up too fast. One minute she's playing with Barbies, and the next thing I know, she's gushing about some kid named TaVonte and experimenting with makeup!"

"You have nothing to worry about—"

Rap music filled the office, and Jada broke off speaking. Deciding she wasn't going to compete with an iPhone, she waited for Max to give her his undivided attention.

Max glanced down at his cell phone, but he didn't pick it up. He nodded at her to continue, as if what she had to say was important, and seemed interested in hearing her advice.

"Your daughter's a smart, spunky girl, with a fantastic personality," Jada continued. "If I had a daughter I'd want her to be just like Taylor. Don't be so hard on her. She's a great kid."

Wearing a pensive expression on his face, Max sat back in his chair and stroked his chin.

"Okay, okay, quit twisting my arm. You can take her shopping on Saturday, but keep it PG," he advised, adopting a stern voice. "Taylor has several hundred dollars on her bank card, but I don't care how much she begs and pleads—*don't* let her buy anything short, backless or see-through, and no hair extensions or fake eyelashes, either."

"Got it. You can trust me, Max. I won't let you down."

"I knew I could count on you," he said with a wink and a nod.

At his words, her heart leaped inside her chest.

"I'll pick Taylor up at breakfast and have her home by three o'clock," she explained.

"Sounds good. My brothers are coming over on Saturday afternoon, and it'll be nice to hang out with them without looking over my shoulder for Taylor. She sneaks up at me at the most inconvenient times, and thinks it's fun to scare me when I least expect it…"

Jada read between the lines. *Oh, like when you're hooking up with one of your girlfriends?*

Max snapped his fingers. "Shoot, I almost forgot. I'm flying to Maui to attend Wendell Coleman's sixtieth birthday bash after the Prescott George holiday mixer on Saturday, and I need you to buy him an expensive gift. Also, book me a suite at the Four Seasons in Maui for two nights, and reserve a rental car. Get me something fast and sexy like a Lamborghini…"

Jetting to Maui for the weekend? Now, that's *what I call the good life!* she thought, wishing she could be his plus-one for the party. Jada hated flying, but she'd conquer her fears if it meant spending the night with Max in one of the most romantic cities in the world. She'd never been on the Moore private plane, but if what her colleagues told her was true, it was the ultimate symbol of luxury and wealth, and Jada would love to see the aircraft up close.

That's not all you'd love, quipped her inner voice. *You'd do just about anything to—*

"Jada, that's all for now." Max put his cell phone to his ear, spun his chair to the window and greeted the caller on the line in Spanish.

Fluent in the language, Jada listened in on his personal call. She pursed her lips. Max was making plans to see a TV sitcom star—the one he'd dumped via text last week—and she suspected he was still romantically interested in the Mexican beauty.

Back at her desk, Jada sat down, put on her headset and logged in to her computer. She found the information for the hotel Max had requested in Maui and stared at the picturesque photographs on the hotel website.

Her cell phone lit up, and she read her newest text message. It was from Shazir. Her first thought was to delete it, but his joke brightened her mood and made a giggle tickle her throat. What was it Aubree liked to tell their single friends? Hearing her cousin's voice in her mind, she wore a wry smile. "Why stress over a man when you can just get *under* another!" the serial dater would say with a wild, boisterous laugh.

Inclining her head to the right, she gave the statement considerable thought. Gave herself a much-needed pep talk. Meeting new people was stressful, but it beat sitting at home alone every night, daydreaming about a man who didn't want her. Jada decided to take her cousin's advice. She wasn't canceling her plans with Shazir. Why should she? Max had actresses and pop stars to keep him busy, and he wouldn't care whom she hung out with after work. Her mind made up, Jada responded to Shazir's text message. She was going out with the flashy executive tomorrow, and she wasn't going to give Max a second thought.

Staring down at his cell phone, Max realized the TV sitcom star had lost her ever-loving mind, and wished he'd never hooked up with Josefina Acosta at

The Dream Hotel three months earlier. Dating her had been a mistake, one Max regretted every time the actress posted lovey-dovey messages on his social-media pages, Tweeted snarky comments to his female friends and showed up at his estate unannounced. Wanting to put an end to her incessant phone calls, text messages and emails, Max had asked Josefina to meet him for coffee, but now questioned his decision. He worried she'd make a scene at the café or do something crazy like propose. Josefina loved the paparazzi more than she loved her weekly Botox injections, and she would do anything to be the lead story on TMZ. Max didn't want to hang up on her, but if she kept talking crazy about them being "soul mates" and having a "loving, committed relationship," he'd have no choice but to end the call. Max didn't want to meet with her tonight, but knew he had to. He had to resign as her agent and make it clear that he didn't have feelings for her.

"I don't have to tell you how much this means to me," she gushed. "I adore my family, and it's important that my parents get along well with the man I love and want to marry…"

Love? Max choked on the word. *You don't love me. You love my wealth, my status and my celebrity connections, but if I lost everything tomorrow you'd be ghost!* Turned off by her speech, he allowed his mind to wander. She talked so much a telemarketer would hang up the phone on her, and Max was tempted to. Josefina wanted him to attend Christmas Day dinner at her childhood home in Guadalajara, and although he'd politely declined—twice—she continued nattering on and on about the menu, her relatives flying in from the States and the expensive Givenchy dress she'd bought on Rodeo Drive for the occasion. Her biggest flaw was that she didn't listen, and it didn't matter how many times Max told her he couldn't attend the dinner, she continued pressuring him to fly to Guadalajara on Christmas Eve.

"This year, I'm going all out for Christmas," Josefina announced. "If the Kardashians can have three Christmas trees, a vintage photo booth *and* a surprise visit from Santa, so can I!"

Bored with the conversation, Max logged in to his computer and checked his emails. He wasn't spending Christmas Day in Mexico with his former fling. It wasn't going to happen. He was spending the holidays with his family at his Santa Monica estate, and he was pulling out all the stops for the big day. He wanted Christmas with his father to be special, and it would be. His personal chef was going to prepare all of Reginald's favorite meals, and had already stocked the pantry with the best champagne and cigars money could buy.

"I have to go," Max said, anxious to get off the phone and back to work. He had scripts to read, contracts to review and sign, and dozens of emails to answer before he left for the day. "I'll meet you at Espresso & Wine Bar at six. Please don't be late. I'm going out of town tonight, so I can't stay long. One coffee, then I'm out."

"Espresso & Wine Bar?" she repeated. "That place is a dump."

Max raised an eyebrow. Not because she'd dissed his friend's coffee shop in Santa Monica, but because he could hear the disgust in her voice, the attitude. She was talking so fast he couldn't understand a word she was saying. "Excuse me?"

"You heard me. It's a three-star café with a bland

decor and menu, and I wouldn't be caught dead there. Let's go to Nobu Malibu. Celebrities flock there every night, and it's the perfect place to run into the paparazzi. I'll tip them off that we'll be in the lounge."

Max scoffed. Couldn't believe that a woman who'd been raised in a poverty-stricken neighborhood in Mexico was acting like an uptight snob born with a silver spoon in her mouth, but he ignored her disparaging comments and said, "You can do what you want, but I'm going to Espresso & Wine Bar tonight."

Josefina let out a long, dramatic sigh and spoke in a haughty tone of voice. "Fine, I'll go, but the next time we meet up you're taking me somewhere fancy and expensive."

There won't be a next time. Max said goodbye, dropped his cell on his desk and reached for the script Jada had handed him that morning when he'd arrived at the office. He needed something to take his mind off his problems, but the poorly written action flick didn't capture his attention. As he flipped to the second page his thoughts turned to his father. Life sucked. Wasn't fair. Didn't make sense. Why did Reginald have to die? Wasn't it bad enough he'd already lost his mother? Was God punishing him for his wild, bad-boy past? Max loved his glamorous lifestyle, but he'd give up everything to have more time with his father.

Wondering how Reginald was doing, he sent him a text message. They'd talked at length that morning, as Max was driving to the office, and his dad had sounded upbeat, like his old jovial self. Yesterday, when he'd worked out with his brother at Champions Boxing Gym, Trey had suggested throwing a cocktail party in Reginald's honor on Saturday night at the Prescott George headquarters, and Max had agreed. Their father's illness had brought their family closer together, and as they'd worked out side by side they'd vowed to make it a night their father would never forget. That morning, he'd mentioned his plans to Jada, and she'd agreed to book his favorite event planner, caterer and florist for the event.

Max accessed his social-media pages. He knew reading Shazir's posts would piss him off, but he couldn't resist checking up on his business rival. To his surprise, the talent agent had posted about a woman he was crushing on.

Frowning, Max scratched his head. She was probably one of his new female clients, someone young and impressionable, whom he could control. Shazir was forty years old, but he had a penchant for twenty-somethings, and the more naive, the better. Max didn't know who the woman was and didn't care. They'd been business rivals for years, but he was sick of Shazir gunning for him. The official motto of the Prescott George organization was From Generation to Generation, Lifting Each Other Up, but Shazir cared about himself and no one else, and seemed to derive great pleasure in getting under Max's skin. Got off on making him angry.

Pushing aside all thoughts of Shazir, he logged off his computer and stood. Max had more pressing matters to deal with than his problems with the ostentatious talent agent. He needed to find more evidence linking Demetrius to the sabotage case—and fast. Max wanted to clear his father's name before it was too late. It worried him to think that he'd run out of time. What bothered him more than anything was that Demetrius had lied to him weeks earlier in his home. Had looked him straight in the eye and vehemently denied setting up his best friend. But, as Max swiped his car keys and cell phone off his desk, he vowed to clear his father's name, even if it meant playing dirty.

Chapter 9

Jada stood inside the reception area of Millennium Talent Agency on Friday night, sipping her warm mulled wine, perusing the round tables covered with appetizers, desserts and cocktails. The event planner had done an outstanding job capturing the winter-wonderland theme Max wanted, and from the moment Jada arrived at the party, her colleagues had been raving about the food, the decor and the entertainment. Guests were crowded around the front desk playing Winter Charades, the line for Name That Song stretched down the hallway, and people from Human Resources were trying their luck at Blindfold Darts.

Tasting a Swedish meatball, Jada admired the extravagant decorations around the reception area. Silver snowflakes hung from the ceiling, the flickering lights from the scented candles gave the space a tranquil ambience, and snowmen decked out in red toques, scarves and sweaters were propped up against the walls. There was faux snow along the windowsill, miniature Christmas trees in every corner and edible gingerbread houses on the ledge.

Catching sight of her reflection in the wall mirror, Jada scrutinized her face. At her cousins' urging, she'd traded her eyeglasses in for a pair of contact lenses, and had been surprised by how much younger she looked without her frames. Everyone had complimented her look—except Max. He didn't notice the change, but Jada wasn't surprised. He dated centerfolds and Miss Universe types. Why would he pay *her* any mind?

Jada's cell phone vibrated inside her clutch purse, and she retrieved it from the bottom of her designer bag. Shazir's name and number popped up on the screen. She debated taking the call, knowing he'd pressure her for a second date if she did, and Jada wasn't sure if she wanted to go out with him again. They had nothing in common, and worse, he'd stolen Max's client. He'd been more interested in discussing Max than getting to know her better. His questions were endless—Had Max read any good scripts lately? Which artists was he excited about? How did he find new clients? His comments made her uncomfortable and troubled her conscience. No, there would definitely be no second date.

Jada tapped Decline, dropped her phone into her purse and tucked it under her arm. She'd touch base with Shazir later, after she left the party. He'd texted her that afternoon and invited her to accompany him to a movie premiere at Grauman's Chinese Theatre, but she'd reminded him about her office Christmas party, then politely declined his offer.

"Max, you cheated! I saw you peeking at the dartboard and I want a rematch!"

Loud voices filled the room, drowning out the Christmas music playing on the stereo system. Max, his brothers and their fiancées were obviously having fun playing Pin the Tail on Rudolph. Jada wanted to join in, but thought better of it. Didn't want to upset the close-knit group. She'd met Trey and Derek several times before, and they'd always been friendly, but Jada couldn't shake her doubts. Couldn't help feeling like she didn't belong. And she didn't. They were all successful, professional people with important careers, and she was just a lowly assistant. Would the Moore family make her feel welcome, or treat her like the outsider she was?

Doubts assailed her mind, and the weight of her insecurities overwhelmed her, making it impossible for her to move. To walk across the room and wow the Moore family with her personality. Jada scoffed at the thought. She was an average-looking woman who'd never measure up to the Beyoncés and the Rihannas of the world, and Max wasn't attracted to her. Never gave her a second glance. Deep down Jada feared she'd never find true love, and wondered if she was destined to be alone. *Will I ever meet that special someone? Will I have a loving husband and children in the future or am I just kidding myself—*

"Wow, you look great!" praised a junior talent scout, sidling up to her with a toothy grin. "It's about time you got rid of those fugly glasses and got contacts."

Jada opened her mouth to thank the Justin Timberlake look-alike for the compliment, but a male voice spoke behind her, and she broke off speaking.

"I vehemently disagree…"

As she realized who it was, a shiver snaked down Jada's spine. She glanced over her shoulder, and goose bumps flooded her skin. What was Shazir doing there? Was he trying to get her fired?

"I think your glasses make you look smart, like a sexy librarian, so get them back!"

Her lips were glued together, but she pried them apart and spoke in a calm voice. "Shazir, what are you doing here?" Jada glanced around the reception area and sighed in relief when she realized her colleagues were too busy partying to notice the impeccably dressed party crasher.

Cocking an eyebrow, he leveled a hand over the front of his slim-fitted burgundy suit jacket, then slowly licked his lips. "I'm your suave, debonair date, of course."

"I don't need a date—"

"Yes, you do," he insisted, in a firm tone of voice. "And I'm the perfect accessory."

"You have to go. This is a private function for the employees of Millennium Talent Agency, not an event open to the general public." Her legs were shaking so hard she felt unsteady on her feet, as if they were going to fall out from under her, but Jada gripped his forearm and hustled him toward the door. "Thanks for stopping by, but you have to leave."

"And miss hanging out with you? No way. Max won't mind that I'm here. We're friends."

Jada bit down on her bottom lip. She knew she shouldn't say anything about Kid Quentin, or Max's explosive temper, but she wanted Shazir gone before her boss spotted him and all hell broke loose in the reception area. "First you steal one of his favorite clients, and then you crash his office Christmas party. What do you *think* is going to happen when he sees you drinking his champagne and eating his caviar?"

"Not a damn thing. We're Prescott George members,

and squabbling in public is beneath us." Shazir winked. "Besides, I'm not here for the appetizers. I'm here for you."

The disappointment Jada felt inside must have shown on her face, because Shazir sobered quickly. Wearing an apologetic smile, he took her hand in his.

"Fine, I'll go, but you're coming with me. Let's ditch this lame party and head to the movie premiere. I want my friends and colleagues to meet the woman who's captured my heart."

Is Shazir for real? I'm not ditching my work party to watch him show off for the cameras! Dismissing his comment, she peered over his shoulder to make sure none of her coworkers were watching them. Jada noticed Alexis—the stunning fashion model who was engaged to Derek Moore—staring at them with a curious expression on her face, and hoped the mother-to-be didn't say anything to her fiancé or future brother-in-law. "I can't. I want to stay here."

"You have to be the most stubborn woman I've ever met," he complained, raking a hand through his curly jet-black hair. "What do I have to do to get through to you? To prove that I'm interested in you and want you to be my number one girl?"

It took everything in Jada not to laugh in his face. Shazir was feeding her a line. Willing to say and do anything to get his way. Reading him like a book, Jada knew what he was doing and wanted no part of it. She wasn't going to let him use her to get under Max's skin, and made up her mind to delete his number from her cell phone once he left the party. He wasn't worth her time, and she had no desire to date the flashy talent agent with a massive ego.

"Please leave," she implored, desperate to get through

to him. Time was of the essence, and if she didn't make Shazir understand the severity of the situation, there could be serious consequences for them both. "If Max sees you he'll lose it, and I don't want to upset him."

A sneer curled his lips. "But I do."

"I won!" Max ripped off his blindfold and stalked toward the laminated picture of Rudolph the Red-Nosed Reindeer taped to the wall. He raised his arms triumphantly in the air. Max knew it was wrong to gloat, but he couldn't resist celebrating his come-from-behind victory over his brothers. "I told you guys I'd win, but you didn't believe me. Said I was all talk and no action," he reminded them, cocking an eyebrow. "Well, how ya like me now, boys?"

His brothers chuckled, their fiancées did, too, and the sound of their boisterous laughter bolstered his mood. Made Max momentarily forget his problems. His business trip to San Francisco had been a bust. He'd decided not to sign the boy band, or the aspiring actress he'd been in talks with for weeks. He didn't think they had the "It" factor, and the only bright spot of his two-day trip had been shopping for Taylor. He'd bought everything on her Christmas list, and couldn't wait to see the look on his daughter's face when she opened her presents on Christmas Day.

"I thought I was competitive," Trey said, "but, Max, you're on a whole *other* level."

Max shrugged. "Guilty as charged. What can I say? I hate to lose."

Kiara's ponytail swished back and forth as she nodded her head. "You're not the only one. I beat Trey at Scrabble and he pouted for an entire week! After that, I just let him win."

Chuckling, Max grabbed his tumbler off the table and finished his candy cane vodka. He enjoyed having his family around, and was glad his brothers and their wives-to-be had agreed to attend his office holiday party.

"I should have known. I knew I was good at Scrabble, but not *that* good." Trey wrapped Kiara up in his arms. "I know how much you love this song, so let's dance."

"Let It Snow" was playing on the stereo system, and Trey belted out the lyrics as he slow-danced with his fiancée. Max felt his eyes bug out of his head. His brother's behavior was shocking. That wasn't Trey. He was an award-winning screenwriter, not an aspiring singer. His brother didn't fawn over women, but watching Trey with Kiara proved he was completely devoted to the businesswoman with the dazzling smile.

"It's time to pay up, so quit stalling." Max stuck out his hand and wiggled his fingers. "I beat you fair and square, and now I want my kizzash."

Derek reached into the back pocket of his charcoal-gray dress pants, took out his leather wallet and opened it. Scowling, he fished out five hundred-dollar bills, slapped them into the palm of Max's hand and said, "There. Happy now?"

"Thanks, bro! It was great doing business with you." Max closed his eyes and fanned his face with the crisp bills. "*Man*, this feels good. You should try it sometime."

"I'm glad you won," Derek said. "Now that you have some money you can go buy yourself some class because you're the worst trash-talker I've ever met."

Max shrugged. "Don't blame me. Blame Dad. He taught me everything I know!"

Alexis winced as if in pain, then exhaled a deep breath.

"Alexis, what's wrong?" Sobering, Max pocketed his winnings and studied his future sister-in-law closely. He remembered how sick Shay had been when she'd been pregnant with Taylor, and hoped Alexis didn't have complications, too. "Everything okay with my nephew?"

An amused expression covered her face. "Your *nephew*?"

"What makes you so sure we're having a boy? There could be a little girl in here, for all you know," Derek joked, reaching out to touch his fiancée's flat stomach. Early in her first trimester, Alexis wasn't sporting a baby bump yet, and still hadn't told any of her friends.

Raising his glass to his mouth, Max nodded in agreement. "Just a lucky guess, but it doesn't matter to me what gender the baby is. I'm going to spoil them rotten, and you can't stop me."

"Is that Jada in the gold sweater dress? I almost didn't recognize her without her glasses."

Mad at himself for not realizing it sooner, Max shook his head. He knew there was something different about her when he'd breezed past her desk that afternoon after returning from his trip, but he was on his cell. Max wished he'd stopped to tell Jada how pretty she looked. Blessed with a slender, curvy body, Jada was humble about her beauty, which made her even more attractive to the opposite sex. Several of his male employees were romantically interested in her, but Max had made it clear from day one that Jada was off-limits.

Damn, Max thought, raising his glass to his mouth. Had her eyes always been luminous and bright and impossible to look away from? And if so, why hadn't he noticed before?

That's what you get for not paying attention, chided his inner voice. *If you had put away your cell instead of responding to Josefina's angry text messages, you would have noticed Jada was wearing contacts, not glasses, and a fitted designer dress.*

"I didn't know Jada and Shazir were a couple," Trey continued. "When did they hook up?"

Max choked on the ice cube in his mouth. *What?* The words blared in his thoughts, and for a moment he couldn't think or speak. Lost all use of his tongue and the ability to form sentences.

Bewildered by his brother's words, Max blinked, then noticed the talent agent with the bad-boy reputation was standing beside his assistant. He'd been so busy admiring Jada he'd failed to notice Shazir gazing at her with lust in his beady little eyes.

Gripping his tumbler, he wished it was the executive's neck. What was he doing here? Who invited him? His thoughts spun. Was he with Jada? Max couldn't understand why Jada—a smart, sensible woman—would want to date the fortysomething bachelor. Sure, Shazir was attractive in a cheesy, boy-band-member kind of way, but he was arrogant as hell, and he didn't have an honest bone in his body.

Searching for answers, his mind raced from one thought to the next. Shazir was standing so close to her Max would need a crowbar to separate them, but what bothered him more than anything was the broad I'm-the-man grin on the executive's face. They were lovers? Why?

"They make a cute couple," Kiara said. "And you can tell by Shazir's goofy, lopsided smile that he's totally into her. He looks happier than a kid at a Pokémon Convention!"

Max slammed his empty glass on the table. "I'll be right back."

Derek clapped a hand on Max's shoulder, and Trey slid in front of him, blocking his path.

"Don't do anything stupid," Trey advised, adopting a stern tone of voice. "This is a party, not Champions Boxing Gym, and if you start a fight with Shazir, it could have serious consequences for all of us, including Dad."

"And the last thing we need is more drama. We have enough on our plate as it is," Derek added.

"Who's fighting?" Max asked, cracking his knuckles. "I just want to talk to the guy."

Derek nodded. "Fine, then we'll come with you."

Annoyed that he suddenly had two chaperones, Max crossed the room, rehearsing in his mind what he wanted to say to his brown-eyed nemesis. Should he curse Shazir out for stealing Kid Quentin from under his nose or play it cool, not give him the satisfaction of seeing him sweat? Deciding the latter was the way to go, Max clapped Shazir hard on the back and thanked him for coming to the party. "It's good to see you," he lied, his smile as fake as a three-dollar bill. "I'm glad you could join us tonight."

"See, baby, I told you Max wouldn't mind me stopping by." Oozing with confidence and pride, Shazir slid an arm around Jada's waist and rubbed her hips. "Jada told me you were upset that Kid Quentin dropped you so he could sign with my agency..."

She. Said. What? Max stared at Jada with wide eyes. He couldn't believe she'd blabbed to the competition about their private conversation in his office days earlier, and figured Shazir was lying, just trying to get under his skin. But when Jada dropped her gaze to the floor, Max knew she'd betrayed his trust.

"Jada said you wouldn't want me here, but I assured her it was water under the bridge."

Water under the bridge? Max thought, inwardly fuming. *It happened two days ago, you low-down dirty snake! And Jada's right, you creep; I* don't *want you here, so leave!*

Trey cleared his throat. He must have sensed Max's rage, because he stepped forward, shielding Shazir with his body and wisely changing the subject. "Are you free tomorrow night? We're having a holiday mixer at Prescott George for our dad, and all members are welcome."

"I'll let you know. I don't know if you've heard, but I'm the star of the Rent-a-Bachelor campaign. I've single-handedly raised more money than any of the other members, and I'm booked solid until Christmas Eve," he bragged, popping the collar on his white dress shirt.

"Then what are you doing here?" Max cocked an eyebrow. "Shouldn't you be at a five-star restaurant wining and dining one of your dates?"

"Jada begged me to come tonight, and I didn't have the heart to disappoint her."

Max scoffed. Didn't believe a word he said. He watched Shazir flirt with Jada and felt such a strong sense of betrayal it rocked him to the core. He'd seen enough. Couldn't stand to be around Shazir another second and feared if he didn't leave he'd slug him in the face. "If you'll excuse us, I need to have a word with my assistant," Max said, stepping forward.

"Okay, but bring her right back." Licking his lips, he let his gaze slide down Jada's fine feminine shape.

"She promised me a dance, and I've been looking forward to it all day."

"See you around, Shazir. Have fun at *my* party."

The grin slid off Shazir's mouth, and a sneer darkened his face. "If Jada's not back here in five minutes I'm coming to get her, got it?"

Ignoring him, Max took Jada by the arm and led her through the reception area and into the conference room. It was empty, but there were dirty plates and Christmas-themed bowls filled with caramel popcorn on the table. Releasing her, Max stared her down. "You had no right to discuss our private conversation with your lover."

"Shazir isn't my lover—"

Relief flowed through his body, and his arms dropped to his sides. "He's not? Then why did he have his hands all over you? Why is he here?"

"Max, I didn't invite him. He showed up unannounced and I was trying to get rid of him, so I told him you were pissed about the Kid Quentin deal, hoping he'd leave, but he didn't."

"I don't want Shazir knowing my private business," he continued. "What happens at *my* agency stays at *my* agency. Understood?"

"Absolutely. It won't happen again. I promise."

Her apologetic smile softened his heart. He felt guilty for ever doubting her loyalty, and wished he'd kept his cool back in the reception area. "Do you love him?"

"Who? Shazir? Don't be silly. I hardly know the guy. We've only been on one date."

Max raked a hand through his hair. It was none of his business whom Jada dated or what she did in her free time, but he couldn't stop himself from asking the question in the forefront of his mind. "Are you lovers? Did you sleep with him?"

"No, and I don't plan to. Shazir's a lot of fun, and he tells great stories, but he's not my type." Jada grabbed a handful of popcorn, tossed one into her mouth and gestured to the door with a nod of her head. "I should get back to the party before Shazir starts a conga line. He said every event needs a signature dance, but I fervently disagreed."

"He's right, but make sure it's not the 'Nae Nae.' I hate that dance!" Jada laughed, and Max did, too. Glad she wasn't mad at him for losing his temper, he thanked her for planning a great office party and chuckled when she asked for a raise. One minute they were cracking jokes, and the next thing Max knew, they were pressed against each other, kissing as if it was the most natural thing in the world. His mind was screaming, "No!" but his body was screaming, "Yes!"

Her lips were sweet, flavored with caramel and addictive. They were intoxicating, the best thing that had ever happened to his mouth since bourbon-flavored cigars. Her perfume was floral and fruity, a subtle feminine scent that tickled his nostrils. Max told himself to stop, that he was making a mistake, but he wanted Jada and wasn't going to deprive himself the pleasure of her kiss. He'd never had romantic feelings for an employee, but he was helpless to resist her. Jada pulled away, but Max tightened his hold around her waist.

Max could hear laughter, conversation and music in the distance, but their moans and groans drowned out the noises of the party. Electricity coursed between them, crackled like lightning. Max imagined himself picking Jada up, putting her down on the table and hiking her legs in the air. He wanted to bury himself deep inside her, could almost see it now. Max couldn't control his thoughts or his wayward hands. He caressed her shoulders, rubbed and stroked her hips. Desperate for her, he cupped her face in his hands and backed her up against the door. When Jada slid her tongue into his mouth and teased his tongue with her own, chills rocked his horny body. Later, when Max told his brothers what happened in the conference room with Jada, he'd have no recollection of who made the first move, but he'd remember how incredible it had been kissing her. He'd never entertained the idea of them hooking up before, but he couldn't deny their sexual chemistry and how much he enjoyed holding her close to his chest.

Someone pounded on the door, then wiggled the knob. Jada jumped back, out of his arms, and Max strangled a groan. It had to be Shazir looking for Jada and Max was pissed about the interruption. Damn him! Why couldn't the pretty boy find someone else? Why did he have his sights set on Jada? The doorknob stopped shaking, and then footsteps echoed in the corridor. Max stared at Jada, couldn't take his eyes off her. He saw her quick intake of breath, the dazed expression on her face, and wondered what she was thinking.

"I shouldn't have kissed you," he admitted, concerned about the fallout from his behavior. He wasn't afraid of her contacting HR or suing him for sexual harassment; he was worried about her quitting. She was the best assistant he'd ever had, and he didn't want to lose her. "Jada, I'm sorry. I don't know what got into me, but I assure you it won't happen again."

Sadness flickered in her eyes, but she nodded her head, as if she wholeheartedly agreed with his statement. "I understand," she said quietly, fiddling with the silver bracelet on her left wrist. "Alcohol makes people do crazy things sometimes."

Yeah, that's true, but I'm stone-cold sober, he thought, staring at her lush mouth. He wished her lips and her curvy body were still pressed against his, but wisely kept his distance.

"Good night, Max. Enjoy the rest of the party." Jada unlocked the door then yanked it open. "I'll be by around noon to pick up Taylor, so see you tomorrow."

Max stepped forward, found himself following her into the darkened corridor like a lost puppy looking for a home. He didn't want Jada to leave with Shazir; he wanted her to leave with him, but when he opened his mouth to confess the truth the words didn't come.

Chapter 10

The blue-eyed stylist in the striped keyhole dress at Luxe Beauty Salon spun Jada's chair around with a dramatic flourish and pointed at the beveled mirror in front of her workstation. "I hope you like the sleek, eye-framing cut. It's the latest hair trend, and *très* chic."

A gasp escaped Jada's mouth. She almost didn't recognize herself, couldn't believe the image staring back at her. Arriving at the salon with Taylor two hours earlier, she'd asked the stylist to make her look sexy but smart, to give her a hairstyle befitting the assistant to a major talent agent, and the brunette had delivered. *Is that* really *me?*

Leaning forward in her seat, Jada studied her reflection for several seconds. *Wow!* echoed in her mind. Her hair had been colored, washed and trimmed, but she'd been so busy reading magazines she hadn't noticed what the stylist was doing. Her transformation was jaw-dropping, and Jada loved everything about it. Long, sweeping bangs were draped dramatically over one eye, and curls cascaded down her shoulders, giving her a youthful look. Best of all, her hair looked vibrant and healthy.

Turning her head from right to left, Jada assessed every angle. Goodbye, dull, boring brown, and hello, radiant honey-blond highlights! She wanted to dance around the salon, but resisted the urge. Didn't want to embarrass herself or Taylor, who was sitting in the chair beside hers reading a graphic novel. Jada couldn't remember the last time she'd been this excited—

Of course you do, challenged her inner voice. *Last night when you kissed Max!*

Jada tried not to think about that kiss, the one that stole her breath, but she couldn't control her thoughts. Alone with Max in the conference room, she'd fallen under his spell, and when he'd swept her up into his arms and pressed his mouth against hers she'd collapsed against his chest. It was the moment she'd been waiting two long years for, and the kiss did not disappoint.

An image of Max filled her mind, and Jada licked her lips. Sensual, passionate and hot, the kiss was everything she'd hoped it would be. She'd never experienced anything like it. Jada only wished it had happened at his estate rather than the office conference room, because there was no doubt in her mind that if they'd been alone at his waterfront mansion, they would have made love. Jada wanted Max to be her first, and hoped when the time came he wouldn't get cold feet. Or worse, reject her. Her ex-boyfriend had freaked out the night she told him the truth—which she didn't like thinking about—and Jada was scared history would repeat itself. Painful memories came rushing back, stealing her joy, but she pushed them aside. She refused to let anything ruin her girls' day with Taylor.

"Jada, dear, what's wrong?" the stylist asked, a concerned expression on her heart-shaped face. "Why are you frowning? You're not feeling your fabulous new hairstyle?"

Blinking, she surfaced from her thoughts. "No, it's great. Thank you so much."

Taylor snapped her fingers in the air. "Get it, Ms. Jada! You look incredible."

"Thanks, sweetie. It's different, but I love it. It's exactly what I wanted."

"My dad's going to love it, too. He likes women with long, curly hair."

Jada raised an eyebrow. Taken aback by the tween's words, she wondered what the fifth grader was up to. All day, Taylor had been making comments about her dad's personal life—*he doesn't like women who curse... he won't date someone who smokes...he falls hard for females he can have smart, intelligent conversation with*—and although Jada changed the subject every time Taylor mentioned her father's "ideal type," she couldn't help feeling guilty for taking mental notes and storing the information about Max in the back of her mind.

The salon, filled with dozens of attractive women wearing the latest fashions, was buzzing with conversation, but the male stylist flat-ironing Taylor's hair gave Jada a toothy smile. "I want to see you again," he announced, vigorously nodding his head, his thick black curls tumbling around his forehead. "So, slide me your number so we can make it happen."

Stunned by how bold he was, Jada stared at him with wide eyes. *Is he for real, or is he pulling my leg?* Cute, with dark features and a lanky frame, he'd been making her laugh ever since she'd arrived at the salon. And if she wasn't crushing on Max, she'd take the Colombian native up on his offer. Jada loved dancing, and often joked that she could beat J-Lo in a dance battle, but she wanted Max to be her dance partner, not the flirtatious stylist.

"Sorry, Gerardo, she's busy," Taylor quipped with a cheeky smile, dropping her graphic novel in her lap. "Better luck next time, *papi*!"

Cracking up, the stylist wagged his finger at the tween. "Good one, *bebita*."

Giving Taylor a grateful smile, Jada flashed her a thumbs-up. The fifth grader wasn't a good girl, she was a *great* girl, and Jada loved spending time with her. Bright and early that morning, she'd driven the forty-five minutes to Max's waterfront estate. Although she'd been nervous about seeing him after their sizzling kiss last night, she'd wiped her damp palms along the side of her skinny jeans, knocked on the front door and greeted Max with an easy-breezy smile. He'd waved her inside, and his calm, cool demeanor had instantly put her at ease. Inside the foyer, Max had given Taylor a stern talking-to about being on her best behavior then excused himself to take a phone call. Or perhaps to avoid speaking to Jada about that explosive kiss that made her temperature soar.

In the car, Taylor had been busy on her cell phone, texting, Tweeting and scrolling, but when they arrived at the Third Street Promenade, she'd linked arms with Jada and dragged her into her favorite clothing store. The upscale shopping, dining and entertainment complex in downtown Santa Monica was only steps away from the Pacific Ocean. With everything from farmers-market produce to designer fashions and electronics, the open-air promenade was a shopper's nirvana, and a hit among locals and tourists alike. Lively street performers and musicians had created a festive mood. The streets were noisy, chock-full of holiday shoppers searching for the perfect Christmas gift, but Jada and Taylor had had fun strolling around the promenade, enjoying the sights and sounds around them. They'd found dresses, accessories and shoes in a popular department store, then had lunch at a burger restaurant famous for its fresh ingredients, homemade sauces and signature drinks. Seated on the patio, eating their entrées, they'd chatted about their families, their favorite Christmas songs and movies, and their celebrity crushes.

"Gerardo, thank you, thank you, thank you!" Taylor shouted, dancing around in her leather swivel chair. "I look prettier than Zendaya!"

Giggling, the tween stroked her lush, silky locks, then whipped her hair back and forth. Taylor blew herself a kiss in the mirror and everyone standing nearby burst out laughing.

"Do you think TaVonte's going to like my hair?" Taylor asked.

"Of course he will, but what matters most is what *you* think. Do you like it?"

Nodding, she scooped her cell phone out of her lap and snapped a selfie.

"Ms. Jada, can I get my makeup professionally done, too? *Please?*" she begged, clasping her hands together. "I've always wanted extra-long eyelashes and glitter lipstick. All my classmates have it done, and it looks *so* cool."

Jada shook her head. She didn't need to think about it, even though the tween had a desperate look on her face. "If you go home with makeup your dad will kill me, and I'm too young to die!"

"One o'clock mani-pedis for Taylor Moore and Jada Allen?" asked a female voice.

"That's us," Taylor said, waving her hands wildly in the air. "We're here!"

"Wonderful. Are you lovely ladies ready to be thoroughly spoiled and pampered?"

Taylor leaped off her chair as if it was on fire, and cheered. "I was born ready!"

Ten minutes later, Jada was soaking her feet in a tub of salt water, sipping a complimentary glass of sparkling lemonade. Everything about the VIP lounge was relaxing—the sky murals painted on the ivory ceiling, the stunning array of potted plants and exotic flowers, and the dim lights. Jada finished her drink, put the empty glass on the side table and closed her eyes. Took a moment to reflect on the day, and how much fun she was having with Taylor.

The air smelled of scented oils, the instrumental jazz music playing in the salon was calming, and the ten-minute hand and foot massage by the technician was heaven. All her stress left her body, and for the first time in months, Jada felt confident, as if she could tackle every hurdle, every challenge, including her feelings for Max. And she wasn't going to wait until Monday to talk to him; she was going to speak to him when she dropped Taylor home. At the thought, every muscle in her body clenched, but it was high time she came clean to Max, and the sooner, the better.

"Ms. Jada, do you like my dad?"

Her eyes flew open. Convinced she'd misheard the question, Jada cranked her head to the right. Before she could gather her thoughts, Taylor spoke, and the fifth grader's boldness blew Jada's mind, proved she was definitely Max Moore's daughter.

"Come on," she urged. "Answer the question. Do you like my dad or not?"

"Of course I do. He's my boss, and we've worked well together for many years."

"No, I mean in a romantic way. Like the way I feel about TaVonte."

A lie fell from her lips. "No, of course not. I'm, ah, dating someone."

"That's too bad. I know my dad can be salty sometimes, but you're definitely his favorite staff."

"I am?" Jada asked, unable to hide her surprise. "Who told you that?"

"My dad, of course. He talks about you nonstop." Taylor affected a deep, masculine voice. "'I'll ask Jada. She knows everything… Jada's an outstanding employee, and I don't know what I would do without her… Jada's the *real* star of the agency, and I'm lucky to have her.'"

Jada read the situation perfectly and asked the fifth grader the question running through her mind. "Taylor, are you trying to find a girlfriend for your dad?"

"I sure am. If he's booed up he'll stop bothering me."

Smiling, Jada reached out and patted her hand. "He's your dad, Taylor. That's his job."

"But he treats me like a baby, and he never listens to me. It's annoying, Ms. Jada."

"I know, but in his eyes you'll always be his baby girl, and that will never change."

"Oh, brother." Sighing deeply, as if she had the cares of the world on her shoulders, Taylor fiddled with the silver mood ring on her left thumb. "Now I'm *really* depressed."

"Don't be. That's just the way dads are. I'm twenty-seven, and my dad *still* calls to check up on me three or four times a day. He reminds me to eat healthy, to set my home alarm at night, and threatens to beat up anyone who upsets me."

Her eyes widened. "Really? But you're an adult."

"I know, and I wish someone would tell my dad that!" Laughing, Jada thought about the conversation she'd had that morning with Ezekiel as she was driving to Malibu. "To be honest, it's kind of sweet. It doesn't matter how old you get, you'll always have your dad's love and support."

"I never looked at it that way."

"You should, and trust me, you could have it much worse," she pointed out.

"I can't think of anything worse than my dad treating me like a baby, especially in front of my friends. It's the worst!"

"My uncle Harrison was a drag queen, and when I was a kid, every day he'd pick up my cousin Aubree from school in a ridiculously long wig and silk Chanel pajamas—"

"OMG! I'd die of embarrassment if my dad did something like that!" Taylor shivered, then rubbed her hands along the arms of her cropped knit sweater. "TaVonte lives with his grandparents, and he's always telling me how lucky I am to have a dad who loves me."

"He's a very wise young man, Taylor. You should listen to him."

A cell phone buzzed, and Taylor and Jada both reached for their iPhones.

Hoping she had a message from Max, Jada punched in her password. She'd texted him at lunch, to let him know how Taylor was doing, but he hadn't responded. That was unlike him. He always answered her texts promptly, and she worried about what his silence meant.

When she saw that her phone had pinged with a text

from Shazir, not Max, her throat closed up and went so dry she couldn't swallow. Did Max regret their passionate, no-holds-barred kiss last night? Had he already moved on to someone else? Did he have female company at his estate? Was that why Max hadn't replied to her message? Because he was—

Jada slammed the brakes on her thoughts, refused to think the worst about him. His divorce had soured his opinion of relationships, but he was a catch, the kind of man she'd be proud to take home to her family in Inglewood, and all she wanted for Christmas was Max. She wanted to know if the kiss meant anything to him, and although she was nervous about asking him point-blank, she needed to know the truth. Frowning, she read Shazir's message.

I want you to be my date for the Prescott George holiday mixer tonight. I have something important to talk to you about, so I'll pick you up from your condo at six.

Taking a moment to consider his invitation, Jada tapped her index finger against her cell phone case. She suspected Shazir was using her to get under Max's skin, and wanted no part of his deception. Days earlier, Max had invited her to the cocktail party they were throwing in his dad's honor at the Prescott George headquarters, and Jada had agreed to go. Reginald had a larger-than-life personality, and Jada loved hearing his hilarious childhood stories about Max. Could listen to him talk for hours about his mischievous son—and all the trouble he used to cause at his exclusive Brentwood private school. Before she could text Shazir back, another message from him popped up on her screen.

I have a life-changing business proposition for you that could take your career to the next level, and fatten your bank account. See you at six, Beautiful, and wear something short, red and sexy!

A life-changing business proposition? What is that *about? And why is Shazir being vague?* Doubts plagued her thoughts. Just then, Taylor spoke, and her loud, bubbly voice captured Jada's attention. Deciding to call Shazir later, she dropped her cell in her purse and faced the tween.

"I'm so excited about the dance I wish I was already there!"

"I bet," Jada said with a laugh. "I hope you enjoy every minute of it."

"I will. To be honest, it's all I can think about." Giggling, Taylor flipped her smooth, silky hair over her shoulders. "There's a lake near my school, and yesterday when TaVonte and I were eating lunch at our favorite bench, he promised to bring me flowers tonight. I can't wait."

Seated side by side, watching the nail technicians work, Jada and Taylor discussed gift ideas for their friends and family, and skating at the holiday ice rink in Santa Monica in the coming weeks. In good spirits, Taylor spoke about her best friends at school, her extracurricular activities and how cool her mom was. When she joked about her dad being a "grumpy old man," Jada spoke up, unable to let the disparaging comment slide. She asked Taylor to be more respectful of her dad, and after an awkward silence, the tween promised she would.

Three hours after arriving at the salon, Jada paid the bill, thanked the staff for their help and ushered Taylor out the front door. The streets were so crowded it was hard to walk. Police officers in orange helmets patrolled the area on bicycles, tourists with selfie sticks posed for pictures all across the promenade, and panhandlers begged for change. Pressed for time, Jada suggested they get ice cream another day, but Taylor poked out her bottom lip and Jada caved like a house of cards. "Okay, we'll stop at Creams and Dreams, but you have to make it quick."

The girl's eyes were brighter than the sun. "Thanks, Ms. Jada. My dad was right. You *are* the best."

"Has anyone ever told you that you're exactly like him?"

"Grandma Virginia says it all the time, but I try not to hold it against her."

Laughing, they strode into the ice-cream parlor and joined the line. While Taylor placed her order with the shop clerk, Jada checked her cell phone for missed calls. Nothing. Still no response from Max. At the thought of him, her pulse sped up. Jada was excited about showing off her new look and hoped she'd be confident, not nervous, when they spoke about their relationship. Max was the one Jada wanted, the man of her dreams, and tonight she was ready to put her heart on the line.

Chapter 11

"Turn it off. I've seen enough." Pushing away from the round table inside Max's gourmet kitchen, Derek jumped to his feet. Pacing in front of the windows, he mumbled under his breath about being emotionally scarred and needing a shot of whiskey. His head bent, he stuffed his hands into the pockets of his faded blue jeans, cursing the midwife who'd posted the natural childbirth video online. "I can't watch anymore. It's too disturbing."

Max chuckled. "Man up, D. We haven't even gotten to the good part yet. Wait until the baby's head crowns. There's nothing quite like it."

Derek shivered, as if he was standing naked inside a skating rink, then pressed his eyes shut. "I don't know why I let you guys talk me into watching that stupid video," he complained. "How am I supposed to sleep tonight after seeing childbirth up close and personal?"

Trey scoffed. "It's nothing you haven't seen before.

You've hooked up with more women than an NBA player, and you brag about it every time we play poker!"

"Yeah, well, that was before I reunited with Alexis. Now that I have my girl, I don't need anyone else, and I don't want to watch any more gruesome videos, so get rid of it."

Max scoffed. "It's a childbirth video, D, not a horror movie!"

"It might as well be," Derek grumbled, leaning against the granite breakfast bar. "I wish I'd plugged my ears when the mother collapsed on the bed, screaming bloody murder. I'll never get that sound out of my mind, and it's all your fault, Max. Thanks a lot."

"Quit whining. You haven't seen nothing yet." Max picked up his beer and tasted it.

"And I don't plan to." Derek stuck out his thumb and rattled off his list of duties when Alexis was admitted to the hospital. "I'm in charge of feeding Alexis ice chips, rubbing her back and taking pictures once the baby is born, and that's it."

"Come on, man. You have to cut the umbilical cord. It's your duty as a father."

"I... I—I don't think I can," Derek stammered, tugging at the collar of his tan lightweight sweater. "And I don't want anything to do with the afterbirth, either. I overheard Alexis on the phone yesterday, and her great-grandmother advised her to take the placenta home and plant it in the backyard. Says it's supposed to bring good luck."

"Ah, hell, naw!" Trey scrunched up his nose. "That's just nasty!"

Derek sighed. "Finally. Now you guys understand what I'm going through."

"And it only gets worse from here," Max said with a

wry smile. His thoughts returned to that morning, and he reflected on the argument he'd had with Taylor after breakfast. Busy watching videos on her cell phone, she'd refused to clean her room, and when Max had threatened to ground her for a month, she'd stomped upstairs and slammed her bedroom door. "Like women, kids are ungrateful, impossible to please and never satisfied."

"Speak for yourself. Kiara's an angel," Trey bragged with a broad, toothy smile. "She's the best thing that's ever happened to me, and if I had my way we'd already be married."

"Alexis is a gracious, compassionate soul, and I have absolutely no complaints." Derek's face softened. "I've met a lot of females, but no one compares to Alexis. She's my heart, my everything, the wind beneath my wings…"

An image of Jada popped in Max's mind, and his heart skipped a beat. Thundered in his ears. There was no denying it. No escaping the truth. Max was taken with her. Attracted to her. Wanted to make love to her in every sexual position imaginable.

Aroused by the explicit thought, his mouth dried, and an erection rose inside his cargo pants, stabbing his zipper. How was that even possible? Max wondered, racking his brain for answers. He'd never once given her a second glance, so why was he lusting after her now? Craving her mouth? Itching to stroke her curves? All day, he'd thought about that kiss, and nothing else. Couldn't concentrate long enough to read contracts or movie scripts, and if his brothers hadn't stopped by to discuss the San Diego chapter's sabotage case, Max would still be in his home office, reliving the moment he'd kissed Jada at the office Christmas party. He'd never experienced anything like it. The kiss was passionate, packed with lust and heat, arousing every inch of his body.

Questions crowded his mind. Was he romantically interested in Jada because they had an undeniable connection, or because Shazir was pursuing her? Sitting back comfortably in his chair, he considered the executive's motives. Shazir was a wolf in sheep's clothing, the kind of man who'd do anything to lure a woman into bed, and Max didn't want to see Jada get hurt. She deserved to be with someone who would cherish her. And although he'd never admit it to anyone, not even himself, Max wanted to be that person—at least during the Christmas holidays.

A cell phone rang, filling the kitchen with hip-hop music, and Derek excused himself from the table to take the call. Glancing at the flat-screen TV mounted to the wall, Trey chuckled at the sportscaster's joke, then vigorously nodded his head in agreement. "I couldn't have said it better myself." Trey grabbed a handful of chips from the plastic bowl and put one in his mouth. "The Lakers are so bad they couldn't *buy* a win!"

Crossing his legs at the ankles, Max listened as Trey reminisced about taking Kiara to her first basketball game. Watching his brother amused him, made him think that true love did exist. He liked his bachelor lifestyle, but deep down he envied the fact that Trey and Derek had both found happiness—even though their relationships intervened with their "guys only" nights. They'd grown close in recent months, but these days his brothers spent most of their free time with their fiancées, and Max missed hanging out with them on a weekly basis. It bothered him that their poker nights, outings to Lou's Diner and workout sessions at Champions Boxing Gym would soon be a distant memory, but he reminded himself that he had a lot to be thankful for. He finally had a good relationship with his brothers, his business was flourishing, Taylor had made the honor roll, Reginald was showing small signs of improvement—

And you kissed Jada! interjected his inner voice.

Max licked his lips. Tried to recall every single detail of their spontaneous make-out session in the conference room. Grinned when he remembered how she'd eagerly responded to his touch. How she'd wasted no time stroking his chest with her soft, delicate hands. It was more than just a kiss. Making out with her had been the highlight of the party, a thrilling, mind-blowing moment Max wanted to experience again and again and again. And he would. No doubt about it. But the next time he kissed Jada he wouldn't hold back. Wouldn't stop until he had his fill of her—if that was even possible. She was one hell of a kisser, and he wondered what other skills she had. Did she enjoy taking the reins in the bedroom? Was she a bold, sensuous lover?

Goose bumps rippled across his skin, then careened down his spine. A light bulb went off in his head, burning brighter than a million stars. He'd spend the holidays with Jada, but keep it quiet. He didn't want anyone to know they were lovers. Couldn't risk someone at the agency finding out about their affair. He shuddered to think what would happen if the truth was revealed. He wasn't a sexual predator who propositioned his female employees, and Max didn't want his business rivals to soil his reputation. A Christmas fling was the perfect antidote for his stress, and just thinking about hooking up with Jada in his office—bent over his desk, on his leather chair, up against the bookshelf—made his mouth wet.

Jada stuck her head inside the kitchen, beckoning Max with her hands, and his thoughts scattered like leaves in the autumn breeze. His eyes froze on her lips. He saw her mouth moving, but he didn't hear a word she said. Was blindsided by her beauty. Couldn't think straight, let alone speak. She'd ditched her hair bun for loose, silky curls, and her burgundy cut-out sweater, skinny jeans and suede booties made her look sexy as hell. If his brothers weren't in the kitchen, Max would have kissed her, but since he didn't want to embarrass Jada he remained in his seat. Clasped his hands in his lap so he couldn't reach out and stroke her dewy brown skin.

"Bro, snap out of it." Trey gave Max a shot in the arm. "Listen up. Jada's talking to you."

Blinking, he tore his gaze away from Jada's curves and straightened in his chair. Mad at himself for zoning out, he wore an apologetic smile. "I'm sorry. You were saying?"

"Taylor's finished getting ready for the dance. Come see. She looks incredible!"

She's not the only one. Max started to tell Jada he loved her hairstyle, but when he spotted Taylor standing in the middle of the staircase, his tongue froze inside his mouth. What in the world? Was this a sick joke?

His stomach churned and a lump formed in his throat, threatening to choke him dead. Max couldn't believe what he was seeing. Five hours ago, his daughter had left the house looking like an adorable tween, but she'd returned from the Third Street Promenade dressed in a provocative outfit. Taylor—his sweet, innocent daughter who used to love finger painting, *Dora the Explorer* and pony rides at Griffith Park—was wearing makeup, a pink strapless dress that revealed an immodest amount of skin and strappy, open-toe heels.

"Dad, what do you think?" Taylor asked, doing a twirl.

"I think you need to go upstairs and change."

The smile slid off her lips, and her face crumpled like a sheet of paper. "Y-y-you don't like my outfit," she stammered. "You don't think I'm beautiful?"

"Of course I do, honey, but your dress is inappropriate."

"No, it's not. Ms. Jada helped me pick it out, and she said it was perfect for a girl my age."

Every muscle in his body tensed. Max glanced at Jada, hoping she'd deny his daughter's claim, but to his surprise, she looked upset, not embarrassed, and glared at him as if *he* was the problem. He rarely got mad at Jada, but he was angry that she'd allowed his daughter to buy a dress that belonged in a pop star's closet, and struggled to control his temper. It was a challenge, but he spoke in a calm voice. "Go find something else to wear."

"But, Dad—"

"This isn't open for discussion. Put on something in your closet."

"I've worn everything in my closet a million times!" Poking out her bottom lip, Taylor folded her arms across her chest. "I bought this outfit specifically for the dance, and I love it."

"What I say goes, and you're not leaving the house in that dress."

"Max, I think she looks lovely—"

"No one asked you," he mumbled, casting a glance over his shoulder. Pretending not to notice the wounded expression on Jada's face, he said, "Stay out of this. It's none of your business."

Max respected Jada and was glad his daughter adored

her, too, but he didn't need any more unsolicited advice from her. When it came to parenting his daughter she was wrong. Taylor was a tween, not a college student, and he wasn't going to give her the freedom to do and wear whatever she wanted.

"I have to wear this dress," Taylor explained, her voice wobbling with emotion. "This is the kind of outfit all the girls will be wearing at the dance, and I want to fit in with my friends."

Max held his ground, wouldn't let his daughter have her way just because she was pouting. If he did, she'd never learn to respect him or anyone else, and he didn't want her to become a spoiled, disrespectful child. "You can change, or you can stay home. It's your decision."

"Come on!" she whined, stomping her foot on the ground. "I have nothing else to wear."

"Yes, you do, and this is not open for discussion, so do as you're told."

Tension consumed the air, polluting the space with hostility and anger. Frowning, Max glanced over his shoulder and peered into the kitchen. He could hear the TV blaring, Kevin Hart's shrill, animated voice and the whirl of the microwave. His brothers were watching a movie and talking smack, but their hearty chuckles didn't bolster his spirits.

"This is so unfair," Taylor complained. "And you're being mean."

"I want you to go to the dance and have a good time with your friends—"

"No, you don't. You're bossy and controlling, and you're trying to ruin my life!"

Her expression was grim, but Max was determined to stand his ground. He had to teach his daughter to make better choices. To be a leader, not a follower. He was her father, not her friend, and nothing mattered more to him than raising a confident young woman who respected herself and her body. The hyper-sexualization of females in society was frightening, and he'd seen first-hand the negative effect on teenage girls. For that reason, he paid close attention to everything his daughter did. Max wanted Taylor to be happy, but there was no way in hell he was letting her go to the dance in a dress that belonged in Rihanna's closet.

A thought struck him. What if Taylor refused to change? What if she decided to stay home? After the dance, she was supposed to have a sleepover at her best friend's house, but if she changed her mind he'd have to cancel his trip to Maui for Wendell Coleman's birthday bash. The three-time Tony Award winner had five teenage daughters, and Max knew his favorite client would understand what he was going through with Taylor. Wouldn't begrudge him for missing the star-studded event at his favorite resort, but to be on the safe side, he'd ask Jada to arrange to have the actor's birthday gift delivered to his LA mansion first thing tomorrow.

"I love this dress, and I'm wearing it to the dance. You can't stop me." Raising her bent shoulders, Taylor fervently nodded her head. "I'm calling Mom. She'll agree with me."

"It won't change anything. This is my house, my rules, and my word is law."

Max started to tell Taylor she was a beautiful girl who didn't need to wear makeup or revealing clothes to be noticed, but when tears filled her eyes and spilled down her cheeks, he broke off speaking. It hurt Max to see her cry. Filled with sympathy, he moved toward the staircase with his arms outstretched.

"Don't touch me!" Taylor spun around and marched

upstairs, her shiny black hair swishing across her bare back. "Leave me alone! I don't want to talk to you."

"Taylor, don't speak to me like that. I'm your father and you will respect me…"

Max wanted to climb the stairs, to follow Taylor into her bedroom, but a hand gripped his forearm, stopping him in his tracks.

"Max, calm down. You're shouting. You're scaring her."

"Don't tell me what to do. Taylor's my daughter, not yours, and I don't need your help."

Jada's head jerked back as if she'd been slapped across the face, and she released his arm.

"This is all my fault," he said. "I should have taken Taylor shopping myself, instead of letting her go out with you, but I thought you could handle it. I thought you'd respect my wishes."

Jada didn't speak, but her dark, menacing gaze chilled Max to the bone.

Chapter 12

Leave before it's too late, or you'll end up saying something you regret! Jada dismissed the thought, refused to heed the warning blaring in her mind. Her inner voice told her to grab her things and leave the mansion, but Jada wasn't going to run off just because Max had yelled at her. His words hurt, but she concealed her emotions. Wouldn't give him the satisfaction of seeing her cry. Stepping forward, Jada met his dark, hostile gaze. Didn't flinch when his jaw clenched and his face darkened. She'd never lost her temper before, let alone hit anyone, but the urge to punch Max was so overwhelming her hands curled into fists.

Jada straightened her bent shoulders. Ignored her damp palms and quivering limbs. She knew what she had to do. She had to take a stand. To speak the truth. Couldn't remain silent because Max was her boss and she was afraid of getting on his bad side. Screw that. And this time she wouldn't let him silence her. Nothing was going to stop her from setting him straight. From showing him the errors of his ways. He'd treated Taylor horribly, had been harsh and unreasonable, and he owed his daughter an apology. "Max, you overreacted about Taylor's outfit, and the things you said to her were incredibly hurtful."

Max scoffed, shook his head as if it was the most ludicrous thing he'd ever heard. "Are you kidding me? Taylor has no business wearing makeup, her hairstyle is too mature for a ten-year-old, and her dress is completely inappropriate."

"Why? Because it doesn't reach her ankles?"

"No, because I don't want horny, pubescent boys ogling my daughter. I'm her father, Jada. It's my job to protect her, and that's what I'm going to do, whether you like it or not."

"Protect her from what? She's going to a chaperoned school dance, not Coachella." Jada wanted to grip his shoulders and shake some sense into him, but she kept her hands at her sides. "The problem isn't Taylor's outfit, Max. It's you."

Max raised an eyebrow. He stood perfectly still, like a guard standing outside Buckingham Palace, but Jada could tell by his narrowed gaze and stiff posture that he was upset. Pissed that she'd disagreed with him. Determined to get through to him, she wore a sympathetic expression on her face and softened her tone of voice. "Taylor isn't five anymore. She's ten. A tween. A feisty, spunky girl who's interested in makeup and boys, and the sooner you come to terms with who she is, the better off you'll be. And Taylor, too."

"Thanks for your concern," he said with false cheerfulness, "but this is *my* family, *my* daughter, and I know what's best for her. Not you. Don't worry, Jada. I've got this."

Vibrating with anger, Jada pursed her lips together to trap the curse on her tongue inside her mouth. She couldn't believe his nerve, the smug, confident grin on his mouth. Who did Max think he was? The second coming of Christ? It took every ounce of self-control Jada had not to storm into the great room, snatch a pillow off the brown suede couch and beat him with it. *How dare Max speak to me like that!* she raged, seething inwardly. *I did nothing wrong!* He's *the one who insulted Taylor and made her cry! Not me!*

Jada took a deep, calming breath. Glanced outside the window and admired the clear, picture-perfect sky. Her gaze swept over the expansive grounds. It was beautifully landscaped, with vibrant floral gardens, shady trees and a lily pond. The sprawling six-acre estate in the most exclusive neighborhood in Los Angeles was fit for a king, and the muted earth tones throughout the main floor created a tranquil mood, but Jada felt stressed, not relaxed. In university, Max had had dreams of becoming an architect, and his keen eye for design had been beneficial when he purchased and renovated the Malibu mansion. Every room offered stunning views of the ocean, the open-floor concept was warm and inviting, and framed family portraits hung on the ivory walls.

This makes no sense, Jada thought, staring at a photograph of Max hugging Taylor. *Max loves his daughter more than anything else in the world, so why would he hurt her feelings? Why would he make her cry?*

"Before you go, let me make one thing clear…"

Curious about what Max was about to say, Jada tore her gaze away from the photograph and gave him her undivided attention. Stopped trying to figure out why Max had blown up at Taylor.

"You're my assistant, not my therapist or a family counselor," he continued in a stern voice. "In future, I'd appreciate if you didn't intervene when I'm disciplining my daughter."

Heat burned her cheeks and shame crawled across her skin. Jada wanted the ground to open up and swallow her. She couldn't think of anything worse than being scolded by Max, in *his* house, with his daughter and brothers listening in, and realized she'd overstayed her welcome. Crossed the line. This wasn't her family. Max was her boss—period—and now Jada knew no matter what she said or did that would never change. They'd kissed last night, and she'd fooled herself into believing it meant something to Max, that he cared about her, but he didn't. He didn't respect her or value her opinion, and Jada had to leave his estate before things got worse.

Max cleared his throat. "One more thing. Keep your thoughts and opinions about my parenting skills to yourself from now on, because I don't want to hear it. Understood? I won't let you or anyone else undermine me in front of Taylor."

Her hands were shaking, but she grabbed her purse off the mahogany table and forced a smile, one that concealed the anger simmering inside her. "Max, you know what? You're right," she said, nodding her head. "I'm a lowly administrative assistant. Who am I to tell you what to do? Or advise you about how to parent your daughter? I'm a nobody."

Max tried to interrupt her, to clarify what he'd said seconds earlier, but Jada cut him off.

"*You* asked for my help, but the moment I disagreed

with you, you decided my opinion was worthless, and now that I know how you *really* feel about me, I can't work for you."

"You're twisting my words. I never said that."

"You didn't have to. I'm quite skilled at reading between the lines..." Her voice wobbled, but she pushed past her emotions and spoke her mind. "I quit. I'll submit an official letter of resignation first thing Monday morning."

Fear flashed in his eyes. "Jada, you can't quit. I need you. You're the heart and soul of Millennium Talent Agency, and I'd be lost without you."

"Nonsense. You're the legendary Max Moore. One of the most revered talent agents in the city. You don't need me or anyone else. You've got this, remember?"

Her mind made up, she turned and strode through the foyer.

Max slid in front of her, blocking her path. His cologne washed over her, and for a moment, Jada forgot why she was mad at him. He licked his lips, and tingles flooded her body.

"You're quitting because I disagreed with you?" he asked, his eyebrows jammed together in a crooked line. "Because we argued about Taylor's outfit for her school dance?"

No, I'm quitting because I love you, and I'm tired of pretending I don't.

"Thanks for everything, Max. It was an honor to work for you. I've learned so much."

"I won't let you quit. We're a team, Jada, and I need you at the agency."

Scared her emotions would get the best of her and she'd burst into tears if she spoke, Jada stepped past Max and yanked open the front door. He called out to her, but she didn't stop. Ignored his apologies. Increased her pace. Fleeing the multimillion-dollar estate with the feng shui fountain, the vibrant flower garden and the winding cobblestone driveway, she willed her heart not to fail and her legs not to buckle.

Jada deactivated the alarm, slipped inside her car and started it. Anxious to leave, she put on her seat belt, then sped through the wrought-iron gates. In her rearview mirror, she spotted Max and his brothers standing on the driveway and wondered if they were discussing her dramatic exit. Jada dismissed the thought, told herself it didn't matter what the Moore brothers were doing. Max was her past, not her future, and she had to stop thinking about him. Gripping the steering wheel, Jada swallowed hard, blinking away the tears in her eyes.

An hour later, Jada parked in front of her condo, turned off the ignition and dropped her face in her hands. Christmas music played from inside her purse, and she knew from the ringtone that it was her cousin calling, but Jada didn't feel like talking to Aubree. Not now. Feared if she did she'd choke up. And even though she wanted to vent about what happened with Max, she didn't want her cousin to worry about her. Or race over to her apartment with a bucket of cookie dough ice cream and an armload of chick flicks.

Jada stepped out of the car. Retrieving her shopping bags from the trunk, she spotted children in red velvet Santa hats playing soccer at the park across the street and joggers, dripping in sweat, racing up the block. She'd lived in the neighborhood for a year, and had easily made friends in the close-knit community. It was a safe area, her neighbors were young and worldly, and best of all, it was a short twenty-minute drive to her father's apartment.

Jada dragged herself inside her condo, dumped her bags on the hardwood floor and dropped into her favorite armchair. Her two-bedroom Santa Monica town-home was smaller than Max's kitchen, but Jada loved everything about her condo. It was bright and cozy, filled with natural sunlight, and decorated with vintage posters, colorful area rugs and suede furniture. Yesterday, while watching *This Christmas* on TV, she'd put up her pine tree and decorated the living room with ribbons, tree lights and greenery, but the soothing, refreshing scent in the air didn't alleviate her stress. Didn't stop her from reliving her argument with Max in her mind.

What a day, she thought, exhaling a deep breath. She'd gone shopping with Taylor, then argued with Max. She hadn't planned on resigning, but in the heat of the moment it had seemed like the right thing to do. The only thing to do. Though now she regretted her rash decision. Jada had enough money saved to pay her bills for three months, but she'd go stir-crazy being home every day, with nowhere to go and nothing to do. First thing Monday morning, she was going to the unemployment office. Working part-time was better than sitting around in her condo thinking about Max, and Jada was hopeful she'd have another administrative position in the New Year, because returning to Millennium Talent Agency wasn't an option.

Jada blinked back tears, staring up at the ceiling until the moment passed and her vision cleared. Her instincts had been wrong. Max wasn't the right man for her. Like her ex, he didn't respect her, and that was reason enough to stay away from him—

Taylor, too, added her inner voice. *You have to make a clean break.*

Sadness filled her heart. Jada adored the tween, but she'd never get over Max if she was still communicating with his daughter, and although she knew Taylor would be upset, she made a mental note to cancel their Sunday afternoon plans at the holiday ice rink.

Her gaze strayed to the coffee table and landed on the framed photograph of her family, and for some strange reason Jada wondered what her dad and siblings would think of Max. Would her father approve of him? Would he get along well with her family? Would they like him? Of course they would, she thought, dismissing every doubt. Everyone always did. Max was more than just a handsome face. He was personable, had a fun-loving nature and an eclectic taste in music, food and movies. Over the years, she'd seen him work his magic on difficult people, so making a connection with her loud, lovable family would be a breeze. *Not that it matters*, she told herself, blinking back tears. *Max doesn't respect me, and we'll never be a couple.*

Her cell phone buzzed, and Jada fished it out of her purse. Her eyes widened. It was six o'clock! She'd been sitting in the living room for over an hour, staring aimlessly at the ivory walls, thinking about Max. Try as she might, she couldn't shake her melancholy mood, couldn't stop wondering how Taylor was doing, and if she'd gone to her school dance as planned.

Jada punched in her password, read her newest text message and surged to her feet, knocking her purse off her lap. Shoot! Shazir was on his way to her apartment to pick her up for the Prescott George party. The event was for members, their family and guests, but Jada didn't want to be anywhere near Max. Not because she hated him, but because she was scared her emotions would get the best of her and she'd lose her temper again. Busy with Taylor, she'd forgotten to respond to Shazir's earlier text message, and now he thought she was his date for the party. It wasn't going to happen. No way, no how.

Hoping to catch Shazir before he left his house, Jada dialed his cell number and put her iPhone to her ear. He answered on the first ring, and relief flowed through her body. His confidence was evident in his flirtatious greeting, but Jada wasn't moved by his performance. Guys like Shazir were a dime a dozen in LA, and although Jada enjoyed his company, she knew they'd never be more than friends.

"Hello, Beautiful. I know you're anxious to see me, but I'll be there soon," Shazir said, his tone dripping with pride. "I hope you're dressed and ready to go to the Prescott George holiday mixer because I'll be at your condo in ten minutes."

"I'm sorry, but I can't go. I meant to call you earlier, but it's been a crazy-busy day."

"Of course you're going. You're my date."

No, I'm not! Jeez, what's wrong with these LA men? Don't they listen?

"Reginald is showing signs of improvement, and the Moore boys want to celebrate the good news with their friends and family at the Prescott George headquarters," he added. "You have to come. It's a momentous occasion, and I'd hate for you to miss it."

Jada was glad Reginald was feeling better, and hoped his health continued to improve, but in light of everything that had happened that afternoon with Max, she didn't think it was a good idea to attend the party. He wouldn't want her there, and that was reason enough to stay home.

"Furthermore, I have a very important business proposition to discuss with you," Shazir continued. "One I know you'll be excited about. Trust me. It's big. Huge. Life-changing."

Intrigued, Jada stared down at her cell phone. She wondered what Shazir had up his sleeve and asked him point-blank. "I'm listening. Tell me more."

"Not now. We'll talk later, after the party."

"Shazir, I'm not going. I don't belong at the Prescott George holiday mixer."

"Is that what Max told you?" He scoffed. "Don't listen to him. Forget him. It doesn't matter what he thinks."

How can I forget a man I've been crushing on for years? A man whose smile makes my heart flutter and my knees weak? Jada hesitated, took a moment to think things through. Going to the party with Shazir was a bad idea, but he wouldn't take no for an answer. Insisted she attend the event as his special guest, and promised to be a perfect gentleman.

"You're going, and that's final."

Jada opened her mouth to protest, but the dial tone buzzed in her ear. She redialed Shazir's cell number, but his voice mail came on. She texted him, but no response. Left with no other options, she marched into her bedroom to get ready for the Prescott George party.

Butterflies flooded her stomach. She wasn't pumped about schmoozing with multimillionaires and powerful business executives; she was excited about seeing Max again, and secretly hoped he'd apologize and beg her not to quit Millennium Talent Agency.

An apology? Keep dreaming! quipped her inner voice in a shrill, sarcastic tone. *You have a better chance of being struck by lightning during a snowstorm!*

Chapter 13

The Prescott George headquarters were located on the twelfth floor of the Fine Arts Building, a historic cultural monument in downtown Los Angeles. As Shazir led Jada through the grand, sophisticated space, bragging about his many contributions to Prescott George, Jada admired the palatial ambience.

Jada composed herself and closed her gaping mouth as they entered the great room. Filled with gleaming marble floors, decorative chandeliers, and eye-catching artwork and sculptures, the penthouse reminded her of a museum. There were large sitting areas surrounded by smaller, enclosed offices for board members, meeting spaces and two grand ballrooms for social events. The penthouse and the elegantly dressed guests milling about exuded wealth and opulence, and Jada felt out of place, as if she didn't belong. And she didn't. From the moment Shazir had picked her up and ushered her inside his yellow convertible, Jada had doubts about attending the holiday mixer. Shazir must have sensed her unease, because he moved in close and tightened his hold around her waist. Pressed his body against hers. The only thing Shazir loved more than boasting about his fabulous jet-setting life was posting about it on social media, and when he suggested they take a selfie, she politely declined. She didn't want Shazir to think she was interested in him romantically. She wasn't. Her heart yearned for Max, her body, too, and she didn't want anyone else. And if not for her curiosity about Shazir's lucrative business proposition, she never would have agreed to be his date for the holiday mixer.

Her thoughts returned to minutes earlier. In the car, while driving to the party, Shazir had flirted with her nonstop and complimented her outfit so many times Jada lost count. She'd paired her green wrap dress with gold tassel earrings, bangles and a beaded clutch purse. Her metallic ankle-strap pumps gave the outfit a youthful edge, and every time Jada glanced in the passenger-side mirror a smile overwhelmed her mouth. She loved her new look and had never felt sexier. Though she'd wished Shazir would quit ogling her. When he stopped at an intersection, he'd tried to kiss her, but she'd turned her face, causing his lips to graze her cheek. Annoyed, she'd glared at him. Was that why he'd asked her to be his date? Because he wanted to put the moves on her? Because he thought he could lure her into his bed? Put off by his sexual advances, Jada reminded Shazir they were friends and nothing more, and told him if he crossed the line again she was going home. Mumbling an apology, he'd jacked up the volume on the stereo and kept his eyes on the road and off her cleavage for the rest of the drive.

The great room held a strong, piquant scent, and her mouth watered at the delicious aromas wafting in the air. Tuxedo-clad servers holding silver trays offered candy cane martinis and star-shaped salmon capers to guests. The instrumental version of "Winter Wonderland" wafted through the grand room, and decorative glass vases filled with poinsettias beautified the round tables. The towering Christmas tree in the corner of the room twinkled with lights and silver ornaments, and lush green wreaths hung on the walls.

Jada stopped abruptly, couldn't get her legs to move. She spotted Max standing in front of the fireplace and sucked in a breath. While Shazir bragged about his prized motorcycle collection and his palatial homes around the world, Jada tried to get her body under control. She had to stop shaking, sweating and fidgeting. No doubt, Max would be surprised to see her at the party with Shazir, but she had to remain calm, no matter what. Couldn't wear her heart on her sleeve, or do something stupid like crash through the emergency exit to escape.

Her gaze slid down his shoulders and lingered on his chest. *Mercy*, she thought, unable to control her wayward thoughts. *He looks good enough to eat, and I'm starving!* He was dressed in his trademark Armani suit, a burgundy tie and polished leather shoes, and it was impossible not to stare at him. To envision him naked in her bed. To desire another kiss. She couldn't take her eyes off him, tried but failed miserably. Jada willed him to turn around, to notice her across the room, but he was standing beside Reginald's wheelchair, chatting with several distinguished-looking men, oblivious to the world around him.

"I'm glad you agreed to be my date tonight," Shazir

said. "You look sensational on my arm, and we make a formidable couple, like a younger, sexier version of the Obamas…"

Jada forced herself not to roll her eyes. *If you say so, but I'm not interested.*

"Damn, you're so fine I'd follow you off a bridge if you jumped!"

His hearty chuckle made her laugh. "You're crazy."

"And you're hardworking, intelligent and sincere. That's why I want you to come work for me." Shazir lowered his mouth to her ear and spoke in a husky voice. "You're the total package, and I need someone with your skill and expertise to be my right hand."

"Shazir, I already have a full-time job."

Guilt pricked her conscience, but Jada ignored it, pretended not to notice the heaviness in her chest. She didn't feel comfortable telling Shazir about her argument with Max. The less he knew about her problems, the better. Jada didn't want to tell him she'd quit her job, feared if she did he'd rub it in Max's face, and she didn't want her ex-boss to be mad at her.

A waiter approached, but Shazir dismissed him with a flick of his hand and continued his pitch. "My assistant quit two weeks ago, and everyone the temp agency sent over was a complete disaster," he complained. "They were lazy and incompetent, and I fired all of them. Needless to say, I'm desperate to find a suitable replacement, and I have my sights set on you."

Realization dawned as Jada slowly nodded her head. Now everything made sense. She finally understood why Shazir had asked her out, why he was relentlessly pursuing her. He needed a new assistant and thought he could lure her away from Millennium Talent Agency, but it wasn't going to happen. Max would lose it if she went to work for his business rival, and although they weren't friends anymore, Jada would never do anything to purposely hurt him. "Shazir, thanks for thinking of me, but I can't work for you—"

"How much is Max paying you? I'll double your salary and give you a hefty signing bonus. Be smart, Jada. Five grand can buy a *lot* of Christmas gifts."

Dollar signs flashed in her mind, and her mouth fell open. She'd been toying with the idea of returning to school next year to finish her degree in human resources, and if she accepted Shazir's job offer she could use the money from the signing bonus to pay her tuition. Every year, Max gave his employees a bottle of expensive wine and a Christmas bonus, but since she'd resigned that afternoon she probably wouldn't be entitled to the gift.

Jada told herself it didn't matter, not to sweat it. Money wasn't everything, and she'd rather be unemployed than work for someone who didn't respect her. "Why me?" she asked. "Why do you want to hire me to be your personal assistant? What makes me so special?"

"Max is always bragging about you being his secret weapon, says you're the heart and soul of Millennium Talent Agency, and I could use someone like you in my corner. So, when my assistant quit I figured this was the perfect opportunity to steal you away from the competition. Was I right?"

Jada didn't answer, dodged his gaze. She needed a moment to collect her thoughts. Jada was no fool; she knew what Shazir wanted, what his motives were. He wanted to make Max jealous and uncover his secrets, but Jada would never betray her former boss. It was a tempting offer, and she could definitely use the money, but she couldn't work for Shazir. And not just because he hated Max. She didn't trust him, and couldn't imagine being his assistant, not even for double her salary.

"There's no rush," he said casually, squeezing her shoulders. "The agency's closed for the holidays, and I leave for Aspen tomorrow, so I don't need your answer right now. Take a few days to think about it, and let me know what you decide in the New Year."

There was nothing to think about, but Jada nodded her head, as if she was going to consider his offer. A server appeared with drinks. Shazir grabbed two champagne flutes from off his tray and shoved one into Jada's hand. "This Christmas," came on the stereo system, and hearing the soulful, upbeat song brightened her mood. Humming the lyrics, she swayed her body to the music. Why was she stressing about seeing Max? Worried about how he would react when he found out she was Shazir's date? It didn't matter what Max thought, didn't matter that they were at odds. It was Christmas, her favorite time of year, and she was going to have fun at the party.

"Jada, I'll be right back." Shazir straightened his navy blue tie. "I need to touch base with Christina North and the board chairman about the Rent-a-Bachelor charity fund-raiser. I've raised more money than anyone else in the organization, and I deserve to be publicly recognized. If not for me, the fund-raiser would have tanked!"

As Shazir left, a female waiter appeared with appetizers. Taking a napkin, Jada helped herself to some hors d'oeuvre and made small talk with the silver-haired gentleman standing nearby. Out of the corner of her eye, she spotted Alexis across the room, giggling and cuddling with Derek. The mom-to-be waved, and Jada did, too. A sucker for a fairy-tale romance, she watched the love-struck couple for several seconds. She liked the

former supermodel, and was happy that Alexis had reunited with her high school sweetheart and was expecting her first child. Unlike other brides, Alexis wasn't
excited about dress fittings, cake tastings and bridal
shows; she was thrilled about marrying her soul mate,
and Jada hoped the model had the wedding of their
dreams and a healthy baby.

Jada touched her stomach, couldn't help wondering
what it was like to be pregnant. From the moment she'd
met Max, she'd dreamed of marrying him and having
his babies, and even though she knew they'd never be
a couple, Jada still fantasized about being a wife and
mother. Over the last two years, she'd met plenty of
great guys, but she'd ignored them because she was
holding out hope for Max. That had been a mistake.
Just because none of them gave her butterflies didn't
mean she shouldn't consider them. Why not give them
a chance? It couldn't hurt. And dating someone new
was a hell of a lot better than sitting around, pining for
Max during the holiday season. Max wasn't interested
in her, and she had to accept it. She had to move on with
her life, and she would.

Clearing her mind, Jada rejoined the conversation,
chatting and laughing with everyone in the group. Several of Max's business associates, whom she'd met nu-
merous times, didn't recognize her because of her new
look, and their effusive praise made heat flood her
cheeks. Jada hated being the center of attention, and
the more they gushed about her appearance, the more
embarrassed she was.

"You're a great conversationalist, and I'd love to take
you out sometime." The cardiologist in the checkered
bow tie and navy suit asked for her cell number. "If

you're free tomorrow, we could have dinner at Nobu. How does that sound?"

Lust shone in his eyes, and his broad grin showcased each one of his pearly white teeth. Jada wasn't attracted to the short, stocky bachelor, but she considered his request. Her cousins had canceled their plans for Sunday, and Jada had nothing else to do, so why not have dinner with the successful cardiologist from Bel-Air? If nothing else, they'd have a nice meal at the chic five-star restaurant, and maybe even spot a celebrity or two.

Warming to the idea, Jada returned his smile. Bound and determined to forget Max, she opened her purse and took out a business card. But when the cardiologist plucked it out of her hand and promised to call her later, Jada felt worse, not better, and knew she'd made a mistake. Once again, her gaze found Max. He was at the bar, surrounded by a bevy of beauties, no doubt wooing them with his charm. Max was it for her, the only man she wanted, and that sucked. *How am I supposed to move on with my life when I can't stop obsessing about Max?*

Max faked a smile, nodded as if he was listening to the redhead's long, convoluted story about her audition with Tyler Perry weeks earlier, but he was actually watching Jada on the sly. He still couldn't believe she'd arrived at the party with Shazir, a man he despised, and wondered for the umpteenth time if she'd lied to him about them being lovers. *God, I hope not*, he thought, downing the rest of the vodka tonic.

"If you were my man, I'd already be a household name, and have my picks of jobs."

"Me, too," chirped a former child star. "Let's hook up later. You won't regret it."

The other women at the bar spoke at once, shouting to be heard, but Max ignored them. His friends and family didn't believe him, but it was hard finding love in the gold-digger capital of the world. Every woman he met in LA had ulterior motives. They were more interested in what he could do for them than in getting to know him as a person. And forget meeting Taylor. They knew nothing about kids, didn't want to learn, and complained when he skipped social events to spend quality time with his daughter. He wasn't ready to settle down, but if he did find love again it wouldn't be with someone in the entertainment business. It would be with someone humble, loving and sincere, who enjoyed the simple pleasures in life like breakfast in bed, picnics in the park, long drives through the countryside and afternoons spent binge-watching his favorite TV shows on Netflix.

"Max, are you going to the Golden Globe Awards next month? I'd *love* to be your date."

"Get in line," joked a news reporter. "We all want to be his plus-one to the awards show."

Tuning the conversation out, he focused his attention on his stunning administrative assistant. Max checked her out from head to toe. He liked how her makeup enhanced her natural beauty, how her money-green dress skimmed her curves and how her high heels elongated her brown, silky legs.

Damn, she's been hiding all that body under shapeless clothes all this time? Why? he wondered. *It doesn't make sense. Most women play up their looks, not downplay them, and females with remarkable beauty like Jada often use their looks to get ahead.*

Max raised his shoulders, straightened to his full height. He'd never expected to see Jada at the Prescott

George party, and watching her socialize with other organization members pissed him off. After she'd quit and stormed out of his house, his brothers had joined him in the foyer, wearing grim expressions on their faces. They'd threatened to disown him if he didn't apologize to Taylor, and encouraged him to make amends with Jada, too.

"You guys agree with Jada?" he'd asked, unable to believe what he was hearing from his siblings. "But you're *my* brothers. You're supposed to have my back."

"We do, but we're not going to tell you you're right when you're wrong, and, bro, you're a hundred percent wrong on this one." Trey had vigorously nodded his head. "You were mean to Taylor and you should go upstairs and apologize."

"And you were horrible to Jada, too," Derek had added. "You're so afraid of striking out at love and getting hurt again you can't even see that Jada's in love with you."

Flabbergasted, Max had lost his voice, couldn't speak. What? Jada? But she was his right hand, not a potential love interest. Nothing made sense to him, and he couldn't understand why his brothers were encouraging him to pursue his longtime assistant.

"Open your eyes, bro, before it's too late," Trey had warned. "Women like Jada are hard to find, and if you take too long to make your move someone else will swoop in and steal her right from under your nose. Someone suave and charismatic like your archrival."

"Shazir might be a lot of things, but he's no fool," Derek had said in a no-nonsense tone of voice. "He knows a good woman when he sees one, and he'll do everything in his power to get Jada in bed. Is that what you want? To see her on the arm of another man?"

The word *No* had blared in his mind, but he'd kept his thoughts to himself.

Scared his brothers would make good on their threat and beat him up, he'd gone upstairs to make things right with Taylor. It hadn't been easy, but he'd swallowed his pride and apologized to her for losing his temper. He'd wiped the tears from her eyes, told her how much he loved her and promised to stop treating her like a kid. To smooth things over, he'd agreed to let Taylor wear the pink strapless dress—with a cardigan—and she'd given him a big hug. Back downstairs, she'd posed for dozens of pictures with her doting uncles, and by the time Taylor had left for the dance with her best friend, she was smiling, giggling and blowing kisses.

Max had hoped his brothers would leave when Taylor did, but they'd followed him into his master suite, giving him unsolicited advice about Jada. They'd advised him to send her flowers, then call and ask her out, but he'd refused. He'd reminded them that he was her boss and he didn't believe in mixing business with pleasure. A Christmas fling was one thing; a long-term relationship was another. Though Max didn't know what Jada wanted. Was she the relationship type? Was she eager to be a wife and mother, or content playing the field? Would she be interested in a fling, no strings attached? Max had dismissed his thoughts and his brothers' suggestions. "It won't work. I'm her boss. It wouldn't look good."

Derek had cocked an eyebrow. "Jada resigned, remember?"

"That's right," Trey had said, with a broad grin. "She doesn't work for you anymore, so you're not breaking the rules. And if I were you, I'd call her ASAP."

Max blinked, gave his head a shake to clear his mind.

His heart brightened and hope surged through his veins. Jada was alone! She was standing beside the Christmas tree, snapping pictures, and Max knew if he didn't make his move now he might not get another chance. All night, he'd watched other men approach her, and wanted a moment alone with her, too, without Shazir or anyone else interrupting them.

Intent on reaching her, Max stalked across the room with one thought on his mind. He grabbed a candy cane martini off a waiter's tray and joined her in front of the ridiculously tall Christmas tree in the corner of the room. Her perfume filled his nostrils, and the floral, fruity scent instantly calmed him. Max couldn't recall ever being this tense, not even when he'd met his idol, Sidney Poitier, at the Palm Springs International Film Festival last year, and hoped he wouldn't embarrass himself. Although he knew she'd never laugh at him. Jada just wasn't that girl. She didn't have a mean bone in her body and treated everyone with kindness. But when Jada glanced in his direction, and the smile slid off her lips, his confidence deserted him and sweat drenched his palms.

"A drink for the most beautiful woman in the room," he said with a nod and a grin.

Jada stared at the glass, then back at him, and shook her head. "No, thanks. I'm good."

"Looks like you lost your date to an Instagram model."

Following the route of his gaze, she shrugged as if she didn't care who Shazir was getting cozy with. "It's to be expected. Shazir is a big-shot Hollywood executive, and I'm an average-looking girl from Inglewood—"

Stunned by her admission, he interrupted her midsentence. "That's the most ludicrous thing I've ever heard. You're smart, witty and beautiful, and there's nothing average about you."

Her eyes narrowed, but Max didn't understand why. Clearing his throat, he put the cocktail glass down on a nearby table and wore a sincere expression on his face. In full swing now, the party was filled with the most successful and influential people in LA, but Max only had eyes for Jada. "You don't believe me?"

"Of course not. Men don't want smart girls with nice personalities. They want girls with big boobs and huge asses, girls who'll put out on the first date."

"Not me. I prefer females with class and substance. Like you." Winking good-naturedly, Max stepped forward and cupped her chin in his hand. Her skin was soft and warm against his. Everyone at the party could see them, but he didn't care. Nothing mattered more to him than making things right with Jada, and he would. "You're intelligent and perceptive and I think the world of you."

Jada laughed, and the loud, shrill sound pierced his eardrum. A scowl darkened her face and bruised her lips. The urge to kiss her was overwhelming, more powerful than gale force winds, but he ignored the needs of his flesh and stuffed his hands into the pockets of his dress pants. It wasn't the time or the place to make a move on her. Not when she was giving him attitude. Max knew he deserved the cold shoulder, but still... He wasn't used to Jada being mad at him, and he didn't like it. Wanted them to go back to being cool with each other, and hoped he'd be able to prove to her that he was being sincere.

"I don't believe you."

Out of the corner of his eye, he spotted Shazir getting cozy with the full-figured model, and thanked his lucky stars. He hoped the talent agent spent the rest of the night with the woman and far away from Jada. "Why would I lie? You're important to me, and I care about you."

"If that was true, you wouldn't have insulted me this afternoon when I tried to talk to you about Taylor. You would have listened to me with an open heart, instead of dismissing my opinion." Jada tucked her purse under her arm. "Now, if you'll excuse me, I need to use the ladies' room. Enjoy the rest of your evening."

Max watched Jada exit the great room, sashay down the hallway and out of sight. He couldn't recall ever feeling so low. *Damn*, he thought, rubbing a hand along the back of his neck. *Walking on water wouldn't be this hard!* He had to make things right with Jada. Tonight, before the chasm between them grew, and he lost her forever. He'd screwed up, and if he wanted her back in his life he had to go all out. Up his game.

An idea came to him, and his frown morphed into a smile. He'd never chased down a woman before, had never begged anyone for forgiveness, but that was exactly what he was going to do. He was willing to be vulnerable if it meant seeing Jada smile again. His pulse sped up as memories of their first kiss came to mind. Just the thought of kissing her, of feeling her warm, soft body pressed hard against his, made his mouth dry.

Glancing around the room to ensure the coast was clear, Max marched purposely through the doors and down the corridor with one thought on his mind: seducing Jada. And Max knew just what to do to make his fantasies about his assistant come true.

Chapter 14

Jada studied her reflection in the oval-shaped mirror in the ladies' washroom and liked what she saw. She still couldn't believe how different she looked with curly hair, professional makeup and a designer dress, and she hoped she'd be able to maintain her chic new appearance in the New Year. She washed her hands with soap, dried them with a paper towel and dumped it in the trash can.

The door swung open, and several females drowning in diamonds and heavy makeup sashayed inside, giggling uncontrollably. Jada recognized them from the party, recalled seeing the quartet huddled up with Max at the bar and wondered which woman was his date. The Gabrielle Union look-alike? The female in the black mesh cocktail dress? Or the Caribbean beauty with the mile-long legs and endearing accent?

Her shoulders drooped, caving under the weight

of her sadness. Did it matter who his date was? Who he was going home with tonight? Max was out of her league, a man who could have anyone he wanted, and it didn't matter how much she desired him—he'd never be her boyfriend.

Giving her head a shake to clear her thoughts, Jada straightened her gold chain-link necklace and fixed her tousled hair. Max had messed it up when he'd touched her. Damn him. He'd waltzed up to her, smelling dreamy and sounding smooth. Jada could listen to Max talk all day, and was so captivated by the sound of his voice she'd almost forgotten that she was mad at him. She'd wanted to ask him about Taylor, was curious to know if the tween had gone to her first school dance, but she was so anxious to get away from Max it had slipped her mind.

Her cell phone chimed and Jada retrieved it from her clutch purse. She'd received a group text from Delilah and Aubree, and reading the message from her cousins made her smile. Their busy schedules had prevented them from getting together last weekend for dinner, and Jada missed them. They wanted to go Christmas shopping at The Grove on Monday, and she agreed to meet her cousins at the mall at five o'clock.

Texting Aubree, she yanked open the bathroom door and strode down the dimly lit corridor. Her feet were on fire, begging to be soaked in warm water. Jada decided she was taking a bath the moment she got home. Yawning, she struggled to keep her eyes open. It had been a long, taxing day, and all she could think about was going home to unwind.

She checked her watch, saw that it was ten o'clock and wondered if her date was ready to go. Wishing she'd driven herself to the Fine Arts Building, she decided to call a cab to pick her up. Shazir was the life-of-the-party type, and loved to mingle and socialize for hours on end, and Jada didn't want to wait for him; she wanted to leave now. Not because she had something important to do at home, but because talking to Max had unnerved her and she feared if he touched her again she'd do something she'd regret—like kiss him.

Jada was so busy texting back and forth with her cousins she didn't see Max until she bumped into him. He folded his arms around her, and she melted against his chest. Jada liked being near him. His cologne enveloped her, making her feel warm and cozy, but when she remembered the hurtful things he'd said to her that afternoon she tried to break free of his hold. "What are you doing? I need to return to the party."

"A female guest booked Shazir for the rest of the night through the Rent-a-Bachelor fund-raiser, and they left a few minutes ago," he explained, gesturing to the elevator with a nod of his head. "Shazir couldn't find you, and asked me to tell you."

Of course he did! Jada thought, annoyed that he'd ditched her for someone else while she was in the ladies' room. *He's a modern-day Casanova who'll bed anything that moves!*

"Jada, don't sweat it. I'll take you home whenever you're ready."

"Don't worry about me. I can find my way home. Now please let go of me."

He tightened his hold around her waist. "Not until we talk."

"We already did, and to be honest, I'm all talked out. I have nothing else to say to you."

"Well, I have a lot to say, and I'm not leaving until I do."

Max didn't raise his voice, but Jada could tell by the

terse expression on his face that he was frustrated. Annoyed with her. Jada forced herself not to suck her teeth and roll her eyes. Didn't want to get on his bad side again. The last time she did, he'd let her have it, and hours later his insults still stung.

"I'm mad at myself for hurting your feelings, and I want to apologize for the way I acted this afternoon. I lost it when I saw Taylor all dressed up, and I know it probably doesn't make sense to you, but my heart broke when I realized she wasn't my little girl anymore..."

Moved by his confession and the vulnerability in his voice, Jada wiped the scowl off her face. In his eyes, Taylor was growing up too fast, and it was obvious Max was struggling to cope with the changes in his daughter. Jada sympathized with him and knew he was going through a rough patch with Taylor, but that was no excuse for his behavior.

As if reading her thoughts, he said, "I was an ass, but I hope you can find it in your heart to forgive me. I'm sorry I yelled at you, but it won't happen again."

"It better not, or I'll put my kickboxing training to good use and take you down!"

A grin curled his mouth. "Bring it on."

His gaze dropped from her eyes to her lips, sending shivers along her spine, but Jada stopped staring at his mouth and asked, "What happened with Taylor? Did she end up going to the dance, or is she home with the babysitter?"

"After you left, my brothers came down on me pretty hard for making Taylor cry, and threatened to kick my ass if I didn't make amends," he explained. "Needless to say, I apologized for upsetting her, and Taylor left for the party with her best friend as planned."

"I'm proud of you, Max. You did the right thing."

Lowering his mouth to her ear, he brushed his lips against her skin and spoke in a deep, throaty voice. "Damn, you feel good. Jada, I'm weak for you, and I'm not afraid to admit it. I've tried, but I can't stop thinking about that kiss in the conference room."

Jada held her breath, waiting, hoping, willing him to make the first move, but he didn't.

Something came over her, and she did something she'd never dreamed possible: she backed Max into the wall, gripped his suit jacket in her hands and kissed him. As if she was starving and he was dinner. Now that she'd resigned, she didn't have to worry about being on her best behavior or doing the right thing, and gave herself permission to lose control. To do what felt natural. What she wanted, what her flesh desired.

Jada was breathless, but she licked his lips, hungrily feasted on them. He tasted even better than she remembered. Caught up in the moment, she moaned and groaned inside his mouth. Couldn't stop. Massaging his chest through his dress shirt, she enjoyed feeling his hard muscles beneath her fingertips, and his erection against her thigh. Her inner voice told her to break off the kiss and flee the corridor, but her body had a mind of its own. And it wanted Max. Feeling confident, Jada whispered against his mouth. "Max, I want to make love to you… It's all I can think about…all I want… Come back to my place…"

Staring down at her, his expression filled with skepticism, he raised an eyebrow. "Jada, are you sure? You've had several cocktails tonight, and I think that might be the alcohol talking."

"I'm positive. I've wanted this for a long time, but I was scared to make the first move."

"Why? Because of Taylor?"

"No, because of you. You date centerfolds, and I'm just a simple girl from Inglewood—"

"You're stunning, and any man would be honored to have you on his arm."

Hope surged through her heart. More excited than a bride on her wedding day, Jada tried to wipe the smile off her face, but couldn't. "Including you?"

"Hell, yeah." Max nuzzled his chin against her bare shoulder. "And if I wasn't your boss I'd take you with me to Maui for the weekend."

"You're not my boss anymore. I resigned this afternoon."

"You can't quit. You're the best employee I have!"

"You'll survive. You always do. You're Max Don't-Need-Anyone Moore. You can do my job and yours, and make it look easy."

"Jada, you're wrong. I need you," he whispered against her ear. "More than you know."

His tone had a hint of sexual innuendo to it, and Jada liked it, loved how he wasn't afraid to speak his mind or kiss her publicly, out in the open, where anyone could see them.

"Come with me to Maui. I don't have a date for the party, and I want to be with you."

Closing her gaping mouth, Jada met his gaze. Convinced she'd misheard him, she said, "You want me to be your plus-one for Wendell Coleman's birthday bash?"

"Abso-freakin'-lutely. With those eyes and that smile, you'll easily wow the other guests."

His words floored her, but she hid her surprise. Acted like his compliment was no big deal, even though it made her heart smile. Traveling with Max to Maui was out of the question, but Jada had to admit she was tempted. She liked the idea of being alone with him in one of the most romantic cities in the world. In her mind, she imagined them frolicking on the beach, feeding each other tropical fruit, kissing under the stars and dancing in the light of the moon. Slamming the brakes on her fantasy before it took an erotic turn, Jada moved out of his arms. She feared that if she didn't she'd lose control again. "Does your invitation have anything to do with me arriving at the party with Shazir?"

Max grinned. "It's not *who* you arrive with that's important. It's who you *leave* with."

Touché, she conceded, hiding a smirk. *And I'd love to leave with you!*

"Shazir isn't the right man for you, but that's not what this is about." Max took her hand in his and squeezed it. "Kissing you last night stirred something inside me, and now I'm seeing you in a whole new light. I think we owe it to ourselves to explore these new feelings, and why not do it in beautiful, sunny Maui?"

Why not indeed? His gaze held her hostage. Her tongue was glued to the roof of her mouth, and it felt like her shoes were stuck to the hardwood floor, but Jada maintained her composure. Didn't break out in song and dance around the corridor, kicking up her heels.

"Jada, you're coming, and that's final," he announced. "I won't take no for an answer."

His lips covered her mouth, and her thoughts scattered. Max slid a hand under her dress, stroking her bottom, palming and squeezing it. No one had ever made her feel so desirable, and making out with Max in the darkened hallway gave Jada a rush. Made her want to continue their intimate party for two on his private jet.

Voices filled the corridor, startling her, and Jada

broke off the kiss before they gave the other guests an eyeful. Fanning her face with one hand, she straightened her dress with the other. *Where are my shoes? And why am I panting like a dog in heat?* Bracing her hand against the wall, she stuffed her feet back inside her stilettos, then fixed her hair. Jada couldn't wrap her mind around what had happened. She'd kissed Max? Licked his lips and massaged his chest? Groaned, moaned and begged him to make love to her?

"We should go. My jet is waiting at the Van Nuys Airport, ready for takeoff."

"But I have nothing to wear," she argued. "Hell, I don't even have a toothbrush."

"Don't sweat it. We'll swing by your apartment and get everything you need."

Her head spinning, Jada could only nod. *Is this* actually *happening or am I dreaming?*

Taking the hand he offered, she snuggled against his shoulder. Excitement rippled across her skin. He'd seduced her, one kiss at a time, and just the thought of making love to him made her panties wet. Jada wasn't going to worry about what the trip meant, or what the future held for them; she was going to enjoy the present. She was heading to Maui with the man she loved, in his private jet aptly nicknamed *Adventure*.

Jada was thrilled, so ridiculously happy she thought her heart would burst. Forty-eight hours in paradise with her dream man? What could be better? What more could a girl want? The two-day trip was a once-in-a-lifetime opportunity, and Jada planned to make the most of her time alone with her suave, debonair crush. Confident they were going to have a magical, unforgettable weekend, Jada followed Max inside the waiting elevator, draped her arms around his neck and kissed him with such passion *her* knees buckled.

The interior of the Bombardier Challenger 850 Learjet was so sophisticated Jada was afraid to touch anything. She stood in the galley, fiddling with the turquoise bangle on her right hand. *Wow*, she thought, suddenly breathless. *So,* this *is how the other half lives!*

Jada admired her plush surroundings. Decked out in leather and gold accents, the private jet had a gleaming cabin, a spacious lounge and entertainment center, and a master bedroom with a king-size bed and a marble shower. Pillows and cushions were embossed with the Moore family crest, Waterford crystal lamps showered the space with light, and furnishings gave off an air of subtle luxury. Everyone in Max's family had access to the private plane to travel and to conduct business and on-site interviews, and since Jada handled all the bookings, she knew the Learjet was used on a weekly basis. It was popular with the Hollywood elite and the ultimate symbol of wealth among them, its cost running to millions of dollars.

"Max, this is a gorgeous aircraft." Jada had seen the plane from a distance several times before, but she'd never been inside the private jet, and was blown away by the opulence around her. "You sure know how to travel in style."

"Thanks, but if you think this is nice, wait until you see the Boeing 727 I ordered last month," he bragged. "It makes the interior of Air Force One look like a shuttle bus!"

A female voice came on over the intercom, greeting them in Spanish, then English, and Jada took a seat as instructed by the first officer. The air hostess, a slender brunette with dimpled cheeks, appeared in the cabin, offering drinks and snacks, but Jada was too nervous to eat. She hated flying, almost as much as she hated spiders, and clutched the armrest to stop herself from bolting from her seat. Max must have sensed her unease, because he reached out and clasped her hand. It helped. Her pulse slowed, and her limbs stopped shaking.

A cell phone rang, and hip-hop music filled the cabin. Max retrieved his iPhone from his pocket, then put it to his ear. Jada could tell by his furrowed brow that he was talking to an ex-lover or a disgruntled client, and decided she wasn't going to compete with his cell phone for his attention. In the past she had, but not tonight.

"Sorry about that," Max said, ending the call. "A client needed to vent, and I knew if I didn't answer she'd keep blowing up my cell, and that's the last thing I want."

His cell phone buzzed, but before he could answer it, Jada plucked it out of his hand. Thinking fast, she unzipped her purse, dropped it inside and slid the clutch under her seat. Keeping her eyes straight ahead, fixed on the flat-screen TV mounted in the corner of the cabin, she pretended not to notice Max staring at her with a bewildered expression on his face.

"What are you doing?"

"Saving you from yourself." Jada voiced her concerns about him having his cell phone during the flight. "Do you want to spend time with me or your cell? Because if you want your iPhone I can grab a cab back to my place."

"Oh, no, you won't. For the next forty-eight hours, you're mine, all mine."

"Just forty-eight hours?" she joked, batting her eyelashes. "That's enough for you?"

Chuckling good-naturedly, Max kissed her cheek. "Only time will tell."

"I can't believe we're flying to Hawaii right now. This is crazy!"

"No, what's crazy is that you've worked with me for years, but we've never traveled together. If you ask me, this trip is long overdue." His eyes dimmed, and the smile faded from his lips. "We have to head back to LA on Monday night, so we won't have much time for sightseeing, but can definitely squeeze in a private tour before we leave the island."

Baby, I don't care what we do or where we go, as long as we're together.

"What time does Wendell's party start?" Jada asked, curious about the event.

Max chuckled. "It started on Friday, and Sunday's the grand finale."

"A three-day birthday bash? I've never heard of such a thing. How indulgent."

"It's the latest celebrity trend, and I've attended several weeklong events for my other clients. If not for the Prescott George holiday mixer, I would have left for Maui days earlier."

"I've always wanted to visit Maui, but I haven't had the opportunity. What's it like?"

"Tranquil, stunning and picturesque,"he explained, reclining in his window seat. Clasping his hands on his stomach, he crossed his legs at the ankles as if he was relaxing in a hammock, and spoke in a soothing voice. "I love the locals, the traditional cuisine and culture, but I could do without the mosquitoes, the obnoxious tourists and the suffocating heat."

The jet climbed in the sky, high above the trees and clouds, but Jada was too busy chatting with Max about his favorite travel destinations to notice the view. His carefree attitude put her at ease, and his jokes made her shriek with laughter.

Yawning, Jada kicked off her shoes and closed her eyes. Seated comfortably in her leather armchair, she listened as Max recounted his most memorable Christmas, but she must have dozed off in the middle of his story, because the next thing Jada knew, he was urging her to wake up.

"Beautiful, it's time to get up. The plane just landed in Maui…"

Jada opened her eyes. Peering over his shoulder, she saw clear blue skies, radiant sunshine and sprawling fields of lush green grass. *I still can't believe it! I'm in Maui with Max!* Her temperature soared and excitement shot through her veins.

"We're here," Max announced, kissing the tip of her nose. "Let the adventures begin!"

Chapter 15

The outdoor lounge at the Four Seasons in Maui at Wailea was filled with so many magicians, clowns, hula dancers and men on stilts that Max thought he was at a summer carnival. The air smelled of popcorn and cotton candy, and although he'd enjoyed a delicious five-course lunch with Jada at one of the upscale restaurants in the hotel, the aroma tickling his nose made his mouth wet. Sweat spilled down his face, clinging to his short-sleeve Ralph Lauren dress shirt. Max needed an ice-cold drink, but held off from ordering a vodka tonic until after he found the guest of honor and wished him a happy birthday.

He stood beside the concession stand, holding Jada close to his side with one hand and a birthday gift for Wendell Coleman in the other. Max scanned the grounds for his favorite client, but he couldn't find the award-winning actor anywhere. Guests had honored the actor's request by wearing red, and the eight-tier birthday cake was the same vibrant shade. Max wanted to call Wendell to find out where he was, but remembered he'd left his iPhone in the suite to appease Jada, and didn't feel like running upstairs to retrieve it.

"Aloha!" chirped a female voice. "Welcome to Maui, the land of promise, allure and adventure. Mr. Coleman is thrilled that you are here to celebrate his sixtieth birthday, and wants you to party the night away, so eat, drink, dance and be merry!"

A resort employee appeared, draped leis around their necks and disappeared into the crowd. *Wendell wasn't kidding about going all out for his party*, Max thought. He looked around the lounge area, noting all the A-list stars devouring caviar, sipping Cristal and snapping pictures. He knew from speaking to the Chicago native earlier in the week that the star had not only booked out the entire resort for his birthday bash, he'd also spent millions of dollars on the event, and the costumes, decor and elaborate food stations were jaw-dropping. With over one hundred films to his credit, Wendell was known and loved worldwide, and Max felt fortunate to be his agent.

Sweating profusely, Max took the handkerchief out of his back pocket and wiped his forehead. Beside him, Jada swiveled her hips to the chart-topping reggae song the female DJ was spinning in her booth. The music was loud, the drinks were flowing, and guests clad in bikinis, swim trunks and evening wear were mingling, laughing and dancing. Photographers scrambled around the lounge, on the hunt for the perfect shot.

Spotting the gift box beside the bar, Max strode through the lounge, smiling and nodding at everyone he passed. He'd been to hundreds of five-star resorts in his life, but he was impressed by the natural beauty of the sprawling property, and decided this would be the first of many visits to the Four Seasons in Maui. Palm trees waved in the breeze, tropical flowers perfumed the air and ocean views created a tranquil ambience. Cabanas outfitted with plasma-screen TVs, chaise lounges and ceiling fans surrounded the infinity pool, and once Max dropped off Wendell's birthday gift he was going to relax inside the private cabana he'd reserved.

Dark gray clouds covered the sky, but the air was hot and stifling. Birds chirped, bees buzzed and insects flew around the lounge, annoying guests. Max put the gift in the oversize box, asked Jada what she wanted to drink and placed their orders with the silver-haired bartender with the jovial disposition.

Whistles, cheers and applause filled the lounge, seizing Max's attention. Glancing over his shoulder, he smiled at the guests on the field. Wendell had thought of everything, including old-school carnival games, and partyers were having so much fun playing Bean Bag Toss, Balloon Pop and Disk Drop that Max considered joining them. But he didn't want to leave Jada. They'd been inseparable since arriving at the resort hours earlier, and Max knew if he left her alone at the bar someone would swoop in and steal his place. Like that afternoon, when he'd stepped out of the hotel gift shop to take a phone call from Taylor. He'd returned five minutes later, to find a musician with Lenny Kravitz hair putting the moves on Jada. She'd laughed, insisted he had nothing to worry about, but Max didn't want to take any chances where she was concerned. Stunning in a flower-printed sundress and caged sandals, Jada attracted male attention everywhere she went, and Max didn't want to lose her to one of the celebrity guests.

"I haven't played Ring Toss since I was a kid." Entering their private cabana, Max sat down on the tan couch, put his feet up on the coffee table and tasted his drink. "My parents used to take me and Bianca to Six Flags practically every weekend, and we'd spend hours on the rides, playing games and goofing off."

"Lucky you. I've never been to Six Flags, or any other amusement park."

"Really?" he asked, surprised by her admission. Though Jada had worked closely with him for two years, and knew all about his personal life, Max didn't know much about her upbringing. He wanted to learn more. "But Six Flags is literally right in your backyard. It's practically a national treasure, and every kid's dream vacation."

"I wanted to go, but money was always tight for my family, and I didn't want to make my dad feel bad by asking him to take me somewhere I knew he couldn't afford…"

Listening to Jada open up about her family and the sacrifices she'd made over the years for them made Max feel close to her. She told him about her broken home, her estranged relationship with her mom and her younger siblings. Max couldn't think of a time when he wasn't attracted to bad girls, women who liked breaking the rules and living on the edge, but he was moved by Jada's sincerity and admired her even more. She charmed him with her childhood stories, made him smile and chuckle. They sat in the cabana, talking, flirting and kissing, oblivious to everyone else at the party, and if not for the deafening applause that erupted in the lounge, Max wouldn't have noticed Wendell, or the mammoth five-ton elephant he rode in on.

Max got up and stood in front of the cabana, watching the actor's grand entrance. Impressed, he couldn't figure out how Wendell had pulled it off, but cheered when his client took center stage. His salt-and-pepper hair gave him a dapper look, his slim-fitted cherry-red suit was eye-catching, and his diamond jewelry complemented his flashy designer ensemble.

The DJ lowered the music, then handed Wendell the microphone.

"Thanks for coming, everyone!" Wendell smiled and waved. "I figured I should get to my party before everyone gets wasted and forgets why they traveled to Maui in the first place!"

Hearty chuckles and snickers rippled through the crowd. The female drummer banged the cymbals, drawing another cheer from the guests, and Wendell flashed a thumbs-up. Despite his staggering fame and fortune, he'd never forgotten his roots, and spoke with warmth and humility about his friends and loved ones.

"None of this would be possible without my soul mate, my ride-or-die for the past nineteen years, Norchelle." Wendell wrapped his arms around his statuesque, dark-skinned wife, kissed the top of her head, then her lips. "Thanks for everything you do for me, our family, and for being the best wife a man could ever ask for…"

Max finished his drink. He was moved by the actor's heartfelt speech. And he wasn't the only one. Jada sniffed, then dabbed at the corners of her eyes with her fingertips. Max draped an arm around her waist. His hands wanted to explore her body, one delectable inch at a time, but he reminded himself they were in public and exercised self-control.

"All this talk about love and happiness is putting me in the mood…"

Max cranked his head to the right and stared at Jada

with wide eyes. He'd never seen this side of her—the bold, provocative temptress with the sultry bed-me voice—and it made him wonder what other secrets the petite beauty was keeping from him.

Leaning in close, Jada brushed her lips against his ear. "Shall we go?"

Lust infected his body, shooting through his veins, and seconds passed before his thoughts cleared. Max hadn't been intimate with anyone in months, not since his dad's dire cancer prognosis, and he couldn't think of anything better than making love to Jada. Max knew the answer to the question in his thoughts, but he asked it anyways. "Go where?"

"Back to your suite, of course. Or mine, if you prefer. It doesn't matter to me."

"Let me touch base with Wendell first. I can't come all this way and not wish him a happy birthday," he explained, kissing her cheek. "You understand, don't you, baby?"

Smirking, her eyes bright with mischief, Jada held a hand in the air and wiggled her long, slender fingers. "You have five minutes, then that ass is mine."

Max erupted in laughter, chuckled long and hard for several seconds at her joke. *That ass is mine?* Why did her bold, unexpected quip turn him on? Max studied Jada closely, noted her glassy eyes and flirtatious demeanor. She was tipsy. No doubt about it. Max prided himself on being a gentleman, and decided he'd be going to bed alone tonight. It wasn't the end of the world. They could make love in the morning, before their private tour, or when they returned to LA on Monday night. As long as Jada didn't catch feelings, they'd have one hell of a holiday fling, and Max was looking forward to every erotic minute of it.

A slide show filled with memorable moments of Wendell's life played on a projector, and guests oohed and aahed during the twenty-minute video. The cake was cut, dozens of speeches were made, and celebrity performers rocked the stage. Wendell worked the resort lounge with the charm and charisma of Obama, and when the actor threw his arms around Max and kissed his cheek, everyone standing nearby chuckled. "You made it! Good to see you, Max."

"There's the man of the hour," Max said, with a broad grin. "Happy birthday, man."

"Thanks, son, and who's this lovely lady beside you with the beautiful smile?"

Before Max could speak, Jada introduced herself to Wendell and told him she was touched by his speech about his wife and their marriage. "You were brilliant, Mr. Coleman."

Smoke curled up from Wendell's cigar as he spoke. "Son, I like her. She's smart, has good taste and a *great* ear. Wife her!"

"Been there, done that, and I'm not doing it again," Max said, with a laugh.

"Spoken like a true player." Wendell clapped Max on the shoulder. "Just wait. Your time will come. You'll find love when you least expect it, and when you do, it will knock you clear off your feet, but you'll be a better man because of it."

Max didn't respond, but the expression on his face must have revealed his disbelief, because Wendell continued, full steam ahead, imparting words of wisdom.

"I've been divorced twice, and swore up and down that I'd never get married again, but the moment I met Norchelle, I was a goner. Done. All in."

His gaze found his wife in the crowd, and a proud smile exploded across his face.

"Do you know what sealed my fate? How I knew Norchelle was The One?"

"No," Jada said in a breathless tone of voice. "What did she do?"

Her eyes were wide and bright, filled with wonder, and Max knew Jada was loving the actor's story. A small crowd gathered around them, and he groaned inwardly, wished they didn't have an audience listening in. Like most actors, Wendell loved being the center of attention—and hearing his own voice—and once he started yapping about his wife and kids there was just no stopping him.

"Days after we met, I got pneumonia and was hospitalized. Norchelle never left my side. She fed me soup, read me comics, and cursed me out every time I snapped at one of the nurses." Wendell laughed at the memory. "Norchelle keeps it real with me, no matter what, and loves me without fail, even when I screw up. Proposing on our third date was the smartest thing I've ever done, and I've never once regretted my decision."

"Liar!" Max joked, cocking an eyebrow. "That's not real life. That's the script for your new romantic comedy on BET, and you know it!"

Everyone laughed. Guests wanted to know more about the TV show, but Max was done shooting the breeze with Wendell. Had had enough of his advice for one day. He didn't want the actor to put crazy thoughts in Jada's head, and knew if they stuck around, listening to him preach about the benefits of marriage, it would ruin his good mood.

"Norchelle is my one true love," Wendell continued in an awe-filled voice. "And I wouldn't be the man I am today without her unconditional love and unwavering support. She's the reason for my every success, and I owe everything I am to her."

Mrs. Coleman appeared, with a photographer in tow, and linked arms with her husband. "Max, you don't mind if I borrow my husband for a minute, do you? I'll bring him right back."

Grateful for the interruption, Max nodded and said, "No worries, Norchelle. He's all yours!" Giving Wendell a fist bump, he promised to touch base with him next week, then escorted Jada through the lounge, into the hotel lobby and to the waiting elevator before the guest of honor could stop them from leaving the party.

Chapter 16

"Max, what can I get you to drink?" Jada asked, unlocking the door to her hotel suite. She turned on the floor lamp and dropped her key card on the chestnut-brown table against the wall. Her cell phone buzzed from inside her clutch purse, but Jada ignored it. Didn't want any distractions while she was with Max, wanted to give him her undivided attention—and more. He'd been quiet in the elevator, hadn't said much when she'd asked him what his plans were for New Year's Eve, and appeared to be deep in thought. "I'm going to grab a raspberry wine cooler from the minibar. Do you want one?"

Her question was met by silence. Jada glanced over her shoulder, saw Max standing in the hallway instead of inside her suite and frowned. Couldn't understand what he was doing, and why he was dodging her gaze. "You're not coming in?"

Stepping back, he stuffed his hands into the front pockets of his khakis and jingled the coins inside. "No. It's late, and we have a full day ahead of us tomorrow. The private island tour starts at seven a.m., and if I want to be alert I need a full night's sleep."

Jada didn't laugh at his joke. He was lying. It was only nine o'clock, much too early for a party animal like Max to retire for the night. Having been his assistant for years, Jada knew that he didn't go to bed until midnight or later, and was awake and raring to go every morning by the crack of dawn.

Questions overwhelmed her mind. *Is he meeting up with someone else?* Slanting her head to the right, Jada studied his face for signs of deception. Had he made a connection with one of the female celebrities at the party? Was that why he was anxious to leave? They'd been joined at the hip since arriving at the resort that morning, and he'd scarcely used his cell phone, but that didn't mean he hadn't made late-night plans with someone else. Instead of wondering what was going on, Jada asked, "Max, what's wrong? I thought we were having fun."

Seconds passed, lasted so long that Jada realized he wasn't going to answer the question. She didn't understand why he was suddenly giving her the cold shoulder. They'd had a great day together—hanging out at the resort, eating delicious food, chatting about their hobbies and interests for hours—and making love inside her suite would be the perfect end to a perfect date. For once, his cell phone wasn't ringing or buzzing off the hook, and having his undivided attention made Jada feel special, as if he cared about her and wanted to make her happy. And he had. He'd been a perfect gentleman since they'd arrived in Hawaii, and Jada wanted to create more wonderful memories with him. Being on his arm was a thrill, and she'd enjoyed meeting his celebrity friends at Wendell Coleman's birthday bash, but the highlight of their trip was hanging out in the private cabana, talking and kissing.

Hearing a pop, Jada glanced around the suite for the source of the noise. Her gaze strayed to the balcony window. Fireworks lit up the night sky, and the dazzling display brought a smile to her lips. *Wendell Coleman sure knows how to party!*

"It's nothing personal," Max said quietly. "You're tipsy, and I don't want you to wake up in the morning and hate me for taking advantage of you."

Please do! Jada had never heard anything more absurd, but instead of rolling her eyes she tried to soothe his fears. "Max, I won't. Furthermore, I'm not tipsy. I feel great!" To prove it, she walked toward him in a straight line, reciting the alphabet. "See! I *told* you I wasn't drunk."

"I still don't think it's a good idea I come in, so I'll see you tomorrow. Good night."

Max turned to leave, but Jada grabbed his arm and pulled him inside her suite. "Not so fast." Determined to have her way, and her man, she said, "I'm not ready for you to go."

Slamming the door shut with the back of her foot, she set her sights on Max.

"What now?" He looked amused, as if he was trying not to laugh. "You're in control."

Desire consumed her. It was so strong and powerful Jada couldn't fight it, and did what she'd been fantasizing about for years. What she'd been dreaming of doing from the moment she'd first laid eyes on him. Kissing him hard on the mouth, with every ounce of passion coursing through her veins, Jada ripped his shirt from his body and caressed his broad, muscled chest with her hands. Stroked his shoulders. Rubbed his nipples. Licked and sucked his earlobe into her mouth. "You feel amazing," she purred, her voice a breathless whisper. "Don't worry. We won't do anything you're not comfortable with. I promise."

"Hey, that's *my* line!"

Laughing and kissing, they stumbled through the suite and collapsed onto the king-size bed. The lights were low, perfect for lovemaking, and classical music was playing in the distance, adding to the romantic ambience in the room. Max took his time undressing her, and Jada reveled in his touch. She loved feeling his mouth against hers, on her neck and shoulders, and giggled when he flicked his tongue against her ears. Pleasure engulfed her body. Her nipples hardened, and her sex tingled.

Max cupped her breasts in his hands. Jada cried out. Begged him for more. Told him to do it again. Moaned to the heavens when he obliged. Her blood pressure spiked, causing the room to spin around her, and Jada feared she was going to pass out. His lips were against her mouth, his hands were in her hair, then between her legs, turning her out with each flick of his long, deft fingers.

Jada sucked in a breath. Every inch of her body was throbbing with need, desperate for him. His fingers played in her curls, parted her fleshy lips, then swirled inside her sex. In and out, back and forth, each move more explosive than the last. Electricity singed her skin, and moans tumbled off her lips. Her throat was hoarse, and her body was on fire, scalding hot. *I'm going to explode, and he isn't even inside me yet!*

To regain the upper hand, Jada rolled on top of Max and pinned his hands above his head. Pressing soft, featherlight kisses along his collarbone and torso, she told him how handsome he was. His body was perfect, flawless, and exploring his chiseled physique with her tongue and hands was the most thrilling experience of her life. "This is amazing… *You're* amazing, and I can't get enough of you…"

Her appetite for him was insatiable, and the longer they kissed and caressed each other's bodies, the harder it was for Jada to control her emotions. She started to tell Max the truth, that she loved him with all her heart, but when he gazed deep into her eyes she got cold feet. Was scared that if she did he'd lose interest in her, and Jada didn't want to chase him off. In one night, they'd gone from zero to one hundred, but she'd been dreaming about this moment for years, and wanted to experience the pleasure of his lovemaking. Couldn't imagine a better Christmas gift.

"What are you doing to me? I've never felt this way before…" His voice was husky, filled with desperation, and it was the sexiest thing Jada had ever heard. An orgasm for her ears. Feeling powerful, as if she could do anything she wanted, she unbuckled his pants, yanked down his zipper and slid a hand inside his boxer briefs.

Pleasure shot straight to her core. Her mouth watered and her heart thumped at the sight of his erection—long, wide and ridiculously thick. She wanted it between her legs, and she shivered uncontrollably at the thought. Jada stroked his shaft until it was good and hard.

Facing him, she watched his eyes roll in the back of his head, his lips part, and heard a groan fall from his mouth. He cradled her head in his hands, holding her in place, giving her a rush. Jada knew what he wanted, what he needed, and answered his unspoken request.

To please him, she lowered her head to his lap, gripped his erection and sucked it into her mouth. Swirled her tongue around it. Licked the length. Tickled and nibbled the tip. Stroked it with her hands. That morning, while waiting in the lobby for Max to arrange their private island tour with the front desk clerk, she'd flipped through the January issue of *Cosmopolitan* magazine. Recalling the sizzling sex tips she'd read, Jada decided to put the article to the test. Increasing her pace, she sucked his erection harder, faster, and moved her body in a sensual way, rubbing her breasts against his skin.

Max groaned, then cursed in Spanish, and Jada knew she was doing something right. She was emboldened by his praise, and her confidence grew. She'd never had sex before, let alone made the first move on a guy, but calling the shots in the bedroom made her feel fierce, invincible, more ballsy than Wonder Woman. Jada liked how he tasted, enjoyed pleasing him, and varied her pressure and speed to excite him. It worked. Max pulled her to his chest and kissed her passionately on the mouth, stealing her breath for the second time in minutes.

"You're something else, you know that?" Kissing the corner of her lips, he tenderly stroked her cheeks with the back of his hand. "Are you sure this is what you want?"

Jada nodded her head. "Yes. I want you to be my first."

The grin slid off his face.

"Come again?" His voice carried a note of confusion. "*What* did you just say?"

"I'm a virgin, and you're the only man I want to make love to."

Max sat up, then shot to his feet.

Panic seized her heart. "What's wrong? Where are you going?"

"I shouldn't be here. This is a mistake."

"No, it's not. I want this, Max. I want you."

Max grabbed his clothes off the floor, put them on, then dragged a hand down the length of his face. "Your first time should be special, with someone who's a hundred percent committed to you, not a casual hookup in Maui that doesn't mean anything."

Is that what this is? A casual hookup that doesn't mean anything to you? Something broke inside her, causing her spirits to sink and her heart to ache. Crushed by his words, she felt her eyes tear up, but Jada willed herself not to cry. Didn't want Max to know his confession was a blow to her self-esteem. Jada snatched a pillow off the bed and covered her naked body. Five minutes ago, she'd been all over him, and now she just wanted Max to leave her suite.

"You're an incredible woman, and I think the world of you, but I don't want a serious relationship," Max said, his smile apologetic.

Ice spread through her veins, chilling her to the bone, but Jada governed her temper. Didn't lash out at him. She'd been fooling herself. This wasn't her. Sex without love was meaningless, and even though she wanted him to be her first, she had to protect her heart. Max was right: she deserved better. As much as she loved him, she loved herself more, and wanted a relationship, not a Christmas fling. One day, she'd meet the right man who'd be worthy of her, and it saddened her that it wasn't Max.

"This is wrong… I shouldn't have come here… I don't know what I was thinking…"

The desk phone rang, and Max broke off speaking.

"Aren't you going to answer it? It could be important."

Shaking her head, Jada lowered her gaze to the carpet as she searched the room for her dress and undergarments. Finding them, she snatched them off the couch, put them on and made a beeline for the bathroom. Jada caught sight of her reflection in the wall mirror and cringed. Wished she could click her heels three times and return to LA. Her hair was sticking up, mascara was smeared across her cheeks, and her outfit was a wrinkled mess. Jada wanted to hide out in the bathroom until Max was gone, but when his voice cracked she stopped dead in her tracks.

"Derek, talk to me," he demanded, shouting into the receiver. "What happened?"

Jada spun around, facing him. Seeing the tension in his jaw, she feared something bad had happened to Taylor while she was with her mom. Was the tween in trouble? Had she been hurt?

Pushing her feelings aside, Jada approached the desk and placed a hand on Max's shoulder. She wanted him to know she was there for him, if he needed her. And it was obvious he did. Hanging his head, he wiped at his eyes with the back of his hand. Jada was hurt that he'd rejected her, but she wanted to comfort him. Ending the call, Max dropped the phone in the cradle and kicked the desk chair so hard it fell over with a thud.

"What's wrong? What happened?"

Closing his eyes, he took a deep breath and raked a hand through his short black hair. "My dad collapsed this afternoon and was rushed to the hospital. He's stable now, and my brothers were able to take him home, but doctors don't think he'll make it through the night."

"Max, I am so sorry. Reginald looked great last night at the holiday mixer, and I thought his health had improved."

"We all did, but his supposed breakthrough was false hope. He's dying, and there's nothing anyone can do about it." Max crossed the room, unlocked the adjoining door and yanked it open. "I'm going to call Captain Woodson, and let her know our plans have changed. I'll be back to get you in ten minutes, so please be ready to go."

Max left, slamming the door behind him, and Jada leaned against the couch. Her heart broke for him. His father was dying, his business rival was gunning for him, and he was having problems with his daughter. No wonder he didn't want a serious relationship. He had enough on his plate, and Jada didn't want to be a burden to him, a nuisance like all the other women in his past who wouldn't take no for an answer.

Reality struck, and her thoughts cleared. It was time for her to face the truth, to stop pretending she could have a successful relationship with Max one day. Sure, they had great conversations about life, and shared morals and values, but they weren't meant to be, and she needed to move on. His well-being was no longer her concern, and once they returned to LA she had to distance herself from him. They were over, and she had to put the past behind her.

Tomorrow, she'd contact Shazir and accept his job

offer. Why not? It was a great opportunity, with a fantastic agency, and she'd be a fool to turn it down. Her mind made up, Jada stood, grabbed her hand luggage from the closet and hurled clothes, shoes and beauty products inside.

Chapter 17

On Thursday afternoon, Max sat beside Reginald at the round walnut-brown table inside the boardroom at the Prescott George headquarters, hoping for his dad's sake that Demetrius would show up for the emergency meeting that had been scheduled for two o'clock. The committee had planned to gather on Monday, to discuss the San Diego sabotage case with all parties involved, but Demetrius had canceled at the last minute. All week, he'd been giving them the runaround, claiming he had the stomach flu one day, a migraine the next, and car trouble yesterday, but Max didn't believe him. Demetrius would do anything to avoid facing Reginald and the board members. Tired of the businessman's games, his brothers had offered to pick him up at his Malibu mansion and agreed to personally escort him to the conference room.

To pass the time, Reginald chatted with the board members. His speech was slow, and talking seemed to require all the strength he had, but he joked around with his long-time friends. Max had a lot on his mind, and couldn't stop his thoughts from racing, but he listened to the conversation, nodding in agreement as his dad reminisced about the past. Despite his failing health, Reginald was in a good mood, and listening to his father crack jokes made Max realize all hope wasn't lost. His dad was still alive, and he was going to cherish every moment they had together.

"Seriously, Reginald, how are you keeping?" a media mogul asked with a sad smile.

"It's true what they say. You can't keep a good man down. Or quiet!"

A software company CEO, with a thick mustache, spoke in a jovial voice. "I believe you, old friend. I haven't seen you this lively since you won a million at the Bellagio in '09. Blackjack always was your game, and I bet you still have a hot hand."

"That was one hell of a weekend." A pensive expression covered Reginald's gaunt face. "To be honest, it's a blur in my mind. I drank a whole *lot* of tequila that night, and so did you!"

Chuckles filled the air as Reginald bumped fists with his friends.

Max drummed his fingers on the table. Pulling back the sleeve of his navy Tom Ford suit jacket, he glanced at his diamond watch. Demetrius was thirty minutes late for the meeting, and hadn't even had the decency to call and explain his tardiness to the group.

Max cursed under his breath. *You've got to be kidding me*, he fumed, gripping the armrest of his leather chair. *Who does Demetrius think he is? The Donald? Why is he jerking us around? Doesn't he realize this is a matter of life and death?*

Struggling to control his temper, Max took his cell

phone out of his jacket pocket and typed in his password. Staring at his screensaver—a selfie he'd taken with Jada at Wendell Coleman's birthday party— brought cherished memories to mind. He tried not to think about their romantic weekend in Maui, but it was a losing battle.

Images of her bombarded his thoughts. The fact that Jada was a virgin who wanted him to be her first lover made him desire her even more. Made him realize how special she was. She was his rock, the only person besides his father whom he could count on, and Max missed seeing her around the office. And venting to her about his problems. He hadn't spoken to Jada since they'd returned to LA on Monday, and although he longed to hear her voice, he couldn't bring himself to call her. Not after the way he'd treated her in Maui. There was no doubt in his mind that she wanted nothing to do with him, and he didn't want to upset her.

His thoughts returned to yesterday's staff meeting, and pain stabbed his heart. He'd learned from one of his employees that Jada had accepted a full-time position as Shazir's personal assistant, and trolling the talent scout's social-media pages had confirmed it. Shazir had bragged about his gorgeous new hire online, making Max feel even worse for his behavior in Hawaii, but it was too late to apologize. He had to move on. He wished her well, but he hated the idea of her working for his rival. Even worse, Jada had cut ties with Taylor, and his daughter was devastated. Max told her not to worry, reminded her that she had friends and family who loved her, but nothing he said made Taylor feel better. That afternoon, she'd called as he was driving to the Prescott George headquarters, upset because Jada wasn't answering her texts or phone calls. Hearing his daughter cry broke his heart, but Jada had made her decision, and even though Max didn't agree with it, he had to respect it.

The conference room door flew open, and Demetrius shuffled inside, wearing a gray fedora, wrinkled golf attire and a long face. Trey and Derek followed behind him, sat down at the table and nodded at Max. Anxious to get the meeting started, Max put his cell phone on the table, cleared his throat and addressed the board members.

"My brothers and I requested this emergency meeting to not only prove my dad had nothing to do with what happened to the San Diego chapter, but that he was framed by his oldest and dearest friend, Demetrius Davis." Max reached into his brown leather satchel at the foot of his chair and searched for the manila folder. It was the smoking gun, the information he'd searched months for, and thanks to the private investigator he'd hired, he finally had the documentation he needed to clear his father's name. From the detailed report, he'd learned that the computer leaks and viruses that had affected the San Diego chapter had originated from a server in Demetrius's office.

And that wasn't all. He'd tracked down Demetrius's ex-wife, Ellen Davis, in nearby San Bernardino, and met with the soft-spoken mother of three on Tuesday afternoon. Ellen had told Max everything he needed to know about her vindictive ex-husband. After Demetrius learned about Ellen's affair with Reginald, he'd vowed to get even during the divorce proceedings and had made good on his threat. He'd seen to it that Ellen was ostracized by their friends and had told their adult daughters about the affair. What he'd uncovered about the celebrated businessman was mind-blowing, more shocking than an episode of *Scandal*, and every salacious word of the five-page report was true. Max was angry about what Demetrius had done to Ellen and Reginald, but a small part of him felt bad for the businessman. Reginald had not only broken the Bro Code, he'd humiliated the man he called his Brother, and nothing his dad ever said or did would alleviate Demetrius's pain.

Unable to find the folder, Max dumped the satchel on the table. He searched through his things, but it wasn't there. He scratched his head. Where could it be? That morning, when Christina stopped by his office to discuss the Prescott George Christmas Eve charity fund-raiser, he'd taken the folder out of his desk and put it in his satchel. Had he misplaced it? Accidentally left it in his office? Max didn't know where the document was and hoped his screwup wouldn't affect his dad's case.

"Find what you're looking for, son?" Demetrius asked with a crooked grin.

Max could smell his arrogance, his pride, and suspected that Demetrius had something to do with the missing document. Choosing to dwell on the positives, not the negatives, he abandoned his search for the folder, clasped his hands in front of him and addressed the balding businessman. "I had a document detailing your involvement in the San Diego sabotage case, but unfortunately, it's gone missing. Thankfully, I have Ellen's cell number. Should I call her, or do you want to man up and come clean about what you did to my father?"

The grin slid off Demetrius's face, and panic flashed in his eyes.

"Demetrius, is this true?" a board member asked, stroking his salt-and-pepper goatee. "Are you responsible for the break-ins, computer leaks and vandalism that plagued the San Diego chapter last summer? Were you angry at Reginald, and framed him to take the fall?"

"This is your last chance. Tell us the truth, or I'm calling your ex-wife." To loosen Demetrius's tongue, and prove he was serious about his threat, Max grabbed his cell phone off the table, accessed his Contacts app and searched for Ellen's number. "I'll put her on speakerphone, so everyone can hear what she has to say about your bitter quest for revenge."

"No! Don't!" Demetrius shot to his feet, mumbling under his breath as he paced the length of the sun-filled conference room. Max couldn't make out what he was saying, but his hunched shoulders, woeful disposition and teary voice said it all: he was guilty.

"Tell us what you did. This is important." Trey stood. He joined Demetrius in front of the window and placed a hand on his shoulder. "My dad is dying, and you owe it to me and my brothers to tell us what happened."

"Reginald is ill, and we want to clear his name before he…" Unable to finish his thought, Derek broke off speaking and hung his head. "Do the right thing, Demetrius—"

"I did it! It's true! I admit it!" Demetrius shouted.

Silence fell across the room.

"I was angry about the affair, and I wanted to get even!" Demetrius fell into an armchair, took off his iron-rimmed eyeglasses and dropped his face in his palms. "I just wanted Reginald to suffer and get kicked out of the organization he loved so much, but I never meant for the San Diego chapter to suffer, or for the LA chapter to get a six-month suspension. That was never my intention…"

Relief flowed through Max, but he stared at Demetrius with disgust. He couldn't believe the man who'd been like a second father to him could be so vindictive and mean.

"I… I—I didn't think something like that would happen," Demetrius continued, his voice wobbling with emotion. "I messed up, and I'm sincerely sorry about the trouble I caused."

Demetrius broke down then, cried so hard his shoulders shook, and his deep, racking sobs filled the air. Reginald rolled his wheelchair across the room, spoke in a quiet voice, just loud enough for the disgraced businessman to hear, and clapped him on the back.

"Reginald, man, I'm sorry about what I did. Can you find it in your heart to forgive me?"

"Of course I can. You're not the only one who's made mistakes. I've done some pretty messed-up things in my life, and if Trey and Derek can forgive me for being a pitiful excuse for a father when they were kids, then I can forgive you, too."

Blown away by his father's speech, Max stared at Reginald with wide eyes. Like his brothers, he'd loved Demetrius deeply, but he was disappointed about the spiteful things he'd done. Max didn't know if he'd ever be able to forgive him. Maybe in time, but not today. Not until he answered for what he'd done to Reginald. Board members, still reeling from Demetrius's confession, looked bewildered.

"What happens now?" Demetrius wiped at his cheeks. "What is my punishment?"

Heads bent, board members spoke quietly for several seconds.

"You owe restitution to both the San Diego and Los Angeles chapters," the committee chairman announced in a stern voice. "Effective immediately, your membership has been indefinitely revoked. We wish we could keep this ugly situation quiet and deal with it in-house, but we have no choice but to contact the authorities. You broke the law, and you have to answer for what you did in San Diego…"

Max glanced down at the table, saw his cell phone light up and stared at the number on the screen. A groan rose in his throat. He didn't want to talk to Shay. Not now. They'd argued days earlier about Taylor going on a "date" with TaVonte to a Sunday matinee movie, and their conversation had left a bitter taste in his mouth. Max didn't understand why his ex-wife was going out of her way to piss him off, and he was sick of her appeasing Taylor. These days, his daughter was acting like a spoiled brat who thought she didn't have to listen to her father. Max knew Taylor was upset that Jada was out of their lives, but that was no excuse for her behavior. Max thought of letting the call go to voice mail, but knew that if he did, Shay would ream him out for being an absentee father, and he didn't feel like hearing her complain.

Wanting privacy, Max grabbed his phone off the table, then exited the conference room. "Shay, what is it? I'm in the middle of an important meeting, and I can't talk."

Deep, racking sobs filled the line, and Max feared his ex-wife had lost her mother. Yesterday, when he'd talked to Taylor, she'd mentioned that her grandma Virginia was back in the hospital due to complications from surgery. "Shay, I am so sorry—"

"You should be!" she snapped. "Taylor is missing, and it's all your fault. I'll *never* forgive you if something bad happens to my baby girl."

Her words didn't register, didn't add up in his mind. "What did you just say?"

"I came to pick her up from school, but she's not here, and no one knows where she is."

Max felt a sinking feeling in his stomach and a painful sensation in his chest.

"I... I—I can't lose her," Shay stammered. "Taylor's my world, and I love her more than anything. She's the best thing that's ever happened to me."

He asked her to speak to school officials, but Shay was too emotional to do what he asked.

"Wh-wh-what if she's been kidnapped? What if someone took my baby?"

"Shay, don't talk like that." Charging toward the elevator, Max noticed the time on the wall clock as he took his car keys out of his pocket. He refused to think the worst. School had ended ten minutes earlier, and Max was convinced there was a good reason for his daughter's absence. "I'm on my way. Don't move. We'll find her. I swear."

"You better, and when we do we're going to court to revise our custody agreement."

His heart dropped, and his car keys fell from his hands. Max tried to speak, but he didn't have the words. He wanted to find his daughter, not argue with his ex-wife.

"I'm going to fight for sole custody to protect Taylor, from the emotional roller coaster of being *your* child," she spit. "You're the problem, Max, and I won't let you hurt her again."

His vision blurred, and fear knotted inside his chest. Max had only cried three times in his life: the morning his mother had died at UCLA Medical Center, the day Taylor was born and the night Reginald had revealed his terminal cancer diagnosis, but the thought of losing custody of his only daughter—his pride and joy—made his eyes well up with tears that spilled down his cheeks.

Chapter 18

Jada found an empty space in the parking lot at Malibu Elementary School, parked under a cluster of leafy palm trees and threw open her car door. Racing up the flower-lined walkway, she noticed kids playing soccer, custodians sweeping the sidewalks and parents chatting on the brick steps.

Entering the school, Jada took off her sunglasses. Sunshine splashed through the windows, casting a glow around the colorful posters, framed artwork and inspirational quotes that covered the vibrant walls. Leafy potted plants flanked the doors, the air smelled of scented markers, and pop music played in the distance. Jada had been to the school once, to attend Taylor's band concert, and remembering how much fun they'd had eating ice cream at a nearby café afterward made a sad smile fill her lips.

"We've looked everywhere," Shay said. "It's time to call the police. They should be involved."

Max disagreed. "It's only been thirty minutes. Let's keep looking. I *know* she's here somewhere…"

Jada entered the office and noticed a large group of people gathered around the front desk, arguing. Max was there with his brothers, school administration officials and a short, stocky man she didn't recognize. The stranger, dressed in a Dodgers baseball cap and navy coveralls, stood behind Shay, and it was obvious by the way he was touching her that they were a couple. Young and fashionable, with a wardrobe that could rival a Grammy-winning pop star's, Shay was always well put together, but today the single mom had tearstained cheeks, a runny nose and a crooked ponytail.

"Jada? What are you doing here?"

At the sound of Max's voice, Jada nodded in greeting and forced a smile. Tried not to let her nervousness show, even though her palms were damp and her knees were knocking together. As usual, he smelled delicious and looked handsome in his tailored suit, silk tie and polished shoes. Days had passed with no word from him, and although they'd never be a couple or work together again, she'd longed to talk to him. To laugh and joke around like they used to. Memories of Max and Taylor were never far from her thoughts, but for her own sanity she had to move on with her life, even though every day without them made her feel worse.

Staring down at her leggings, she shifted her sneaker-clad feet and tugged at the sleeve of her sweatshirt. She wished she'd had time to shower and change before driving to the school, but Shay had called her in a panic while Jada was working out with Aubree and Delilah at LA Fitness, and she'd grabbed her bag and left without any thought to her appearance.

"I called her," Shay answered, stepping forward.

"Jada loves Taylor, too, and I thought she could help us find her. The more people looking for her, the better, right?"

"Yes, of course. Good thinking," Max said, slowly nodding his head.

"Thanks for coming, Jada. We really appreciate it." Holding a wad of Kleenex, Shay dabbed at her eyes, then blew her nose. "Taylor's classmates said she was in the band room at the end of the day, but we searched the entire building, with no luck. We checked out her favorite areas in the neighborhood, too, but came up empty. I don't know what else to do."

"Has anyone called TaVonte Williams?" Jada asked, thinking aloud. "He's her best friend, and if anyone will know where Taylor is, it's TaVonte. These days they're practically joined at the hip, and they like to hang out after school."

The vice principal stepped forward and shook his head. "Unfortunately, TaVonte was absent today. I spoke to his grandmother several minutes ago, and she explained that he's home sick with the flu."

Something hit the window, drawing Jada's gaze across the room. Students were playing soccer, and every time the ball hit the glass the group giggled. Noticing the man-made lake across the field, Jada remembered something Taylor had said weeks earlier, while they were having their pedicures done at the beauty salon. *There's a lake near my school, and TaVonte and I have lunch at our favorite bench every day... Sometimes we throw rocks into the lake and make wishes... Sometimes we listen to music or record videos...*

"We should check the lake," Jada said. "It's a long shot, but you never know."

"Y-y-you think Taylor's in there?" Shay stammered, her eyes wide with alarm.

"No, she might be there with some of her friends. It's her favorite hang-out spot."

Max touched her forearm. "Are you sure?"

Her thoughts scattered, but she found her voice. "It's just a hunch. I could be wrong, but it's worth checking out. We have nothing to lose."

Everyone filed out of the office and through the front door. Jada wanted to run across the field, shouting Taylor's name, but resisted the urge. Feeling guilty for not responding to the tween's earlier messages, she hoped her silence hadn't pushed Taylor to run away, and purposed in her heart to do something special for the fifth grader during the Christmas holidays.

"She's there!" Shay yelled, breaking out into a slow jog. "Taylor's wearing her school uniform, but I'd recognize her floral jean jacket anywhere!"

From where Jada was standing, she could see the bewildered expression on Taylor's face and hoped the tween wasn't mad at her for leading her parents to her secret hiding spot. Mother, father and daughter embraced. Then Max picked Taylor up off the ground and swung her in the air. One by one, everyone hugged Taylor, but when Jada waved at the tween, her gaze darkened.

Regret flooded Jada's body, making her feel low, but she smiled in greeting. "Hey, kiddo," she said, ignoring the painful knot in her throat. "How's it going?"

Shrugging, Taylor stared down at her black Mary Jane shoes. "Okay, I guess."

"Are you mad at me?"

"Not anymore." She kicked a rock across the field. "If you don't want to talk to me anymore, that's fine.

It's no big deal. I have lots of friends, and they think I'm great."

"You are, Taylor. You're the smartest, funniest fifth grader I know, and I love hanging out with you."

Hope sparked in Taylor's eyes, brightening her face. "You do?"

"Of course I do." Reaching out, Jada took Taylor's hand in her own and squeezed it. "If it's okay with your mom and dad, maybe we could go ice-skating this weekend. My treat. What do you say?"

Taylor cocked her head to the right and flashed a cheeky smile. "Throw in some cookie dough ice cream *and* a chocolate milkshake from Creams and Dreams, and you're on!"

Everyone laughed. Plans were made for the group to have dinner at a local restaurant, and as they started back across the field, Jada realized she'd made a huge mistake distancing herself from Taylor. *What's wrong with me? What was I thinking? How could I* not *be friends with the bubbly, fun-loving tween with the outrageous sense of humor?* That was like living without the sun, and just because she wasn't friends with Max didn't mean she shouldn't be friends with his daughter. Jada adored Taylor, and made up her mind to talk to Shay and Max about having a girls' day with the tween once a month.

"Jada, hold up." Max gripped her arm, then slid in front of her. "We need to talk."

Her mouth dried. Was he bothered by what she'd said to Taylor? Did he have a problem with her making plans with his daughter? Opposed to them spending time together? Jada didn't want to talk to Max, but he was blocking her path to the parking lot, and since she didn't want to cause a scene she decided to hear him out.

He had two minutes to say his piece, and that was it; she wasn't giving him a second more of her time. Tired and hungry, Jada wanted to go home and make dinner, not shoot the breeze with her former crush.

Former crush? repeated her inner voice. *Who are you kidding? You* still *love him!*

"You're incredible." His gaze and his tone were filled with awe. "You did it again."

Jada raised an eyebrow. "Did what?"

"Saved the day. I don't know how you do it, but you always say and do the right thing, and as usual you were bang on. Thank you for helping us find Taylor. We couldn't have done it without you."

Her brain was filled with conflicting thoughts, and she struggled to focus on what Max was saying. Max sounded sincere, and he was wearing an earnest expression on his face, but she wasn't moved by his compliments or his effusive praise.

"I owe you an apology for the way I acted in Maui. I never meant to hurt you…"

Jada held up a hand to silence him, but he continued on with his speech. His apology meant nothing to her. She had a strength and confidence she'd never had before, felt as if she'd grown in leaps and bounds over the last few weeks, and she wasn't afraid to tell Max what she thought of him.

"Do you forgive me?"

"No, I don't. I'm done with you."

His jaw dropped, but Jada pretended not to notice the shell-shocked expression on his face. When it came to Max, she was a two-time loser, but from now on she was putting herself first—not him—and if that meant keeping him at arm's length, so be it.

"Jada, you don't mean that. We've been a team for a while, and we have a long history—"

"One minute you want to be with me, and the next you don't. I can't win with you, Max, and I'm sick of trying," she confessed. "I deserve to be with someone who appreciates me, someone who isn't going to run off at the first sign of trouble, and that person isn't you."

"Jada, I screwed up, and I'm sorry." Sighing deeply, he leaned against the hood of his Porsche. "I was scared, and I didn't want history to repeat itself. That's why I pulled away from you in Maui."

"Scared of what? I'd never do anything to hurt you. You know that."

"I've seen relationships that started with promise, passion and love turn to hate all too often, most notably my marriage, and I didn't want it to happen again. Add to that, I have to think about Taylor, and what's best for her, too."

"Relationships are full of ups and downs, but if couples are committed to making things work they'll be successful. I'm not a relationship expert, but my grandparents were happily married for over fifty years, and I plan to imitate their example. Love is hard work, but anything worth having is worth fighting for, and I'm a fighter."

"I believe you." Clasping her hand, Max pulled her to his chest and folded his arm around her waist. "Jada, I'm tired of running. I know what I want and it's you. I'm all in, and if you give me a chance you'll never regret it."

Taken aback by his words, Jada stood silent for several seconds before she spoke.

"Talk about a dramatic turnaround," she said, unable to believe what she was hearing. "Five days ago you didn't want to settle down, and now you're ready to commit. What gives?"

"Jada, you're the right woman for me because you're honest, trustworthy and ridiculously kind. You want the best for me and my daughter, and I love your sincerity…"

Love? The word ricocheted around in her mind, then shot straight to her heart. She couldn't take her eyes off him. Jada was drowning, sinking fast, and there was nothing she would do about it. She was weak for Max, always had been, and there was nowhere else she'd rather be than in his arms. He'd won her over with his gentle caress, his honesty and his boyish smile, and Jada believed he was genuinely sorry about the way he'd treated her in the past.

"That's right, Jada. I love you, and I want to be with you more than anything."

Max nuzzled his face against her cheek, and she giggled as he nibbled her earlobe.

"And I need you to come back to the agency…"

He smelled divine, of expensive cologne and aftershave, and when he licked his lips her mind wandered. His touch was warm, wanted against her skin, and it was hard to concentrate on what he was saying when all Jada wanted to do was kiss him.

"I don't know how much money Shazir offered you, but I'll double it," he vowed. "I won't lose you to him, so I hope that creep is ready for a fight."

Jada hid a smile. There was nothing to think about, nothing to consider. She'd return to Millennium Talent Agency in the New Year and resume working for Max, but she decided to play it cool, didn't want him to know she was overjoyed by his generous, unexpected offer. Not only would she have enough money for her university tuition, she'd be able to help her dad pay off his outstanding credit card bills. "Max, I'm not making any promises, but I think we can work something out. We'll discuss your proposition in the New Year."

"Anything you say, baby." Chuckling, he patted her hips. "I like your new look, but you don't have to get hair extensions or wear revealing clothes for me to notice you. Just be yourself, Jada. That's more than enough."

The smile in her heart spread to her mouth.

"Did you know kissing is good for your health?" Max asked, cupping her chin in his hand. "Studies show it floods the body with endorphins and instantly improves your mood."

Jada arched an eyebrow. "Really? I had no idea. Let's put the theory to the test."

"I was hoping you'd say that." Max crushed his lips to her mouth, slowly and deliberately kissing her as his hands stroked her neck, shoulders and arms.

Sparks flew, and electricity singed her skin.

Cheers and whistles filled the air, and Jada knew they had company in the parking lot. She suspected it was Trey and Derek hooting and hollering like fans at a Lakers game, but Jada didn't care who was watching them. She continued kissing the man she loved, couldn't get enough of his warm, sensuous mouth. They had a lot to discuss—her career, smoothing things over with Taylor, improving his relationship with his ex—but now that they were a couple, Jada was confident they could tackle any challenge, any obstacle, as long as they did it together.

Chapter 19

"It's going to be damn hard for me to keep my hands to myself tonight," Max confessed, a glimmer in his eye and a grin on his mouth. "You look like a sexy Christmas angel, and I'm dying to get you home and *out* of that stunning gown."

Heat flooded Jada's cheeks. Her boyfriend was as handsome as he was charming, and entering the glittering Prescott George grand ballroom on Max's arm made Jada want to pinch herself to prove she wasn't dreaming. He was her dashing ebony prince, and she reveled in his closeness.

"You are the best Christmas gift I have ever been given, and I'm proud to have you on my arm." Max kissed the tip of her nose, then her lips. "*Woman*, I want to ravish you."

Happiness filled her as she snuggled against his chest. They were a new couple, but her heart had always belonged to Max. Her boyfriend was the dictionary definition of a perfect gentleman, and every time he rushed to open a door for her or pulled out her chair, her admiration for him grew. They'd been inseparable since the afternoon they'd left Malibu Elementary School, and now that Jada was returning to Millennium Talent Agency as Max's executive assistant, life was perfect. A dream. Everything she'd ever wanted. "Be patient," she whispered. "Good things come to those who wait, so pump your brakes, Mr. Man."

Max chuckled. "Fine, but don't blame me when I pounce on you later!"

Please do, she thought, her body tingling at the thought of them finally making love. Jada was ready to consummate their relationship, but Max wanted to wait. He said there was no rush since they had the rest of their lives to please each other, and she'd agreed with him. Though once they started kissing it was hard to stop, and if not for Derek knocking on the window of Max's Escalade, they'd still be in the parking lot, making out in his SUV.

"I'm thrilled to welcome everyone to our annual Prescott George Christmas Eve Charity Gala," said the president, waving from the stage. "Tonight isn't just about celebrating with friends and associates. It's about raising funds for a worthy, life-changing cause..."

The über-exclusive event raised hundreds of thousands of dollars for charity every year, and the extravagant silver and gold decorations, esteemed guests, world-class menu and surprise performers made the black-tie party the most coveted ticket in LA. Mingling with city officials, former presidents, television personalities and international superstars, Jada tried not to gawk at the celebrities in attendance. Max loved to socialize with his fellow Prescott George members and their families, while Jada was content in the background, admiring the man she loved.

Gazing down at her outfit, an early Christmas present from Max, she smoothed a hand over her waist and along her hips. She'd fallen in love with the teal off-the-shoulder tuxedo dress the moment she'd tried it on at the Rodeo Drive boutique, and when Taylor declared it was *The One*, Jada had agreed. To complement the dress, she'd styled her hair in an elegant braided bun, added diamond accessories and silver-tone stilettos. When Max picked Jada up at her town house, they'd snapped dozens of pictures and texted them to Taylor, and the tween's witty messages had made them both laugh out loud.

Thinking about the sweet fifth grader filled Jada's heart with love. After the stunt she'd pulled at school, her parents had grounded her for a week, and after several closed-door meetings between mom and dad, things were running more smoothly in the Moore household. Max still hadn't come to terms with the fact that his baby girl wasn't a "baby" anymore, but he was making a concerted effort to be more understanding. The schism between Shay and Max wasn't going to be solved overnight, but Jada was confident their relationship would improve in time. These days, she texted his ex regularly, and planned to have a spa day with Taylor, Shay and her cousins Aubree and Delilah to celebrate Jada's twenty-eighth birthday in February.

Finding table three, they joined the Moore family for cocktails and appetizers. Max introduced Jada to his stepsister, Bianca Duvall, and her blue-eyed date. They discussed the menu for Christmas Day, their plans for New Year's Eve and Prescott George affairs. Jada had fun chatting with Kiara and Alexis about their careers, and when the mom-to-be needed to use the ladies' room and insisted her friends join her, they kissed their boy-friends goodbye and grabbed their clutch bags.

Exiting the ballroom arm in arm, the women giggled and gossiped about the celebrities in attendance. In the lobby, they snapped pictures of the extravagant Christmas decorations, and when Jada's iPhone rang she answered it on the first ring. "Hello! Welcome to the North Pole!" she joked, laughing. "It's Ms. Claus!"

"I wish I could trade places with you," said a female voice with a British accent.

"Hello? Who is this?"

"Someone who envies you. You are *so* lucky to be dating Max Moore…"

Jada held her breath. She wanted to hang up, had a sinking feeling in her chest that the call was bad news, but was curious about what the woman had to say.

"I rented him last Saturday through the Rent-a-Bachelor fund-raiser, and he rocked my world. Literally. Toe-curling sex. Multiple orgasms. All. Night. Long."

A bitter taste filled Jada's mouth.

"Girl, it was the best sex of my life," the stranger purred, her tone one of awe. "You have no idea how lucky you are. Max is an exceptional lover, with a magic tongue, and just thinking about the things he did to me last weekend is making me wet—"

Disgusted, Jada narrowed her gaze. Not wanting to hear another filthy word, she pressed the end button, shoved her cell phone into her clutch purse and slumped against the wall. Glad Alexis and Kiara were in the bathroom and she was alone in the corridor, Jada took a moment to compose herself.

Resting a hand on her chest to slow her raging heartbeat, Jada tried to catch her breath. She wanted to make sense of what had just happened, but couldn't. Her thoughts were muddled, racing in circles, and she couldn't think straight. *Where was I last Saturday? What did I do?* Jada wondered, racking her brain for answers. *More important, where was Max?*

Seconds passed, but when Jada heard "What You Mean to Me," playing in the grand ballroom, she remembered where she had been last Saturday night. Hearing her dad's favorite song reminded Jada how much fun she'd had with her family. They'd eaten too much, drunk too much sparkling apple cider and watched the Christmas-movie marathon on BET. She'd invited Max to join them, but he'd had plans with his brothers, and promised to make it up to her in the New Year. Had he lied to her? Hooked up with someone else last Saturday night? Slept with another woman because Jada was an inexperienced virgin?

"You look like you could use a drink," Christina North, Demetrius's assistant, said, raising her cocktail glass in the air. Jada was glad that Christina was enjoying the party instead of hiding out, given what her former boss had admitted to. "Here, try some of my White Christmas Mojito. It's delicious."

Jada shook her head. "No, thanks. Christina, can I ask you something?"

"Sure, sweetie, anything. What's on your mind?"

"Did a woman rent Max last Saturday through the Rent-a-Bachelor program?"

"Probably. He's our most popular bachelor, and women can't get enough of him…"

Jada felt her eyes tear and her throat close up. She wanted to cover her ears, but she kept her hands at her sides and listened intently to what the brunette had to say.

"Apparently, he plans incredible evenings for his dates *and* gives them their money's worth, if you know what I mean." Giggling, Christina took her iPhone out of her purse, and after several swipes and taps, she fervently nodded her head. "Yup, I checked the logs, and an adult-film star named Nia Pearl paid five thousand dollars for a night with Max. She used her American Express card to pay, and also placed three more bookings for next week."

Christina's cell phone rang, and she excused herself to take the call. Jada was glad to see her go. She needed a moment alone, to process everything she'd just learned about Max. It was hard to believe he'd cheated on her, especially after everything they'd been through, but she'd be a fool to ignore the truth, and had to confront him. Now, before she lost her nerve.

"Sorry we took so long," Kiara said with an apologetic smile. "We were touching up our makeup, and got carried away discussing bridal shows and floral arrangements."

They returned to the ballroom, and the moment Jada saw Max, tension flooded her body. Guests mingled, took pictures and exchanged business cards, and danced to the live jazz band, but the festive, celebratory mood made her feel worse, not better. Max was an esteemed millionaire with celebrity friends, a private jet and gorgeous admirers, and Jada didn't belong in his world. *What was I thinking? Why did I think that we could ever work?*

"There you are." Max slipped an arm around her waist. "You were gone so long I thought you were lost. Baby, let's go. The party's on the dance floor, not over here."

"Who's Nia Pearl?" Jada blurted out, desperate to

get to the bottom of things. "And why did you lie to me about being with your brothers last Saturday?"

His eyes darkened and lines wrinkled his forehead. "Baby, what are you talking about? I didn't lie to you. We took my dad for steak, then watched the UFC fight at the Staples Center."

"Are you hooking up with a woman named Nia Pearl?"

"No, of course not. I'd never cheat on you, Jada. You're everything I need." Max cupped her face in his hands. "I don't know who that is. I've never met her, and I don't want to. All I want is you."

They stared at each other for a long, quiet moment, and her anger slowly dissolved.

"A woman just called my cell, claiming that you hooked up with her last Saturday, and I don't know what to think." But as the words left her mouth, Jada realized it wasn't true. She trusted Max and knew in her heart he didn't do the things the caller said he did. He was her future, the only man she wanted, and Jada believed in him. It didn't matter that they were from two different worlds; he was her soul mate, and she loved him with every fiber of her being.

"Max, I'm sorry," she said, wearing an apologetic smile. "I asked Christina to check the Rent-a-Bachelor logs, and when she confirmed the payment I got jealous. I thought you were cheating on me with another woman, and I freaked out."

His eyes thinned, his nostrils flared, and Jada feared Max was going to lose his temper. It was Christmas Eve, one of her favorite days of the year, and Jada didn't want anything to ruin the Prescott George charity bash. His brothers were slow-dancing with their fiancées, but Jada hoped that if she needed them they'd be able to help her calm Max down. "Baby, it doesn't matter. I believe in you, and that's all that matters."

"What did Christina say?" he roared, speaking through clenched teeth. "Tell me *now.*"

Max balled his hands into fists. He wanted to punch something, to take his frustrations out on the nearest wall, but since he didn't want to scare the other guests he took a deep breath. It didn't help, but when Jada kissed his lips his anger waned. A conversation he'd had with Demetrius weeks earlier played in his thoughts, and a light bulb flashed in his mind. All at once, the pieces of the puzzle fit. Why Christina had lied to Jada about his whereabouts last Saturday. Her unexpected visits to his office in recent weeks. Why his manila folder, filled with damning information about Demetrius, had suddenly gone missing. Why Christina couldn't look him in the eye when they spoke.

Fuming, he struggled to control his temper, the rage boiling up inside him. Searching the ballroom for Christina, he found her standing alone at the bar and decided to put his theory to the test. Waving his brothers over, Max shared his suspicions with his family and agreed with Derek: they had to talk to Christina before the party was over.

"If we don't confront her tonight we might not get another chance," Trey pointed out, speaking in a hushed tone of voice. "Let's do this, bro. It's now or never."

Alexis tucked her purse under her arm. "I'll come, too. Just in case you need backup."

Max took his iPhone out of the pocket of his white tuxedo jacket, found the Recorder app and hit the record button. Careful to conceal his iPhone, he marched across the room and joined Christina at the bar. "I finally figured it out," Max said, keeping his tone calm, even though he was pissed. "Demetrius didn't carry out his sinister plan alone. He needed help, and paid you well to do his dirty work."

Christina made her eyes wide. "I have no clue what you're referring to, and I resent what you're implying. And for your information, I'm a college graduate, not a common criminal."

"Yes, you are. You helped Demetrius frame my father and I want to know why. What did he ever do to you? You don't know him, and you had no right to destroy his reputation."

"I wish I'd done more!" she spit, molding her hands to her hips. "Your family doesn't care who they hurt or how many lives they ruin. I used to have a cushy job and a gorgeous condo in Santa Monica, but now I'm unemployed and it's all *your* fault."

Max stared at her with wide eyes. He couldn't believe he'd ever thought that Christina was a good person, or that he'd considered hiring her to be his administrative assistant after Jada quit. The more Christina badmouthed his family, the more he despised her.

"Why couldn't you leave Demetrius alone?" she asked, her gaze filled with venom. "Your dad screwed his wife and ruined his picture-perfect life. Hasn't he suffered enough? And, now because of your old man, I lost the best job I've ever had."

Derek stepped forward. "This is about money, plain and simple. You ruined my father's reputation, and destroyed the San Diego chapter to earn a few extra bucks. Just admit it."

A sneer curled her glossy lips. "Damn right, I did, and I'd do it again!"

"Good," Trey said, with a nod. "You can tell your

story to the LAPD because we're going to encourage our father to press charges. You need to answer for what you've done."

Christina sucked her teeth. "He's a sick, old man. No one will believe him. It's his word against mine, and I'm an upstanding citizen with a stellar reputation."

"Your *stellar* reputation won't save you this time. I recorded everything you just said." Max raised his cell phone in the air. "If you ever cause trouble for my family, or any of the other Prescott George members, I'll share this recording with the authorities. Understood?"

Wide-eyed, Christina opened then closed her gaping mouth.

Max gestured to the uniformed security guards standing at the ballroom doors. "Christina, you're not welcome here anymore. Please leave, and don't come back."

The guards appeared at Christina's side and took her arm. "Ma'am, come with us."

Security escorted her out, and Christina walked with her head down and her shoulders bent.

"There are my boys. Come over here and have a drink with your old man…"

Max turned around, saw Reginald in his wheelchair and smiled. Frail, but holding on, Reginald wore a tailored suit, burgundy bow tie and a black top hat. Max ordered a round of drinks with the bartender, then handed a champagne flute to everyone in his family. "We can toast to your reinstatement in Prescott George," Max said, raising his glass in the air. "Dad, you're a full ranking member again, with all the rights, privileges and—"

Reginald interrupted him. "But I don't want my membership back. I only came tonight to say thank-you and a final goodbye to my friends in an organization that meant so much to me."

Max didn't get it, and he could tell by the bewildered expressions on his brothers' faces that they didn't understand what Reginald was talking about, either. "You don't want your membership back? Isn't that what this was all about? Why Derek, Trey and I spent the past three months trying to clear your name? So you could be reinstated in Prescott George?"

"No." Reginald's voice was firm. "It was about making peace with my three sons, earning your forgiveness for not being a good father and, most important, bringing you boys together."

Max lobbed an arm each around Derek's and Trey's necks, and his brothers grinned.

"I have my Christmas present, and this holiday season I discovered what matters most in life. Integrity, love and family." Reginald winked. "*And* the love of a good woman! Way to go, sons. You did well!"

Everyone clinked glasses.

Max clasped Jada's hand and gazed deep into her eyes. "Merry Christmas, Beautiful."

Her face lit up. "Merry Christmas, baby."

"Jada, I love you so much it scares me sometimes," he confessed, unable to keep his feelings bottled up inside anymore. "You're irreplaceable, and the only woman I want is you."

"I love you, too, Max. You are the best thing that has ever happened to me, and I want to make more amazing memories with you and Taylor, and this Christmas we will."

Wrapped up in each other's arms, they swayed to the music playing in the ballroom. Max couldn't recall ever being so happy. Life was good. His father was still alive, he had a strong bond with his brothers, a healthier relationship with his daughter, and he had the woman of his dreams. Cupping his face in her hands, Jada kissed his lips, and Max knew in his heart that their love would last a lifetime.

* * * * *

BLAME IT ON CHRISTMAS

JANICE MAYNARD

This book is for every guy or girl who has found the courage to ask someone out and then been shot down. It hurts. But true love finds a way. :-)

One

"The answer is no!"

Mazie Tarleton ended the call, wishing she had a good old-fashioned receiver she could slam down on a cradle. Cutting off a phone conversation with the tap of a red button wasn't nearly as satisfying.

Behind her, Gina—her best friend and coworker—ate the last bite of her cinnamon crunch bagel and wiped cream cheese from her fingers. "Who's got you all riled up?"

The two women were in Mazie's office, a cramped space behind the elegant showroom that drew tourists and locals to All That Glitters, Mazie's upscale jewelry store in Charleston's historic business district.

Mazie dropped into a chair and scowled. "It's J.B.'s real estate agent again. He's making her badger me."

"You mean J.B. who wants to offer you a ridiculous amount of money for this building that's falling down around our ears?"

"Whose side are you on anyway?" Mazie and Gina had met as freshmen at Savannah's College of Art and Design. Gina was aware of Mazie's long-standing feud with Charleston's highly eligible and incredibly sexy billionaire businessman.

Gina flicked a crumb from her cashmere-covered bosom. "We have dry rot in the attic. A heating system that dates back to the Civil War. And do I need to mention that our hurricane policy rates are set to triple when the renewal is due? I know you Tarleton people are richer than God, but that doesn't mean we should thumb our noses at a great offer."

"If it were anybody but J.B.," Mazie muttered, feeling the noose of inevitability tighten around her neck.

J.B. Jackson Beauregard Vaughan. The man she loved to hate. J.B. Vaughan had been on her personal hit list since she was sixteen years old. She loathed him. And she wanted to hurt him as much as he had hurt her.

"What did he ever do to you?" Gina asked. Her perplexed frown was understandable. J.B. Vaughan was the prototype for tall, dark and handsome. Cocky grin. Brilliant blue eyes. Strong features. And shoulders that were about a million miles wide.

"It's complicated," Mazie muttered, feeling her face heat. Even now, the memories were humiliating.

Mazie couldn't remember a time when J.B. hadn't been part of her life. Way back when, she had even loved him. As an almost-brother. But when her hormones started raging and she began seeing J.B. in a whole new light, a spring formal at her all-girls prep school had presented itself as the perfect opportunity to do some very grown-up experimentation.

Not sex. Oh, no. Not that. She was aware, even then, that J.B. was the kind of guy who *knew things*, and she wasn't ready to go down that road.

She called him on a Wednesday afternoon in April. With her nerves humming and her stomach flopping, she blurted out her invitation.

J.B. had been oddly noncommittal. And then, barely four hours later, he had showed up on her doorstep.

Her father had been locked in his study with a nightcap. Both Jonathan and Hartley, her brothers, had been out on the town doing something or other.

Mazie had answered the front door.

Because she felt weird about inviting J.B. inside—though he'd been there a hundred times before—she stepped out onto the wide veranda and smiled at him tentatively.

"Hey, J.B.," she said. "I didn't expect to see you today."

He leaned against a post, his posture the epitome of cool, high school masculinity. In a few weeks he would be eighteen. A legal adult. Her heart beat faster.

"I wanted to talk to you face-to-face," he said. "It was nice of you to ask me to the dance."

"Nice?"

It seemed an odd choice of words, especially coming from J.B.

He nodded. "I'm flattered."

Her stomach curled defensively. "You didn't actually give me an answer on the phone," she said. Suddenly, her hands were ice, and she was shaking all over.

J.B. shifted from one foot to the other. "You're a cute girl, Mazie. I'm glad you're my friend."

He really didn't have to say anything else. She was smart and perceptive and able to read between the lines. But she'd be damned if she'd let him off so easily. "What are you trying to say, J.B.?"

Now a dark scowl erased some of his cocky charm, but none of his brooding sexuality. "Damn it, Mazie. I can't go to that dance with you. You shouldn't have asked me. You're little more than a baby."

Her heart shriveled. "I'm not a child," she said quietly. "I'm only a year younger than you are."

"Almost two."

The real surprise was that he had kept track. Because of the way their birthdays fell on the calendar, he was right. She took three steps toward him. Inside, she was falling apart. But she wouldn't let him see what he was doing to her self-esteem. "Don't make excuses, J.B. If you won't go out with me, please have the guts to say so."

He cursed vehemently. With both hands, he scraped his slightly-too-long blue-black hair from his face. "You're like a sister to me," he said.

The words were muttered, barely audible. In fact, he spoke them in the direction of the floor. A less-convincing lie would have been hard to find. Why was he throwing up walls between them?

Mazie was breathing so rapidly she was in danger of hyperventilating. Clearly she had misread the situation. J.B. hadn't come here tonight because he was fond of her, or because he wanted to see her.

He was standing on her front porch because he was too much of a Southern gentleman to say no to her over the phone.

A nicer person might have made the situation easier for him. Mazie was tired of being nice. She slipped her arms around his waist and rested her cheek on his broad chest. He was wearing a navy T-shirt and faded jeans with old leather deck shoes. Decades ago, he would have been a classic James Dean. Bad boy. Rule breaker.

When she touched him, his entire body went rigid. Nothing moved. Except one thing. One startling and rather large thing.

Jackson Beauregard Vaughan was aroused. Since Mazie had plastered herself against his front, it was rather impossible for him to hide. She found his mouth with hers and threw every ounce of her undiluted teenage passion into an eager, desperate kiss.

J.B. tasted wonderful, exactly like he did in her dreams, only better.

For a moment, she thought she had won.

His arms tightened around her. His mouth crushed hers. His tongue thrust between her lips and stroked the inside of her mouth. Her legs lost feeling. She clung to his shoulders. "J.B.," she whispered. "Oh, J.B."

Her words shocked him out of whatever spell he'd been under. He jerked away so hard and so fast, she stumbled.

J.B. never even held out a hand to keep her from falling.

He stared at her, his features shadowed in the unflattering yellowish glare of the porch light. The sun had gone down, and the dark night was alive with the smells and sounds of spring.

Very deliberately, he wiped a hand across his mouth. "Like I said, Mazie. You're a kid. Which means you need to stick to the kiddie pool."

His harsh words, particularly coming on the heels of that kiss, confused her. "Why are you being so mean?" she whispered.

She saw the muscles in his throat work.

"Why are you being so naive and clueless?"

Hot tears sprang to her eyes. She wouldn't let them fall. "I think we're done here. Do me a favor, J.B. If you ever find yourself in the midst of an apocalypse—zombie or otherwise—and if you and I are the only two humans left on the planet, go screw yourself."

"Mazie…hello… Mazie."

Gina's voice shocked Mazie back to the present. "Sorry," she said. "I was thinking about something."

"About J.B., right? You were ready to tell me why you loathe the man after all these years, and why you won't sell this property to him, even though he's offered you three times what it's worth."

Mazie swallowed, shaking off the past. "He broke my heart when we were teenagers, and he was kind of a jerk about it, so yeah… I don't want to hand him everything he wants."

"You're being illogical."

"Maybe so."

"Forget the money. Hasn't he also offered you two other

properties that are prime locations for our shop? And he's willing to do a trade, easy peasy? What are you waiting for, Mazie?"

"I want him to squirm."

J.B. had bought up every single square foot of property in a two-block strip near the Battery. He planned a massive renovation, working, of course, within the parameters of historic Charleston's preservation guidelines. The street-level storefronts would be glitzy retail space, charming and Southern and unique. Upstairs, J.B.'s vision included luxurious condos and apartments, some with views of the picturesque harbor and Fort Sumter in the distance.

The only thing standing in J.B.'s way was Mazie. And Mazie's property. And the fact that he didn't own it.

Gina waved a hand in front of Mazie's face. "Stop spacing out. I understand wanting to torment your teenage nemesis, but are you seriously going to stonewall the man just to make a point?"

Mazie ground her teeth until her head ached. "I don't know if I'm willing to sell to him. I need time to think about it."

"What if the agent doesn't call you back?"

"She will. J.B. never gives up. It's one of his best qualities and one of his most annoying."

"I hope you're right."

J.B. slid into the dark booth and lifted a hand to summon a server. He'd worn a sport coat and a tie for an earlier meeting. Now, he loosened his collar and dispensed with the neckwear.

Jonathan Tarleton was already sitting in the opposite corner nursing a sparkling water with lime. J.B. lifted an eyebrow in concern. "You look like hell. What's wrong?"

His friend grimaced. "It's these bloody headaches."

"You need to see a doctor."

"I have."

"Then you need to see a better one."

"Can we please stop talking about my health? I'm thirty, not eighty."

"Fine." J.B. wanted to pursue the issue, but Jonathan was clearly not interested. J.B. sat back with a sigh, nursing his beer. "Your sister is driving me crazy. Will you talk to her?" He couldn't admit the real reason he needed help. He and Mazie were oil and water. She hated him, and J.B. had tried for years to tell himself he didn't care.

The truth was far murkier.

"Mazie is stubborn," Jonathan said.

"It's a Tarleton trait, isn't it?"

"You're one to talk."

"I've literally put my entire project on hold, because she's jerking me around."

Jonathan tried unsuccessfully to hide a smile. "My sister is not fond of you, J.B."

"Yeah, tell me something I don't know. Mazie refuses to talk about selling. What am I supposed to do?"

"Sweeten the pot?"

"With what? She doesn't want my money."

"I don't know. I've always wondered what you did to piss her off. Why is my little sister the only woman in Charleston who's immune to the famous J.B. Vaughan charm?"

J.B. ground his jaw. "Who knows?" he lied. "I don't have time to play games, though. I need to break ground by the middle of January to stay on schedule."

"She likes pralines."

Jonathan drawled the three words with a straight face, but J.B. knew when he was being taunted. "You're suggesting I buy her candy?"

"Candy…flowers… I don't know. My sibling is a complicated woman. Smart as hell with a wicked sense of humor, but she has a dark side, too. She'll make you work for this, J.B. You might as well be prepared to crawl."

J.B. took a swig of his drink and tried not to think about Mazie at all. Everything about her flipped his switches. But he couldn't go there. Ever.

He choked and set down his glass until he could catch his breath.

Hell's bells.

The Tarleton progeny were beautiful people, all of them. Though J.B. barely remembered Jonathan's poor mother, what he recalled was a stunning, gorgeous woman with a perpetually sad air about her.

Jonathan and Hartley had inherited their mother's olive complexion, dark brown eyes and chestnut hair. Mazie had the Tarleton coloring, too, but her skin was fairer, and her eyes were more gold than brown. Amber, actually.

Though her brother kept his hair cut short to tame its tendency to curl, Mazie wore hers shoulder length. In the heat and humidity of summer, she kept it up in a ponytail. But during winter, she left it down. He hadn't seen her in several months. Sometimes J.B. dropped by the Tarletons' home on Thanksgiving weekend, but this year, he'd been tied up with other commitments.

Now it was December.

"I'll take the candy under advisement," he said.

Jonathan grimaced. "I'll see what I can do," he conceded. "But don't count on any help from me. Sometimes if I make a suggestion, she does the exact opposite. It's been that way since we were kids."

"Because she was always trying to keep up with you and Hartley, and you both treated her like a baby."

"I suppose we could have been nicer to her. It wasn't easy growing up in our house, especially once Mom was gone. Poor Mazie didn't have any female role models at all."

J.B. hesitated. "You know I would never do anything to hurt her business."

"Of course I know that. Don't be an ass. Your wanting to buy her property makes perfect sense. I can't help it if she's being deliberately obstructive. God knows why."

J.B. knew why. Or at least he had a fairly good idea. One kiss had haunted him for years, no matter how hard he tried not to remember.

"I'll keep trying. Let me know if anything works on your end."

"I'll give it my best shot. But don't hold your breath."

Two

Mazie loved Charleston during the holidays. The gracious old city was at her best in December. The sun was shining, the humidity occasionally dipped below 60 percent, and fragrant greenery adorned every balustrade and balcony in town. Tiny white lights. Red velvet bows. Even the horse-drawn carriages sported red-and-green-plaid finery.

She'd be the first to admit that summer in South Carolina could be daunting. During July and August, tourists had been known to duck into her shop for no other reason than to escape the sweltering heat.

She couldn't blame them. Besides, it was the perfect opportunity to chat people up and perhaps sell them a gold charm bracelet. Or if they were on a tight budget, one of Gina's silver bangles set with semiprecious stones.

Summer was definitely high season. Summer brought an influx of cash. The foot traffic in All That Glitters was steady from Memorial Day until at least mid-October. After that it began to dwindle.

Even so, Mazie loved the holiday season best of all.

It was funny, really. Her own experience growing up had certainly never been a storybook affair. No kids in matching pajamas sipping cocoa while mom and dad read to them in front of the fire. Despite the Tarleton money, which provided a physically secure environment, her parents were difficult people.

But she didn't care. From Thanksgiving weekend until New Year's Day, she basked in the season of goodwill.

Unfortunately, J.B.'s sins were too heinous to include him on Santa's good list. Mazie still wanted to find a way to make him suffer without putting her own business in danger.

When the real estate agent called the following day with another offer from J.B., Mazie didn't say no.

Not immediately.

Instead, she listened to the Realtor's impassioned pitch. When the woman paused to catch her breath, Mazie responded in a well-modulated, exceptionally pleasant tone of voice. "Please," she said politely, "tell Mr. Vaughan that if he is hell-bent on buying my property, perhaps he should come here and talk it over with me in person. Those are my terms."

Then once again, she hung up the phone.

This time, Gina was polishing an enormous silver coffee service they kept in the front window.

She hopped down from the stepladder and capped the jar of cleaner. "Well," she said. "You didn't hang up on her. I suppose that's progress."

Mazie frowned at a smudge on one of the large glass cases. "I thought I was nauseatingly nice."

"Most people think being nice is a good thing."

"True. But not always. We'll see what happens now. If J.B. wants this place, he's going to have to show his face."

Gina blanched and made a chopping motion with her hand.

Mazie frowned. "What's wrong with you?"

The other woman was so white her freckles stood out in relief. And her eyes bugged out of her head. She made a garbled noise.

When Gina continued her impersonation of a block of

salt, Mazie turned around to see what was prompting her friend's odd behavior.

A gaggle of middle-aged women had entered the shop together. The tiny bell over the door tinkled, signaling their presence.

While Mazie and Gina were deep in conversation, J.B. Vaughan had slipped in amid the crowd of shoppers, topping the women by a good six inches.

"I think she's surprised to see *me*," he said. His smile was crooked, his gaze wary. "Hello, Mazie. It's been a while."

His voice rolled over her like warm honey. Why did he have to sound so damn sexy?

The man looked like a dream. He was wearing expensive jeans and a pair of even more expensive Italian leather dress shoes. His broad shoulders were showcased in an unstructured, raw linen sport coat that hung open over a pristine white T-shirt. The shirt was just tight enough to draw attention to his rock-hard abdomen.

Oh, lordy. She had demanded he come in person, but she hadn't realized what she was asking for.

She swallowed her shock and her confusion. "Hello, J.B." A quick glance at her watch told her there was no way he could have gotten there so quickly. Unless he had *already* decided to challenge her refusal to sell face-to-face. "Have you talked to your real estate agent this morning?"

J.B. frowned. "No. I just came from the gym. Is there a problem?"

Mazie swallowed. "No. No problem."

At that precise moment, J.B.'s phone rang.

Mazie would have bet a million dollars she knew who was on the other end of the line. Because she saw his expression change. A huge grin flashed across his face. The Realtor had just passed along Mazie's message.

Damn the man. *She* had wanted to call the shots…to *make* him come plead his case in person.

Instead, he had cut the ground from beneath her feet. J.B. had walked into her shop because it was *his* idea, not because he was toeing some imaginary line or meeting a challenge she had thrown down.

Her temper sparked and simmered. "What do you want, J.B.? I'm busy."

He lifted an eyebrow. "Cleaning a glass counter? Isn't that above your pay grade, Ms. Tarleton?"

"It's my shop. Everything that happens here is *my* business."

Gina squeezed past Mazie. "Excuse me," Gina muttered. "I need to check on our customers."

Mazie should have introduced her redheaded friend to J.B. The two of them might have met at some point in the past, though it was unlikely. But Gina seemed bent on escaping the emotionally charged confrontation.

J.B. held out a red cellophane bag. "These are for you, Mazie. I remember Jonathan saying how much you liked them."

She stared at the familiar logo. Then she frowned, sensing a trap. "You brought me pralines?"

"Yes, ma'am." His arm was still extended, gift in hand.

It might as well have been a snake. "You realize the shop is half a block from here. I can buy my own pralines, J.B."

His smile slipped. The blue irises went from calm to stormy. "A thank you might be nice. You weren't spanked enough as a kid, were you? Spoiled only daughter…"

She caught her breath. The barb hit without warning. "You know that's not true."

Contrition skittered across his face, followed by regret. "Ah, damn, Mazie. I'm sorry. You always bring out the worst in me." He grimaced and pressed the heel of his hand to his forehead. "The candy was a peace offering. Nothing sinister, I swear."

She grabbed the bag of pralines and set it on the counter behind her. She and J.B. were standing at the far back of the store in front of a case of men's signet rings. Hopefully, all of the current customers were shopping for themselves.

"Thank you for the candy." She straightened her shoulders. "Is that all?"

J.B. stared at her, incredulous. "Of course that's not all. Do you really think I wander around Charleston dropping off candy to random women?"

Mazie lifted one shoulder. "Who knows what you do?"

Watching J.B. rein in his temper was actually kind of fun. It helped restore her equilibrium. She *enjoyed* getting the upper hand.

After a few tense moments of silence, he sighed. "I'd like to show you one of my properties over on Queen Street. You could double your square footage immediately, and the storage areas are clean and dry. Plus, there's a generously sized apartment upstairs if you ever decide to move out of Casa Tarleton."

The prospect of having her own apartment was tempting, but she and Jonathan hadn't been able to leave their father on his own. Stupid, really. He'd been a less-than-present parent, both emotionally and otherwise. Still, they felt responsible for him.

Over J.B.'s shoulder, Gina telegraphed her concern like a flamingo playing charades.

Mazie decided to play J.B.'s game. At least for a little while. What she really wanted was to make him think she was seriously considering his offer. And then shut him down. "Okay," she said. "I suppose it couldn't hurt to take a look."

J.B.'s reaction to her quiet statement was equal parts pole-axed and suspicious. "When?"

"Now is good."

"What about the shop?"

"They don't need me." It was true. Mazie was the owner and CEO. In addition to Gina, there were two full-time employees and three part-time ones, as well.

J.B. nodded brusquely. "Then let's get out of here. I'm parked in a loading zone."

"You go ahead. Text me the address. I'll be there in fifteen minutes. All I need to do is grab a coat and get my purse."

He frowned. "I can wait."

"I'd rather have my own car, J.B."

His eyes narrowed. He folded his arms across his chest. "Why?"

"Because I do, that's why. Are you afraid I won't come? I said I would, and I will. Don't make a big deal out of this."

He ground his jaw. She could almost see the hot angry words trembling on his lips. But he said nothing.

"What?" she whispered, still very much aware that they had an audience.

J.B. shook his head, his expression bleak. "Nothing, Mazie. Nothing at all." He reached in a pocket and extracted his cell phone, tapping out a text impatiently. "I sent you the address. I'll see you shortly."

J.B. should have been elated.

The first hurdle was behind him. He had finally convinced Mazie Tarleton to look at another location for her jewelry business. That was *huge*. And it was certainly more than his real estate agent had been able to accomplish in the last twelve weeks. Even so, his skin felt itchy. Being around Mazie was like juggling a grenade. Not only was she an unknown quantity, he was in danger of being sabotaged by his own uneasy attraction.

He was determined to keep his distance.

Nothing with Mazie was ever easy, so he paced the sidewalk in front of the empty property on Queen Street, praying she would show up, but fearing she wouldn't.

When her cherry-red Mazda Miata turned the corner at the end of the street and headed in his direction, he felt a giant boulder roll from his shoulders. Thank the Lord. He was pretty sure Mazie wouldn't have come today unless she was ready to take him up on his offer.

She parallel parked with impressive ease and climbed out, locking her snazzy vehicle with one click of her key fob. He saw her, more often than not, in casual clothes. But today, Mazie was wearing a black pencil skirt with an ivory silk blouse that made her look every inch the wealthy heiress she was.

Her legs were long, maybe her best feature. She walked with confidence. In deference to the breezy afternoon, she wore a thigh-length black trench coat. To J.B. she seemed like a woman who could conquer the world.

As he watched, she tucked her car keys into her coat pocket and joined him. Shielding her eyes with one hand, she stared upward. He followed suit. Far above them, etched in sandstone, were the numerals 1-8-2-2, the year this building had been erected.

He answered her unspoken question. "The most recent tenant was an insurance firm. The building has been sitting empty for three months. If you think it will serve your purposes, I'll bring in an industrial cleaning crew, and we can get you moved with little to no interruption of your daily business."

"I'd like to see inside."

"Of course."

He'd made sure there was nothing to throw up any red flags. No musty odors. No peeling paint. In truth, the building was a gem. He might have kept it for himself if he hadn't so badly needed a carrot to entice Mazie.

For years he had tried to make up for his youthful mistakes. Becoming a respected member of the Charleston business community was important to him. The fact that he had to deal with Mazie and a very inconvenient attraction that wouldn't die was a complication he didn't need. He'd learned the hard way that sexual attraction could blind a man to the truth.

"Look at the tin ceiling," he said. "This place used to be a bank. We're standing where the customers would have come to speak to tellers."

Mazie put her hands on her hips. Slowly she turned around, taking in every angle, occasionally pausing to use her smartphone to snap a picture. "It's lovely," she said.

The comment was grudging. He knew that much. But at least she was honest.

"Thanks. I was lucky to get it. Had to scare off a guy who wanted to use it for an indoor miniature golf range."

"Surely you're joking."

"Not really. I'd like to think he'd never have been able to get the permits, but who knows?"

"You mentioned storage?"

"Ah, yes. There's a finished basement below us, small but nice. And more of the same above. The best part for you, though? There's a safe. We'll have to bring in an expert to get it working again. But you should be able to secure your high ticket items overnight, and thus eliminate any concerns about theft when you're not open."

When he showed her the ten-foot-square safe— stepping aside for her to enter—she lifted an eyebrow. "Kind of overkill, don't you think? My jewelry is small. I don't need nearly this much room."

He followed her in. "Not the way you do it now. But you've been removing every item and putting it all back each morning. If you use the shelves in this safe, you can carry entire trays in here at night and save yourself a ton of hassle."

Mazie pursed her lips. "True."

Her lips were red today, cherry red. It was impossible not to think about those lips wrapped around his—

"Tell me, J.B.," she said, interrupting his heated train of thought. "Is a bank safe this old really secure?"

He swallowed against a dry throat. "Well, it hasn't been used in some time but…"

Mazie pushed on the door. "It's crazy heavy. I suppose it would make a good hurricane shelter, too."

The door was weighted more efficiently than it seemed. Before J.B. could intervene, it slipped out of her grasp and slammed shut with a loud *thunk*.

The sudden pitch-black dark was disorienting.

Mazie's voice was small. "Oops. Guess I should have asked if you have the keys."

"Doesn't matter," he said. "They told me this thing isn't operational." He stepped forward cautiously. "Stand back. I'll grab the handle." That part was easy. Unfortunately, when he threw all his weight into it, nothing moved. "Damn."

He heard a rustle as Mazie shifted closer. "Isn't there a light?"

"Yeah." Reaching blindly, he slid his hand along the wall until he found the switch. The fluorescent bulb flickered, but came on.

Mazie stared at him, eyes huge. "I am *so* sorry. I didn't mean to close it."

"I know you didn't." His heart raced. Aside from the uncomfortable situation, he didn't want to get too close to Mazie. The two of them. In the dark. Very bad idea. "Don't worry," he said. "We'll be fine." He tried the handle a second time. Nothing budged. He pulled out his phone. "I'll call somebody."

He stared at the ominous words on the screen.

No service.

Of course there was no service. The vault was constructed of steel-reinforced concrete, designed to keep out intruders. And the building itself was of an era when walls were built several feet thick. The nearby coffee shop he frequented had terrible cell service because it also was housed in a historic structure.

"So you really *don't* have keys?" Mazie gnawed her lower lip, her arms wrapped around her waist.

"I have keys to the building. Not the safe."

"Someone will notice we're missing," she said. "Gina, anyway. She and I text twenty times a day. What about you? Did you tell anyone you were coming here?"

"I called your brother."

Mazie frowned. "Jonathan? Why?"

J.B. grimaced. "Because he knew I was having a hard time convincing you to sell. I told him you had agreed to at least consider this Queen Street property as an alternative."

"I see." She stared at him. "How often do you and my brother talk about me?"

"Almost never. Why would we?"

Mazie shrugged. "Maybe Jonathan will want to know whether or not you convinced me."

"If he calls, it will just go to voice mail. He'll assume I'm busy and leave a message."

"Well, that sucks." She exhaled sharply and kicked the wall. "You realize that if we die here, I'm going to haunt you for eternity."

"How can you haunt me if I'm dead, too?" He swiped a hand across his forehead, feeling the cold sweat. Her nonsense was a welcome distraction. He would focus on the woman in touching distance.

"Please don't ruin my fantasy," she said. "It's all I've got at the moment." She wrinkled her nose. "We don't even have a chair."

J.B. felt the walls move inward. He dragged in a lungful of air, but it was strangely devoid of oxygen. "Fine," he stuttered. "Feel free to haunt me."

Three

For the first time, Mazie noticed that J.B. seemed decidedly tense.

"Are you okay?" she asked, moving closer and putting a hand on his forehead.

She almost expected to find him burning up with fever, but he was cool as the proverbial cucumber. To her alarm, he didn't move away from her touch or offer even a token protest, and he didn't make some smart-ass remark.

"I'm fine," he said.

"You're definitely not fine."

She got in front of him and put both hands on his face. "Tell me what's wrong. You're scaring me."

His entire body was rigid.

He swallowed, the muscles in his throat rippling visibly. "I'm a tad claustrophobic. I might need you to hold me."

Fat chance. Her heart stumbled at his teasing. And then she remembered. When J.B. was eight years old, he'd been playing in a junkyard with some friends and had accidentally gotten closed up in an old refrigerator during a game of hide-and-seek. He had nearly died.

The incident traumatized him, understandably so. His parents had hired a therapist who came weekly to their house for over a year, but some deep wounds were hard to shake.

She stroked his hair, telling herself she was being kind and not reveling in the chance to touch him. "We're going to be okay. And I'm here, J.B. Take off your jacket. Let's sit down."

At first she wasn't sure he even processed what she was saying. But after a moment, he nodded, removed his sport coat, and slid down the wall until he sat on his butt with his legs outstretched. He sighed deeply. "I'm not going to flake out on you," he muttered.

"I never thought you would." She joined him, but it was far less graceful. Her skirt was unforgiving. She shimmied it up her thighs and managed to sit down without exposing too much.

For an eternity, it seemed, they said nothing. J.B.'s hands rested on his thighs, fists clenched. He was breathing too fast.

Mazie was no shrink. But even she knew he needed to get his mind on something else besides their predicament. "How are your parents?" she asked.

J.B. snorted and shot her a sideways glance. "Really, Mazie? I'm having an embarrassingly public meltdown, and that's the best you can do?"

"You're not having a meltdown," she said. "You're fine."

Maybe if she said it convincingly enough, he would believe her. They were sitting shoulder-to-shoulder, hip-to-hip with less than twelve inches separating them. It was the closest she had been to J.B. in forever. Close enough for her to catch an intoxicating whiff of his aftershave mixed with the entirely ordinary and yet exhilarating man smell of him.

He was big and strong and darkly masculine. Her stomach quivered. *This* was exactly why she normally kept her distance.

J.B. was dangerous.

When she glanced toward the ceiling, she saw tiny air vents up above. They were in no danger of suffocating. Even so, J.B.'s response was understandable. Her skin crawled, too, at the thought of being stuck here for hours.

J.B. was expending every ounce of concentration on not surrendering to the phobia. So any chitchat or small talk would have to be initiated by *her*. The trouble was, she knew J.B. too well, and not well enough.

Charleston wasn't that big a place. Anytime there was a charity gala or a gallery showing or a theater opening, Charleston's elite gathered. Over the years, Mazie had seen J.B. in formal wear on dozens of occasions, usually with a gorgeous woman on his arm. Not ever the same woman, but still…

Because he and Jonathan were best buds, she had also seen J.B. half-naked on the deck of a sailboat and at the basketball court and by the beach. If she really applied herself to the task, she could probably come up with a million and one times she had been in the same vicinity as J.B. and yet never exchanged two words with him.

That was her choice. And probably his. He had been inexplicably cruel to her at a vulnerable point in her life, and she had hated him ever since.

Now here they were. Stuck. Indefinitely.

The tile floor underneath her butt was cold and hard. She drew her knees up to her chest and circled them with her arms. J.B. was right beside her. It wasn't like he was going to look up her skirt.

She sighed. "You doin' okay, stud?" His shallow breathing was audible.

"Peachy."

The growled word, laden with surly testosterone, made her grin. "Why have you never married again?"

The words flew from her lips like starlings disturbed by a chimney sweep. They swirled outward and upward and hung in the air. *Oh, crap.*

Her muscles were paralyzed. Out of the corner of her eye she saw J.B.'s head come up. He went perfectly still. Not looking at her. Gazing straight ahead. The seconds ticked by. A minute passed. Maybe two.

"My parents are well," he said.

It took half a second for the subtext to process, and then she burst into laughter. "Very funny. Message received. The oh-so-mysterious J.B. Vaughan doesn't talk about his private life."

"Maybe I don't have a private life," he said. "Maybe I'm a workaholic who spends every waking hour trying to coax beautiful jewelry merchants into selling their property to me."

With one carefully placed adjective, the dynamic in the room changed. J.B. added flirtation to the mix. Did he do it on purpose? Or was he so accustomed to schmoozing women that the word *beautiful* slipped out?

She pretended not to hear. "If you're a workaholic at this age, you'll be dead before you're fifty. Why do you work so hard, J.B.? Didn't you ever want to stop and smell the roses?"

"I tried it once. Roses have thorns." He sucked in a breath of air. "Are you going to give me your property or not?"

"Did you lock me in here on purpose to make me say yes?"

"God, no. Even I'm not that desperate. Try *your* phone," he said. "You use a different carrier. Maybe it makes a difference."

She glanced at her cell. "Nope. Nada."

J.B. groaned. "How long have we been in here?"

Mazie peered at her watch. "Twenty-two minutes."

"Maybe your watch stopped."

She reached out and squeezed his hand. "Think about something else. Do you have all your Christmas shopping done? What do your sisters want?" J.B.'s two siblings were both younger and female. That's probably why he spent so much time hanging around the Tarleton house when he was growing up.

"They're great," he said. "Do we have to do this?"

"You're the one who didn't want to talk about anything serious."

"Are those my only two choices?"

She hesitated half a beat. "We *could* talk about why you were such an ass to me when we were teenagers."

J.B. cursed beneath his breath and leaped to his feet. "Maybe we shouldn't talk at all."

For the next five minutes, he paced the small space like a tiger in a cage. Mazie stayed where she was. His body language shouted louder than words that he was unraveling.

At last, he paused in front of the impregnable door and slammed it with his fist. He bowed his head, his shoulders taut.

"I can't breathe," he whispered.

The agony in those three words twisted her heart. J.B. was a proud, arrogant man. Having her witness his weakness would make his frustration and anger and helplessness worse.

Without overthinking it, she scooted to her feet and went to him. "Listen to me." Fluorescent lighting was the most unflattering lighting in the world. It made both of them look like hell. His skin was sallow, cheekbones sharply etched. She took his face in her hands again. "Look at me. I want you to kiss me, J.B. Like you mean it. If you can't breathe, I might as well join you. Do it, big guy. Make me breathless. I dare you."

He was shaking, fine tremors that racked his body. But gradually, her words penetrated. "You want me to kiss you?"

"I do," she said. "More than anything." She touched her lips. "Right here. I haven't been kissed in ages. Show me how J.B. Vaughan woos a woman."

He blinked and frowned, as if sensing danger. "You're not serious."

She went up on her tiptoes and brushed her mouth over his. "Oh, yes I am. I'm so damn serious it ought to be against the law." She slid her fingers into his silky hair, cupping his skull, massaging his neck. "Kiss me, J.B."

If this worked, she was going to write a book about curing claustrophobia.

His hands landed on her shoulders, but she wasn't entirely sure he knew what he was doing. There was still a glassy-eyed element to his gaze.

"Mazie?" The way he said her name made the hair on her nape stand up. She knew exactly the moment his arousal broke through the grip of the visceral fear.

This time, the shudder that racked him was entirely hedonistic.

She didn't have to ask again for a kiss.

J.B. took control as if he had been kissing her always. His mouth settled over hers with a drugging sensuality that took the starch out of her knees and left her panting and helpless in his embrace.

Her arms linked around his neck. "This is nice."

"Screw nice…"

His rough laugh curled her toes. No wonder she had kept her distance all these years. At some level she had always known this could happen. She wanted to kick off her shoes and drag him to the floor, but everything was dusty and cold and hard. Not a soft surface in sight.

Once upon a time she had fantasized often about kissing J.B. Vaughan. The reality far outstripped her imaginings.

He was confident and coaxing and sexy and sweet, and she wanted to give him everything he asked for without words.

Thank God there wasn't a bed in sight. Otherwise, she might have done something really stupid.

His tongue stroked hers lazily. "I know what you're doing, and I don't even care. I should have kissed you years ago."

"You did," she reminded him.

"That didn't count. We were kids."

"Felt pretty grown-up to me." In fact, the adult J.B. was reacting much as the teenage J.B. had. His erection pressed against her belly, making her feel hot and dizzy and very confused.

This wasn't real. All she was doing was taking his mind off their incarceration.

He tugged her shirt loose and slid his hand up her back, unfastening her bra with one practiced flick of his fingers. Stroking her spine, he destroyed her bit by bit. "I always knew it would be like this," he groaned.

"Like what?" The two words were a whisper, barely audible over the loud pounding of her heart.

"Wild. Spectacular. Incredibly good." He put just enough space between them to let him cup her breasts in his hands. "Ah, Mazie."

His hands were warm. When he thumbed her nipples, the rough caress sent fire streaking throughout her body.

"Wait," she said. "My turn." She tugged at his soft shirt and sighed when she uncovered his muscled rib cage and taut abdomen. He was smooth and hard and had just enough silky hair to be interesting. She stopped short of his belt buckle.

J.B. nibbled the side of her neck. "Have you ever had sex standing up?"

"Um, no." Her brain was screaming at her to slow things down, but other parts of her body were having so much fun that sensible Mazie didn't stand a chance. "Have you?"

"No. I think it's one of those movie things that might not be so great in real life." He paused, his chest heaving. "But I'm willing to give it a try."

This was insane. They had gone from Mazie trying to distract J.B. from his claustrophobia to jumping each other's bones at warp speed. Though she knew it was suicidal, she couldn't seem to stop herself.

"Kiss me again," she begged. Anything to keep his mind off doing something they both would surely regret.

He granted her wish and then some. First it was her breasts. He bent and tasted each one with murmurs of approval that did great things for her self-esteem. Then he moved up to her neck and her earlobes, and finally, her lips.

Oh, wow, the man knew how to kiss. She didn't even care how many women he had practiced on. The result was mesmerizing.

There were really only so many ways a man and a woman could put their lips together. Yet somehow, J.B. managed to make each ragged breath and groaning caress new and desperate.

He tasted her, and shuddered when she slipped her tongue between his lips and returned the favor. Need— hot and heavy—poured through her limbs and pulsed in her sex. It had been an eternity since she had experienced this level of arousal. Suddenly, she knew she would die if she couldn't have him right here, right now.

Trembling and weak, she clung to his broad shoulders. "I'm not on the Pill," she said. "I don't have any protection."

He bit her bottom lip, tugging it, turning her legs to spaghetti.

"Condom," he moaned. "Wallet."

"Yes." One part of her stood as an onlooker, marveling at her reckless behavior.

Really, Mazie? J.B. Vaughan? After he shot you down all those years ago and ignored you ever since?

Do you really want to do this?

She did. She really did. Maybe she always had.

J.B. removed her top and bra and draped them carefully over the door handle of the safe. Then he turned and stared at her.

She crossed her arms over her chest, unable to pretend sophistication. There had been two men in her life. Not a big number.

He ran his hand from her bare shoulder down her arm, manacling her wrist and reeling her in. "You're exquisite, Mazie."

The recollection of a teenage J.B. had always messed with her head. The popular boy with the raw sexuality and the wicked grin had rejected her and made her feel less than feminine, less than desirable.

It was difficult to reconcile that memory with the present.

"I'm glad you think so."

His slight frown told her he recognized her equivocation. He kissed her temple.

"I love your hair." He ran his hands through it. "It bounces with life and passion. Like you, Mazie."

The sudden segue from frantic hunger to tenderness unsettled her. It was one thing to get caught up in the moment. She didn't trust J.B.'s quiet gentleness. A man could use sex to get what he wanted. Maybe in the midst of their madness, J.B. had recognized her vulnerability where he was concerned. Maybe he hoped to use it to his advantage.

"Kiss me again," she begged. Boldly, she cupped the length of his sex through his pants. He was hard and ready, so ready that the evidence made her want to swoon like some fainthearted Victorian maiden.

Mazie had been abstinent by choice for the past two years. No man had tempted her, not even a little. Now here was J.B. All wrong for her in every way. But at the moment, oh so right.

When she touched him intimately, he shuddered. This

time, she knew the tremors that racked his big frame had nothing to do with a fear of enclosed spaces. J.B. wanted her. Badly. The realization was exhilarating.

They were still mostly clothed, though her bare breasts nestled delightfully against his warm, hard chest. It should have felt weird and odd to be standing here like this. Instead, it was the most wonderfully terrifying thing in the world. In his embrace, she felt torn in a dozen dizzying directions.

She hated this man. Didn't she? Or was this a delightful dream?

The illusion was worth any price. She had waited a decade and more for J.B. to admit that he wanted her. Surely the fates would grant her one outrageous walk on the wild side.

She could call it off. The end would be ugly and awkward and far more scarring than what had happened when she was sixteen. But J.B. would never force himself on a woman, even if Mazie had been the one to initiate the encounter.

"I want you, darlin' Mazie." When he whispered her name and touched her thigh beneath her skirt, she knew the moment was at hand.

It was no contest. "I want you, too, J.B."

What happened next was sheer madness. He scooped her up and backed her against the wall. Her hands tangled in his hair. They were both panting as if they had run a marathon.

He cupped her bottom, grinding his lower half against hers until she wanted to scream with frustration.

He slid his hands beneath her skirt and found bare skin. "Put your legs around my waist."

"The condom," she said. "Don't forget the condom."

"In a minute." He kissed her wildly, his teeth bruising her lips. She pulled his hair, fighting to get closer. Her bikini panties were damp. Her entire body wept with the need to have him inside her.

She crossed her ankles behind his back, ripping at his shirt. "Take this off," she pleaded.

He managed it without breaking the kiss. Now she could run her hands over acres of warm male skin. His body was toned and tanned and sleekly muscled. For a man who supposedly spent a lot of time with spreadsheets and architectural plans, he had the build of an athlete.

"Hang on tight," he demanded. With a muffled groan, he ripped her underpants and held the scraps aloft. "Mission accomplished."

"Those were new," she protested.

J.B.'s grin was feral. "I'll buy you more."

Now he could go where no man had gone in a very long time. He caressed her intimately, inserting one finger…feeling the embarrassingly welcome state of her sex.

"Oh, wow…" She dropped her head to his shoulder and closed her eyes.

J.B. chuckled. "If you like that, I've got lots more."

Without warning, a thunderous pounding on the huge door reverberated in the enclosed space. A muffled shout sounded. "Anybody in there?"

"Holy damn. Lord have mercy."

J.B.'s incredulous response would have been hysterically funny if Mazie hadn't been poised on the brink of a really spectacular orgasm. She groaned and buried her face in his neck.

The voice came again. "Stand back. I'm going to open the door."

"Oh, my God." She jerked out of J.B.'s arms and grabbed for her bra and shirt.

J.B. stared at her, his gaze hot enough to melt all of her inhibitions. "Saved by the bell…"

She should be glad—right? Glad that she hadn't done something stupid and self-destructive?

What was he thinking? His expression was grim.

Her heart sank, incredulous at the way she had let herself fall into old patterns. Suddenly, the situation seemed a thousand times worse.

Four

J.B. cursed beneath his breath, stunned at his run of bad luck. Then again, maybe he should admit the truth. No matter his physical frustration, he had escaped certain catastrophe. He'd spent years avoiding Mazie Tarleton, and yet he'd come perilously close to doing the very thing he knew he couldn't do.

His beautiful enemy was barely decent when a loud scraping ensued, and the heavy door began to swing inward. At the last second, J.B. shoved her torn underwear into his pocket and slipped his shirt on again.

The lights from outside the vault were so bright they both blinked. Their rescuer crossed his arms over his chest. Jonathan Tarleton. Mazie's brother. With a smug smile on his face. "Well, look at you two."

J.B. took a step forward, shielding Mazie in case she had anything else she needed to tuck away. "What are you doing here?"

Jonathan moved back, allowing them to exit. "I though maybe I could convince Mazie to give you a fair hearing. When I arrived, I saw both of your cars, but neither of you. So I put my CSI skills to work and found footprints leading to the vault. Fortunately for you, this hardwood floor is dusty as hell."

For J.B., the rush of cool air was blissful. He inhaled deeply, feeling the last tentacles of his brief ordeal slip away.

Truth be told, Mazie had rescued him quite effectively.

Her methods were almost beguiling enough to make him drag her back into the vault and shut the door again.

Almost, but not quite.

"Thanks for rescuing us," he said. "If you hadn't come by, we might have spent an uncomfortable few hours locked up in there."

"The mechanism was jammed on the outside. I had to hit it with my shoe to knock it loose."

Mazie hadn't said a word up until now, though she had hugged her brother briefly. She edged toward the front of the building. "It was my fault. I didn't mean to close the door." She grimaced. "Not to be rude, but I'm in dire need of the ladies' room. I'll see you later, Jonathan." She gave J.B. an oddly guarded look for someone who had only recently been wrapped around him like a feather boa. "Thanks for the tour."

And then she was gone.

He stared out the window, wondering if the sick feeling in the pit of his stomach was sexual disappointment or something far more alarming.

Had he actually *connected* with his prickly nemesis? Surely not. He couldn't. He wouldn't. The only reason he was spending time with her at all was to seal a deal. He dared not let himself get sidetracked by an almost irresistible attraction.

That kind of thing made a man stupid. He should know.

Jonathan cuffed his shoulder. "Well," he said. "Did you convince her? What did she say?"

J.B. ran his hands through his hair. "She didn't say anything. We'd barely started looking the place over when we got stuck. I have no idea if she liked it or not."

"Of course she liked it," Jonathan said. "Mazie is a sucker for historic buildings. This one has tons of original features, but unlike the dump she's in now, your building is rock-solid."

"Yeah." J.B. nodded absently, reliving every incredible moment of his incarceration. Now that it was over, the whole thing seemed like a dream. Did Mazie Tarleton really let him touch her and nearly make love to her?

"Hey, J.B." Jonathan eyed him strangely.

"What?"

"You have lipstick on your chin."

J.B. froze inwardly. This was a minefield. Mazie wasn't a child anymore, but Jonathan was very protective. That was part of the reason J.B. had kept a healthy distance from her over the years. "Do I?" he said.

Jonathan's expression segued into a frown. "What the hell went on in that vault?"

"None of your damn business. Your sister is an adult. Besides, nothing happened. I got claustrophobic, and Mazie tried to distract me with a little kiss."

"Claustrophobic?" Jonathan's distrust vanished. "Oh, man, J.B., I'm sorry. You must have freaked. That was nice of her, especially considering she doesn't like you all that much."

She seemed to like me just fine a few minutes ago when she had her tongue down my throat.

J.B. swallowed the sarcastic words and managed a noncommittal nod. "Not my finest hour. It's humiliating as hell to have something that happened almost twenty-five years ago still yank my chain. For a minute in there, I thought I was going to lose it."

"You should be glad it was Mazie with you and not someone else. At least she won't ever tease you about it. That girl has a tender heart."

"She's a lot like Hartley in that way. The two of them were always bringing home strays. Have you heard from him at all? I still can't believe he simply vanished."

"No. But it's only a matter of time. Hartley was born and bred here. The Lowcountry is in his blood."

"You don't sound happy about that."

"He abandoned the family business...left me to deal with Dad. I don't have a lot of sympathy for my brother right now."

"He's your twin. Twins are close."

"We were at one time. Not anymore."

"You say that, Jonathan, but I know you. And I know Hartley. The two of you were practically inseparable when we were growing up. You can't pretend that tie isn't there. It always will be."

"Not if I don't want it...not if I don't want *him*."

J.B. let the subject drop, but only because he saw beneath Jonathan's angry response to the deep hurt that still festered.

He rotated his shoulders and took one last look around the room. "I think this will work for Mazie. I didn't get a firm *yes* from her, but I'll follow up."

"And I'll continue to put in a good word for you."

They exited the building. J.B. locked up. "You on for basketball next weekend?"

"Yeah. Seven o'clock?"

J.B. nodded. "I'll see you then."

When Jonathan climbed in his car and drove away, J.B. should have followed suit, but he felt oddly out of sorts. Perhaps because he wanted to get this project settled. He needed Mazie's property.

Who was he kidding? Every bit of his current angst was because of a frustrating, completely off-limits woman who had bedeviled him for years. He wanted her. End of story.

He took out his phone and pulled up her contact info. A short text in this situation would be perfectly acceptable.

Hope you liked the property. Let me know what you think.

But he couldn't do it. Mazie had muddied the waters. Or

maybe they both had. He was accustomed to closing deals. In business. For pleasure. Never both at the same time.

This was exactly why he was screwed. He had resisted temptation all this time, and then in one short afternoon he'd undone all his good intentions.

Thinking about Mazie was a mistake. Half an hour ago, he had been primed to make love to her. His body had been denied satisfaction, and now he was itchy, restless.

One thing he knew for sure.

Kissing Mazie Tarleton was an experience he planned to repeat. Some way. Somehow. Maybe *she* didn't know it, but J.B.'s intentions were crystal clear.

Now that he had touched her, tasted her, there was no going back...

Mazie wanted to go straight home and take a long cold shower, but it was too early in the day to be done with work, and besides, Gina was expecting her to return.

There was no choice but to brazen it out.

Which was not easy when a girl was commando under her skirt.

Fortunately, the shop was swamped with customers. Mazie barely did more than wave at Gina and say hello to her other employees before she was pulled into the fray. Thank goodness for tour ships that dispatched groups of passengers ashore, eager to tick off items on their Christmas lists.

At last, the furor subsided. Mazie sent two of her employees on lunch break. She glanced at her watch. It was almost one.

Mazie had advertised heavily during the last year in several of the cruise lines' brochures. Her print ads were paying off, despite the digital age. Today, she'd had several customers come in clutching their maps of the historic district. All That Glitters was clearly marked, along with the small rectangle showcasing a beautiful necklace and the store's phone number with other contact info.

She glanced in one of the larger cases. "We're going to need more sweetgrass basket charms in gold."

Gina nodded. "Yep. One lady bought six of them for her granddaughters. I'll call Eve this afternoon and place an order."

They were eating pizza standing up, a common occurrence. Gina swallowed a bite and grinned. "Don't keep me in suspense. How did it go with Mr. Gorgeous? Did you like the building?"

"Honestly, I did. The place J.B. wants us to have was originally a nineteenth-century bank. He was showing me the vault when we had a little accident and got locked inside."

Gina's eyes rounded. "You got locked in a bank vault with J.B. Vaughan? God, that's so romantic."

"Um, no. Not romantic at all." You couldn't call what happened with J.B. romance. Sexual frenzy, maybe.

"So it was too scary to be romantic?"

The other woman's crestfallen expression might have been funny if Mazie hadn't been walking on eggshells. She wasn't going to betray J.B.'s secret weakness. Instead, she skirted the truth. "Not so much scary as tense. We were awfully glad to get out of there when Jonathan showed up."

"So are you going to take it? The building, I mean? Will it work for our purposes?"

"It's perfect. Doesn't mean I'm ready to give J.B. what he wants. Surely there's another way."

"Has anyone ever told you that you're contrary?"

"You," Mazie said, finishing her meal. "Every other day." She wiped her hands on a napkin. "My...*conversation* with J.B. got derailed when my brother showed up. I'm sure I'll hear from him soon. J.B., that is."

"And what will you say when he asks you again?"

Mazie flashed to a mental image of the real estate developer's chest. His tousled hair. His eyes, heavy-lidded with desire. Her throat tightened. Her thighs pressed together. "I don't really know."

Unfortunately, the afternoon crowd picked up, and Mazie never found a moment to scoot home and restock her wardrobe. By the time the shop closed at five, she was more than ready to call it quits.

The Tarleton family had lived for decades on the tip of a small barrier island just north of the city. They owned fifteen acres, more than enough to create a compound that included the main house and several smaller buildings scattered around.

An imposing, gated iron fence protected the enclave on land. Water access was impossible due to a high brick wall Mazie's grandfather had erected at the top of the sand. The beach itself was public property, but he had made sure no one could wander onto Tarleton property, either out of curiosity or with dangerous motives. Hurricanes and erosion made the wall outrageously expensive to maintain, but the current Tarleton patriarch was by nature paranoid and suspicious, so security was a constant concern.

At times, Mazie felt unbearably strangled by her familial obligations. Perhaps that was why being around J.B. felt both dangerous and exhilarating all at the same instant.

She punched her security code into the keypad and waited for the heavy gate to slide open. She and Jonathan both wanted to move out, but they were trapped by the weight of love and responsibility for their father. She suspected her brother kept an apartment in the city so he could have a private life, but she didn't pry. Someday she might find a place of her own, as well.

She had let the long-ago debacle with J.B. cast too long

a shadow over her romantic life. Heartbreak had made her overly cautious.

It was time to find some closure with J.B., one way or another. Time to move on.

The house where she had grown up was a colossal structure of sandstone and timber, on stilts, of course. Supposedly, it had been built to withstand a Category Four hurricane. Though the family home had suffered damage over the years, the original structure was still mostly intact.

An imposing front staircase swept upward to double mahogany doors inlaid with stained glass. The images of starfish and dolphins and sea turtles had fascinated her as a child. When she grew tall enough, she liked to stand on the porch and trace them with her fingertips.

The sea creatures were free in a way that Mazie couldn't imagine. All her life she had been hemmed in by her mother's illness and later, her father's paranoia. Jonathan and Hartley—when they had been in a mood to tolerate her—had been her companions, her best friends.

And J.B., too.

The Vaughan family was one of only a handful in Charleston as wealthy as the Tarletons, so Gerald Tarleton had condoned, even promoted his children's friendship with J.B. But Mazie was younger, and Hartley was a loner, so it was always Jonathan and J.B. who were the closest.

Mazie had adored J.B. as a child, then had a crush on him as a teenager, and finally, hated him for years. No matter how she examined her past, it was impossible to excise J.B. from the memories.

Mazie found her father in the large family room with the double plate-glass windows. The ocean was benign today, shimmering shades of blue and turquoise stretching all the way to the horizon.

"Hi, Daddy." She kissed the top of his curly, white-haired head. Her father was reading the *Wall Street Jour-*

nal, or pretending to. More often than not, she discovered him napping. Gerald Tarleton had been an imposing figure at one time. Tall and barrel-chested, he could bluster and intimidate with the best of them.

As he aged, he had lost much of his fire.

He reached up and patted her hand. "There you are, pumpkin. Will you tell cook I want dinner at six thirty instead of seven?"

"Of course. Did you have a good day?"

"Stupid doctor says I can't smoke cigars anymore. Where's the fun in that?"

The family physician made twice yearly visits to the Tarleton compound. Mazie wasn't sorry to have missed this one. "He's trying to keep you alive."

"Or take away my reasons for living," he groused comically.

Her father had married later in life, a man in his midforties taking a much younger bride. The story wasn't so unusual. But in Gerald's case, it had ended tragically. His bride and her parents had hidden from him the extent of her mental struggles, leaving Gerald to eventually raise his young family on his own.

Mazie and her brothers had each paid an invisible price that followed them into adulthood.

She ignored his mood. "I'll speak to cook, and then I'm going to change clothes. I'll be back down in half an hour or so."

"And Jonathan?"

"He's home tonight, I think."

After a quick word with the woman who ran the kitchen like a drill sergeant, but with sublime culinary skills, Mazie ran upstairs and at last made it to the privacy of her bedroom. She stripped off her clothes, trying not to think about J.B.'s hands on her body.

His touch had opened her eyes to several disturbing

truths, not the least of which was that she had carried a ten-dresse for him, an affection, that had never been stamped out.

She had spent a semester in France her senior year, only a few months after he had rejected her. The entire time she was abroad, she had imagined herself wandering the streets of Paris with J.B.

What a foolish, schoolgirl dream.

Yet now, when she stared in the mirror and saw her naked body, it was impossible to separate her former day-dreams from the inescapable reality. She had allowed J.B. Vaughan to caress her breasts, to touch her intimately.

Had Jonathan not intruded to *rescue* them, would she have regrets?

Confusion curled her stomach. She wasn't the kind of person who jumped into bed with a man. Especially not J.B.

Something had happened in the vault.

Yet however she replayed the sequence of events, J.B. didn't come out the villain. *Mazie* had been the one to ac-cidentally close the door and lock them in. *Mazie* had been the one to kiss J.B. *Mazie* had been the one who decided that a nod to her past infatuation would serve to distract J.B. from his claustrophobia.

Was it any wonder he had taken her invitation and run with it?

She stayed in the shower a long time, scrubbing and scrubbing again, trying to erase every vestige of his touch from her skin. She still wanted to hate him. He was still off-limits. And damn it, she *still* wanted to see him squirm.

Today had weakened her position in their face-off.

J.B. was a highly sexual man. When a woman gave him every indication she *wanted* sex, it was no wonder he had obliged.

Mazie had to live with the knowledge that she had done something extremely foolhardy. Self-destructive even.

Circumstances had saved her from the ultimate humiliation.

She didn't have to face J.B. as an ex-lover. Thank God for that.

But the unseen damage was worse, perhaps.

Now she knew what it felt like to be in his arms, to hear him whisper her name in a ragged groan that sent shivers of raw pleasure down her spine. Tonight when she climbed into bed, she would remember his hands on her breasts, her bare body, her sex.

How could she think about anything else?

Five

Even now, her hands trembled as she dried herself with a huge fluffy towel that smelled of sunshine and ocean breezes. The housekeeper liked pinning the laundry on an old-fashioned clothesline when weather permitted.

Mazie put on soft, faded jeans and a periwinkle cashmere sweater with a scoop neck. A short strand of pearls that had been her mother's dressed up the outfit enough to meet her father's old-school dinner requirements.

Sooner or later, J.B. would call about the property swap. She would have to speak to him as if nothing out of the ordinary had happened. And she would have to give him an answer.

His offer was generous. There was no denying the truth.

But she didn't want to give him what he wanted.

Though it was childish and petty on her part, something inside her wanted to hurt him as much as he had hurt her. For J.B., that meant she needed to hurt his business. She was certain he didn't have a heart or real emotions. All he cared about was stacking up more money and more accolades for his financial acumen.

If he really cared about *her*, he'd had plenty of years to make up for the past. But he hadn't.

At last, she could delay no longer. The sun had set in a blaze of glory, and darkness had fallen over the island. She heard a car in the driveway and recognized her brother's voice as it floated up from the foyer.

This mess with J.B. would have to wait.

She had time. Time to come up with a plan. When she saw him again, she wanted to be in control.

Passionless.

Absolutely calm.

There was a very good chance he had used their interlude in the vault to sway her to his side. Though he had not instigated the encounter, he was intuitive and fiercely intelligent. If he had sensed her weakness where he was concerned, he wouldn't have hesitated to use it against her. Nor would he in the future.

She had to be on her guard. She couldn't let her vulnerabilities where J.B. was concerned fool her into thinking he might really care about her.

Troubled and unsettled, she made her way downstairs. Jonathan might quiz her about the incident earlier in the day when she and J.B. had been trapped, but her father would be oblivious. If the subject came up, she would steer the conversation in a safer direction.

She walked into the dining room, ruefully aware that as usual, the full complement of china and silver and crystal adorned the table. A low arrangement of red roses and holly nestled in a Waterford bowl. Despite the fact that there were only three of them, the Tarletons would dine in style.

Grimacing inwardly, she stopped short when she saw the fourth place setting.

"Who's coming to dinner?" she asked Jonathan, a dreadful premonition already shaking her foundations.

Behind her, a familiar velvet-smooth voice replied.

"It's me," J.B. said. "I hope you don't mind another mouth to feed."

J.B. was accustomed to women's flirtatious maneuvers and their attempts to secure his attention. Rarely had he seen a woman with an expression on her face like Mazie's. She recovered quickly, but for a split second, she was startled, her unguarded look revealing a mixture of dismay and sensual awareness.

He'd be lying if he said the dismay didn't puncture his ego. Nevertheless, he kept his smile.

Mazie circled the room, keeping the dinner table between them. "Of course not. This is my father's house. There's always room for one more."

Gerald and Jonathan sat at the head and foot of the table, leaving J.B. and Mazie to face each other from opposite sides. Just for the hell of it, he moved quickly to hold out Mazie's chair as she took her seat. At the last moment, he unobtrusively brushed the side of her neck with a fleeting touch.

He was almost positive she inhaled a sharp breath, but Gerald was talking in a loud voice, so J.B. couldn't be sure. When the four of them were in place, the housekeeper brought out the first course.

By any culinary standards, it was an amazing meal. The Tarletons' cook was more akin to a chef, and she specialized in Lowcountry dishes that included the best of Charleston's local seafood. Tonight's offering was shrimp and grits with a Caesar salad on the side. J.B. was hungry, so he ate well.

But simmering beneath the surface of the lively conversation was the knowledge that Mazie never once looked him straight in the eye. Nor did she address a single comment directly to him. Her behavior was frustrating.

Things were different between them now...whether Mazie liked it or not.

While J.B. nursed his growing indignation, Gerald Tarleton dominated the evening's debate. Despite his declining health, he continued to go into work every day. He and Jonathan commanded a vast shipping empire that had made the family even more wealthy than it had been in the early days when Gerald took over the reins from *his* father.

At one point, J.B. caught his host's attention. "Mr. Tarleton, my dad wanted me to extend an invitation. He'd love to take you out deep-sea fishing on his new boat."

Gerald shook his head, sipping his wine and for a moment looking oddly fragile. "Tell him thanks, boy. But I don't get out and about much anymore. These old bones give me fits. And call me Gerald. You're not a kid anymore."

"The boat is a honey, Gerald. Almost as comfortable as my own house. The crew would pamper you. Think about it, why don't you? Dad respects you a great deal. I know it would tickle him to have a chance to pick your brain about business."

Gerald's pleased expression told J.B. that he had made inroads into the old man's instinctive refusal.

J.B. turned his attention to Mazie. "What about you, Mazie Jane? I seem to recall that you like to fish. We could make a party of it." He tried to get a rise out of her. Mazie had always hated her full name, because she thought it was too old-fashioned.

She choked on a bite of shrimp. Had to dab her mouth with a napkin before she could answer.

"Sounds fun," she said, clearly lying. "If I can find a free Saturday, I'll let you know."

Her Saturdays would be free when hell froze over. That much J.B. knew.

She was blowing him off, and none too subtly. Her evasion brought out his fighting instincts.

Jonathan's cell phone buzzed. He pulled it from his jacket pocket, gave his three companions an apologetic look and stood. "I have to deal with this. Sorry to interrupt the meal."

Cook spirited his plate away to keep the food warm.

Now it was only J.B., Mazie and an elderly man who was already nodding off, his chin on his chest.

J.B. crooked a finger. "I need to speak to you," he whispered. "In private." He motioned toward the door that led to the covered veranda.

Mazie glanced at her father and then at her plate. "I'm eating."

"This won't take long."

"I don't have anything to say to you."

"But I have things to say to *you*," he said firmly. "Or I can wait until your brother returns, and he can hear it all."

"You're a bully," she said, but she rose to her feet. "Make this quick."

Quietly, they stepped outside onto the porch and closed the door behind them.

Mazie wrapped her arms around her waist. "What?" she asked. "What's so damned important?"

"I want to know why you're looking at me like gum you scraped off the bottom of your shoe."

"I'm not," she said, backing away from him half a step.

"Yes. You are. I'm not an idiot. This morning you and I were—"

She shoved a hand against his chest, halting his words in midsentence. "Stop it. Right there. This morning was a mistake." Then she backed up again, almost as if she were afraid to let herself get too close to him.

He lifted an eyebrow. "You didn't enjoy yourself?"

"That's beside the point. It shouldn't have happened. And it won't again."

He chewed on that for a moment. "What are you afraid of, honey?"

Her eyes flashed. "Typical male response. If a woman doesn't want you, she must be afraid. That's bull crap, J.B."

"No," he said, trying his best to tamp down his anger and frustration. "What's bull crap is you trying to pretend that something extraordinary didn't happen between us today…" He hesitated, unwilling to give her ammunition, but itching to get at the truth. "That kind of connection is rare, Mazie."

She stared at him, eyes wide, posture shouting her unease. "I bet you use that line with a lot of women. You have a reputation, you know."

It was true. He couldn't deny it.

But her wariness went much farther back than that. Yes, he dated plenty of women. Mazie had made her judgments about him a long time ago, though.

"Have dinner with me tomorrow night," he said.

"Why? So you can badger me about my property?"

"Would you rather call it a date?"

He had boxed her into a momentary corner. Even as a child, Mazie never backed down from a dare. Now, he used that knowledge against her.

She lifted a shoulder and let it fall. "Fine," she said. "I'll meet you for a business dinner."

"I'll pick you up instead."

"Something casual."

"I'm taking you to Étoile de Mer."

"Absolutely not."

The French restaurant was intimate and extremely formal. In a century and a city that welcomed tourists in virtually any state of dress, Étoile de Mer maintained the old standards. Men in dinner jackets. Women in long dresses. Dancing beneath an antique Baccarat chandelier. The ambiance was unapologetically romantic and luxurious.

He smiled cajolingly. "It's December, Mazie. Jonathan talks about how much you enjoy the season. The hotel will be decorated to the nines. And Chef Marchon has a special holiday menu. The orchestra will play Christmas songs. Say yes. We'll have fun."

A tiny smile lifted the edges of her lips. "Do you always get your way?"

"Most of the time."

"Why are you doing this?" she asked.

He frowned. "I want to spend time with you. Is that so strange?" It *was* strange. And unprecedented. Both of them knew it. He was supposed to be closing a business deal, not chasing an attraction that could burn them both and end very badly.

He was her brother's best friend. It wasn't as if he could walk away and never see her again.

Her wariness was almost palpable. "I won't give you an answer about selling my property for a couple of weeks. I need time to think it over, to discuss the big picture with Gina. To decide how complicated it would be to move the store. If you're hoping to wine and dine me tomorrow night, so I'll be all mellow and sign on the dotted line, that's not going to happen."

"What if I said this wasn't about business at all?"

The words slipped out before he could snatch them back. To be honest, he hadn't known he was going to say something so revealing.

She put a hand to her throat, nervously playing with the strand of pearls. The necklace was nice, but if he had his way, the pearls would be an entire rope, and he would drape them around her neck while they were in bed.

Mazie made no move to break the silence, so he rephrased the question. "What if I swear that tomorrow night will be entirely personal?"

"You're scaring me."

She said it with humor, but he took her words at face value. "Nothing scary, Mazie. Nothing at all. Just two friends enjoying dinner." He was lying through his teeth. This was about much more than dinner. He was courting danger.

"If this is about what happened in the vault, I have to tell you that I'm not usually so…"

Her wrinkled nose and wry embarrassment touched

him. "You were incredible. I've had a hard-on the entire damn day."

"J.B.!"

Her mortified expression made him chuckle. "I get it, Mazie. You're telling me not to expect anything after dinner. That I get my dessert at the restaurant and not in my bed."

"You make me sound naive and ridiculous."

"You're neither of those things. But I'd be lying if I said you didn't shock me this morning. Hell, Mazie. I guess I've had sex a little more than you have, but you and me today…" He leaned against the porch railing and stared out at the ocean. The sound of the waves usually soothed him. Not tonight.

"What about us?"

There was a world of feminine emotion wrapped up in those three little words. Asking for reassurance.

"We connected," he muttered.

He didn't know how else to explain it. He couldn't even make sense of it himself. Was he headed down a familiar road? Letting sexual attraction drag him into a relationship that was doomed to failure?

"We should go back inside," she said quietly. "Jonathan will wonder where we are."

Something clicked. "Is Jonathan part of the problem? Are you worried about what your brother will think?"

"I don't want to cause discord between the two of you."

"Leave that to me." He sounded more confident than he felt.

Jonathan was likely to punch him, at the very least, if he found out J.B. was dallying with his baby sister. After all, Jonathan was partly to blame for the fact that Mazie had held a grudge against J.B. for so long.

"Daddy's awake," Mazie said. "I can see him waving his arms. Probably bossing the cook. Let's go in."

J.B. took her wrist, holding it lightly, needing to touch her, but not wanting to spook her. "I want to kiss you again."

"You do?"

"Yeah. Pretty badly. Just a kiss, Mazie. That's all."

Slowly, waiting for her to lean in and exhaling on a sigh of relief when she did, he drew her against his chest and wrapped his arms around her. She was tall for a woman. Their heights matched perfectly.

She was soft and warm. He buried his face in her neck, dragging oxygen into his lungs. Reminding himself he wasn't a horny teenager. He could control his emotions and his body.

When his mouth found hers, she murmured his name. Hearing her say it, all low and husky like that, made him nuts. He tangled a hand in her hair and deepened the kiss.

He hadn't imagined it. The fire. The wanting.

Whatever happened with Mazie in that bank vault this morning had nothing to do with his claustrophobia or a stress-induced jolt of adrenaline from being trapped.

It was all Mazie.

Now, she kissed him back. Unmistakably. When he would have pulled away, her hands clung to his shoulders, and she pressed against him. His erection was hard and heavy between them. Nothing he could do about that.

"Mazie," he croaked, trying to back away from the edge of insanity. "We need to go back inside. You said so. You're right."

"Don't listen to me," she said, unbuttoning a button on his shirt and stroking his collarbone.

The little tease was tormenting him on purpose.

He dragged her with him to a less exposed section of the veranda, around the corner of the house. This was not the time for Jonathan to burst through the doorway and find his sister in a compromising position.

"Enough," J.B. begged, wondering when exactly he had

lost the upper hand. He batted her hand away and rebuttoned his shirt. "Say yes to tomorrow night. It's the only answer I'll accept."

She smiled up at him, her eyelids heavy, her lower lip plump and shiny where he had sucked on it. "Yes."

Something inside him settled. "And you'll wear a kick-ass dress so I can make all the other men jealous?"

"I want to dance with you," she said. "If we're going all out for this *date*, I'll expect dancing."

"Duly noted."

"And expensive champagne. Maybe even caviar."

"Yes, ma'am."

"I still don't know why we're doing this," she said, the humor fading from her voice. "It seems awfully dangerous. Southern mamas warn their daughters about men like you."

He rubbed his thumb over her cheek, cupping her face. "You should have had a mother, Mazie. I'm sorry about all you lost."

She pulled away from him as if the sudden switch to a serious topic was more than she could bear.

Though her back was to him now, he saw her shrug. "I was luckier than most kids. My father indulged me."

Sliding his arms around her from behind, he rested his chin on top of her head. "It's easy to do. I have the same tendency myself."

"Which doesn't explain why you're trying to steal my livelihood."

He snorted. "Cut the drama. Besides, we're shelving the business negotiations for now. Isn't that what you wanted?"

It was getting more and more difficult to tell himself that this new détente with Mazie was all about business.

She turned around and looked up at him. "We don't always get what we want, J.B."

Six

Mazie wanted another kiss. But she knew her limits. Already she was playing with fire. Common sense was no match for the beat of her heart and the yearning in her blood.

Could she pursue this attraction and not get hurt? Could she indulge in her passion for J.B. and yet still make him pay for all the pain he had caused her in the past?

She fled the porch, not waiting to see if J.B. followed. Fortunately, her father was enjoying his favorite dessert—warm peach cobbler with ice cream. And Jonathan still hadn't returned.

Her father looked up when she walked into the room. "I wondered where everybody had gone."

"You were dozing," she said, seating herself at the table and picking up the napkin. "J.B. and I were talking business."

Her father raised an eyebrow. "Is he trying to sell you something?"

"No, sir," Mazie said. "He wants to buy the building I'm in."

"Make him work for it."

J.B. sat down as well, smoothing his hair and giving Mazie a steely-eyed glance. "No worries there, sir. Your daughter drives a hard bargain."

Fortunately for Mazie, Jonathan returned at that moment, and she was able to consume her dessert in peace while the men grumbled about sports and politics and whether or not South Carolina was going to have a colder-than-normal winter.

It was the occasional heated glances from J.B. that kept her on edge. Even in the midst of male conversation, he made it clear that his thoughts were on her.

Soon after, J.B. said his goodbyes.

Mazie considered walking him out, but Jonathan beat her to it, so she stayed where she was, telling herself she wasn't disappointed. She had kissed J.B. Vaughan entirely too many times for one day.

When Jonathan came back inside, he shut the front door and began punching in numbers to set the alarm. Mazie stopped him. "Are you in the mood to walk the beach?" she asked in a low voice. "I need to talk to you about a couple of things, and I don't want to do it in the house where Daddy can hear."

Jonathan looked tired and stressed, but he nodded. "Sure. You do know it's December?"

It was a running joke between them. A sort of dare as to which of the two would cry uncle when the temperatures dropped. "I'll bundle up," she said.

As she found her earmuffs and a heavy scarf and slipped on an old thigh-length coat, she couldn't help but wonder if J.B. would have welcomed an invitation to stay for a while. Had Jonathan not been home tonight, she might have been tempted.

On the way down the hall, she stopped by her father's bedroom.

"Jonathan and I are going for a walk on the beach," she said. "We won't be gone too long."

Her father lifted his head from his task and frowned. "It's not safe. I like having you both inside the house, so I know where you are."

She hugged him. "We need the exercise. Jonathan seems awfully stressed. Is everything okay at work?"

"The usual kerfuffles. He's fine."

"Have you heard anything at all from Hartley?"

Her father paled, his gaze haunted. "No. Go for your walk. And make sure you lock up when you get back."

"Yes, Daddy."

Jonathan was waiting for her. He tugged a toboggan over his head. "All set?"

She nodded. "Let's go."

In the brick wall on the back side of the house, a heavy wooden gate with electric voltage across the top provided an exit point. Jonathan disarmed the system and held the door for her to pass. In the soft powdery sand at this level, her feet slipped and slid. They crossed the beach to where the tide was going out, then turned left and started to walk.

Jonathan altered his stride to hers immediately. They found their rhythm and strode briskly. Occasionally, another intrepid beach walker passed by going in the opposite direction, but for the most part they had the beach to themselves.

Sometimes when they walked so late, they carried flashlights. This week, the nearly full moon provided plenty of illumination.

Mazie stared out at the almost invisible horizon. Tonight, the line between sea and sky was barely perceptible. As children, she and Hartley and Jonathan—and often J.B.— had loved watching the huge ships coming in and out of Charleston's historic harbor. They had learned how to spot Tarleton vessels, and how to read the bits of foreign language markings on others.

Often, especially on rainy days when there were no good outdoor activities to entertain a quartet of rambunctious children, they spun stories for each other about mysterious cargoes and whether or not it would be possible to stow away and make a sea voyage on the company's dime.

If they had been particularly well behaved, their father would bring out his expensive, high-powered binoculars and teach them how to focus the lenses. Mazie had stared at the ocean for as long as she could remember.

It was vast and inscrutable. She had seen the sea as placid as a baby's bath or angry and punishing in the midst of a hurricane. Sometimes it seemed as if all the answers to life's weighty questions resided in that enormous expanse of water.

Tonight, though, she sought a more human connection. She loved her brother dearly, but she wondered if he could be objective under the circumstances.

"Jonathan?"

"Hmm?" Her brother was lost in thought, his expression serious.

"Do you trust J.B.?"

Jonathan's head whipped around, his gaze incredulous. "He's my best friend. What kind of question is that? Of course I trust him. Surely you're not worried he's going to stiff you on this business deal. Is that why you're dragging your feet?"

"No, it's not that. I know he'll make me a fair offer. He already has, in fact. The only reason I haven't committed yet is because I wanted him to swing in the wind for a little while. The man is so damned arrogant. I couldn't stand the thought of giving in to him so easily."

Jonathan chuckled. "Well, he *is* arrogant, I'll grant you that. But he comes by it honestly. Everything he touches turns to gold."

"And on a personal level?"

"He and I have never done business together."

"That's not what I meant."

Jonathan stopped and faced her. "You're talking about women." He said it flatly. A statement. Not a question.

"I suppose I am."

"J.B. and I are grown men. We don't share locker room stories. What are you asking me, Mazie?"

She wrapped her arms around herself, feeling a chill now that they had stopped and their blood was cooling. "I'm not sure. I'm wondering what you know about his private life."

"As much as anybody, I guess." He started walking again, leaving Mazie to scamper in his wake to catch up. "He likes variety."

Her heart sank. She had come to the same conclusion. "Yeah…"

"Where's this coming from, sis?"

"He's asked me out on a date."

She threw it out there bluntly. No frills. Wondering what Jonathan would make of it.

For the second time, her brother ground to a halt. This time, his expression was thunderous. "Are you serious? I thought you hated the guy."

"Hate is a strong word. It seems like a bad idea, doesn't it?"

Jonathan made a motion with his hand. "Let's turn around." He walked in silence for a few moments. "Why ask me?"

"Well…" She shrugged. "You and I both agree he flits from one woman to the next. If he and I get something going and then it's over, everything will be awkward. Especially for you."

"Do you *want* to go out with him, Mazie?"

Ah, there was the question. She took a deep breath, inhaling the scents of salt air and somewhere in the distance, meat sizzling on a grill. "I do. Even knowing it's probably self-destructive. I like him. A lot. But J.B. has always been our *friend*. It's weird for me."

"How do you think I feel?"

Her brother's wry comment made her smile. "Well, don't worry. It will probably be a one-time thing. I can't imagine that he and I have what it takes to be a couple." Even talking about it sounded bizarre. There was a very good chance the *date* was an attempt to butter her up.

"Don't sell yourself short. J.B. isn't *only* a successful businessman. He does have a life."

"Unlike you," she said, suddenly eager to change the subject.

"Don't start on me, Mazie. Work has been hell lately. Dad goes in every day and creates messes I have to undo. And then I still have *my* projects to deal with. I don't know how much longer we can keep going like this."

"Is it time for him to step down?"

"I think so, yes. But how do I tell him that?"

"What about Hartley? Couldn't he help you?"

Jonathan's low curse shocked her. It was totally unlike him.

His voice was tense and angry. "There is no Hartley," he said. "He's not coming back. And even if he did, it wouldn't matter. Dad has cut him out of the will."

Sick dismay rolled through her chest. "But why?"

"I can't tell you. Or I don't want to tell you," he said, his voice weary. "He's your brother. I don't want to ruin your illusions. But trust me when I say there are some sins a man commits that are unforgivable."

"But I—"

He cut her off with a sharp slash of his hand. "I won't talk to you about this, Mazie. I love you dearly, but the subject is closed."

Jonathan's vehement tone ended the conversation. Their peaceful walk was ruined.

Tears stung her eyes. Jonathan complained about chaos at the shipping company, but for Mazie, All That Glitters was the stability in her life. At home she had a rapidly declining parent, one brother who was working himself to death and another who had apparently abandoned them all. Even worse—though he didn't say much about it—Jonathan's headaches were increasingly severe. It worried her.

They were almost back to the house. She touched his arm. "I'm sorry. I know you're carrying the business. I wish I could help."

He put an arm around her waist and hugged her. "It will all work out. It always does."

She sighed. "I feel like I should head up to Vermont to see Mama…sometime in the next two weeks."

Jonathan stopped. He rolled his shoulders. "I'm not ready to go inside yet."

They dropped down onto the sand. Mazie linked her arms around her knees. "I'll feel guilty if I don't make the effort."

"She doesn't even know who we are. Hasn't for years."

"I know. But she's my mother. And it's Christmas."

"We were there a month ago."

"Yes." The two of them had flown up to Stowe for a ski trip with friends. Afterward, they had stayed over a day, rented a car and driven to a tiny town near the New Hampshire border to make the sad, difficult visit.

"Have you ever wondered," Mazie said, "why Daddy found a place so damned far away from Charleston?"

Jonathan laughed, but there was no humor in it. "Oh, yeah. To his credit, Ravenwood is tops in the nation for residential care facilities. Believe me, I've checked. So no one can fault him there. He's paying a king's ransom to keep her in safety and comfort."

"But my cynical side tells me he doesn't want to have to think about her. It's easier if she's a thousand miles away."

"That about sums it up."

"When was the last time he went up there?"

"I'm not sure. Two years ago. Three?"

"He could have divorced her."

"I think he probably still loves her, Mazie."

She winced inwardly. Maybe the Tarletons were *every one* cursed...doomed to give their hearts unwisely. After all, wasn't Mazie contemplating doing the same thing? She knew how J.B. had treated her in the past, yet she was still hoping against hope that he had changed.

They sat there in silence, listening to the crashing waves, noting how exponentially many more stars there were the longer they let their eyes adjust to the darkness.

She rested her chin on her knees. "I used to wish we were a family like the Vaughans. Normal. Ordinary. Together."

Jonathan tousled her hair. "I'm not sure I'd call my buddy ordinary, but yeah. I get your point." He leaned back on his hands. "I guess we're all a little screwed up because of what happened. I hated it for you the worst. I remember the day Mom left you cried for hours."

"And you skipped baseball practice so you could come home, sit on my bed and read *Little House on the Prairie* to me."

"She wasn't much of a mom even when she still lived with us. We pretty much raised ourselves."

"I know. It used to scare me when she would sit in front of the window for hours on end and not speak."

"Don't go to Vermont, Mazie. It will make you too sad. Wait until January, and I'll go with you. Or maybe February."

"I'll think about it."

"And J.B.?"

She stood up and dusted the sand from her pants. "I'll think about him, too. Who knows, Jonathan? Maybe you and I are both too messed up to have serious relationships with anyone."

He rolled to his feet and shook himself like a dog. "Speak for yourself. I plan to get laid this weekend on a tropical island with a drink in one hand and sunscreen in the other."

"Really?"

He headed toward the gate, his laughter dancing on the breeze. "You're too gullible, Mazie Jane. I'd work on that before you go out with J.B."

Mazie gulped her coffee, burned her tongue and said an unladylike word. "Can you unlock the door? I don't know what I did with my keys."

Gina scooted past her, punched in the alarm code and wrestled with the cantankerous lock. "I hope we do move. I hate this door."

The two of them entered the shop and dumped their things in the back office. Mazie was usually the bubbly one in the mornings. Gina was slower to wake up. But Mazie had spent a restless night tossing and turning and wondering if she had the guts to call J.B. and cancel.

She didn't know which was worse. Going, or not going. Now she was exhausted *and* conflicted.

Gina sifted through the mail she had picked up from their postal box. "Two bills, an invitation to a reception at the Gullah Cultural Center and seven catalogs. Maybe *we* should consider doing a catalog. The bulk mailings must produce business, or we wouldn't be drowning under the weight of them."

"It's even worse at home. The recycle bin overflows this time of year."

"Look at this one," Gina said. "It's an English company that sells organic scented soaps. Their packaging is really nice. We could add some little things like that to put pops of color in the shop. Even jewelry can get monotonous when it's all gold and silver."

"Bite your tongue," Mazie said, laughing.

As they ran through their morning rituals, Mazie felt the strongest urge to tell Gina everything that had happened in the bank vault, and then last night on the veranda. She needed advice. Support. A dose of impartial sanity.

She was supposed to be planning her revenge, not thinking about how good it felt to kiss J.B. To touch him. To feel his hands on her body.

Gina waved a hand in front of Mazie's face. "Hellooo… you spaced out on me, boss. I need you to focus. We've got not one, but two cruise ships today. And it's Friday, so the Holiday Weekends festival starts. We're going to be run ragged."

"You're right."

Gina cocked her head. "Are you okay, Mazie?"

Seven

Mazie changed the subject and busied herself unwrapping a shipment of earrings.

As the afternoon passed, one thought kept spinning in her brain. She wasn't going to sleep with J.B. Of course she wasn't.

But the whole time she was getting ready after work that afternoon, she couldn't help wondering if he was contemplating taking her home with him after dinner. Given what had transpired in the bank vault, it wasn't an entirely out-in-left-field idea. Clearly he knew that going back to *her* place was out of the question.

She left the shop at three in order to get a mani-pedi before going home. Tonight's encounter required all the confidence she could muster. Whether the evening turned out to be business or pleasure or both, she had to be prepared, mentally and physically.

Fortunately, her wardrobe wasn't a problem. A year ago, for a black-tie charity gala, she had ordered a beautiful holiday dress from an online catalog. At the last minute, she had come down with a twenty-four-hour bug and didn't get to attend the event. The gown had been hanging in her closet ever since.

It wasn't really the kind of thing she could use during another season of the year. The floor-length dress was deep green velvet. The fabric was elegant and classic, the design even more so. A plunging neckline showcased her breasts.

The back of the dress also dipped in a deep vee, leaving her arms and shoulders bare.

She debated longer over her hair than anything else. If it were summer, she would put it up, no question. But the weather was perfect today, and with all that bare skin showing, maybe having her hair down around her shoulders was a good idea.

Fortunately for her nerves, Jonathan hadn't yet returned from the office when it was time for J.B. to arrive. Her father was out of the house also, having dinner with friends. Mazie had said goodbye to him earlier as he left with his driver.

Mazie sent the cook and housekeeper home early, so when J.B. pulled up in front of the house in his luxury SUV, no one was around to witness the moment. She peeked out and watched him lope up the front stairs.

He was a gorgeous man, beautiful enough to make her breath catch in her throat. J.B. would hate being called *beautiful*, but the adjective fit. Though his features weren't perfectly symmetrical, and he didn't have the kind of slick sophistication of a model, there was something intensely masculine about him.

He was a chameleon, really.

In a business setting, she had seen him play the part of the successful entrepreneur, both charming and hard-dealing. But when J.B. and Jonathan headed out to North Carolina to camp in the mountains or took off on a weeklong cruise down the coast in J.B.'s sailboat, his tanned limbs and casual clothing made him look like a rugged outdoorsman.

She took one last quick peek before opening the door.

Tonight, in a classic black tuxedo and crisp white shirt, he was a heartbreaker. Mazie knew that side of him better than most.

J.B. was stunned to find that he was nervous as hell. When Mazie opened the door, his heart slugged hard in his chest. Her glorious chestnut hair spilled across her shoulders, thick and wavy. The green dress she wore showcased her slender figure. His fingers itched to stroke all that soft fabric.

But his sense of self-preservation sounded an alarm.

Instead of touching her, he cleared his throat and smiled. "You look stunning, Mazie. I've got the heat running in the car, in case you don't want to bother with a wrap. It's not really all that cold tonight. You could always throw a coat in the back seat for later."

She had stepped back to allow him to enter. Now he stood in the foyer, wanting to sweep her up in his arms and kiss her senseless. Instead, he jammed his hands in his pockets and practiced self-control.

Mazie's smile was guarded. "Thank you. I'll do that."

The current atmosphere could best be described as wary. The physical awareness between them was on a slow boil, but because he had hurt her once, she didn't trust him. He'd have to work on that.

It took Mazie only a matter of moments to lock the door and set the alarm. When she was done, he put a hand beneath her elbow and steadied her as they descended the stairs. The minimal physical contact was enough to make his blood heat.

He helped her into the front seat before closing the door. Then he ran around to the driver's side. As he had promised, the car was toasty warm.

Mazie buckled her seat belt and folded her hands in her lap, her spine straight. It wasn't the posture of a woman prepared to enjoy an exciting evening. If anything, she seemed to be braced for unpleasant news.

"I don't bite," he said teasingly.

They exited the main gates, and he steered the car toward the Ravenel Bridge.

She shot him a sideways glance. "I'm not sure this was a good idea," she said. "We have nothing in common."

Her tone was prissy enough to annoy him. "It didn't seem that way when you locked us in that bank vault."

"That was an accident."

"So you say." He loved teasing her. "We have history, Mazie."

"I'm surprised you'd want to bring that up."

Bingo. Now he knew for sure what land mines lay in his path. She was pissed, even now, about him turning her down years ago.

"You're still mad about that prom thing?"

"Don't flatter yourself." Her fingers made patterns in the velvet. "I got over my embarrassing crush pretty quickly after that night. You were an arrogant jerk. And unkind on top of that. But I learned from that experience."

"Learned what?"

"Not to trust you."

He flinched inwardly. There were extenuating circumstances, explanations that could clear his name, but he wasn't the only person involved, and he didn't want to cause a rift between her and Jonathan. Even now, J.B.'s behavior was risky. It was the reason he had kept his distance for years.

"I'd like to propose a truce," he said lightly, his fingers clenched on the steering wheel. "What if we start over? A new relationship. A new beginning." He told himself he needed her goodwill so she would sell him her property. Surely he wasn't really considering something so much more unpredictable.

"Why would we do that?"

"It's the season of peace and goodwill. Isn't that enough?" He reached across the small distance separating them and touched her wrist. "This isn't about me stealing your property, Mazie. I want it, yes. But we can do business another day. Tonight, I'm only interested in *you*."

He hadn't meant to be so honest, but her inability to accept him at face value was frustrating.

At the hotel, J.B. handed off his keys with a large tip, large enough to guarantee he'd get the car back with no dings or scratches.

The front door was only steps away. He glanced at his passenger. "Do you want to keep your coat?"

"No. I'm fine."

The seat of the SUV was high. Mazie's legs were long, but her dress was fitted. Without asking permission, he put his hands on her waist and lifted her down to the narrow red carpet that led to the entrance.

Overhead, a canvas awning protected them from nonexistent rain. Huge concrete urns on either side overflowed with holly and magnolia blossoms and burgundy satin ribbons.

Mazie's face lit up, her reserve melting in the festive atmosphere. "This is lovely." She actually squeezed his hand momentarily, leaving him to grin like a kid who'd just gotten a gold star for a perfect spelling test. Unfortunately, the moment was far too short.

He curled an arm around her waist and ushered her inside.

Étoile de Mer was old Charleston at her finest. Five years ago, the series of narrow buildings tucked away on a side street had been an aging inn past its prime with a different name. But new owners had completely renovated the connected eighteenth-century row houses.

The result was a chic, luxurious boutique hotel that catered to travelers with the means to splurge, whether that be millennials or baby boomers. The main floor of the hotel included a bar and lounge along with a five-star restaurant that was booked for six months in advance.

J.B. had called in a few favors, made a handful of promises and wrangled a prime reservation for seven o'clock.

Seeing the expression on Mazie's face was worth every bit of hassle.

The host led them up a shallow flight of stairs to the mezzanine level. Their table was tucked inside a bay window overlooking the street.

Once they had ordered an appetizer and wine, J.B. leaned back in his chair and studied his companion. "Have you eaten here before?"

Mazie shook her head. "No. I do go out with friends often, but we generally pick something more casual. And my social life isn't nonstop. Jonathan and I take turns looking after Dad when we want to be gone overnight."

"He can't be on his own?"

"Oh, he could be," Mazie said. "But Jonathan and I are his emotional crutches. Once Hartley disappeared, I think Daddy gave up and started thinking like an old man."

"Do you know where your brother is?"

Mazie shook her head, her expression bleak. "No. I don't even know what happened. Jonathan won't tell me. Do *you* know?"

J.B. shook his head. "Sorry. No idea. Jonathan and I are tight, but he hasn't said much at all about Hartley."

"Oh." She sighed. "I was hoping you could clue me in. The whole thing is frightening. To be honest, it hurts. He and I were very close. I can't believe he left without saying a word." Mazie traced a pattern in the condensation on her water glass with her fingertip. "I used to be terribly jealous of your family," she said. Her rueful sideways glance told him she wasn't kidding.

"Really? Why?"

"The Vaughans are all so incredibly normal. I never had normal in my life. You're lucky, J.B."

The comment caught him off guard. "I suppose I am,"

he said. The waiter interrupted the conversation, arriving to take their order. Mazie chose shrimp étouffée on a bed of fluffy rice. J.B. asked for the rare filet topped with a crabmeat garnish.

When they were alone again, he picked up the threads of the conversation. "What happens to your father when you or Jonathan decide to get married?"

Mazie wrinkled her nose. "I don't know that either of us has to worry about that. My dear brother doesn't let himself get close to anyone, and I'm…" She trailed off, looking uncomfortable.

"You're what?"

"Scared." She tossed the word at him with an almost visible chip on her shoulder.

"Scared of what?"

"I don't want to love someone so much that it blinds me or traps me. My parents are hardly a shining example of marital success. You know the statistics. You've lived them. No offense."

He winced inwardly. Mazie had faced more than her share of abandonment. She must surely have been conflicted about her father sending her mother away, no matter the circumstances.

"I hear what you're saying, but I'm not sure your argument holds water, though. I had the greatest example of marriage in the world, and still I got duped by a money hungry social climber who ruined my credit and cleaned out my bank accounts in the divorce."

"Did your parents try to stop you?"

"Of course they did. Several friends weighed in, too, Jonathan included. But I was blinded by physical infatuation." Wasn't that what he risked now?

"Not too blind to see what you were getting out of the arrangement."

Mazie's humor soothed old wounds. "I was twenty-two

years old and driven by my hormones. It wasn't my finest hour."

"To be honest, I was away at college most of that year, so I didn't hear more than the occasional flurry of gossip. But I remember being very surprised."

He cocked his head. "Why?"

"Because you were always so sure of what you wanted. At the risk of pumping up your already enormous ego, I couldn't imagine any woman walking away from you after only a few months, even if you *were* difficult to live with. Maybe she had the money thing planned from the start."

"If you're trying to make me feel better, it's not working."

Her grin was impish. "Sorry. I've known you and hated you for too long to tiptoe around your feelings…always assuming you *have* feelings." The smile told him she was making a joke at his expense. She wasn't trying to impress him, that was for sure.

"I have feelings," he said, deadpan. "I'm having a feeling right now." He flirted deliberately, for nothing more than the sheer pleasure of watching her react.

Mazie didn't seem to know what to make of him.

She concentrated on her food, most likely disconcerted by his deliberately intimate teasing. When at last she lifted her head and pinned him with an amber-eyed gaze, he knew in an instant that he had waded into deep water.

"Let me ask you something, J.B.," she said.

He waved a hand. "Anything at all. I'm an open book."

"If we hadn't gotten locked in the bank vault and ended up in an extremely compromising position, would you ever have considered asking me out?"

His fork was halfway to his mouth. The bite of tender beef went untasted. Slowly, he set down the utensil, dabbed his lips with a snowy napkin and frowned. "I feel like this is one of those questions women throw out to trip a guy up."

"It's no trick. I'm merely asking—would we be sitting here right now if you didn't have claustrophobia, and we didn't use sex to take your mind off the fact that we were trapped? You've had a decade to ask me out on a date. Why now?"

Mazie watched J.B.'s face, zeroing in on every nuance of expression. She'd like to think her intuition could spot any dissembling on his part. Then again, the man was a practiced charmer. Girls had been throwing themselves at him since he was in middle school.

It was no wonder he was so confident he could acquire her property. He was accustomed to the dominoes always falling his way. The world cooperated with J.B. Inevitably.

While it was true that his youthful marriage had been a bad misstep, he had survived. He'd been humiliated and chastened and perhaps, at the time, even heartbroken. Still, it seemed unlikely he had suffered any lasting damage.

His silence in the aftermath of her question was ominous. Was he inventing a pretty story? Concocting a tale that would flatter her and woo her?

"J.B.?"

He shook his head. "You ask difficult questions, Mazie Tarleton. Maybe I wanted to be sure I was giving you a thoughtful response. Maybe I needed to comb through my own motives. Maybe I'm not even sure why I invited you to dinner. Or maybe I was afraid the truth would make you angry."

She gaped at him, unprepared for this level of transparency. "So what did you come up with? Don't keep me in suspense."

While she waited, breathless, needing to hear what J.B. had to say, their waiter arrived with the main courses. Though the food looked and smelled amazing, Mazie wanted to banish the poor man to the kitchen. J.B. had been hovering on the verge of complete honesty. She wanted desperately to hear his response.

Instead, she had to be content with a seemingly endless parade of servers and sommeliers and even the manager who wanted to make sure every single thing about the dinner was to their liking.

By the time the two of them were finally alone again, the moment had passed.

Mazie sighed inwardly. An orchestra on the level below them had begun playing a medley of familiar Christmas songs. The restaurant buzzed with laughter and the clinking of crystal.

On any other occasion and with any other companion, Mazie would be basking in a haze of warm contentment.

Instead, she ate her meal automatically. All she could think about was the man sitting across from her. Why was he stalling?

He poured each of them another glass of wine, finished his steak and then stared at her.

"The answer is no," he said. "I wouldn't have. The reason I asked you out has *everything* to do with what happened in the bank vault."

Eight

Mazie froze, sensing danger. J.B.'s eyes were dark…intense. More navy blue tonight than royal. And nothing about him suggested lighthearted teasing.

She swallowed, her throat suddenly as dry as sandpaper. "I see."

He drank recklessly, the muscles in his throat rippling as he swallowed. Without warning, some line had been crossed, some barrier breached.

Gone was the good-natured, sophisticated businessman. The wealthy entrepreneur.

In his place was a primal male with flushed cheekbones, glittering sapphire eyes, and a big body that radiated warmth and raw masculinity.

In his right hand, he held a crystal goblet. His left hand moved restlessly on the white linen tablecloth. Against the pristine fabric, his tanned fingers drummed a rhythm only he could hear.

At last he stared at her moodily, his brows dark, his mood volatile. "Is that all you have to say?"

"I may have given you the wrong impression about me," she whispered, conscious of people coming and going nearby.

"Or maybe you hide the real you from the world."

"I'm not that kind of woman," she said desperately. "It was the adrenaline or something."

"Or something…" He laughed without humor. "You're

a sensual woman, Mazie. Sexy and beautiful and damned appealing in every way. We've been dancing around each other for years, always careful never to get too close. I've seen you move across a crowded room to avoid me. Why?"

"You're imagining things," she said, aghast that he had noticed. But of course he had. The man never missed anything. She'd been protecting herself, plain and simple. And he had known, damn him.

"No." His rebuttal was flat. Certain. "I'm not imagining *anything*. You've kept the width of this city between us, but yesterday when I had my embarrassing meltdown, your compassion was stronger than your need to keep your distance. When we touched, it was gasoline on a fire."

"Please don't say things like that," she begged. "It isn't true."

"You can deny it all you like, but I was there, Mazie. So yes…that's why I asked you out. Even though I knew it was a bad idea. I couldn't wait to touch you again." He stood and tossed his napkin on the table. "Dance with me, sweet girl. Dessert will keep."

His hand closed around her wrist. Gently, inexorably, he drew her to her feet.

Mazie trembled. It was impossible to meet his gaze. Not now. Not when her heart slammed against her ribs and her breasts ached for his touch.

He led her down the carpeted stairs and into the salon where a polished dance floor stretched from wall to wall. Overhead, a phalanx of miniature crystal chandeliers, draped in mistletoe and bows, cast a rainbow of shimmering light over the dancers.

The room wasn't large. J.B. pulled her into his arms and held her tightly. They fell into the music as one, barely missing a note or a step. Some men hated dancing. J.B. moved as if he knew the music by heart.

She felt cosseted in his embrace, but at the same time shiveringly aware of the shark-infested waters that might lie ahead. Already her body responded to his caress. His heart beat a steady rhythm beneath her palm. His fingers were warm on the bare skin of her lower back. They didn't speak.

Words weren't necessary.

It wasn't her imagination that other women sneaked peeks at the man who held her so carefully. His breath was warm at her temple. The scent of his crisply starched shirt teased her nostrils.

Her body warmed and melted into his. They were in a very public venue. Dancing was the only acceptable, legitimate reason for a man and woman to be so close.

One song segued into the next. Mazie knew every word, every chorus. For so many Christmases she had wondered about her future. For so many Christmases, she had told herself she despised J.B.

Now the whole world was changing.

She could have danced all night. Her feet barely noticed the pain in her toes, the strain in her calves. For a woman who spent her days in flats or athletic shoes, tonight's escapade was a dose of reality.

Being glamorous hurt.

At last, J.B. was the one to call a halt. He brushed a strand of hair from her hot cheek. "How about a drink?" The words were commonplace. The look in his eyes, anything but.

She nodded, flushed with a confusing mixture of excitement and dread. Whatever happened tonight was up to her. No matter how many times she told herself she had to stay away from J.B., the truth was far simpler.

He was her kryptonite.

She wanted him.

Hand in hand, they ascended the stairs to their intimate table for two. Dessert menus appeared. She downed two glasses of ice water. Her wineglass was refilled, as if by magic.

When their caramel-laced bread pudding arrived, Mazie shook her head. "I don't think I can. I'm stuffed."

J.B.'s heavy-lidded gaze never left her face. "A taste at least," he coaxed. He scooped up a bite. It was covered in whipped cream.

Mazie opened her mouth automatically when he held out the spoon. Her thighs clenched beneath the table. "Yum," she mumbled, chewing and swallowing.

The man was a devil. She wanted to strip him out of that tux and do naughty things to his body.

His slight smile told her he knew exactly what thoughts were running through her head. Without warning, he leaned forward and kissed the edge of her mouth, his tongue delicately swiping a residue of sweet cream. "You taste delectable."

"Stop," she said, breathing hard. "People are watching."

"It was barely a kiss. Don't worry. No one can see."

She realized he was right. The restaurant lights had been dimmed. A trio of short red candles flickered on their table. With the antique privacy screens and artfully placed foliage, Mazie and J.B. were in a world of their own.

The waiter still stopped by, of course, but not as often now that dinner was almost done.

She sipped her wine, awash in a haze of incredulity. Not only was she enjoying herself, but she was spending time with J.B., and she didn't want to kill him. That was progress, right?

Fortunately for her emotional equilibrium, he didn't try to feed her any more dessert. She ate another couple of bites and left it to him to finish. The man was tall and athletic. He could afford the calories.

While they were dancing, J.B. had left his cell phone on the table, silenced of course. Suddenly, it vibrated. He glanced at it automatically, and before he could say anything, another call came in from the same number.

"It's my sister Leila," he said. "She never calls this time of day. Will you excuse me, Mazie?"

"Of course."

As he stood, the phone buzzed a third time.

Something told her it wasn't good news. As she watched, J.B. hurried down the stairs and out the front door where he could talk in private. Though she was at the window, she couldn't see him on the street.

Less than five minutes later, he returned, his face white beneath his tan. "I'm so sorry," he said. "But I have to go. It's my mother." He swallowed hard. "She's had a massive heart attack. They don't know the damage yet. She may have to have surgery tonight."

Mazie's eyes widened. J.B.'s family was close. The matriarch was beloved. "Go," she said, waving her hand at him. "I'll take care of the bill and grab a taxi. Go. Hurry." She lifted a hand and summoned the waiter.

J.B. hesitated, his usual expression robbed of its suave confidence. "I hate to leave you."

She jumped off the emotional deep end. "I could come with you." Even strong men needed support occasionally.

The waiter handed over the check. J.B. pulled out his credit card. When the man walked away, J.B. looked at her and sighed. "I'd like that. If you're sure you want to."

Were both of them thinking about what they were giving up tonight? "Will it seem odd to your family if I show up with you?"

"You know them all. Nobody will notice."

That was debatable.

The waiter dropped off the bill. J.B. scribbled his name and pocketed his credit card. And they were done.

The valet brought the car in record time. J.B. handed over another generous tip and tucked Mazie into the front seat.

She was hardly dressed for a hospital visit. Neither was he.

J.B. drove the maze of downtown streets with a reckless intensity that was only slightly alarming. At the hospital, he screeched into a parking spot in the emergency room lot and hopped out, pausing to help Mazie.

"I can wait in the car," she said, feeling conspicuous in her fancy dress.

He gripped her wrist. "I want you to come."

Once they were inside, it was only a matter of moments until a nurse directed them to the appropriate cubicle. The heart surgeon had just arrived to talk to the family. They were standing in the hall, though Mazie could see J.B.'s mother through the partially open door. The older woman was hooked up to a multitude of machines.

Most families would probably be scolded for having too many visitors. Since the Vaughans had outfitted an entire pediatric wing in recent years, they were VIPs.

The man's face was grave. "Mrs. Vaughan suffered a very dangerous cardiac event. She is weak and not entirely stable. I don't think we should wait until morning for the surgery."

Mazie recognized J.B.'s father and his two sisters, Leila and Alana. As children, Mazie and Jonathan and Hartley had spent large amounts of time at the Vaughan home. But it had been years since she had been close to them as a friend.

Both of J.B.'s sisters had red-rimmed eyes. His father looked exhausted and stressed. Mr. Vaughan nodded. "We're in your hands, Dr. Pritchard. Tell us what to do."

The doctor made a note on his clipboard. "She's been

asking for her son." He looked at J.B. "Once you've had a chance to spend a few minutes with her, we'll prep her for surgery." He paused, grimacing. "I don't want to alarm you unnecessarily, but I need you to know that the surgery carries significant risk. Without it, she'll suffer another heart attack, possibly fatal. So we don't really have a choice."

Mr. Vaughan spoke up, his eyes sunken and underscored with shadows. "You're saying that her other health conditions make it complicated."

The doctor nodded. "Yes. Her autoimmune disease and the high blood pressure are problematic." He looked at all of them. "We need her to fight and to believe she is going to be okay. So no crying, no drama."

J.B.'s expression was grim, his jaw taut. "Understood."

"If you'll excuse me," the doctor said, "I'll go make sure the OR is being prepped. Once the surgery begins, we'll keep you posted in the surgical waiting lounge." With a brief nod, he disappeared down the hall.

J.B. squared his shoulders. "I'll talk to her," he said.

His father hugged him tightly. "We can't lose her, son. She's the center of this family. She's our rock."

"I know, Dad. I know."

J.B. shot Mazie a look she couldn't read. He hugged his sisters. Then he stepped through the door. "Hey, Mom. What's this I hear about you scaring Dad? That's not nice."

The four people left standing in the hallway strained to hear.

Mrs. Vaughan's expression brightened when she saw her firstborn. "Don't you look handsome. A date tonight?"

"Yes, Mama."

"That's nice."

Tears stung Mazie's eyes when J.B. perched on the edge of the bed and carefully took his mother's hand in both of his. He kissed her fingers. "You gave us a scare, but you're going to be fine."

His mother's wrinkled nose and half frown told Mazie that the woman was well aware of her situation.

"I want you to promise me something, sweetheart." Her voice was hoarse and weak.

J.B. nodded. "Whatever you need, Mom. You name it."

"If anything happens to me, I want you to take care of your dad and your sisters. They will depend on you, J.B."

Leila moaned and burst into tears, though she muffled her sobs and moved away from the door. Alana curled an arm around her father's waist.

Mazie's eyes were damp, as well.

Through the door, she saw J.B. lean down and kiss his mother's cheek. "We're not going to talk like that. I have a surprise for you. I was going to wait until Christmas to tell everybody, but you should know tonight. I've asked Mazie Tarleton to marry me. We're engaged. And the good Lord willing, she and I won't wait too long to get started on those grandchildren you've always wanted."

Mrs. Vaughan's face lit up, and a tear rolled down her cheek. "Really, son? Oh, that's wonderful."

Mazie was stunned for thirty seconds until she realized what J.B. was doing. He was giving his mother a reason to fight, a reason to live. Mazie expected the three Vaughans in the hallway to give her the third degree, but they were too focused on what was happening in the emergency room cubicle.

She sucked in a sharp breath. For a moment, J.B.'s play-acting hit a nerve. If she really hated the man, why did his pretend words reach deep inside her and squeeze her heart?

Mrs. Vaughan peered around her son. "Is she here, J.B.? I haven't seen her in ages."

J.B. looked over his shoulder, his gaze clashing with Mazie's. She nodded slowly, alarmed by how appealing it was to play this unexpected role. Had she honestly blinded herself to the truth so completely? Did she want to be J.B.'s fiancée, even as part of a benevolent lie?

Heaven help her. It felt wrong, but what could she do?

Mr. Vaughan and the two girls stepped aside. Mazie smoothed her skirt. She was still holding her small evening purse. She passed it off to Alana and eased the door open. "I'm here, Mrs. Vaughan."

J.B.'s mother held out her hand. "Come sit where I can look at you. And call me Jane. Oh, honey, you're stunning. That dress makes you look like a model. I know your mother would be so proud."

J.B. stood up so Mazie could take his place. She sat down on the bed gingerly, not wanting to disturb any of the medical equipment. "I haven't seen you in forever, Mrs. Vaughan. Jane, I mean. I'm so sorry you've been ill."

Jane Vaughan beamed, her hand touching the soft velvet of Mazie's skirt. "I couldn't be happier," she said. "Let me see the ring." She reached for Mazie's left hand.

Mazie curled her fingers defensively. "J.B. wanted me to help pick out the ring. So we don't have it yet."

J.B. moved closer. He rested a hand on Mazie's shoulder. His fingers were warm on the bare skin at the curve of her neck. "I won't make her wait long, Mom. This just happened."

"I see."

For a moment it seemed as though J.B.'s mother saw through their subterfuge. But her smile didn't waver.

J.B. hugged Mazie and then leaned down to brush his lips across his mother's brow. "When you're on the mend, we'd like your help with wedding plans."

"Oh, yes," Mazie said. "You know all the venues in Charleston and all the best vendors. I'll need all the backup I can get."

Jane was misty-eyed. She gripped her son's hand...and Mazie's. "I wouldn't miss this wedding for the world."

J.B. chuckled. "Consider it good practice for when Leila and Alana tie the knot."

Mazie stood, keenly aware of the warmth of J.B.'s big frame at her back. "I'll let you rest now."

J.B. nodded. "I love you, Mama. And I'll be here during the surgery. We all will. Don't be afraid."

Jane smiled weakly, obviously tired out by the conversation. "I'm not scared. Your father and I have lived a good life. If it's my time to go, don't let him be sad."

Mazie leaned down and kissed her cheek, realizing how much she had missed having a maternal role model as she reached adulthood. "You can't go," she said firmly. "We all need you."

As she slipped out of the room, the others came in to say their last words of encouragement. The nurse arrived with pre-op sedation.

Mazie leaned against the wall in the hallway and said a prayer for Jane's safety.

When J.B. exited the room, he eyed her warily. Unspoken feelings simmered between them.

She shook her head in bemusement. "You always did think fast on your feet." It wasn't really a compliment.

He scraped his hands through his hair. "I don't mean to make light of marriage, but I wanted her to have a reason to fight."

"Of course you did. But the rest of your family?"

"Let's keep the truth to ourselves for now. Explaining the ruse is unnecessary. They have enough on their plate."

This lie might keep her tied to him indefinitely. She wasn't sure how she felt about that. "I'm going to call a cab," she said quietly.

"I'll drive you home."

"No. You need to be here. I'll be fine." The J.B. she knew had disappeared. In his place, she saw a man who was worried and trying not to show it.

She was getting in too deep. She didn't want to admire him or feel sympathy for him. Her years-long antipathy was the only thing protecting her from doing something stupid.

No one would blame her if she ran far and fast. Getting too close to J.B. threatened her hard-won composure.

For a decade and more she had convinced herself that she didn't even like the man. How could her feelings have changed so radically? Her heart pounded. *Walk away, Mazie. Walk away.* Despite her best intentions, emotionally charged words tumbled from her lips. Words that said her heart was far more involved than she was prepared to admit. "Would you like to me to come back after I change clothes?"

Nine

J.B. looked stunned. Somehow the lie he had spouted was changing everything. This felt intimate. Emotionally charged. She found herself offering help and comfort as if she were a real fiancée.

He nodded slowly, his gaze unguarded for a surprising moment. "Yes, please."

"Do you want me to go by your place and bring you something else to wear?" She knew where he lived. She and Jonathan and Hartley had been to parties there. It was a fabulous home overlooking the Battery.

"You don't mind?" He seemed to be weighing his words as if afraid of spooking her.

"Not at all. I'll call Jonathan and tell him what's going on so Dad won't worry."

He nodded. "I'll text you the alarm code and what to grab for me." When he handed her his keys and their fingers brushed, his touch burned. "Do you feel comfortable driving the SUV?" he asked.

"Not entirely, but I'll take it slow. It's late. There won't be much traffic."

He cupped her chin in his hand. "Thanks, Mazie. I never expected the evening to end this way."

He kissed her softly. At first, it was a kiss of gratitude… of kinship. But in a flash it went somewhere far darker. It seduced her, cajoled her and made her heart beat faster.

His lips were firm and demanding, his smothered groan

telling her that the reluctant connection between them, the one neither of them really wanted or needed, was not easy to eradicate.

This wasn't how they had anticipated the evening would end.

She pulled away. "I should go."

Having J.B. look at her this way was alarming and disconcerting. They had moved from a romantic, flirtatious evening to something far more real.

He nodded, his gaze heavy with emotions she couldn't decipher. "Be careful. And call me if you have any problems."

"I'll be back as soon as I can." She touched his hand. "She'll pull through, J.B. She's a strong woman."

"I hope you're right."

Back at home, Mazie peeled out of the velvet dress with a wistful sigh. After changing into soft jeans and a lemon-yellow cotton sweater, she grabbed a canvas tote and stuffed it with water and snacks. There was no telling how long she would be with J.B. during his vigil.

Entering his home a short while later gave her an odd feeling in the pit of her stomach. Though they had known each other for years, they were not on intimate terms. Or at least they hadn't been until the episode in the bank vault.

She walked through the elegant living room and dining room and climbed the stairs to the upper floor. J.B.'s bedroom commanded the best view in the house, not that she could see anything at this hour.

Though she had already accessed his text for the alarm code, now she checked again, making note of the items he wanted and where to find them. Pants, shirt, socks. A sweater. Casual shoes. A clean pair of boxers. Her cheeks heated. It was a good thing there was no one around to see her reaction.

In his closet she found the leather carry-all he had requested. She stuffed everything into it and took one last look at his text. These few items would hold him until he could come back home. A man didn't need to spend the night wearing a tux, even if it *was* hand-tailored just for him.

She stood in the center of his bedroom for a moment, making sure she hadn't forgotten anything. It was impossible not to look at his massive king-size bed. The wood was dark and heavy, the comforter crimson damask. How many women had J.B. entertained in this luxurious space?

Not her business. Not at all.

Ignoring her hot cheeks, she ran back downstairs, reset the alarm and scooted out the front door. This time, driving the huge SUV was not quite so intimidating.

When she made it back to the hospital, it was the middle of the night. The surgical waiting room was deserted except for the four Vaughans. J.B.'s two sisters were asleep, curled awkwardly on a duo of love seats. Mr. Vaughan was dozing also.

J.B. paced restlessly, looking darkly handsome despite his fatigue.

He greeted her quietly. "That was fast."

"There's no traffic at this hour." She held out the leather satchel. "Here you go. I know you must be ready to get out of that tux."

His sexy grin was a shadow of its usual wattage. "Is that an invitation, Mazie? I'll have to take a rain check."

She pretended his teasing didn't fluster her. "Try to behave. Is there any word yet?"

He yawned. "No. The surgery actually started thirty minutes ago. They said it could take hours."

"Go change," she said. "I'll wait right here."

Though J.B. in a tux was eye candy of the best kind, she

almost preferred the man who returned moments later. A rumpled J.B. in casual clothes was dangerously appealing.

She raised an eyebrow. "Where's your tux?"

"I wadded it up in the bag. Has to go the cleaners anyway."

"Ah. Do you want to sit, or shall we walk the halls?"

"You're probably tired," he said.

"My adrenaline is still pumping. If you want to make a few laps of the building, I'm game."

J.B. poked his head into the lounge long enough leave his bag and to tell his dad where to find him. Then he rejoined Mazie. "Let's go. I can't stand to do nothing but wait."

J.B. was ridiculously glad to see Mazie.

He was a selfish bastard for asking her to stay, but her presence gave him something to hang on to. In front of his sisters and his dad, he had to be strong and unflappable. With Mazie, he could be himself. The distinction should have worried him, but he was too tired to think about the reasons why.

For now, he would ignore his ambivalent reactions to being with her in this charged situation.

They walked the halls in silence. His name and his face were well-known in Charleston, particularly to the hospital staff. His family had been major benefactors for years.

No one bothered Mazie or him. A few nurses here and there said hello. With the lights dimmed and most patients asleep, the building was sleepy and secure.

He ignored the elevators and climbed the stairs, Mazie on his heels.

When they were both breathing hard, he pushed open the door on 4B and crooked a finger at her. "Let's take a look at the babies."

Though the nurse on the other side of the glass frowned, she didn't shoo them away. He could almost watch Mazie's heart melt into a puddle of maternal instinct when she scanned the row of clear plastic bassinets. "They're so tiny," she whispered. "How can they be so small?"

"We were all that little once upon a time."

She bumped his hip with hers. "Not you, surely. I can't even imagine it."

They stood there in silence. A third of the infants slept peacefully. Another third blinked and examined their surroundings with myopic interest. But it was the last third who demanded all the attention. They wailed and scrunched up their faces, making their displeasure known.

He shuddered. "How do new parents do it? You can't Google how to take care of a newborn."

"Sure you can. You can Google anything. Besides, you promised your mother grandchildren. You'd better get over your fear of babies in a hurry."

"Are you volunteering?" His heart squeezed at the thought of having a daughter who looked like Mazie.

"Heck, no." She chewed her bottom lip. "To be honest, I've always been afraid that I might turn out like my mother. I love the idea of kids, but parenting scares me."

"And what about marriage?"

"What about it?"

He sneaked a sideways look at her, noting how intently she studied the helpless infants. "I thought every woman wanted to get married. You didn't object to being my fake fiancée." Under the circumstances, maybe he hadn't given her a chance to protest.

"C'mon, J.B. You can't be serious. This is the twenty-first century. Women have lots of choices."

"That doesn't answer my question." He was inordinately interested in her answer.

She shrugged. "I don't know if I'll *get* married. Watching what my father went through…"

"Did he ever consider divorcing your mother?" Divorce was a painful subject for J.B. His failure still stung deeply.

"No. At least I don't think so. Jonathan thinks he's still in love with her after all these years. But he never goes to see her."

"Because she doesn't recognize him?"

"I guess that's the reason. It must be very painful."

J.B. glanced at his watch. When Mazie let down her guard with him, he actually thought the two of them might finally be able to heal the decade-old rift. But no matter how appealing that prospect was, their timing was off. "We've been gone a long time. I'd better get back to the cardiac floor."

When they reached the surgical lounge, a nurse had just come out of the OR with an update. The surgery was going well. It would be at least another hour and a half, and then recovery.

J.B. grimaced. He took Mazie's arm and drew her away from the others. "Go home," he said. "I shouldn't have asked you to stay." Her skin was smooth and warm beneath his fingertips. He had to resist the urge to stroke her.

"Don't be silly. I'm here. Relax, J.B. I've got nowhere else I need to be." Her smile seemed genuine, though still cautious perhaps.

"This isn't the evening I had planned," he said, his voice husky with fatigue and something else he was too tired to hide.

She cupped his cheek in her hand. "If you're talking about sex, we already took that off the table…remember?"

"Says who?"

His teasing wasn't up to its usual wicked voltage.

"Says me." She paused. "I enjoyed tonight," she said. "Dinner. Dancing. When you're not being a condescending jerk and breaking a girl's heart, you're a pretty nice guy."

* * *

Mazie hadn't meant to be so honest, but it was hard to hold a grudge at 3:00 a.m.

J.B.'s jaw was shadowed with dark stubble. His hair was rumpled. The clothes she had brought him smelled of starch and laundry detergent. The blue button-up shirt and navy cotton pullover strained across his broad, hard chest.

The man looked like he had just crawled out of the covers and thrown on whatever was at hand. And yet he was still the sexiest thing she had ever seen.

She flashed back to his bedroom, for one brief moment imagining herself sprawled on that ruby comforter with J.B. leaning over her.

Her breathing quickened.

To make things worse, she couldn't help remembering the pink and blue swaddled babies. No matter what she'd said to JB, she *wanted* to have a normal family like his. But it just wasn't in the cards for her.

Even her own brother had disappeared.

The Tarletons were a mess.

J.B. took her arm. "Let's sit down. Are you hungry?"

"No," she said. They settled onto a padded bench. Once she was off her feet, the fatigue came crashing over.

He pulled her into his chest, wrapping an arm around her. "Close your eyes. Catnaps are my specialty."

The man wasn't kidding. In seconds he was snoring softly.

Mazie sighed and tried to do the same. But she couldn't relax. Being this close to J.B. lowered her defenses. She didn't *want* to like him. She didn't want to empathize about his worry for his mother. And she surely didn't want to be engaged to him.

Once upon a time, she would have welcomed the chance to be part of J.B.'s life. Those dreams had been crushed early and well. Now, she was almost positive that this sudden affability on his part was a calculated effort to win her trust.

The reality of selling her building to him was not the point. If she decided to go through with it, she would make him pay dearly for the privilege of relocating her.

No, what was really dangerous to her peace of mind was the possibility that J.B. could worm his way into her heart and then walk away when he got what he wanted.

While Mazie struggled internally with the extraordinary feeling of being wrapped in J.B.'s arms, Leila awakened and crossed the room. She tapped Mazie on the knee. "I need coffee," she whispered. "You want to come with me?"

Mazie nodded, welcoming the rescue from her own rapidly eroding good sense. Slipping out from underneath J.B.'s heavy arm, she grabbed her phone and wallet and followed his sister out of the waiting room. The sandwich shop and the main dining room were closed, but near the front entrance, a sleepy barista dozed over her iPad at a coffee counter.

Leila ordered her drink tall and black. Mazie couldn't face that much caffeine in the middle of the night, but she asked for an iced green tea. They found seats in the nearby atrium.

Mazie smiled sympathetically at the other woman. "This must have been really scary for all of you."

"Terrifying." Leila buried her nose in her cup. "My mom is a superhero. Seeing her like this…" She sniffed and wiped her nose.

"Were there any symptoms?"

"Honestly? I don't know. She's the kind of person who would badger the rest of us to get flu shots and go to the dentist, but she might have ignored her own warning signs 'cause she's always so busy."

"Heart surgeons perform miracles these days."

"Yeah." Leila yawned and set her empty cup on a nearby

table. "I'm sorry our family drama ruined your special night."

"Oh, that's okay," Mazie said quickly, wincing inwardly. The ground beneath her feet was quicksand. How did a recently engaged woman react? "The important thing is for your mom to be okay."

Leila grinned, seemingly fortified by her java. "To be honest, I was pretty shocked about this engagement. After the debacle of J.B.'s first marriage, he swore he'd never tie the knot again." Her eyes rounded, and she slapped a hand over her mouth. "Oh, lordy. Please tell me you already knew about that…the marriage, I mean."

"Of course. He's been very upfront with me. You do remember that my brothers and I used to hang out at your house all the time? Not so much as adults, but enough to keep up with J.B. and his escapades. He told me his wife was pretty awful."

"Mom and Dad tried to stop him, but he was madly in love. I was just starting high school, so I thought it was all terribly romantic. It didn't take long for the truth to come out. All she wanted was money. Poor J.B. was collateral damage."

"He seems to have bounced back pretty well," Mazie said, hoping she didn't sound cynical.

"I haven't seen him go out with the same woman more than two or three times. He's rabid about not giving anyone of the opposite sex the wrong idea. He's a workaholic, and he's not interested in anything permanent." She frowned and cocked her head. "How did the two of you hook up? I've watched you avoid each other for years."

"Ah, well…" This was the tough part. She was a terrible liar. "We occasionally crossed paths at a party or a gallery opening. But I suppose we got closer when he started this renovation project down near the Battery. He wants to buy my property. I kept saying no, and he continued to beg."

"Interesting. I've known my brother to do just about anything to seal a deal, but marriage? That's a new one."

Mazie knew Leila was teasing. But her careless comments underscored Mazie's own insecurities. If Mazie had said yes when J.B.'s Realtor called the first time, or even the second, Mazie never would have gone out with J.B., and she never would have been put in the situation of lying to his family.

"Shouldn't we get back upstairs?" she said.

Leila nodded, all animation fading from her face. "Definitely."

As they walked into the surgical lounge, Alana updated her sister with the latest progress report. J.B. and his dad appeared to be asleep.

Mazie kept to herself in one corner of the room until she realized that a *real* fiancée would never be standoffish. Instead, she moved to sit close to J.B., hoping that his sisters would think she didn't want to wake him.

At four fifteen, a weary surgeon came in to talk to them. The siblings formed a united front around their father. The doctor was upbeat. "The surgery went as expected. We did a quadruple bypass, so she'll have a long road ahead of her. Healing takes months, not weeks."

J.B.'s expression was strained. "When can we see her?"

"She'll be in recovery for some time. We'll rouse her slowly. When she's awake, we want everything to be low-key and calm. Nothing stressful at all. I'd recommend all of you go home and get a few hours of sleep. Come back later in the morning. If there's any problem, a nurse will contact you immediately."

Mr. Vaughan didn't like that answer. Mazie could tell. But the poor man looked dead on his feet.

Leila put an arm around her dad. "Alana and I will go back to the house with you, Papa."

J.B. kissed the top of her head. "Thanks, sis." He hugged

his father and Alana. "I'll take Mazie home and then see you guys around lunchtime."

Leila frowned. "But you live the closest of any of us to the hospital."

J.B. didn't miss a beat. "Mazie doesn't," he said.

Mazie could see the speculation in their gazes, but she was too tired to play her part. Did the girls think J.B. would have a fiancée living under his roof already? Fat chance. She'd had it from his own sister's lips that the man didn't like relationships.

In the parking lot, she tried to lobby for common sense. "Let me call a car," she said. "There's no reason at all for you to drive me home."

They had come straight from their date to the hospital. Her car was out at the beach house.

J.B. destroyed her argument by kissing her deep and slow. His tongue stroked hers. "There's a better option," he muttered, as he turned her legs to spaghetti. "For once, just trust me."

Ten

"Trust you?" Mazie eyed him warily.

He grimaced. "I'm so tired my eyeballs ache. Leila was right. It will be dawn soon. I don't really want to spend the next hour driving you to the beach and then heading back to my own place. Come home with me," he said huskily. "My house is five minutes away. We both need sleep."

Mazie hesitated. This family crisis had thrust her into a position of intimacy that was difficult to handle. She was a compassionate person. She could see that J.B. was dealing with stress and fatigue. Still, her sense of self-preservation was strong.

She'd been avoiding this connection forever, and now here it was, rushing her far too quickly into the quicksand of shared desire and impulsive choices.

"I'll be fine in a cab."

He took her wrist and reeled her in, wrapping his arms around her and pulling her close. "Pretty please, Mazie Jane. I don't want to be alone."

She examined his face in the harsh glow of the security lights. If she had seen even a shred of evidence that he was playing her, she would have walked away. But the hell of it was, she thought he was sincere.

"Okay," she said, giving in more or less gracefully. "It will only be for a few hours anyway."

They both climbed into the vehicle without further conversation. J.B. drove with a steady hand on the wheel. His profile was stark. Bold forehead, straight nose, firm chin. Mazie felt as if she was seeing him for the first time. It was clear that his family adored him and that he was someone they leaned on.

At his house, she hovered in the hallway. "I'll crash down here," she said. "Why don't you go on upstairs and get comfortable?"

He frowned. "I have a perfectly lovely guest room right across the hall from my suite."

"I don't want to argue about this J.B. Not right now." If she climbed those stairs, all bets were off. Too cozy. Too everything.

His gaze cooled. "Fine. We'll share the sofa."

She'd had no sleep. Her eyes were gritty, and her body was limp with exhaustion. "If that's what you want."

Most of J.B.'s beautiful home was decorated in true Charleston fashion. No doubt one or both of his sisters had helped, maybe even Jane. But at the back of the house in his personal den, he had opted for masculine comfort. An enormous flat-screen TV. A couple of huge recliners and an oversize sofa that looked as if it was covered in the soft, scarred leather of old aviator jackets.

He kicked off his shoes and grabbed two afghans from the cabinet to the left of the TV. "Make yourself at home. Are you hungry? Thirsty?"

She shook her head, wondering why she had voluntarily stepped into the lion's den. "I'm fine. Go to sleep, J.B. You'll have to be back at the hospital soon." Without waiting to see if he would take her advice, she curled up on one end of the couch and laid her head on the arm. At the last minute, she remembered to send a text to Gina letting her know that Mazie would not be coming in to the store this morning…or at least not until much later. Then she silenced her phone.

Out of the corner of her eye, she saw J.B. sprawl a few feet away from her and prop his feet on the coffee table.

The lure of sleep was strong. How did she end up here? Was this really as innocent as it seemed?

J.B. groaned and rolled his neck. "I'm too damn tired to relax."

Mazie sighed. "Lie down, for heaven's sake. Let me rub your head."

"I can think of other places I'd rather have you rub." His fake leer didn't have enough energy to be insulting.

"On your back, Mr. Vaughan."

As she sat up, J.B. stretched out full-length, his feet propped on the other arm of the sofa. With his head in her lap, he relaxed. Thick lashes, unfairly beautiful for a man, settled on his cheeks.

"Thank you, Mazie," he muttered.

She stroked his forehead, feeling the silkiness of his hair. Keeping her touch light and steady, she watched as the lines of tension in his face and shoulders gradually eased.

Some strong emotion slid through her veins and weakened her resolve. She couldn't fool herself any longer. She was dangerously close to falling for him again. How reckless could she be?

Soon, he was asleep. Only then did she allow herself to lean back and close her eyes.

J.B. dreamed about angels. Perhaps he should have been alarmed. He wasn't prepared for his life to end. But this particular angel whispered to him, words he couldn't quite catch.

He awoke with a start. For several long seconds confusion reigned. Then the familiar surroundings grounded him. Worry for his mother arrived first. And then concern about Mazie.

Good Lord. How long had he been sleeping in her lap?

The poor woman must be a glutton for punishment. He sat up carefully, noting the awkward bend to her neck. A glance at his watch told him it was not quite eight thirty. Still time to rest. And no messages on his phone.

Without overthinking it, he grabbed a pillow and scooped Mazie up long enough to change their positions. She murmured in her sleep but didn't wake. With his back against the couch, he tucked her up against him and sighed. This would do.

The scent of her hair tickled his nose. He had danced around his attraction to her for years, never quite willing to admit it existed. Now here she was. In his house. In his arms.

This relationship was *snakebit* from the beginning. Even if Mazie learned to trust him, what did he need from her? Marriage was out of the question. He'd learned that lesson the hard way.

Women were duplicitous. And he was bad at reading their wants and intentions.

He closed his eyes for the second time, and slept.

When next he awoke, the sun poured into the room through a crack in the draperies. As he crooked his arm to see his watch, Mazie stirred. "J.B.?"

"Right here, darlin'. We both went out cold."

She appeared charmingly befuddled. "Oh."

He stroked her cheek with the pad of his thumb. "Are you always this beautiful in the morning?"

It was a cheesy line. But hell, it was true. Her skin was soft and flushed. Those big golden eyes were underscored with shadows, but still deep enough for a man to lose himself.

Mazie bit her lip. "I must look a mess."

He threaded his fingers through her thick, glorious hair. The waves clung to his hand. His heart beat faster. "I'm going to kiss you."

It was a warning and a plea all wrapped up in one. He felt remarkably off his game. Ever since that incredible episode in the bank vault, he'd been obsessed with the need to touch her again.

He'd been compelled to ask her out. Some would say it was his subconscious that had taken over and proclaimed the false engagement.

He shifted his weight and leaned over her on one elbow. "Mazie," he whispered.

She put a hand behind his head and pulled him closer. "Yes."

The single word shot arousal through his veins like a powerful stimulant. He was trembling, almost out of control. Yet they had barely begun.

Her lips clung to his, not submissive, but challenging. He was hard in an instant. Desperate. Ready to beg. But the incredible woman beneath him was not erecting any barriers at all. She arched into his embrace, melding their bodies from shoulders to hips, completely his except for the fact that they were fully clothed.

The look in her eyes was his undoing, part yearning, part caution. She didn't completely trust him. He'd have to work on that.

"Easy, love." He distracted her with a hungry kiss while he wrestled with her thin sweater. Once he ripped the garment over her head, he was treated to the sight of raspberry-tipped breasts cupped in a lacy confection that was meant to drive a man wild.

He teased her nipples through the semi-transparent cloth. "I've pictured you like this in my head," he groaned. "But I never thought it would happen."

She nipped his bottom lip with sharp teeth. "And why is that? I thought the larger-than-life J.B. Vaughan was irresistible to the female sex."

"You're sassy. And no, I'm not irresistible. You aren't

even sure you like me, Mazie Jane. And you sure as hell don't trust me."

The flicker of her gold-tipped eyelashes told him he had hit a nerve. But her voice when she answered was steady. "I discovered something in that bank vault, J.B. Something that shocked me. Apparently, it's possible to crave someone even if he's a bad boy with a terrible reputation."

His smile widened. "You *crave* me, darlin'? Well, I must be doing *something* right."

"Does your ego ever take a rest?" She caressed his chin, smiling faintly.

He ignored her gibe. "Get undressed before someone like your brother decides to interrupt us."

Mazie wriggled away from him long enough to dispense with her pants and socks. J.B. did the same. He leaned forward to grab his wallet and extract a condom. His hands were shaking.

She curled her arms around him from behind and rested her cheek on his back. "We're probably going to regret this."

"Yeah. Maybe." He pulled her in front of him, standing her on her feet and kissing her cute, tiny belly button. Gooseflesh rose on her pale skin. "You have no idea how much I want you."

"That might be the sleep deprivation talking."

He slid her bikini underwear down her legs and sighed. "Nope. It's you, Mazie Jane." He parted her damp folds with his thumbs and caressed her intimately. Her whimper of pleasure hardened his erection a millimeter more, if that was possible.

In another situation, he would have taken his time with her. He might have paused to savor the smorgasbord of delights. But he'd only been half kidding about Jonathan. Given the situation at the hospital, someone could call at any moment. He dared not turn off his phone.

"We should hurry," she panted, perhaps reading his

mind. "I'm ready for you. More than ready." She played with the shell of his ear, leaning down to whisper naughty suggestions.

J.B. cursed. He shed his boxers with more speed than finesse and sheathed his sex. Mazie was still wearing her bra. It was too late to do anything about it. He had to have her in the next thirty seconds, or he was going to die.

Moving to the edge of the sofa, he gripped her wrist. "Come here, sweet thing. Let me love you." He took her by the waist and helped her straddle his lap, her long, smooth legs spread on either side of his hips.

Mazie took over before he could do more than groan and bury his face in her chest. She sank down onto him, taking him inside her, joining their bodies with the sweet wild slide of passion.

His vision went dark. Everything inside him focused on the sensation of Mazie's tight, hot sex accepting him. Sweat broke out on his brow. "Slower," he begged. He was close to embarrassing both of them.

Mazie combed his hair with both hands, massaging his scalp, toying with his ears. "What if I like it fast and hard?"

He gripped her soft butt so tightly it might leave bruises. "Bad girl." He thrust upward, filling her, claiming her.

Mazie laughed. The soft, husky chuckle drove him mad. Suddenly, he was sorry he had chosen this position. It was too passive. He was in a volatile mood. Lack of sleep blurred the edges of his control.

"Put your legs around my waist." He stood abruptly. Mazie was a tall woman, but he was extremely motivated. He eased past the coffee table and tumbled them both to the carpet, their bodies still joined.

Mazie smiled up at him, her eyelids half closed, her breath coming in short pants. "Who knew you were so strong? I'm impressed Mr. Vaughan."

His chest heaved. "You make me nuts. Why is that, do you think?"

"Mutual antipathy?"

He pumped his hips.

Her eyelids fluttered shut. She arched her back, gasping.

"Look at me, Mazie. I want to see your eyes when you come."

She obeyed. Her amber-gold gaze locked on to his. He felt naked suddenly, raw and exposed. Those eyes saw everything.

Mazie wet her lips with the tip of her tongue. She reached up and traced his features with her thumbs. "I won't break, J.B. Give it all to me."

The sexual challenge dissolved the last of his rapidly winnowing willpower. With a groan of helpless inevitability, he pounded into her, thrusting again and again until his world went black, and his entire body spasmed in hot, desperate pleasure.

Dimly, he heard Mazie's cry of release and felt the flutters of her sex on his shaft as she came.

When it was over, they lay in a tangle of arms and legs and fractured breathing. Mazie was still wearing her bra. J.B. couldn't feel his legs. Her body was soft and warm beneath his. He never wanted to move, though that wasn't a viable choice under the circumstances.

After several long moments of silence, he rolled to his back and cleared his throat. "I don't know what to say. I'd offer to fix you bacon and eggs, but that seems a paltry thank-you for what just happened."

He was dizzy, and his feet were cold.

Mazie patted his cheek. "Don't be silly. It was sex. Great sex, I'll admit. But just sex. I can grab breakfast at home."

When she stood up, found her undies and began to get dressed, he gaped at her. "What are you doing?"

She pointed at the antique clock on the mantel. "It's late,

J.B. Your family will be expecting you at the hospital. And even though I told Gina that I wouldn't be there to open the shop, I still need to get to work." She fastened her jeans and sat down to put on her socks and shoes.

"But you're the boss." What the hell was happening? The sex had been incredible, wild and hot. How could she pretend as if nothing had happened? Was she really as un-affected as she seemed?

"It's the Christmas shopping season. I need to be at my store. But more important, your mother will be asking for you soon. Grab your shower, J.B. I'll call a car service. No worries."

She picked up her purse and jacket. "I'll be in touch to check on your mom later today." She blew him a kiss. "Gotta run."

As he rolled to his knees and stood up, he heard his front door open and shut.

Eleven

Mazie leaned her back against J.B.'s front door for half a second, barely long enough to catch her breath, and then she fled. She jogged three blocks before she called a car service, desperate to make sure J.B. wasn't going to follow her. With her heart pounding and her eyes blinking back tears, she felt like a crazy woman.

Her whole world was upended.

How could puppy love have stayed alive all these years? She *knew* what kind of man J.B. was. Thanks to his sister's candid remarks, Mazie also knew J.B.'s views on relationships and marriage.

Only the worst kind of masochist would allow herself to be sucked back into his realm. Pretending like morning sex was no big deal had required all of her acting abilities. Harder still was erasing the mental image of a naked J.B. sprawled on the plush carpet.

The man had a seriously ripped body.

He was also funny and smart, and kind to his mother and the rest of his family. That didn't erase his willingness to squash other people in his drive to get what he wanted in business.

He had hurt her once before. If she allowed him to get too close, odds were, it would happen again.

Despite her panic and all-out flight from J.B., she arrived home in a slightly calmer frame of mind. She would survive whatever this was. She had to…the past was not worth repeating.

Jonathan was at work, of course. She had texted him from the car to let him know Mrs. Vaughan was stable. He had answered with a single word. *Good.* That kind of clipped response was typical of her brother when he was neck deep in shipping crises.

Her father was dozing in the living room with a paperback novel in his lap. Mazie sat down beside him and touched his arm. "Hi, Daddy."

He opened his eyes. "Hello, baby. What are you doing home this time of day?"

She explained about Mrs. Vaughan's heart attack, glossing over the details about her date with J.B. and why Mazie was at the hospital at all.

Her father nodded. "I'll have Jonathan's assistant send flowers."

"That would be lovely." She paused, shifting gears. "How was *your* dinner last night? Did you have a good time?"

He grew animated as he shared details of his evening.

Mazie spotted an opportunity and took it. "Daddy, have you ever thought about moving to one of those places where your friends live? Here at the house you're awfully isolated and lonely, and besides, you know that Jonathan and I might not always be around."

"I like it here," he said. "It's safe." Then his smile grew wistful. "Are you planning on leaving your old dad, Mazie? I knew it would happen one day."

"No plans," she said lightly, witnessing his frail emotions. This thing with J.B. had made her even more aware of how dysfunctional her family was. She sighed, needing reassurance, wanting answers. "Daddy, please tell me what happened with Hartley. Jonathan won't talk about it."

His face darkened. "And neither will I. It's best you

don't know. Just understand that he's probably never coming back."

She wasn't a child. What secret was so terrible that it had ripped their small family apart?

With an inward sigh, she stood and stretched, feeling the strain of not enough sleep and the fact that several of those hours she did doze were sitting upright on J.B.'s sofa. It was frightening to realize that she already missed him. "I'm going to take a shower, grab a quick lunch and head to work. Do you need anything before I go?"

His eyelids were already drooping. "I'm right as rain. Don't worry about me."

Fortunately for Mazie, All That Glitters was madly busy on this bright, sunny Saturday in December.

She waded into the fray, grateful for something to distract her from the unanswerable questions about her fake engagement and her enigmatic fiancé.

Since Gina was far too busy to dig for details about Mazie's date and the events that followed, Mazie was able to shut out the past twenty-four hours. Mostly.

The day passed quickly. Sales numbers were gratifying. If she took the new building J.B. was offering her, she would have ample room to expand.

The Tarleton shipping business would have had room for her if she had been interested. But she had needed something she could control, a part of her life where she was in charge, where she didn't have to worry about being abandoned.

If she couldn't have J.B.—and did she really want him?—her work was going to be her future.

As they prepared to lock up and head home at five, Mazie cornered Gina. "You want to grab a bite of dinner?"

"Oh, gosh, Mazie. You know I would. But we're having a big extended-family Christmas thing at my aunt's house tonight. Kind of a command performance. You're welcome to come with me."

"No, no. That's fine. Go. Don't be late. I'll wrap things up."

"Are you sure?"

"Positive. You covered for me this morning. Get out of here."

When the store was empty, Mazie turned the deadbolt and flipped the sign in the window to Closed.

She told herself she wasn't jealous of Gina, but it was a lie. Gina came from a huge Italian clan. She had more cousins than she could count. Mazie's parents were both only children.

All Mazie had ever wanted was to belong, to have a big, loving family. First her mother was sent away. Then Hartley left. Now her father's health was precarious. Soon it would be just Jonathan and Mazie. When Jonathan eventually married, Mazie would be on her own.

The prospect was dismal. Was that why she had let herself be drawn back into J.B.'s orbit? Was it the memory of her old crush on him that drove her now, or was there more to this dangerous liaison?

It must be the holidays making her maudlin. As much as she loved the holly and the mistletoe and the beauty of the season, at times all the hoopla amplified her aloneness. She finished the last of the chores that were rote to her by now, and went to the back to get her jacket and purse.

When she returned, her heart stopped. There, standing half-visible in front of the top glass pane of her door, was a huge man. But a familiar one. He was dressed casually in khakis and a forest green sweater.

After her heart started beating again, she opened the lock and let him in. "You scared me to death," she said. It was already dark outside.

"It's dangerous for you to be closing up alone. Anyone could bust in here and hurt you or rob you."

"We have a system," she said calmly, though her fingernails dug into her palms. "Gina and I usually walk out together, but she had a *thing* tonight. I sent her on, so she wouldn't be late. What are you doing here, J.B.?"

He lifted an eyebrow. "Collecting my fiancée?"

"That's not funny." Even so, his teasing smile made her heart wobble. The fact that they had been naked together only a few hours before made her skittish.

"Mom's asking for you," he said.

"Well, crud." She frowned. "I know why you did what you did, but how are we supposed to handle this now?"

"We need to buy a ring. I asked my friend Jean Philippe to give us a private appointment at six."

Mazie heart clenched in alarm. "We're not engaged," she said firmly. "And I'm not picking out a ring."

"You have to."

"I don't have to do anything."

"Be reasonable, Mazie. She's awake and she wants to see you. She's worried that her heart attack messed up our special evening. She's ragging my butt to make sure I put a ring on your finger. Sooner, not later. I couldn't disappoint her."

Mazie was appalled at how much she wanted to play his game. At this rate she would end up abandoned at the altar because she didn't have enough sense to guard her heart. "Tell her I'm picky. Tell her no one in Charleston has a loose stone big enough or perfect enough to suit me. Tell her you and I will be flying to New York after the holidays to hit up Harry Winston and Tiffany's."

"I can't tell her that," he said, visibly grinding his jaw.

"Why not?"

"Because she would insist I book two tickets right now.

The woman is like a bulldog, Mazie. Sick or not sick, she'll grill you until you cave."

"Why don't you borrow a ring from a friend, then. Or pick out something by yourself. It can be anything. Why does it matter?"

J.B. didn't like not getting his own way. His eyes glittered. "I've never had to work so hard to buy a woman jewelry."

Mazie didn't want to think about all those women. "Sorry to inconvenience you," she muttered.

"My mom has spies all over the city. If I don't do this the right way, somebody will spill the truth and she'll be devastated."

"And you'll say it's my fault." She stared at him, shocked. "Maybe."

Mazie saw a million reasons why this was a terrible idea. "She came through the surgery really well. Why don't you just admit the truth?"

"You mean I should say that I flat-out lied to her on her death bed? Oh, yeah. That's an awesome idea."

"Well, when you put it like that…" Mazie grimaced. That was the trouble with lies. One thing always led to another. "This is ridiculous, J.B. I *know* Jean Philippe. Not as well as you, maybe, but I'm pretty sure he's not going to buy my act as an adoring fiancée."

"I thought about that. We'll just tell him that we've kept our relationship under wraps."

"Why?"

"I don't know. Maybe your brother doesn't approve."

"Oh, crap." She rubbed the center of her forehead where a headache bloomed. "I'm going to have to tell Jonathan and Daddy what we're doing. If word gets back to them that I'm *engaged*, and I haven't told them, they'll be so hurt."

"Can your father keep a secret?"

"Are you asking me if he's senile?"

"Well, he does seem to be slipping."

Mazie shook her head slowly. "He's not as sharp as he was, but he'll understand this. I'll just have to remind him not to talk about it at all. That's the safest bet. Besides, it's only for a week or so…right? Until your mom is recovering well? Then you and I can have a huge fight and end things."

"You don't have to sound so happy about it," J.B. groused.

She moved toward the door and stopped to pat his cheek. "It's going to be the highlight of my Christmas season."

If there was one thing Mazie knew about J.B., it was that he never left any detail to chance. That's why he was such a success in business. That and the fact that he was way smarter than his smiling blue eyes and surfer physique might suggest.

She stood on the sidewalk outside her shop and argued with him. "I'm taking my own car," she said. "It's the only plan that makes sense. That way I can drop by the hospital after we do this jewelry thing, and then head home."

"A couple buying an engagement ring doesn't arrive in multiple vehicles," he said stubbornly. "You have to commit to the role, Mazie."

"We'll improvise. It will be okay." She wasn't going to let him push her around. It was a matter of principle.

"Fine."

J.B. wasn't happy, but she didn't care. She was tired, and this pretending was breaking her heart. Didn't she deserve a man who *really* wanted her?

As far as she could tell, J.B. was simply being himself… taking care of problems. His determination to bend her will to his shouldn't have hurt. She knew who and what he was. But her emotions plummeted.

Jean Philippe's shop made All That Glitters look like a thrift store. He was a fixture in Charleston. He sold wedding rings and engagement rings, fabulous necklaces and even the occasional tiara. The fifty-something jeweler knew all there was to know about gem stones and their provenance.

Clearly, he didn't offer private appointments to anyone and everyone. He was expecting a big sale.

The store was closed, of course, since it was after business hours. A uniformed guard, fully armed, unlocked the front door and let them in. Then he relocked the plate-glass entrance and stationed himself beside the exit.

Jean Philippe was effusive. "Mr. Vaughan, Ms. Tarleton. I am honored that I can serve you in this special way."

Mazie's cheeks heated. "We'll try to be fast. I wasn't sure I wanted a ring, but J.B. insisted."

The older man raised a scandalized eyebrow. "Of *course* you need a ring. Oh, I know how you girls think these days. You're independent. You can buy your own jewelry. You don't need a man. But trust me, young lady, it means far more coming from the love of your life."

When Mazie glanced at J.B., he had an odd look on his face. Maybe he was jittery about the *L* word. "So how do we start?" she asked.

Jean Philippe glanced at J.B. "Would you like to select a handful of rings and let your fiancée pick from those, or do I—"

J.B. shook his head ruefully. "I'll let her have free rein. I trust her."

The other man's carefully manicured eyebrows shot to his hairline. There were pieces in this store that would bankrupt a lot of men. "Well, I…"

"Anything she wants, Jean. Anything."

It was all Mazie could do not to roll her eyes. Her *fiancé* was having entirely too much fun at her expense. It would serve him right if she picked out the biggest, gaudiest bauble in the store.

Unfortunately, she was too squeamish to spend that kind of money for a two-week stint of playacting.

Without much fanfare, she glanced in the nearest case. "That one's nice," she said.

Jean Philippe pulled out the ring she had indicated, a tiny frown marring his forehead. "A decent stone," he said grudgingly. "But rather pedestrian. It's only a single carat."

Mazie jumped, startled, when J.B. slid an arm around her waist. He murmured in her ear. "I'm a wealthy man, darlin'. We need something that befits my bride-to-be. Something that's as beautiful as you are. Don't hold back."

The jeweler nodded eagerly. "Indeed."

Oh, good grief.

She stared at the rows of rings blindly, wishing J.B. didn't smell so good. Also wishing that he would back up so she could breathe.

One at a time, she pointed out rings. One at a time, the two men shot them down. Finally, she began to lose patience.

She took J.B.'s arm. "Perhaps we should come back another day when we have more time. I want to visit your mother."

J.B. ignored her, his attention riveted on a nearby case she hadn't perused.

"That one," he said. "Top row on the right."

Jean Philippe practically danced in his polished cordovans. "Wonderful eye you have, Mr. Vaughan. That is an exquisite yellow diamond from Brazil. The rich color and dazzling clarity are unmatched by anything I've seen in the last ten years. Five and a half carats, cushion cut. The setting is platinum, very simple. Designed to showcase the stone, but if the lady prefers something else, we could always reset."

J.B. narrowed his eyes and picked up the loupe. "Let me take a look."

As he examined the stone, Mazie freaked inwardly. The ring had to be well over six figures. That was a heck of a lot of money for a play prop.

She tugged his sleeve. "That one's too much. Be sensible."

J.B. turned to face her, his half smile intimate, toe-curling. "It's you, Mazie. Rare. Unique. Stunning. The stone picks up the sunshine color in your amber eyes and the gleams of gold in your hair." Before she could stop him, he took her left hand and slid the ring onto her third finger.

For a split second, the world stopped. J.B.'s hands holding hers were warm, his grasp strong. The ring nestled in place as if it had been sized for her and her alone.

She swallowed. "It's beautiful." The stone was actually heavy on her hand. Weighty. Serious.

Everything this engagement was not.

He frowned, perhaps sensing her unease. "We can go with a traditional diamond if you'd prefer. I realize this color is not the usual bridal choice."

Mazie knew J.B. was playing a part. He was pretending to care, pretending to consult her wishes. No matter how much she told herself this fairy-tale moment wasn't real, the little girl inside her who dreamed of fairy tales and Prince Charming was jumping up and down.

Her throat was tight. "I love it," she said huskily.

J.B. turned to the jeweler, pulling his wallet from his jacket pocket and extracting his platinum credit card.

"We'll take it."

Twelve

Mazie found a parking spot at the hospital, turned off the engine and sat for a moment, staring at her newly adorned hand. If alien civilizations actually existed, she could probably pick up communications from other planets on this thing. The ring was huge, stunning.

Even here, in the semidarkness, it seemed to have a life of its own, much like J.B.'s impromptu engagement for his mother's benefit.

Before Mazie and J.B. had left the jewelry store, Mazie had been forced to hover for long embarrassing minutes while the two men conducted the business portion of the transaction. The ring came with a two-page appraisal and a fancy box wrapped in plum satin paper and silver ribbon.

The fact that the box was empty didn't seem to bother anyone. It was part of the pomp and circumstance of purchasing a ridiculously expensive piece of jewelry.

She glanced out the window, suddenly aware—as never before—of the possibility of getting mugged in a parking lot. Because she had insisted on having her own car, she and J.B. had gotten separated on the way to the hospital. He might be close by or on the other side of the building.

As far as she could tell, no was one lurking in the shadows ready to snatch a ring off her finger. Shaking her head at her own vivid imagination, she got out and locked her car.

Before she could take more than a few steps, J.B. appeared, loping across the pavement. Clearly, he had found a parking spot more quickly than she had.

"Did you spend most of the day here?" she asked.

He folded his arms across his chest. "The part of it that I wasn't having sex with you, Mazie. You can't pretend it didn't happen."

"Watch me," she muttered, taking off for the hospital entrance as if she were being pursued.

J.B. kept pace with her mad dash, but he didn't touch her. She told herself she was glad.

In the elevator, they were surrounded by strangers. On the CCU floor, the other three Vaughans kept their vigil. J.B.'s mother was doing very well. The nurses had had her up walking, and all her stats were good. In another twenty-four to forty-eight hours, she would likely be moved to a regular room.

Alana motioned for everyone's attention. "Mama wants to tell us something. But we have to make it quick. They're bending the rules right and left, but we're running out of goodwill, I think."

The five of them entered the cubicle. The two sisters took one side of the bed, J.B. and his father the other. Mazie hung back near the door.

"Okay, Mama," Alana said. "What's up?"

Mrs. Vaughan looked at her son. "You four have been here most of the day." She patted her son's hand. "J.B., I want you to take your sisters and your dad, and go have a nice restaurant dinner somewhere. *Not* the hospital cafeteria. Mazie will sit with me while you're gone."

They all turned and looked at Mazie. She felt her face heat. "I'd be happy to do that."

Leila grimaced. "But Mazie needs dinner."

"I have peanut butter crackers in my purse. I'll be fine." She curled her fingers around the ring. Maybe she could slip it off for the moment.

J.B.'s face had no expression at all. If Mazie had to guess, she'd say he was sifting through his mother's statement for hidden grenades and wondering if it was safe to leave Mazie behind.

Mrs. Vaughan waved a hand. "Go. I'm serious." Her voice was weak, but her color was healthy, and she was clearly in good spirits.

"Okay, Mama." J.B. turned to Mazie and kissed her on the cheek. "Make my mother behave."

"I'll do my best." Having J.B. be so casually affectionate after what had happened between them this morning rattled her composure. What would happen if his careful attentions were rooted in truth? Could she trust him? Would she be glad?

When the room emptied, Jane Vaughan exhaled and smiled at Mazie. "I love that crew, but when they hover, I want to smack them up the side of the head. I'm not accustomed to being out of control. I don't much care for it."

"Yes, ma'am. I understand."

"Pull that chair closer to the bed, Mazie."

"You probably should rest until they bring your dinner tray. I have things to read on my iPad."

J.B.'s mother shook her head. "This may be our only chance to speak in private. I have to carpe diem," she said.

Seize the day? Mazie frowned inwardly. "I'm not sure I understand."

"I want to talk about my son, dear girl. And your relationship to him."

Mazie froze, sensing danger. Here was a woman who had undergone serious surgery. She couldn't be upset or shocked or any other emotion that would impede her recovery. "Okay…"

Jane chuckled. "Don't look so petrified. I know the engagement is fake. You can relax."

Mazie gaped at her. "Why would you say that?"

"Jackson Beauregard is my firstborn. I know him, and I love him. Ever since that stupid woman coaxed him into marriage and humiliated him, J.B. has closed himself off emotionally. I've prayed that he would come to terms with the mistake he made, but J.B. is harder on himself than anyone else. He can't forgive his own youthful blunder. He swore never to let any other woman get that close to him again. And he's kept that vow. He has multiple women in his life, but to him they're as interchangeable as a pair of socks."

"But…"

The older woman grimaced. "He was trying to give me a reason to live. And it was sweet of him, dear boy. But I'm not a fool. Nobody does a one-eighty that fast. If he had been falling in love with you, I would have gotten wind of it." She grinned. "I have *spies* all over the city."

"That's what J.B. told me." Mazie paused, trying to understand. "So you're saying there's no reason to continue with the charade?"

"Oh, no, my dear. Just the opposite. I'm begging you to keep up the pretense in hopes that my sweet boy will see that true love is worth fighting for."

Mazie's head was spinning. In the midst of this extraordinary conversation, a nurse had come in to draw blood and check vitals. Close on her heels was an employee with a dinner tray.

When the medical staff finally wrapped up their assigned tasks and left the room, Mazie uncovered the meal. "Looks like a grilled chicken breast, rice and lemon Jell-O."

"Oh, goody."

Jane's dour sarcasm made Mazie laugh. "You need the calories to get better. Which do you want first?"

"If I eat all that dreadful stuff, you have to agree to my plan."

Mazie cut up the chicken, added sweetener and lemon

to the tea at Jane's request, and raised the head of the bed. "I'm feeling a little bit under the gun, Jane. You have to understand, J.B. and I are…" She trailed off.

How exactly did one define what she and J.B. were to each other? She was letting his masculine charm drag her under his spell all over again, and he was using her as a convenient ploy.

Jane, true to her word, was working her way through the bland food. "Have you slept together?"

"Ah…" A hot flush rose from Mazie throat to her hairline. This woman had endured major, life-threatening surgery, and yet still had the capacity to do an interrogation that would make a seasoned professional proud. "I'm not comfortable discussing that with you."

"Fair enough." Jane finished the rice. "I'm aware you've known each other forever, but how did you come to be on a fancy date last night?"

Mazie chose and discarded explanations rapidly. "J.B. was wining and dining me because he wants to buy my building. It's smack in the middle of his big restoration project. I'm the last holdout."

"How delicious. I hope you haven't made it easy for him."

Were they talking about business or sex?

Mazie uncovered the tiny serving of Jell-O and added a plastic spoon. "I'll have to admit, it made me mad that he thought I would simply give him what he wanted. So I've been cranky and obstructive. But he's offered me another property for my store that is lovely. I've decided to let him stew until after Christmas, and then give him what he needs."

"Well, I'm glad his business dealings are doing well, but I'm more concerned about his emotional well-being. Please let the engagement stand, Mazie. He already trusts you. That's a huge step forward."

"Why would you say that?" She couldn't let herself believe the fantasy that J.B. actually cared for her. There would be too far to fall when the truth was revealed.

"No man enters into a fake engagement unless he is absolutely sure the woman in question will let him off the hook when the charade is over. Clearly, he trusts you not to sue him for breach of promise or something awful like that. And he doesn't have to worry that you're after his money, because you have plenty of your own. You're the perfect woman for him."

But she wasn't.

J.B. didn't want to be married. And no matter how great the sex, no man was going to tie the knot when he wasn't emotionally involved. Mazie wasn't convinced J.B. would allow himself to be that vulnerable.

If she went along with this plan, he might destroy her all over again. Still, she couldn't say no to his mother, not under these circumstances.

"I don't know that I am, Jane. But if it will make you happy, I'll let this arrangement ride for the moment."

Jane beamed. "Thank you dear. Now let me see the ring."

Mazie blushed again. "How did you know?"

"You've been hiding your left hand since you walked into the room. Not only that, I practically ordered my son to take you ring shopping today, and I was fairly certain he wanted to pacify me."

"It's a little over the top," Mazie confessed.

She held out her left hand. Even now, in this sterile, medical setting, the ring blazed with life.

Jane took Mazie's hand in both of hers and studied the diamond from all angles. "Wow," she said.

Mazie wrinkled her nose. "I know. It's too much, isn't it? I don't know what he was thinking."

"I always told my children to go big or go home." Jane closed her eyes, rubbing her chest absently.

"Mrs. Vaughan? Jane?" Mazie looked at her in alarm. "Are you okay?"

"Just tired, my dear. Why don't you read your book now, and I'll nap for a few minutes…"

"Of course." Mazie tidied the mostly empty food tray and covered everything. Then she rolled the little table away from the bed so Jane could relax in comfort.

When she glanced at her watch, she saw that the Vaughans had been gone only fifty minutes. If they followed Jane's directive, they would stay away another hour. Mazie pulled her iPad mini from her purse and queued up the book she was reading. It was a romantic comedy about a dyslexic librarian and a handyman who liked to work after hours. The story was charming and funny, but it failed to hold her interest.

At last, she dropped the device into her purse and studied the woman in the bed. Mothers, in general, were supposed to have keen instincts when it came to the love lives of their children. Jane was more dialed in than most. The fact that she saw through the false engagement ruse meant that she really did understand how J.B.'s mind worked.

What the other woman *didn't* know was that J.B. had already rejected Mazie once. He had broken her heart. He'd left her vulnerable and hurting.

You could argue that something so long ago wasn't real or even very important. But Mazie still carried the scars. For J.B.'s mother, she would let this charade continue a few days or weeks.

Nothing more, though.

She was not going to be foolish enough to believe that the ring and the situation were anything more than a son's desire to cheer up his mom.

J.B. stood in the doorway of his mother's hospital room and studied the two women inside. His mother was napping. Every report they had received so far was promising. Surely that meant she was beyond the worst of the danger.

Beside the bed in an ugly recliner covered in faux leather, Mazie snoozed as well, one hand tucked beneath her cheek. It was no wonder. She had waited at the hospital with him a big chunk of the night, and then this morning at his house, she had been otherwise engaged.

The memory of making love to Mazie disturbed him. He liked keeping things in neat compartments. His feelings for the woman with the whiskey-colored hair and the amber eyes slopped over into several boxes.

Business contact. Longtime family friend. Childhood confidante. Lover.

Most disturbing of all, she was his best friend's sister. It was the last designation that gave him heartburn.

A physical relationship with Jonathan's sister seemed fraught with danger. For years he had kept her in a box labeled *not for* me. Now, to make things worse, J.B. himself had invented a fake engagement to give his mother something on which to focus her goals for recovery. How far would he have to play out that scenario before he put a stop to it?

Not that he thought Mazie would take advantage of the situation. If anything, she was a very reluctant fiancée.

He must have made a sound, because Mazie's eyes flew open.

"Oh, hey," she said. "You're back. Where are the others?"

His mom roused, as well. "Hello, son. Did you all get something good to eat?"

He nodded. "We did, Mom. Dad and the girls have gone home to sleep. I'm taking first shift. I'll be here overnight."

"I don't need a babysitter."

He leaned down and squeezed her hand. "Humor me."

He glanced at Mazie. "If you're ready, I'll walk you down to your car."

"Take your time," his mother said with an arch smile.

Mazie's cheeks heated.

He rolled his eyes. "Behave, Mom."

She was unrepentant. "The moon is out. It's a beautiful night. I'm not going anywhere. And by the way…"

"Yes?"

"You did well on the ring. It's gorgeous."

For some reason, the tops of his ears got hot. "We're glad you like it. I wanted something unique and special… like Mazie."

His fiancée stood and stretched. The stone on her hand flashed and sparked as she moved. "Enough blarney," she said.

She gave his mom a smile. "I enjoyed talking to you, Jane. Maybe I'll see you tomorrow? If you feel like having a visitor?"

J.B.'s mother waved her arms. "Come here. Give me a hug. And yes, I'll be expecting you. I'll send the rest of them out for coffee, so we can gossip."

"As long as you're doing everything the doctor orders, we can gossip to your heart's content. Good night, Mrs. Vaughan. See you tomorrow."

"I'll be back shortly," J.B. said.

He took Mazie's arm and steered her toward the bank of elevators. "Thanks for doing that. It makes her feel good to know that the rest of us are obeying her orders."

"She's not that bad," Mazie protested. "She only wants what's best for all of you."

"Uh-oh," he said, faking alarm. "She's indoctrinated you."

Mazie punched his arm. "Don't be mean. Your mom is a sweetheart."

He tapped the button for the lobby. "I agree one hundred

percent. But don't let her fool you. She'll have you dancing to her tune in no time."

Outside, he walked Mazie across the courtyard and to the far parking lot where she had left her car.

She unlocked the door and tossed her purse on the passenger seat. "You should hurry back inside," she said. "In case she needs something."

He leaned an arm on the roof of the car, boxing her in. "Trying to get rid of me, Ms. Tarleton?"

Mazie looked up at him, her features shadowed. "No."

He stroked a wisp of hair from her cheek, wishing they weren't in a public arena so he could kiss her the way he wanted, needed. "I missed you today."

She murmured something that was neither agreement nor dissent.

He frowned. "You *are* my fiancée, after all."

Her head snapped up, her demeanor indignant. "Fake fiancée," she insisted.

"What are we going to do about this *thing* between us?"

"You're talking about sex."

"Yes. But it's not easy and fun, is it? We're digging ourselves into a pretty big hole."

"I agree. It seems smarter to end things now."

"What if I don't want to? You and I are crazy in bed—crazy good."

"I'd like to point out that we haven't actually tried sex in a bed. We seem to go for more inappropriate locations. Bank vaults. Your living room sofa."

He kissed her temple. "Nothing wrong with a sofa." It struck him suddenly that he didn't want her to leave. He liked having her at arm's length in the midst of his family crisis. She made everything easier.

The implications of that shot alarm and adrenaline coursing through his veins, but he ignored the internal upheaval, intent on having his way.

"I have an idea," he said. "Why don't you move into my place for a few days? My mother likes you, and you could help us keep an eye on her. Plus, my house is close to All That Glitters. Cut your commute time in half."

"That's a fairly elaborate setup just so you and I can have the occasional booty call. What's your end game, J.B.?"

Why did women always want to strangle a man with emotion and romance? This was physical. Nothing more. Mazie had to know that.

"There is no end game," he said gruffly. "With Mom sick and you working and me *trying* to work, this is the only scenario I can come up with for you and I to get a moment alone."

"For sex."

"Yes," he said, grinding his jaw. "For sex."

"How long are you thinking about?"

"I don't know. A week, maybe. Or two."

"That takes us up until Christmas."

"I guess it does." He slid his hands into her hair and cupped her head, tilting it back so he could kiss her. "Spend Christmas with me, Mazie. Today wasn't enough," he said, his body already taut with need. "I want you. Beyond reason. Tell me you feel it, too."

She was soft and warm in his arms, her body a feminine foil for his harder, bigger frame.

"Yes," she said, her voice barely audible. She sounded more resigned than happy. "But I like a lot of things that are bad for me. Rich chocolate mousse. Salted caramel ice cream. Bad boys who insist on getting their own way."

He dragged her closer, closing the car door and leaning Mazie against it until his lower body pressed hers. His erection ached.

"I have to go back inside," he groaned.

Mazie cupped his face in her hands and kissed him slow and deep, her tongue teasing his. "I'll think about your offer, J.B." She flattened her palms on his chest and shoved. "We're not having sex in a parking lot. I have to draw the line somewhere."

He might have whimpered. He nearly begged. But she was right, damn it. Gulping in huge breaths of the chilled night air, he forced himself to back up. "Pack a bag tonight. Please."

"Don't push me. I said I'll think about it." Ducking out of his embrace, she opened the driver's door and got into her little sports car. "See you tomorrow."

Thirteen

Mazie was starving when she finally got home. She'd never actually gotten around to eating the peanut butter crackers in her purse. All of the household staff were long gone by now, but she could cook well enough on her own. Which was pretty surprising for a woman whose mother hadn't been around when she was a teenager. Fortunately, more than one housekeeper had taken pity on a moody preteen and let her putter around the kitchen.

Jonathan found her there. The smell of bacon frying had clearly drawn him away from his home office.

"Late dinner or early breakfast?" he asked, sniffing the air with an appreciative sigh.

She took a carton from the fridge. "I missed supper. You want any scrambled eggs?"

He sat on a stool at the counter. "Actually, that sounds pretty damn good. I had a salad with a client, but I wasn't in the mood for a big meal."

"Still feeling rotten?"

He nodded. "I haven't wanted to tell you this, but I guess it's time. My doctor wants me to go to some hippie-dippie holistic retreat out in the desert to see if we can break the cycle of these headaches. The doctors and counselors who run the program use a combination of meditation and medical assessment and organic or natural medicines."

She tended the eggs carefully. The strips of perfectly crisped bacon were already draining on a paper towel.

"No offense, Jonathan, but that doesn't sound like you at all." His air of brooding exhaustion made her worry about him.

"You're right. In fact, you couldn't be *more* right. But I'm getting desperate."

"Here. I'll have toast ready in a minute. Start on this." She gave him the eggs and bacon. "But why wouldn't you want to tell me that?"

"Because the retreat center is booked months in advance. The only opening they had was the week that includes Christmas."

"Oh." Disappointment curled in her stomach. "Well, it's just one day on the calendar. Daddy and I will be fine."

Jonathan grimaced. "That's the other part. Dad's been invited to go on a cruise with his college buddies. He asked me what I thought, and I told him it would be good for him to get out of the house. But that was before I knew I'd be leaving, too. I feel terrible about this, Mazie. I've dreaded telling you."

She managed a smile. "Don't be ridiculous. I'm a grown woman. Besides, there are tons of places I can celebrate the holiday. Don't worry about me at all. The important thing is for you to get well."

Relief lightened his face. "I'll make it up to you, I swear."

"I'll be fine. Eat your eggs before they get cold."

She added the toast to their plates and joined him. For several minutes, peace reigned in the beautiful kitchen. Mazie often thought about having her own place. A man to cook for, or one who might cook for her. A couple of kids running through the halls, leaving toys scattered about. Maybe a mongrel dog, or two…

"Jonathan?"

"Hmm?" He had cleared his plate and was now slathering butter and honey over a piece of toast.

"J.B.'s mother came through the surgery well. But right

before she went under the knife, J.B. did something kind of dumb. They were all afraid she wasn't going to make it. Even Jane, his mom, wasn't sure."

"And?"

"J.B. told her we were secretly engaged. He said she had to get well so she could play with all the grandchildren we're going to have."

"Stupid bastard." But he said the words with wry affection.

"I know. I couldn't even be mad at him, because he was so worried and scared."

"But now you have to wait a little while before you can break it off so you won't upset her."

"Something like that." She didn't bother explaining that Jane Vaughan had already seen through the ruse. What did it matter?

Jonathan opened the dishwasher, tucking his few items inside. "If you want my advice, I wouldn't bother telling Dad. It will only confuse him. I hate to say it, but I see him slipping a little more with each week that passes."

"And you think that won't be a problem on a cruise?"

Jonathan grinned. "It's not like he can wander off. Seriously, though, I know all of his gang. They'll look out for him."

"As long as none of them is like Daddy."

"The cruise is billed as an all-inclusive event for older adults. Much older. He'll be fine."

"I hope so."

Jonathan glanced at the clock. "Don't move. I have something I want to show you."

When he disappeared, Mazie tidied up the kitchen. The housekeeper could have done it in the morning, but Mazie hated leaving a mess overnight. She had just wiped down the counter when Jonathan returned carrying a small box, much the size of the one that had come with her ring.

This box was red leather, and it wasn't wrapped. Mazie was standing at the sink when Jonathan tucked his arms around her from behind. "I hate like hell to miss Christmas, sis. I want you to have your present early."

He hopped up on the granite-topped island and folded his arms across his chest. "Go ahead. Open it."

Mazie pulled on the hinged lid and caught her breath. Inside was a delicate necklace. A gold chain, featherlight, coiled in the box. It supported a single, gorgeous pearl, as fat as a child's marble.

She lifted the necklace carefully, rubbing a fingertip over the luminescent sphere. "It's beautiful, Jonathan."

"Dad put my name with his on a lot of legal stuff recently. When I was going through the safety deposit box, I found a bunch of Mom's jewelry. Evidently, when he sent her away, she had to leave it all behind. I know how much you miss her, especially during the holidays. I thought you could wear this and feel close to her...until you and I can go to Vermont after the first of the year."

Mazie eyes were damp. "Thank you, Jonathan. I adore it."

He waited as she wrestled with the clasp. "It will all be yours someday anyway."

She frowned. "No. That's not fair. You and Hartley will take a share for your spouses."

"Hartley is out of the picture, and I don't know that marriage is in the cards for me."

"Why do you say that?"

His gaze was stormy, troubled. "I've wondered if these headaches are a precursor of something worse. What if I've inherited Mom's instability? I don't want to doom a wife or a baby to the kind of life you and I experienced. It wouldn't be fair."

She was shocked. Had he been wrestling with this possibility for months? Shaking her head vehemently, she touched his knee. "Oh, Jonathan. I had no idea. I don't think that could be true. You're brilliant. You run a multinational shipping empire. Hundreds of people depend on you, and you handle it all with such grace, including your ability to make sure Daddy still feels needed. You're *not* going crazy. I would tell you if I saw any inkling."

Some of the clouds left his face. "Thanks," he said gruffly.

"Don't worry about the holidays," she said. "I might spend Christmas somewhere else since you and Daddy will both be gone." Was she rationalizing her decision? Trying to put a positive spin on a choice she knew she should never make? "J.B. offered a room at his house." And a whole lot more…

"For a fake fiancé, he sure has a hell of a nerve. Are you sleeping with him?" Jonathan's tone was truculent.

She scowled at him, long accustomed to his protective nature. "I love you, big brother. And I love my gift. But I won't have this discussion with you. Are we clear?" Some things were far too private.

"What will you tell Dad?"

"The truth. That I'm helping out a friend. I'll drop by here and see him every other day or so until he leaves. By the time he gets back from the cruise, all of this will be over."

"So you'll spend Christmas with the Vaughans? That would make me feel better about leaving you."

"Maybe so, or if that doesn't work out, maybe with Gina's crew. She has so many cousins they would never notice one more person. She's always asking me to come to family things. I don't know that Mrs. Vaughan will feel up to having much of a Christmas, anyway."

"Okay. As long as you're not alone."

"Being alone isn't so bad," she said. "It's not the same as being *lonely.* I have you and Dad and all kinds of friends. I'll be fine."

The question remained, would she spend Christmas in J.B.'s bed?

* * *

Her brave statement to Jonathan was tested a few hours later.

With the lights out and the room dark, all she could think about was how much she wanted J.B. here beside her. The strength of that yearning was a wake-up call. How had he wormed his way into her heart so quickly?

It occurred to her that over the years she had whipped up her antipathy toward him for no other reason than to keep from admitting that she still had feelings for him. Not teenage heart palpitations, but full-blown, adult emotions that left her weak and vulnerable and afraid.

J.B. was playing with her. Not cruelly, but for fun. He was intent on having a grown-up sleepover.

A holiday affair.

She would be a fool to let him have that much control over her happiness. To let him lure her into his home and into his bed.

Even knowing every single reason that she had to guard her heart, she couldn't resist the pull of the perfect holiday with J.B.

Admitting the truth was both elating and terrifying.

Come morning, she was going to pack a bag and cast her lot with Charleston's *baddest* bachelor.

When she reached the hospital on Sunday just before noon, she was suddenly unsure about going in. J.B. hadn't called. Or texted. They had left things between them at a rather volatile crossroads last night.

Maybe he was regretting his impulsive invitation.

It wasn't too late to undo that. Her bag was in the trunk. No reason for him to ever know she had come prepared.

Because she had dropped by work briefly before coming to the hospital, she was dressed nicely in a black pencil skirt, emerald green silk blouse and her new necklace. The large pearl nestled just at the top of her cleavage.

She touched the cool stone. Jonathan understood all she had missed as a child...all they both had missed. The pearl couldn't bring her mother back, but it was a tangible link to all the might-have-beens.

Inside the hospital, she headed straight for the information desk and confirmed that Mrs. Vaughan had been moved to a regular room. That was definitely good news. When Mazie made her way upstairs, she found only Alana in residence. Even the bed was empty.

The woman who was only a couple years younger than Mazie smiled. "They took Mom one flight up for cardiac rehab. She'll be back soon."

"And the rest of your family?"

"Dad's an early riser. He got here at six this morning and sent J.B. home to sleep. Pop is downstairs grabbing a snack right now. Leila and I were here by eight. Mom's asking for her favorite coffee. The doctor okayed it, so Leila went to get her some."

"Well, it sounds like you have everything under control. Perhaps I'll swing by later in the day."

Alana hopped up, tossing the paperback book she had been reading into her tote. "Actually, I have a favor to ask."

"I'd be happy to help," Mazie said. "What is it?"

"My sister and I have matinee tickets for *The Nutcracker* at 2:00 p.m. today. Mom remembered and is insisting we go. One of the tickets was for her, so she wants Daddy to take her place. Which is stupid, because the man is *not* a ballet fan, but what can he do? He wants to make her happy."

"I'd be happy to sit with your mother," Mazie said.

"J.B. will be back soon. You wouldn't be here alone."

"I've already said yes," Mazie teased. "No need to oversell it."

"Perfect," Alana said.

At that moment, an orderly wheeled Mrs. Vaughan back into the room and helped her into bed. Mazie hovered in the hall during the transfer, not wanting to be in the way. Soon, Mr. Vaughan and his other daughter arrived, as well. The controlled chaos lasted for several minutes.

Mazie could hear J.B.'s mother directing everyone's movements. Mazie grinned to herself. No wonder the Vaughans loved and feared Jane. She was a formidable force.

At last the hoopla settled and the room quieted. Mazie could hear Jane asking for her. She stepped to the door. "I'm here."

Jane kissed her husband and daughters as they leaned over her bed. "Go have fun, my loves. Mazie and J.B. will look after me until you get back."

Soon the room emptied, and it was just Mazie and Jane. For the first time since Mazie had arrived, the older woman seemed to deflate.

"I'm toast," she grumbled. "I hate feeling this way."

"You had a major heart attack and serious surgery. It's going to take some time. Why don't you rest until they bring your lunch tray?"

"I'm tired of resting. Tell me about your family. I need distractions. I'm going crazy in this place."

Mazie pulled up a chair. "Okay. What do you remember?"

"Not much," Jane said. "When you children were small, I knew your parents well, but the years passed, you all grew up, and we lost touch."

"You know about my mother, though?"

Jane's expression softened. "I do. The poor woman had demons, I suppose. And you were just a babe."

"Old enough to remember her leaving."

J.B.'s mother patted the bed. "Come sit here." Jane took her hand. "Everyone in Charleston knew what was happening. But the scuttlebutt was never unkind. Your parents were well respected, and to see you children lose your mother..." She shook her head, her gaze sober. "We all grieved for you and your brothers. And your father, too, of course. How is Gerald doing these days?"

"His health is precarious. He's twenty-two years older than my mom, so he's beginning to slow down."

"It must have been hard for him. Sending her away."

Mazie stood up and paced, her arms wrapped around her waist. "Yes. My brothers and I visit her occasionally. Up in Vermont. But she hasn't known us for years. She seems happy, though."

"If you marry my son, I'd be honored to be your mother-in-law."

It sounded like a joke, but when Mazie turned around and stared at her, Jane was clearly dead serious. Mazie hesitated. "You told me you understood that J.B. was inventing this whole engagement charade."

"I do. But sometimes a man does things for reasons he can't even understand until later."

"Mrs. Vaughan... Jane. Please don't set your heart on this." She bit her lip. "It's not real."

"I've seen the way he looks at you."

Mazie swallowed, desperately wanting to believe that Jane was right. "He's physically attracted to me. For the moment. I think it's probably the thrill of the chase. As soon as I sell my property to him, he'll lose interest."

"It's time he settled down."

"J.B. has a great life. I don't think he's missing out on anything."

"And what about you, Mazie?"

Fourteen

J.B. heard just enough of the conversation in his mother's hospital room to realize that poor Mazie was floundering. He bumped the partially open door with his hip and entered. "I brought Chinese for Mazie and me. Sorry, Mom. We can eat in the lounge if it makes you too hungry."

He smothered a grin at the naked relief on Mazie's face. "Thanks, J.B."

A young woman in pink scrubs brought in the noon meal and set it on the bedside table. While J.B. set out the more appetizing of the two feasts, Mazie helped Jane get organized.

As everyone was digging in, Jane smiled genially.

"We should settle on your wedding date immediately," she pronounced, staring at her broiled codfish with distaste. "All the best summer venues will be booked soon."

J.B. took his mother's outrageous efforts in stride. He was used to her tactics.

Poor Mazie, on the other hand, choked on a bite of moo shu pork, her expression impossible to read. Her cheeks turned pink. Was she appalled or intrigued about the mention of wedded bliss?

For his part, the idea didn't bother him as much as it should have.

J.B. shook his head. "Back off, Mom. I love you, but this is between Mazie and me."

Mazie nodded. "Please don't be offended. But we're in

no rush, Jane. J.B. has this big project ahead of him, and besides, we haven't been together all that long."

His mother shook her head, picking at a cup of out-of-the-can fruit cocktail. She shot a sly glance that J.B. intercepted, though he didn't think Mazie saw. "You know how much I hate downtime, son. This wedding could be the perfect thing to occupy me while I'm having to take it easy."

"Nice try, Mom. Guilt and coercion are not going to work on either of us. Mazie and I are adults. You'll have to trust us to decide when the time is right. Now eat your lunch and behave."

The remainder of the afternoon passed without fireworks. His mother napped off and on. In between, he and Mazie entertained her with lighthearted conversation about anything and everything. Mazie was great with his mom. For a woman who had grown up without a female role model, she was remarkably astute when it came to handling a difficult parent.

Caring for her father had shaped her adult life.

By the time the next shift arrived at five, J.B. was more than ready to spirit Mazie away. Watching her all afternoon had been slow torture. He wanted to make love to her again. Badly. And this time in a comfortable bed with soft sheets where he could take his time with her. The prospect dried his mouth and tightened his body.

She was an elegant woman, graceful, fun loving, and above all, kind. Which didn't explain why she had given him such grief about selling her building. The place was a mess. Heating, wiring, water issues in the basement. Everything he had offered Mazie as a trade was far and away better. But she had clung to her hatred of him. He liked to think he had mended fences with her now…that what happened so long ago no longer mattered.

Some people said love was the flip side of hate. Did he

want that from Mazie? Surely not. He'd been vulnerable once, had trusted a woman. The betrayal that followed had cost him his heart, his pride and his fortune.

Mazie wasn't like his ex-wife. He'd stake his life on it. But did he really want to take a chance?

His mother's heart attack had diverted his attention. But now that she was on the mend, he needed to focus his attention on persuading Mazie to sell.

Perhaps he could combine business with pleasure. He had asked her to spend Christmas with him. Was she going to say yes? The prospect was far more personal than he wanted to admit.

When his father and sisters shooed him on his way—after heaping gratitude on Mazie for spending her Sunday afternoon at the hospital—J.B. followed Mazie outside, breathing in the crisp evening air with a groan of relief.

"God, I hate hospitals," he said. "The smells. The sad faces. I hope Mom doesn't have to stay long."

Mazie rolled her shoulders. "It's a great hospital, J.B. But I know what you mean."

"Are you hungry?"

"Not yet."

"You want to walk the bridge?" The Ravenel Bridge, completed in 2005, had been constructed with both a pedestrian path and a bike lane. It was a popular destination any time of the year, but in December when the weather was kind, it couldn't be beat.

Mazie nodded. "I'd love to. I've been feeling like a slug." She glanced down at her slim skirt and high heels. "I'll have to put on other clothes."

They had made it out of the lobby and were standing on the sidewalk near the main parking lot. J.B. took her arm, his fingertips rubbing lightly over the narrow bones of her wrist. "Did you bring what you needed to stay over?" He felt her pulse jump.

She nodded slowly. When she lifted her gaze to his, he saw deep vulnerability. "I'm not sure why, but I did."

Exultation flooded his veins, though he kept his expression noncommittal. Words he couldn't say hovered on his lips. Words that would change everything. He couldn't do it. He wouldn't. It wasn't really necessary to upset the status quo. Too much at stake. "Good. Let's meet at my house, and we'll both get changed."

Was that disappointment he saw on her face? He felt a lick of shame, but it didn't sway him.

The distance was short, ten minutes at the most. Even so, he held his breath until he saw Mazie's distinctive car pull into his narrow driveway and squeeze in beside his SUV.

He slammed his car door and waited, rifling though his pockets for what he wanted to give her.

Mazie got out as well, with her purse slung over her shoulder and a stylish duffel in her hand.

"I made you a set of keys," he said. "I'll remind you how to use the alarm before we go to bed tonight." He took the heavy bag from her.

She wrapped her arms around her waist. "That's not really necessary, is it? I won't be here long."

"I want you to feel at home."

As he said the words, something about them set off warning bells in his head. When had he *ever* said that exact phrase to a woman? Never that he could recall.

He would have to tread carefully. Mazie might get the wrong idea. Even worse, so might he.

Inside, he led her upstairs, bypassing his bedroom and ushering her into a beautifully decorated guest room. The celadon hues were soothing.

"This is beautiful," Mazie said.

He set her bag on the dresser. "I hope you won't want to spend too much time in here."

Her mouth dropped open in a little O of shock. Hot pink color flooded her face. "J.B., I…"

He held up a hand. "It's your room. Completely private. No strings attached. But I reserve the right to remind you how sweet it is when we both give in to temptation."

She lifted an eyebrow. "Sweet? More like insane."

"So you admit it."

Mazie shrugged, her gaze moody and restless as she dropped her purse on a chair and examined the amenities.

"It would be hard not to," she muttered, running her hand over the bedspread.

Watching her touch the bed was almost tactile. His skin quivered as if she were stroking *him*. He kept his distance, though it strained every ounce of his control.

He loved her.

The admission slapped him like a jolt of cold water on a winter morning. He wanted to snatch her up and kiss her senseless and bury himself inside her until he couldn't breathe with wanting her.

But the consequences of such abandon were very nearly life and death.

He couldn't dive into this thing without remembering the past. Failure. Humiliation. Self-loathing.

Instead, he did the mature, nonreckless thing. "Get dressed," he said gruffly. "We'll walk the bridge, and then I'll take you for fresh shrimp and hush puppies at Lolita's."

This time, Mazie's smile was open and untinged with the wariness that was so much a part of her personality.

"For that kind of positive reinforcement, I'll follow you anywhere."

J.B. needed exercise. Badly.

And though he would have preferred the kind between the sheets, it was probably better this way.

Mazie changed clothes as quickly as he did. Soon they

were on their way toward the bridge. Beneath the magnificent structure with the two triangular sets of silvery spires, an enterprising city had installed parking and a labyrinth of short trails.

While Mazie hopped out and began stretching, J.B. locked the car and tried not to look at the way black spandex cupped her cute butt. Lord help him. He did a few stretches, too, but he was antsy. "Let's go," he said. "We can walk the first quarter mile to warm up."

They were far from the only people enjoying the bridge. Though the sounds of cars whizzing by a few feet away on the other side of the concrete barrier was not exactly relaxing, being able to look down on the city of Charleston made up for it. They started out at a brisk walk.

When Mazie shed her jacket and tied it around her waist, he gave her a nod. "Ready?"

"Yep. I'll drop back when people pass us."

They set off at an easy jog. Tension winnowed away from his body step by step. For weeks he had been totally immersed in the huge project that included Mazie's shop. And then the scare with his mother had left their entire family on edge.

But the emotions that had truly kept him tied in knots day and night were all because of Mazie.

At the top of the arc, he expected her to stop, but she kept on running, her ponytail bouncing in the wind. He kept pace with her, curbing his stride to match hers. At the other end, they did an about-face and headed back. This time, when they hit dead center on the bridge, Mazie paused long enough to stare down into the inky black Cooper River far below.

On sunny, bright days, you could spot dolphins frolicking. Tonight, the deep water was mysterious.

He bumped her hip with his. "We can't stand here too long, or we'll get cold. And I'm starving."

A smile curved her mouth. "Have you ever heard of delayed gratification?"

He took her arm. "Not a fan."

They walked quickly, using the last segment to lower their heart rates. Unfortunately, being near Mazie kept his blood pressure and respiration perpetually in the red zone.

For the moment, he would sublimate with food.

Lolita's was a hole-in-wall place. The kind of eatery the locals patronized and tourists rarely took the time to find. Not on the beach, but near enough the water to have the best seafood in Mount Pleasant.

Even better, the ambiance was definitely casual. He and Mazie didn't look out of place in their running clothes.

The hostess led them to a scarred table beneath a huge stuffed tarpon wearing a Santa hat. She handed them plastic-coated menus. "Wreckfish is the special tonight. Two sides. Thirty-five bucks. It's worth the price. Soup of the day is seafood gumbo. Let me grab you a couple of waters, and I'll be back to take your order."

Mazie yawned. "Sorry," she said as the waitress walked away. "I didn't sleep great last night. Jonathan and I had eggs and bacon late, and I drank half a cup of coffee. I was able to do that in college, but I guess I'm getting old."

J.B. leaned back in his chair and chuckled. "Yeah. You're ancient." He glanced around the restaurant, noting the multiple strands of Christmas lights and the ubiquitous tinsel garlands. "I suppose I should confess something. My housekeeper decorated my place for the holidays. Garlands and lights and such. But I don't have a tree. Seems kind of a waste for just me."

"No worries," she said. "We never have a tree up at our house."

He frowned. "You're kidding. I thought you were the one who loved Christmas. Jonathan jokes about it and how he has to hide his Scroogish tendencies when you're around."

"I do love Christmas," she said. "But we haven't decorated since my mom left. At first, we kids were too little, and by the time we were in high school, the moment had passed. The boys weren't particularly interested, and I was self-conscious about tackling it on my own. Plus, I was afraid it would make my father sad. So we don't deck the halls." She shrugged. "There are enough decorations elsewhere for me to enjoy. It's no big deal."

But it was a big deal. He hated the thought of a little girl yearning for candles and ornaments and wreaths and a tree and having no one to get them for her.

Their meal arrived. Both of them cleaned their plates.

Mazie finished her last plump shrimp and her last crispy hush puppy. "This place is amazing. I'm glad you thought of it."

The blissful appreciation on her face was aimed at the food, but J.B. was equally willing to accommodate any other appetites she might have. His body ached for her. The urgency of his desire was outrageous enough to slow him down for a moment.

Though he would like to take her straight back to the house and strip her naked, he needed to take a deep breath and get some perspective. Besides, she needed some pampering.

After taking care of the check, he ushered her outside. "I have a surprise," he said.

As usual, Mazie's response was laced with suspicion. "I hope it doesn't involve bank vaults."

Was she flirting with him? Or simply giving him a hard time? It baffled him that he still had difficulty understanding her. Usually he could read people like open books. Mazie was a whole damned library with the doors padlocked.

He opened the car door for her and tried to help her up

into the passenger seat, but she waved him away. "I can do it."

"Fine," he muttered. He waited until she was settled and slammed the door. Loping around to the driver's side, he quickly composed and discarded several versions of a plan to make her smile.

It was Christmas. The season of peace and goodwill. He and Mazie were mending fences, but he wanted more. He was tired of living in the shadows of his own failures.

Suddenly, he knew he had to give her the perfect, special holiday.

For a split second, he envisioned a year in the future with the two of them gathered around a fireplace reading books to a toddler. The image shocked him so much, he almost ran a red light. Tonight was about Mazie's broken childhood. He didn't want to examine his other motives too closely.

Mazie shot him a glance. "You okay?"

He swallowed the lump in his throat. "Yeah. Sorry. My mind was on something else."

She patted his thigh. "I understand. You must be so worried about your mom. But she's doing well, J.B. Honestly, she is. When you all were gone today, she told me she's feeling stronger every day."

"Yeah, I know." His mother was definitely on his mind. But her condition was stable. This thing with Mazie was definitely *not* stable.

Up ahead, he finally spotted what he was looking for. He turned into a parking lot and shut off the engine.

Mazie looked through the windshield and then sideways at him. "What are we doing here?"

"What do you think?" He reached across the small space between them and caressed her cheek with the pad of his thumb. "I think you've been a very good girl this year. Santa wants you to have all the trimmings."

Fifteen

Mazie's throat tightened. Tears stung her eyes. How dumb was this? She surely wasn't going to get all emotional because a man was being sweet and kind and indulging her love of the holiday.

J.B. stared at her with a quizzical smile on his face. He had charisma in spades. No wonder he'd dated his way through half the women in Charleston. He was a young George Clooney. Charming. Funny. Hard to pin down.

"Are you sure?" she asked. "Real Christmas trees shed needles everywhere. And they can be hard to set up."

J.B. grinned. "Challenge accepted."

"Okay, then. You asked for it."

She hopped out of the car and inhaled a deep lungful of balsam-scented air. "Take a whiff," she said. "No artificial tree can give you this."

Though it had been dark now for several hours, the proprietor had strung up long swaths of colored lights among his offerings. Christmas carols played in the background from an old-fashioned boom box. Because it was getting closer to the main event, the Christmas-tree lot was crowded with browsers.

Moms and dads and excited children. Young couples. Families with teenagers.

For a split second, Mazie felt like a child again with all the anticipation and wonder and hope of innocence. And she owed it all to the man who had once broken her heart.

But he had changed, she was sure of it. And now his sensual charm was irresistible.

J.B. tagged along behind her with an indulgent smile on his face as she walked through the rows of freshly cut trees. Half a dozen varieties were represented, but the Fraser firs were her favorites.

She bypassed the six-and seven-foot trees and headed for the bigger ones. J.B.'s living room had high ceilings. No need to skimp.

At her request, he held up one tree at a time, twirling them around so Mazie could inspect all sides. Finally, she found the one she wanted. It was perfectly symmetrical, and it was fat and healthy. It topped J.B. by almost two feet.

For the first time, he winced. "You sure about this? It's gonna look bigger when we get it inside."

"It's the perfect tree," she said. "You'll see."

While J.B. paid for the expensive fir, and the man tucked it in a mesh sleeve for the trip home, Mazie gave herself a stern lecture. She would *not* let herself be sucked into a fantasy where J.B. doted on her and actually cared about her. Everything about this weird December aberration was make-believe.

He liked having sex with her. And maybe he was also stringing her along so she would sell him her property, or he was worried about his mother and using Mazie's sympathetic heart to help him get through these difficult days, or both.

That was all this was.

At the moment, he looked like a ruggedly sexy lumberjack. He had hefted the heavy tree on top of the car, and was now securing it with bungees.

She joined him and slid an arm around his waist, feeling his muscles strain as he worked.

"You're my hero," she said, only half joking.

He stepped back and wiped sap from his forehead. "You

owe me for this. Just so you know, I plan to collect later tonight."

His wicked grin curled her toes. "The tree was your idea," she pointed out, leaning into him and inhaling the scent of warm male. "I merely went along with the adventure."

"Smart woman." He kissed her nose and then found her mouth with his. The second kiss started out lazy for five seconds and then hardened.

Mazie arched her neck, kissing him back. "You drive me crazy," she muttered.

"The feeling is mutual." He backed her against the side of the car, his lower body pinning hers to the vehicle. "I haven't needed anyone like this in a very long time. You make me want to be sixteen again."

"No," she groaned, her arms tightening around his neck. "Not that. I want the J.B. who knows all the naughty secrets about women."

He pulled back, his gaze oddly abashed and serious for the moment. "I don't know all *your* secrets, Mazie."

"I don't have anything to hide," she said lightly. The lie was both easy and disturbing.

He sucked in a sharp breath, his chest heaving, as he looked around at all the people keeping them from a private moment. "We still have to buy decorations," he muttered.

"Then let's go."

They hit up a fancy department store nearby, cleaning out a huge percentage of their handblown ornaments and silvery tinsel. Mazie added box after box of multicolored lights to the haul.

When the cashier rang up the total, J.B. never flinched. He handed over his platinum card and scrawled his name on the credit slip, giving the poor woman a smile that made her blush from her throat to her hairline, though she was old enough to be his grandmother.

Mazie rolled her eyes. The man couldn't help himself. His masculinity was electric and compelling.

Back in the car, she yawned. "It's probably too late to decorate tonight."

"I hope that means what I think it means."

She fidgeted in her seat, trying to get comfortable, her breath coming faster. "I could be persuaded."

"Oh, no," he said, staring at the traffic and not at her, so that she saw only his profile. "You're a guest in my home. I'll need a firm, unequivocal invitation."

There was a tongue-in-cheek tone to his voice, but what he said made sense. It would be cowardly on Mazie's part to pretend reluctance when the truth was, she wanted him every bit as badly as he wanted her.

Sliding her hand across the leather bench seat, she placed it on his upper thigh, gripping the taut muscle beneath his pants. "I'd like to have sex with you, J.B. In a bed, in a chair, heck, even in your fancy kitchen." She sighed. "You're a very tempting man. And I'm in a mood to indulge."

He shot her a sideways glance. "You sound like someone prepared to go off a diet. Am I really that bad for you?"

She pretended to mull it over. "Hmm. Let me see. A commitment-phobic bachelor. A relationship that will possibly hurt other people when it ends, including me. That's a yes, J.B. I don't think you're my smartest choice, but I'm not going to run away. You're exactly what I want for Christmas."

They were parked in his narrow driveway now, with two houses looming on either side. The vehicle was dark. What was he thinking? Had she startled him with her plain speaking?

After a long, tense silence, he handed her his keys. "Unlock the front door. I'll carry the tree in."

She did as he requested, and then stood aside while he brought the large Fraser fir into the house. Immediately, the foyer filled with the fragrance of outdoors. Crisp, clean. If they invented a name for this particular scent, Mazie would call it *mountain morning.*

They had bought a tree stand, a fancy one that held a good supply of water but could be tilted carefully to straighten the trunk. Somehow, they had to unwrap the tree, lift it into the container and tighten the bolts.

Suddenly, Mazie realized that she should be the one to call the shots. J.B. was trying to give her a Christmas experience she had missed for many years. He wouldn't stop until the whole damn tree was ablaze with lights and sparkling with expensive ornaments.

After he leaned the tree in a corner and dusted off his hands, she went to him and laid her head on his shoulder. "I'm serious. I don't want to decorate this tree tonight."

She felt his body tense. "You're sure?"

"I'd rather decorate you. Maybe a dab of whipping cream. A little chocolate. What do you say?"

His laugh sounded breathless. "Don't toy with me, woman."

It came to her in that moment that she was in over her head. She had wanted him forever, it seemed. But for years, she had been afraid to admit those feelings or to fight for what she needed and deserved.

In spite of the risks, she was all in now. When it came to a choice, she would always choose J.B. Maybe the aftermath of this little experiment was going to suck, but that was in the future. For now, she wanted him so much it left her breathless.

"No games," she whispered. "But I think I'd like a quick shower first."

He grabbed her hand and dragged her toward the stairs. "We'll do it together and save time."

"I can't remember if I shaved my legs."

"Doesn't matter."

His desperation might have been flattering if she hadn't been so scared of letting him know how she felt. She had to keep this light and physical. No messy emotional connection.

That was hard to do when he was so damned cute.

In his bathroom, he released her only long enough to turn on the water in the shower enclosure and adjust the temperature. When he turned around, Mazie was naked from the waist up.

His cheeks flushed dark red. "I think you're getting ahead of me," he croaked.

"Maybe you should try harder." She stripped his shirt over his head and kissed his nipples. They were flat and copper colored, and he hissed with pleasure when she licked them.

His running pants were thin nylon. They did little to disguise the fact that his sex was rising to the occasion rapidly, thick and eager.

By unspoken consent, they each removed the remainder of their own clothes. She was bashful, but not reluctant. The look in J.B.'s eyes made a woman feel invincible.

When they were both completely nude, he took her hand, lifted it to his lips and kissed her fingers. "After you, my lady."

Her hair was in a knot on top of her head, because they had been running earlier, so she didn't have to worry about putting it up. It would be easy enough not to get it wet. At least that's what she thought until J.B. joined her.

Even though his hedonistic shower was huge, the guy was big. He took up a lot of room.

Mazie backed against the corner, her heart beating far too fast.

"Face the other wall," she said. "I'll wash your back." Anything to keep him from staring at her. When he turned away, she breathed a sigh of relief.

With shaking hands, she picked up the washcloth and soaped it. Then she started at the back of his neck and rubbed hard enough to make his skin pink. Next, his shoulders, his broad back and his narrow waist.

J.B. groaned as if she was torturing him…when all she was doing was playing the role of a bathhouse girl. She kneeled on the slick floor and soaped the backs of his legs… powerful thighs, muscular calves. Even his bare feet were sexy. Now that it was time for him to turn around, she nearly lost her nerve.

She rose to her feet and put both hands on his shoulders. "All done here."

He spun slowly and stared at her. The heat in his blue-eyed gaze made her stomach clench with desire. "You gonna wash the rest of me?" he asked, a tiny smile tipping the corners of his mouth.

"I think you're perfectly capable of handling that," she said primly.

"Then I'll do *your* back. You know…tit for tat."

She tried not to laugh. "I don't believe that word is politically correct anymore."

He lifted an eyebrow. "Tat?"

"You're impossible."

He put his wet hands on her shoulders and turned her away from him. Soon, the feel of his hands on her body made her legs shaky. Especially when one particular part of *him* kept bumping her bottom.

J.B. put a lot of effort into making sure she was clean from head to toe. He seemed particularly taken with her bottom. When he had soaped it up to his liking, he rested his erection in the cleft and slowly massaged her with his sex.

Oh, lordy.

He'd barely gotten started, and she was falling apart. "J.B.?"

"Hmm?" He kissed the back of her neck, nibbling gently. "We're using an awful lot of water. Seems irresponsible."

Without warning, his arms came around her from behind. "Let me finish this one part," he muttered. "Then we'll get out."

He abandoned the washcloth. Instead, his big soapy hands caressed her breasts.

Her head fell back against his shoulder. "I don't think my boobs are all that dirty," she panted, trying not to beg him to take her then and there.

"Maybe not." He tweaked her sensitive nipples. "But they're so damned pretty when they're wet and slick."

She was wet and slick somewhere else. Embarrassingly so. But it seemed rude to mention it. Not when J.B. was doing such a bang-up job of bathing her. His hands were gentle and thorough. Much more of this and she would melt…maybe slide right down the drain.

When the water started to run cold, she seized the chance to move their interlude to somewhere less wet and more horizontal. After all, she didn't want to be responsible for either one of them cracking their skull in the shower.

"Bed," she begged. "Let's get in your bed. The water is freezing."

J.B. couldn't argue with that. He turned off the faucet and grabbed towels for both of them. "Your lips are blue," he said. "Poor baby. I'll have to warm them up."

She scrubbed her body with the dry towel and grabbed a robe off the back of the door. "Meet you on the mattress. Bring condoms."

He followed her, pausing only to rummage in a bathroom drawer. "Plural," he teased. "I like how you think."

J.B.'s bed was a testament to fine linens and the ingenuity of an American mattress company. She climbed beneath the covers, tossed her damp towel on the floor and reveled in the unmistakable luxury of thousand-thread-count sheets. It figured that J.B. would have only the best in his bachelor paradise.

Instead of joining her immediately, he stood with his hands on his hips and stared at her.

Mazie clutched the covers to her chin. "I thought you'd be in more of a hurry." The part of him that reared strong and proud against his flat belly seemed not inclined to wait.

One masculine shoulder lifted and fell. "I'm enjoying the prelude," he said, the words low and husky. "You look delicious in my bed."

"Like an apple waiting to be picked?"

"Like a moment I want to paint and record for posterity."

The sappy romantic comment stunned her. Not because he said it jokingly, but because of the utter sincerity in his quiet words.

"I want you here with me," she begged. "Come warm me up." His steady regard made her self-conscious.

He dropped the towel wrapped around his hips. "I can do that."

When he joined her underneath the covers, something inside her sighed with contentment. Which was odd, because she was a long way from satisfied.

She ran her hand down his flank. Questions trembled on her lips. Requests for reassurance. Demands about the future.

What did J.B. want from her? Was any of this more than a lark for him?

Swallowing her uncertainties was much harder than it should have been.

"Thank you for the Christmas tree," she said.

He turned on his side and faced her, resting his head on his hand. This close she could see his thick eyelashes and the sparkles of gold in his blue irises.

"I'm glad we skipped decorating for this instead," he said.

Despite her best efforts, her insecurity slipped out. "What is *this*, J.B.?"

The faint frown on his face told her she had overstepped some invisible boundary. "Do we have to ask that question right now? Can't we enjoy the moment?"

She nodded slowly, swallowing her disappointment. "Of course we can."

Hurt bubbled in her chest, but she ignored it.

J.B. wasn't a forever kind of man. She had known that when she climbed into his bed. She would take this temporary affair and wallow in the magic of Christmas. Reality was something that could wait for the cold, bleak days of January.

"Make love to me," she whispered.

Her words galvanized him. Bending over her, he suckled her breasts and slid a hand between her thighs. When he entered her with his finger, she cried out. Her body was taut with arousal.

A lock of his hair fell over his forehead. His face was flushed. "I want you, Mazie Jane. Insanely, as it happens. Why do you think that is?"

"Maybe you got tired of women who won't stand up to you."

He choked out a laugh, as if her blunt honesty had surprised him. "You're prickly and unpredictable. I've had easier women, that's for sure."

When she reached for his erection, he batted her hand away. "Next time, love. I'm too primed for that." He sheathed himself and moved on top of her, fitting the blunt head of his sex at her entrance. "Lift your arms," he demanded. "Hold on to the headboard."

She obeyed automatically, clenching her fingers tightly around the wavy iron bars. Her eyelids fluttered shut.

J.B. pushed inside her slowly. The feeling was indescribable. She heard a ragged curse, as if he, too, was surprised at the way their bodies fit together. Yin and yang. As old as time. As new and fragile and precious as a morning mist on the beach.

"Open your eyes, sweet girl. Don't hide from me."

She tried. The intimacy was painful. His features were taut, his expression impossible to read.

But she, on the other hand, felt naked. Surely he could see everything she had hidden for so long. Her wrists weren't immobilized. She could have touched him if she wanted.

Still, she didn't move. She held her breath, her body straining against his, her heart soaking up every tender, muttered endearment, every rough thrust, every unbelievably raw emotion.

"J.B.," she cried out, feeling the peak rush toward her.

He buried his face in her hot neck. "Come for me, Mazie."

She wrapped her arms around him, arched her back and obeyed...

Sixteen

Mazie had never enjoyed *sleeping* with a man. Actually *sleeping*. But somehow, curling up with J.B. and letting drowsiness roll over her was the most wonderful feeling in the world.

By the time she awoke the next morning, something had changed. Not in him, maybe, but in her. No matter how foolish or self-destructive, she had to admit the truth.

She had fallen in love with J.B.

There hadn't been far to fall. Deep in a sixteen-year-old girl's heart the memory of her feelings for him had lived on, just as strongly as the memory of her mother's leaving home when she was twelve.

Traumatic events, world-changing events, never really went away. A person just learned to bury them. She had covered her desire for J.B. with animosity, trying to pretend he was nothing to her. It had worked for a long time—years even. But no more.

The covers were warm. J.B.'s big body was warm. He held her cradled in his arms, her head on his shoulder.

What was she going to do? How far could she let herself be pulled into his orbit and still be able to break free?

He stirred and gave her a sleepy smile. "Hey, there, gorgeous."

She cupped his stubbly chin. "Shouldn't you be at work?"

J.B. yawned and glanced at the digital clock on the bedside table. "I've got it covered."

"What does that mean?"

"Isn't All That Glitters closed on Mondays?"

She was surprised he had paid that much attention. "Yes."

He kissed her nose. "I wanted to spend the day with you. My partner is on call for any emergencies. It's almost Christmas. Things are slow."

It bothered her that he hadn't said a word about their long-standing feud or her property or his big project that included her. After his mother's heart attack, he had backed off completely. Two weeks ago, his Realtor had been contacting Mazie every three or four days. Now, nothing.

Was J.B. playing a game with her? Did he think she would cooperate if he wrapped her in romance and soft sheets?

Once before, she had been positive he had feelings for her. When the teenage J.B. had exhibited arousal, she'd been naive enough to believe it was going to lead to something. To a relationship. To a future.

He had disabused her of that notion cruelly.

Was she courting heartbreak a second time? Was J.B. even capable of love? Did he want more than her body and her business?

Was J.B. Vaughan her soul mate or her worst nightmare?

She wanted to take this experience at face value. She wanted to live in the moment. Sadly, she had never been the kind of woman to enjoy sex for the sake of sex. Before this thing with J.B., she had been celibate for two years.

"What did you have in mind?" she asked, snuggling closer.

His eyes were heavy-lidded, his hair tousled. Without his fancy suits and his billionaire persona, he looked far more dangerous.

"I thought after breakfast we could decorate the tree," he said. "Then take a shift at the hospital sitting with Mom."

"I like it."

"But first…" He reached for a foil packet on the night-stand and turned back to press a possessive kiss on her mouth. "I want to play."

After last night's excess, this morning should have been lazy and indulgent. Instead, it was as if the world was ending and this was their last chance to find a mate.

J.B. touched her everywhere, whispering her name, showering her with endearments and compliments. Her first climax hit sharp and hard and left her shaking. Before she could do more than gasp for breath, he was driving her up again…raking her nipples with sharp teeth, pressing kisses to her belly and below. Filling her with his power-ful thrusts.

When she came a second time, he was there with her, a muffled shout buried against her throat. She wrapped her legs around his waist and held him tightly, her eyes damp.

They slept again.

When she woke up the next time, her stomach was growling.

"Feed me," she begged, shaking his shoulder.

J.B. rolled out of bed and padded to the bathroom, giv-ing her a tantalizing view of his male beauty. "You're so demanding."

She could hear his laughter, even after he closed the door.

While J.B. was getting dressed, she took a quick shower, fetched her bag from the guest room, and pulled out fresh clothes. It sounded like the day would be casual, which suited her just fine. Mondays were usually lazy days, her one indulgence in a week that was typically crammed with work and looking after her father.

She followed her nose to the kitchen and found J.B. knee deep in eggs and bacon.

"Shall I make toast?" she asked, pausing to lean her cheek against his arm.

He gave her a quick kiss. "Butter's on the counter right behind me. There's a loaf of bread in the pantry. Coffee's ready if you want some."

The homey scene was entirely bogus. J.B. Vaughan was not a domesticated animal. Mazie didn't even want to calculate the number of women who had wandered into this charming kitchen scene over the years.

She knew this wasn't the same place J.B. lived during his short marriage. That knowledge should have made her feel better. And it did…a tiny bit. Truthfully, she adored his carefully preserved row house.

The copper-bottomed pots hanging over the island might be only for show, but as far as she could tell, J.B.'s kitchen was outfitted like a chef's dream. Mazie liked to cook when she had the time. It wasn't hard to imagine herself right here in the midst of preparing a big dinner for a group of friends.

While J.B. scrambled and fried, she found a cookie sheet and decided to do the toast in the oven. When it was done, she joined him at the table and slid two pieces of perfectly browned sourdough onto each plate.

A jar of homemade plum preserves she had found in the fridge was the finishing touch.

J.B. devoured the meal as if he were starving.

Truth be told, they had expended a great deal of energy since they ate shrimp the night before. And it was already midmorning.

She reached across the table and removed a drop of jam from his chin. "How are you at putting Christmas lights on a tree?" She vowed to keep the day light and easy. No more personal questions that would make both of them uneasy.

He finished the last bite of eggs and sat back in his chair. "Don't know. I guess we'll find out."

J.B. was in trouble.
And he knew it.

Part of him wanted to get Mazie out of his house and out of his bed. It was beginning to feel as if she *belonged* here.

That wasn't possible.

He liked her. A lot. Still, he had done the marriage thing, and he was really bad at it. So he needed to put a stop to this *playing house* gig.

As the morning progressed, he watched her, searching for any sign that she thought this was leading to something bigger. Other than a single, logically female question last night, she hadn't pressed for answers. Maybe because he had shut her down.

He felt bad about that.

By the time they finished the tree, his living room was a mess, but Mazie was glowing. She stood back and put her hands on her hips. "Look at it, J.B. It's glorious." She threw her arms around him in a big bear hug. "I can't wait until it's dark tonight, and we get the full effect."

Her enthusiasm was contagious. He felt a sense of pride that he had been able to give her something so simple and yet so profound. Mazie was a confident, happy, successful woman, but deep inside was that sad little girl who had lost her mother and had spent multiple Christmases on the edges of someone else's celebrations.

Damn Jonathan and Hartley for not noticing. Maybe they were too close to the situation, and maybe they had other interests. It was women who usually created the warmth of holidays, women who knew how to make an occasion memorable.

But J.B. wished her family hadn't dropped the ball where Mazie was concerned.

He tugged her ponytail. "I can't wait until dark either."

She headed for the stairs. "We need to leave for the hospital. You promised we'd be there at one."

He followed her a moment later, only to find that she

had taken her overnight bag and all her things to the guest room to get ready.

Why, damn it? And why wasn't he glad? He felt like he was losing his grip. Nothing made sense.

At the hospital, the news was not quite as upbeat as it had been. His mother was wan and listless. According the doctor, there was infection somewhere in her body. They were pumping her full of antibiotics.

Only Leila was there.

His sister stepped out into the hall to speak to them. "I'm not sure what happened overnight, but she was like this when I got here this morning. Dad is a wreck. I sent him home to sleep. Alana is with him."

J.B. hugged his sister. "You go, too. Mazie and I can be here as long as we need to be."

The afternoon crawled by. His mother alternated between resting and waking, barely speaking at all. Mazie sat beside her and rubbed her hand, the one that wasn't encumbered with the IV.

J.B. paced.

At one point, when their patient was sleeping, he pulled Mazie to a far corner of the room. "I feel like we should be doing something."

She grimaced. "Hospitals are all about waiting. They must think the medicine will work eventually. She's not getting worse."

He pressed the heel of his hand to his forehead. "I hate being helpless."

Mazie wrapped her arms around him. "Whatever happens, she knows how much you love her. That's the important thing."

His blood chilled. Mazie was obliquely referencing what all of them had been thinking. Jane Vaughan might not pull through this. His heart pounded and his knees felt funny. He loved his mom.

For the first time, he truly understood how Mazie must have suffered when her mom was taken away. It would have been like a death.

"I'm sorry," he said, his hands on her shoulders.

"For what?"

"For not realizing how much it has hurt you to have your mother several hundred miles away."

Mazie paled. "She doesn't even know who I am."

"So you feel guilty if you don't go and even sadder when you *do*? That's the worst of it, isn't it? You want to believe that it will be different every time you visit, but it never is."

She nodded slowly. Tears welled into her eyes and spilled onto her cheeks.

He held her close, his heart expanding with an emotion that confused him. Being so close kindled a spark of sexual arousal, but it wasn't only that. He wanted to protect her and make her happy and give her the family she had always wanted. Holy hell. What was he thinking?

Before he could make himself release her, Mazie slipped free of his arms. "Excuse me," she muttered. "I'll be back."

When he turned around, his mother's eyes were open. "You love her, don't you, son?"

He started to deny it, but at the last moment remembered the faux engagement. "Of course I do, Mom." He pulled up a chair beside the bed and studied the machines beeping softly. "How are you feeling?"

She pursed her lips. "Tired. Glad to be alive."

"I don't want you to fret. Can I go get you a hamburger? Medium rare with onions?"

The little joke made his mother smile. "You would do it, wouldn't you?"

"If you asked me. I love you, Mama."

His heart was cracking inside his chest. Breaking wide open. Between his fear for his mother and his need for Mazie, he was turning into someone he didn't recognize.

His mother put her hand on his head, almost like a blessing. "You don't have to worry about me, J.B. I'm going to live to see those grandbabies you promised me."

Guilt choked him. He couldn't tell her the truth. Not now.

Mazie returned at that moment, rescuing him from the need to deal with his mother's loaded statement. His fiancée was pale, but she seemed calm. She had been to the hospital gift shop by the looks of it. In her hand, she carried a vase of pink sweetheart roses.

"Alana told me these were your favorites."

His mother perked up visibly. "Oh, thank you, sweet girl. They're beautiful. Set them right there where I can see them."

J.B. stood. "I'm gonna grab some coffee." He was suffocating. He *wanted* Mazie here. Of course he did. But seeing her interact with his mother signaled an intimacy he was trying his damnedest to avoid.

After that particular Monday, the days fell into a pattern. Christmas was barely over a week away. J.B. and Mazie both went to work every morning, but the evenings were for taking care of family, and later for making love beneath the beautiful, fragrant Christmas tree.

J.B. had discovered Mazie's particular fantasy when it came to holiday sex, so he capitalized on it.

She had no complaints.

It was the happiest she had ever been.

Still, hovering in the back of her mind was the knowledge that she would have to leave eventually. The longer she stayed, the harder it would be to extricate herself from a relationship that was definitely lopsided when it came to the emotional component.

J.B. gave her his passion and his compassion, but his heart wasn't up for grabs.

It hurt. Badly. She couldn't lie to herself. She tried not

to think about it, but deep down was a tiny stupid glimmer of hope that he would come around…that he would feel what she felt.

Because he never said the words, neither did she.

On December 22, she was so glad she had not.

It was an ordinary day, nothing to indicate that her bubble of perfect joy was about to pop.

On that morning, it was raining. J.B. kissed her goodbye as she left for work. She was wearing a black raincoat with a hood, so she thought it would be enough to keep her dry. When she got outside, though, she realized that the light showers had turned into a downpour. Not only that, she had forgotten to pick up her umbrella.

She was running late, but she scooted back inside to grab it.

As she did, she heard J.B. on the phone talking to someone. He must have been in the den, because his voice carried clearly to the foyer.

"I don't think we have anything to worry about. I've got her eating out of my hand. It won't be a problem."

All the blood drained from her heart to the floor. Numbly, she grabbed the umbrella, backed out of the house and fled.

Unfortunately, it wasn't far to her destination. She parked and gripped the steering wheel. Her mind was blank one minute and filled with pain and terror the next. Surely it couldn't be true. Surely J.B. hadn't moved her into his house and slept with her so she would give him a stupid building.

She had noticed him pulling back emotionally over the last few days. Though they had been as close as a man and woman could be from a physical standpoint, it was if J.B. had put up a mental wall between them.

She had assumed, had hoped actually, that it was because his feelings for her were changing. That maybe he was fighting the connection between them.

He had failed at commitment and marriage in the past and was too afraid to try again.

But what if his retreat was more sinister? What if he was getting ready to reject her again now that he had accomplished his goals?

Try as she might, she couldn't think of another interpretation for his words. Especially because he had sounded happy and upbeat.

With his mom on the mend and Mazie no longer a problem, he was going to have a very merry Christmas.

Mazie couldn't bear it. Why did no one she cared about stick around for the long haul?

What was wrong with her?

Seventeen

Somehow, she made it through the day.

Gina looked at her oddly several times, but they were too busy with customers for her to grill Mazie. With only two shopping days left after this one, the store was a madhouse.

Jewelry flew out the door like fake gold doubloons being tossed in a Mardi Gras parade. Fake doubloons. Like everything else in Mazie's life at the moment. Her engagement, her blackhearted lover. Even her smile. Because inside, she was nothing but a child crying in the driveway when everything she loved best was being taken away from her.

At last, the interminable day was over. She had to figure out a way to extricate herself from J.B.'s house. First, though, she had to go by the hospital. Jane was doing much better, but she wasn't entirely out of the woods.

Mazie knew J.B. was working late, so she wouldn't have to see him. Please God, let that be so.

Both Alana and Leila were with their mother. Mr. Vaughan had been home napping during the afternoon but was due back soon.

The three women in the room greeted her warmly. Mazie hung her purse on a chair and cleaned her hands with hand sanitizer.

"How's our patient today?" she asked.

Jane wagged a finger at her two daughters. "If these two will quit worrying, we'll be fine." But J.B.'s mother didn't look healthy. If anything, she seemed frail and pale.

Alana spoke up, looking chagrined. "You're not as well as you think, Mama."

"Oh, pooh. I'm determined to be home for Christmas. You wait and see."

Leila grimaced. Mazie sympathized. Jane wasn't a bad patient, but she was strong willed.

Leila hugged Mazie unexpectedly. "You've been so great to our mother. She told us that you're not actually engaged to my brother. So you've really gone above and beyond. Thank you, Mazie."

Alana hugged her, too. "I was disappointed. I think he needs someone like you in his life, but the guy is stubborn as a rock."

"Don't I know it," Mazie said lightly.

The lump in her throat was more of a boulder. Though the Vaughans didn't realize it, this was Mazie's goodbye visit. She had agreed to J.B.'s charade when she thought something real might grow out of it…when she had trusted him. Now, though, she had to leave him.

Without warning, the door swung open and J.B. strode into the room. He carried with him the crisp masculine scent that was like a drug to her. She put the width of the bed between them and barely acknowledged his presence.

It wasn't so hard. He was chatting with his sisters and sitting on his mother's bed to speak with her.

Suddenly, every alarm in the room began to beep. Jane's eyes fluttered shut and her breathing was raspy. In an instant, three nurses ran into the room and surrounded the bed.

The three siblings clung to each other, ashen faced.

Mazie huddled in the corner, out of the way.

J.B. was wild-eyed as if he couldn't believe what was happening. He looked for Mazie.

"Come where she can hear you," he begged. "Tell her she has to hold on."

Mazie didn't know if he was asking for himself or his mother or both. But she would do whatever he asked, because she loved him desperately.

Before Mazie could move closer, Leila, tears streaming down her cheeks, patted her brother's arm. "Stop, J.B. Quit pretending. It doesn't matter now. Mom knows the engagement isn't real."

His jaw dropped. He stared at Mazie with hot eyes. "You told her?"

Humiliation burned her cheeks. "Well, I…"

His face was stony, his gaze both judge and jury. "We'll talk about this later."

A doctor joined the fray. "I'll need all of you to step into the hall, please." As a team of medical professionals swooped in, J.B. and his sisters and Mazie were kindly but firmly evicted.

J.B. took her arm and steered her a short distance away, far enough for the two of them to speak in private.

His expression was tight with fury. His grasp was firm enough to leave bruises. "Go home," he said. "I have to concentrate on my family now. They are all that matters to me."

The intimation was sharply painful. He blamed Mazie.

This wasn't the time to exonerate herself. And besides. What was the point? It didn't matter what J.B. thought of her. Their relationship—if you could call it that—was over. And this time the pain of his rejection was far more devastating than she could have imagined.

She stumbled her way to the parking lot and got into her car. Driving to J.B.'s house, dealing with the alarm, and unlocking the door took all the courage she had, even knowing that he was not going to interrupt her.

With shaking hands and a stomach curling with nausea, she packed up her clothing and personal items. Most of it was in the master bedroom. A few things in the guest room. There wasn't a lot, really.

Her holiday affair hadn't lasted all that long.

Back downstairs, she went into the den and plugged in the lights on the Christmas tree. The beautiful fir mocked her. The tears came then, hot and painful. She had gambled and lost.

J.B. hadn't cared about her when she was sixteen, and he didn't care about her now.

She was a means to an end.

When she was calm enough to drive, she headed for home. For the last week, Jonathan had been working like a madman, preparing to be gone, so he was keeping late hours. Her father was distracted with chores for his trip and would be leaving in the morning. He was the most animated she had seen him in months.

Mazie had dinner with her father and helped him pack afterward. As she was folding a pair of socks, she blurted out a question she had wanted to ask him for years but had never had the guts.

"Daddy?"

"Hmm?"

"Why do you never go see Mama? Why did you send her so very far away?"

He turned slowly, his face paling. He sat down hard on the side of the bed. "I wondered when one of you kids would finally ask me that." His voice rasped with emotion.

"I don't want to upset you, but I need to know."

He shrugged, playing with a loose thread on one of his sweaters. "When your mother had her complete psychotic break, I took her to the best and most expensive doctors in the country. Your mother was the love of my life. When she came to me, she was young and charming and so full of animation. It was only after we married that I discovered her demons."

"And nothing helped?"

"No. Not really." His jaw worked. "We went through

months and years of diagnosis and treatment. She seemed better for a time, but then her father killed her mother and took his own life. That was too much for her to handle."

Dear God. "But you told us our grandparents died in a car accident."

"I didn't want to frighten you. And as for your mother…" He stared out the window, obviously seeing some painful scene from the past. "I couldn't bear the thought of her taking her own life. When I found the facility in Vermont, it was reputed to be one of the best in the entire world. Your mother thrived there, though she no longer knew me or even that we were married."

"I'm so sorry, Daddy."

He shrugged. "We had eight or nine good years together. They had warned her not to have children, but she was adamant about wanting a family. I've always prayed that none of you would be affected. She continually sabotaged her birth control, and each time she got pregnant, she refused to take the medicines that controlled her mania. By the time you were ten, things had gotten very bad indeed."

"I remember."

"The tipping point was the day I found her playing with knives in the kitchen. She had cut her fingers badly. Swore it was a mistake. But I knew we were nearing the end. Not long after that, she woke up from a dream in the middle of the night and thought I was a burglar trying to strangle her in her sleep."

He stopped and gasped for air, clearly still traumatized after all these years. Shaking his head, he gazed at Mazie bleakly. "I brought doctors here to the house. A dozen of them. They all said the same. The end of her mental competence was coming soon, and if it happened while she was alone with you kids, she might harm you."

"So you sent her away."

"I did. I missed her so badly I thought my heart would break in two. But I had to protect you and your brothers."

Mazie went to him and wrapped her arms around him. "Thank you for telling me."

"I should have done it long before now, but it was so hard to face it…to talk about it."

He was shaking. Mazie felt the lash of guilt for putting him through the retelling, though she was glad to know the truth. "You're a good man. And a good father. I'm so happy you're going with your friends on this trip."

"I'm sorry I won't be here for Christmas."

"No worries," she said blithely. "Gina has asked me to spend the day with her family."

That part was true. He didn't have to know that Mazie had declined the invitation.

She fell into bed that night, but slept only in snatches. Alana and Leila had taken turns answering Mazie's texts. Jane Vaughan had a pulmonary embolism. It was serious… likely a complication from her surgery. But she was being treated with the appropriate medications and would be monitored closely.

Mazie begged both of J.B.'s sisters not to let him know that she was in contact with them.

There was to be no Christmas celebration at the Vaughan homeplace. If Jane stabilized, she might be allowed to leave the hospital for a few hours to celebrate with her family at J.B.'s house, since it was so close to the hospital.

On the twenty-third, Mazie worked all day and then drove her father and brother to the airport. Their flights were only an hour apart, and fortunately in the right order. Jonathan was able to make sure his father got safely on the plane to Fort Lauderdale where he would meet up with his college buddies. Soon after, Jonathan flew out to Arizona.

Hopefully, he would find some relief for the headaches that plagued him.

That night, Mazie walked the floors in the empty house. She felt like a ghost. A phantom. A woman who wasn't actually real.

The pain had receded for the moment, leaving her pleasantly numb.

She slept on the sofa for five hours. Showered. Went in to work.

Christmas Eve was normally her favorite day of the year. This time, she suffered through it, watching the clock, waiting for the moment she could return home and pull the covers over her head.

Her acting skills were top-notch. When Gina asked once again about Christmas Day, Mazie declined with a smile on her face. Gina assumed—and Mazie didn't correct her—that Mazie was spending the holiday with J.B.

There would be plenty of time later for the painful truth.

All That Glitters closed at four on the twenty-fourth. Mazie handed out beautifully wrapped gifts to all her staff, gave a brief emotional speech and sent everyone on their way.

With the inventory secured and the shop locked up and the alarm set, she headed for home. She had to get through the next thirty-six hours. After that, maybe she could find a way forward. Perhaps she would move to Savannah and open another branch of her popular jewelry shop. That would put her far enough away from J.B.'s orbit not to bump into him, but still close to her family.

Maybe Jonathan could hire someone to help out with their father. Mazie couldn't stay in Charleston any longer. She had to change her life.

The long hours of Christmas Eve were a mockery of all her dreams. As a teenager, she had imagined she would be married by now. With a house of her own, children, a husband. Having a career had been important to her, but no more so than building a future with people she loved. Starting traditions. Sharing special moments.

She sat in front of the TV and watched bits and pieces of movie classics. Funny ones. Sad ones. Hopeful ones.

When that pastime lost its allure, she walked the beach in the dark. From the water's edge, she could look into the windows of large rental houses. Families celebrating. Eating. Laughing.

Never had she felt so alone.

Christmas morning dawned sunny and mild as it so often did in Charleston. As soon as she woke up, all the awful memories came rushing back, not the least of which was the look on J.B.'s face when he exiled her from his mother's hospital room. It had shriveled her soul.

She knew now what she had to do to bring closure to this painful episode of her life. Perhaps she had dreamed the solution in her sleep.

First she showered and dressed for the day. Lycra running pants and a long-sleeve tee would suffice. Then she visited the safe in her father's office.

She riffled through a stack of documents, selected the appropriate one and tucked it in a brown envelope. Next she Googled twenty-four-hour delivery services.

Soon, she would never have to see or speak to J.B. Vaughan ever again.

Eighteen

J.B. was in hell. And operating with a split personality. Thankfully, his mother had recovered to the point that her doctor was comfortable releasing her for a few hours on Christmas Day.

The family had strict instructions to rush her back if certain symptoms occurred.

But Jane Vaughan was glowing. Surrounded by her children and her husband, she was ecstatic to be celebrating the holiday in something other than a hospital gown.

Alana and Leila had thrown together a very creditable feast. Roast turkey with all the fixings. Grandmother Vaughan's sweet potatoes. A few other side dishes, and—procured from a local bakery—a stunning red velvet cake.

Since J.B. didn't own any china—only masculine earthenware dishes—the womenfolk had opted to break with tradition and use disposable plates to minimize cleanup. J.B.'s drop-in-thrice-a-week housekeeper had been given the week off between Christmas and New Year's to spend with her family.

The meal was outstanding… J.B. felt deep relief and gratitude to see his mother doing so much better. His father was equally exuberant to have his bride back on her feet. Alana and Leila were in a celebratory mood, as well.

The only nagging thorn in J.B.'s soul was Mazie's absence. He had started to call her a dozen times, but he was still so angry that she had revealed their secret to his mother without asking him. In the midst of all the drama, he had actually been convinced that Mazie's mistake caused his mother's relapse.

Later, he realized the truth. He had overreacted.

He owed Mazie an apology for that. But his righteous anger was justified. The secret about their fake engagement hadn't been hers to reveal.

She had gone behind his back. That was why he was angry—right?

Or was he so devastated, because in the midst of everything that had happened, he had finally realized the complete truth. Not only was he heels over ass deep in love with Mazie, he might be willing to believe he had a second chance at forever.

The three recent nights without her in his bed were interminable. He had come to depend on her soft warmth to help him sleep. He worked too hard and had trouble relaxing. Mazie's presence in his life in the midst of his mother's traumatic illness had helped steady him.

Why had she told his mother the engagement was not real? What did she hope to gain?

Her unexpected and dangerous choice felt like a betrayal.

After the midday meal, his parents dozed in the den. J.B. helped clear the table, but his sister shooed him out of the kitchen.

Leila kissed his cheek. "We love you, J.B., but we can do this faster without you. Relax. Check your email. We've got this."

He wandered toward the front of the house, reluctant to go into the den. There were too many memories there. Seeing the beautiful Christmas tree he and Mazie had decorated hurt. He didn't want to remember. He wanted to throw the damned thing out to the curb, ornaments and all.

When the doorbell rang, his heart leaped in shock and

momentary hope. But of course it wasn't Mazie. Why would it be? He had sent her away most emphatically.

The barely-twenty-something man standing on the doorstep wore the familiar uniform of a well-known delivery service. He handed J.B. a manila envelope. "Sign here, please."

J.B. scribbled his name on the magnetic screen. "Did you draw the short straw today?"

The young kid shook his head and grinned. "Nope. Jewish. I volunteered. Merry Christmas, sir."

J.B. closed the door and opened the envelope. At first he couldn't process what he was seeing. It was a deed. Not just any deed…but a deed to the building that housed Mazie's jewelry store. And she had signed it over to him.

Leila exited the kitchen, drying her hands on a dishcloth covered with reindeer. "What's that?"

He frowned. "I'm not sure. It seems as if Mazie has finally agreed to let me have her property for my renovation project."

"That's good, isn't it?"

"Yes. But I…"

"But what?"

"I don't know why she's giving it to me now after stonewalling for so long. And why the hell did she tell Mom we weren't engaged without asking me first? The shock could have killed Mom."

"And you're still angry."

"Hell, yes," he said.

Alana gave him a pitying look. "You're such a dope. You don't know Mazie at all. Of course she didn't tell Mom anything. Mom guessed the truth from the very first day you lied to her. She knew you wanted to give her something to cling to before heart surgery."

"She did?"

"Yeah. Mazie kept your secret, J.B. And she kept pretending because Mom asked her to. But you yelled at her and humiliated her in front of all of us and a bunch of nurses and doctors. Bad karma, my brother."

His heart sank. The enormity of his blunder crushed him. "I've got to talk to her," he muttered.

"We're about to open presents," Alana said. "And besides, I don't think you should go rushing over there if you don't have your head on straight. You've hurt Mazie. You'd better decide what you want from her, or you'll make things even worse."

J.B. made it an hour and a half before he cracked.

He *had* to go talk to Mazie. It couldn't wait. He needed to apologize and tell her he loved her. Or both.

Fortunately, his mother decided she was ready to go back to her hospital bed. The cardiologist had promised that if this next set of tests was acceptable, he would release her on the twenty-seventh.

When the house was finally empty again, J.B. grabbed his keys. He drove across town and on toward the beach, barely even registering the empty streets. His heart pounded in his chest. Would Mazie be willing to talk to him? He had treated her terribly.

When he got to the Tarleton property, the front gates were locked. Fortunately, J.B. had the security codes. Jonathan had given them to him a few months ago when all the family was out of town at the same time. J.B. had checked on the property for them.

Now, he prayed the codes hadn't been changed.

He breathed a sigh of relief when the gates swung open. All the cars were visible, parked in the partially sheltered bays beneath the house. But there was no sign of life anywhere.

Patience.

He took a deep breath, trying to silence his galloping

heartbeat. He loped up the front steps, entered a second code and eased open the door.

"Mazie? Jonathan?"

As far as J.B. could tell, no one was home. He walked through the main floor of the house. There was no sign of any activity. No meal. No televisions running. No wrapping paper.

He stopped at the bay window and gazed out at the aquamarine ocean.

And then he saw her. Down by the water's edge, a lone figure, unmistakably feminine, strolled along the shore, bending now and again to pick up a shell.

His body moved instinctively. Exiting the back of the house, he peeled off his socks and shoes, rolled up his pants legs and let himself out of the gate, using the same codes he had memorized earlier.

Mazie had stopped now and was looking toward the horizon, her hands on her hips. The sound of the waves masked his approach.

He stopped a few feet away so as not to scare her.

"Mazie," he called hoarsely.

She spun around, flinching visibly when she saw it was him. "Go away, J.B. This is my beach."

"You can't own beaches in South Carolina," he said. "Please, Mazie. Let me talk to you."

"Didn't you get my package? It's over. You have what you want. Leave me alone."

The scales fell from his eyes. The angel choirs sang. His own stupid brain finally clicked into gear. If he hadn't been such a clueless idiot when he was a younger man, he could have had Mazie by his side and in his bed all these years.

Instead, he'd been saddled with a terrible marriage that had almost destroyed him. He had ended up all alone and had convinced himself that he liked it.

"No," he said soberly. "No, I don't have what I want."

He swallowed hard, not quite able to say the words. But he was trying. "I need you, Mazie. I *want* you in my life. I'm sorry I yelled at you and accused you of something you didn't do. I rejected you. Again. Only this time, it was far worse. Alana told me you didn't spill the secret. I should have known better."

She folded her arms around her waist, her posture brittle with *something*. "Apology accepted. And as for the other, I'm no longer interested. Find another woman."

"I can't," he said. "There's only you."

Pain drenched her beautiful eyes. Tears welled in them.

"You don't need to play the game anymore, J.B. I know what you were after. I gave it to you. We're done."

Now he was confused. "Are you talking about the property?"

"Of course," she shouted. "Does any of this sound familiar? *'I don't think we have anything to worry about. I've got her eating out of my hand. It won't be a problem.'*" She paused to catch her breath. "You didn't want me when I was sixteen, and you don't want me now. You've been *using* me, and I was fool enough to go along with it. But I'm done."

All her anger seemed to winnow away. She stared at him, stone-faced.

He swallowed hard. "You misunderstood," he said carefully.

"Liar."

"I wanted to go out with you when you were sixteen, I swear. I had a huge crush on you. But your brother promised to neuter me if I went through with it because he knew my reputation with girls. So I turned you down. And I've regretted it ever since."

She blinked, her expression wary. "That doesn't excuse the fact that you used sex to coerce me into selling my property to you. I *heard* you, J.B. You can't talk your way out of this one."

His knees felt funny. "I love you, Mazie. I think I have in some way or other my whole life. But I got married, and I screwed that up, and after that, I was too embarrassed to talk to you."

"You don't love me," she whispered. "You *don't*. I heard you on the phone."

God, he had hurt her so badly. He'd tried to protect himself from making another mistake, but in the process, Mazie had become collateral damage.

"I was talking about the mayor," he said. "That was my partner on the phone, yes. But we weren't discussing you. I've been sweet-talking the mayor and the city council into letting us build a city park. They have grant money for beautification. We've offered to go in with them, if they agree, and do the project in tandem."

"The mayor?"

He nodded. "The mayor. Not you. In case you haven't noticed, you've been leading *me* around by the nose, and not the opposite. I adore you, Mazie. I'm sorry it took me so long to admit it, but I'll spend the next six months convincing you if you're interested in a June wedding. Or if we're both scared, we can wait a year. Or two. Or four. But nothing will change on my end. I love you, Mazie Jane."

The sun was hot on the top of his head. He felt dizzy and sick and terrified. Nothing in his life had ever been as important as this. And he had bungled the hell out of it.

"Say it again," she whispered.

"I love you?"

She shook her head. "No. The part where you wanted to take me to the dance when I was sixteen."

His heart lightened. "When you grew up, Mazie—overnight it seemed—it socked me in the stomach. For years you had been this cute, spunky little kid trying to keep up with your brothers and me. Then suddenly you were a princess. I got tongue-tied just trying to talk to you."

"But you let Jonathan get in your head."

"To be fair to your brother, I was kind of a jerk in those days. He was probably right to wave me off."

"I adored you back then," she said, the words wistful.

He tasted fear. "And now?"

She didn't say a word for the longest time. He could almost *feel* the struggle inside her. Finally, she held out her hand. "I love you, Jackson Beauregard Vaughan. I didn't want to, but I do. As embarrassing as it is to admit, I think I loved you way back then and somehow never got over it."

He closed his eyes and inhaled sharply, tilting his face toward the sun, feeling the weight of the world dissipate. Then he smiled at her and dragged her into his arms.

"I think I've been waiting on this moment forever." After kissing her long and thoroughly and reveling in her eager response, he pulled away at last. "Why are you alone on Christmas Day, sweet girl?"

She laid her cheek against his shoulder. "I'm not alone, J.B. I have you. Merry Christmas, my love."

"Merry Christmas, Mazie." He scooped her into his arms. "Is that house behind us really empty?"

She grinned at him, her hair tumbling in the breeze. "Completely. Would you like to join me in my bedroom and open your Christmas present?"

He laughed out loud, startling a trio of seagulls. "Oh, yeah. And just so you know, great minds think alike. I got you the very same thing…"

Epilogue

Jonathan sat in his luxurious Arizona hotel room at the retreat center and read through the packet of meditation techniques that were supposed to diminish his headaches. Nothing seemed to be working. Not expensive pharmaceuticals. Not hippie-dippie mumbo jumbo. With each passing week, he became more fearful that something in his mother's messed-up DNA had triggered a cataclysm in his. A mental meltdown that might change everything about his life.

Or destroy it completely.

The intensity of the headaches scared him more than he wanted to admit. He didn't want to end up like his mother, drugged and helpless in a facility somewhere.

A phone call from his sister had soothed some of his other concerns. Mazie and J.B. were together. With a capital *T*. It boggled the mind, but both of them sounded happy.

He wished them all the best, even if it was a little weird for him personally.

More important, it was a relief to know that whatever happened to him, J.B. was going to make sure Mazie was okay.

At least one member of the Tarleton family would find happiness...

* * * * *

LET'S TALK
Romance

For exclusive extracts, competitions
and special offers, find us online:

- facebook.com/millsandboon
- @MillsandBoon
- @MillsandBoonUK

Get in touch on 01413 063232

MILLS & BOON

THE HEART OF ROMANCE

A ROMANCE FOR EVERY READER

MODERN

Prepare to be swept off your feet by sophisticated, sexy and seductive heroes, in some of the world's most glamourous and romantic locations, where power and passion collide.

HISTORICAL

Escape with historical heroes from time gone by. Whether your passion is for wicked Regency Rakes, muscled Vikings or rugged Highlanders, awaken the romance of the past.

MEDICAL

Set your pulse racing with dedicated, delectable doctors in the high-pressure world of medicine, where emotions run high and passion, comfort and love are the best medicine.

True Love

Celebrate true love with tender stories of heartfelt romance, from the rush of falling in love to the joy a new baby can bring, and a focus on the emotional heart of a relationship.

Desire

Indulge in secrets and scandal, intense drama and plenty of sizzling hot action with powerful and passionate heroes who have it all: wealth, status, good looks…everything but the right woman.

HEROES

Experience all the excitement of a gripping thriller, with an intense romance at its heart. Resourceful, true-to-life women and strong, fearless men face danger and desire - a killer combination!

To see which titles are coming soon, please visit

millsandboon.co.uk/nextmonth

JOIN US ON SOCIAL MEDIA!

Stay up to date with our latest releases, author news and gossip, special offers and discounts, and all the behind-the-scenes action from Mills & Boon...

 @millsandboon

 @millsandboonuk

 facebook.com/millsandboon

@millsandboonuk

It might just be true love...

GET YOUR ROMANCE FIX!

Get the latest romance news,
exclusive author interviews, story
extracts and much more!

MILLS & BOON
MODERN
Power and Passion

Prepare to be swept off your feet by sophisticated, sexy and seductive heroes, in some of the world's most glamourous and romantic locations, where power and passion collide.

Eight Modern stories published every month, find them all at

millsandboon.co.uk/Modern